In the Darkness . . .

"Please, I know you're there," said Chandal. "I won't hurt you. I just want to speak to you."

The girl maintained a rigid posture.

"Can you hear me? I promise you—you'll be all right." Chandal moved closer.

The young girl moved, her mannequin head turning slightly at first, until it finally managed to rotate completely around to face the wall. The rest of her body remained facing front. Chandal edged slowly toward her.

The girl's head suddenly spun around on her shoulders and snapped into a frontal position. Her expression was distorted and ugly—she hissed at Chandal.

Above her now, a face, vaguely visible, teeth bared. Chandal hadn't noticed. Caught her breath —the only sound.

Then the silence was fractured. She heard a female voice. "I will not be disturbed here. I will not be disturbed. . . ."

THE BROWNSTONE

KEN EULO

PUBLISHED BY POCKET BOOKS NEW YORK

Another *Original* publication of POCKET BOOKS

POCKET BOOKS, a Simon & Schuster division of
GULF & WESTERN CORPORATION
1230 Avenue of the Americas, New York, N.Y. 10020

ISBN: 0-671-83459-2

First Pocket Books printing October, 1980

10 9 8 7 6 5 4 3 2 1

POCKET and colophon are trademarks of Simon & Schuster.

Printed in the U.S.A.

This book is for my wife, Elena
—just as I promised.

Acknowledgment

My special heartfelt thanks to Meg Blackstone, my editor at Pocket Books, for her invaluable assistance and generosity in the preparation of this book

Lakewood Sanitarium
Dusk, September 4, 1980

And now his time had run out.

Seated alone behind his polished mahogany desk, Dr. I. Luther leaned back and closed his eyes. The electrical shock authorization form lay in front of him unsigned. In the quiet stillness of the room, he took up the old question of just how much electrical shock the brain could withstand before a vital part of it closed down forever.

Tiredly, he pressed his fingers into the corners of his eyes and tried to reason past the blankness of his mind. He still could not get a hold on the source, the beginning.

Why, after obvious progress, had the patient suddenly reverted back to speaking in the third person? How to explain this setback? Had the self-destructive forces taken hold again?

His mind skipped backward, trying to reach into the abyss of mental illness, to shine the light of his profession into the darkness of a mind turned to shadows.

He reached for his tape recorder. Only once had the patient spoken in the first person. The words had been recorded. Dr. Luther had listened to those words a hundred times. He still was unable to understand their meaning. Nervously, he pressed the button.

Click.

"Because I have seen what I have seen,
Because I have been where I have been,
Because I have communed with those who know . . .
I am who I am."

He rewound the tape and listened once again.

"Because I have seen what I have seen . . ."

PART ONE

"Because I have been where I have been . . ."

❧ 1 ❧

THE DAWN GREW—RED, STREAKED, DULL, AND cloudless. From the brownstone window the old woman watched the sleeping city, rise and begin to murmur.

The night was over.

Silently, swiftly, a shadowy figure slipped from a neighboring doorway, robbing the street of its solitude. In a shaft of dim light, the face loomed closer, then moved up the street to disappear around the corner.

The old woman shuddered. It was beginning.

A bead of sweat popped from her brow as she imagined the parade of ghostlike figures who would soon fill the sidewalks below, marching their way into life. She would not be one of them.

Shifting her weight from one leg to another, she stared down at the stains on her white lace dress— blotches that ravaged her dreams. As her gaze moved from one rose-colored stain to the other, her expression turned briefly sad; vacant eyes grieving in a wrinkled face.

She had been seriously ill for more than a year now and loathed the wasted old woman she had become. What was it? Vanity? Fear of death? No. Something else. Her increasing helplessness and dependency on others. Her mind filled with the shock and the absolute certainty that she no longer had the ability to function entirely on her own.

And so, she had called on the power of Ahriman. Ahriman, she knew, would take her outstretched hand and lead her back through the darkness; he would guide her past the worst shadows and free her from the dark terror of reality that surrounded her. The small bedside table filled with medication. The bed that had restrained her for most of the day—the stairs that were increasingly harder to climb, the withered flowers, faded pictures and lost loves. That was her reality, that and the hatred she sometimes felt for her sister.

With a faint tremor of misgiving, the old woman brought her hand up to her breast and sighed. Her mind went back to the morning it all began. "It's a great day, mother. A great day," her father had said, holding her sister high so that everyone could peer at the new arrival. She was so tiny, head no bigger than an orange, tiny hands and feet exposing themselves through the green blanket, yet she had filled the room with her presence, stealing the energy, the breath from the other little girl who sat alone in the corner.

No matter. She was not alone now.

The goat had been with her again for sometime. When she had first summoned him, he had appeared as a thin shadow. Now, when the Woden tin whistle sounded, he sprang before her in flesh and savagery.

But daylight could not sustain him.

Bands of hazy sunlight fanned out from the window's edge, and the old woman in lace knew that it was morning. A breeze wafted suddenly across her face and something brushed her cheek. She started and turned swiftly around.

From the center of the room, a cloud of red fumes rose toward the ceiling. As it spread and thinned, the goatlike image, which had stood magnificently by her side throughout the dark hours, began to dissolve. Part illusion now and part reality, it spread its ancient wings, lashing its tail gently, as it continued to disappear.

With a sudden motion, the old woman thrust her forearm directly into the flame of the candle. At once the air of the musty room rang with her long, woeful cry.

Her groan rose higher as her flesh became scorched by the flame. The sulfurous odor of her own burning

3

flesh made her gag. There was no other way—before the goat departed, she had to display her devotion and obedience.

The goat bared its teeth and released a stream of vaporous blue gas, cold, yet comforting. Then it vanished, leaving the old woman in lace to herself. In her mind echoed these words—*let me enter you. You may enter me. We will become one.*

Chandal stepped, naked and wet from the shower, and began to dry herself with the soft blue-green bath towel. Her firm body moved in perfect rhythms, the towel moving briskly over her taut limbs. Through the half-opened door, she watched Justin hurrying between the two rooms, looking for his notebook. In it, he had written: 1. Traveling expenses—$840; 2. shipment of furniture—$2,200; 3. purchase of secondhand car—$1,500. The list went on in detail for an entire page, and now it was useless. Justin had decided to stay in New York instead of heading to California as planned.

That was how quickly things could happen. Lives could change. It had happened to them, and their lives had changed. The brownstone had happened to them. The brownstone, that decrepit, dingy, musty symbol of New York elegance, in which no one from suburbia would be caught dead. Justin hadn't been able to resist it.

It was the wildest coincidence. It couldn't have happened, but it had. Justin had been on his way home from unemployment and he'd done the good Samaritan thing, helped an old lady carry her package. A few fateful words had passed between them and the incredible had occurred. The old lady and Justin had something in common. He was without living accommodations as of the first of the month, and she and her sister had an apartment to rent. But what an apartment. What a mouth-watering, once-in-a-lifetime apartment, an entire floor of a brownstone. Justin had immediately thought of high ceilings and fireplaces and huge rooms and said we'll take it. Chandal had known

4

his mind was made up as soon as he had mentioned it.

"Honey, have you seen the damn notebook?"

"It was on the dresser the last time I looked."

"Well, it's not there now!"

Chandal made no comment, but lifted her arm and stretched her long torso. "You still think we're doing the right thing?" she asked, and Justin said, "Absolutely!"

She wrapped herself in the towel. "Yes, well— I'm not so sure."

"Ah! But I am." He stuck his head inside the door and smiled, with the same perfect teeth of his Scottish mother. His eyes, deep green with long lashes, and his nose, average size and straight, were from his Hungarian father. The scar over his left eye was his own invention. Fascinating, Chandal had thought, the night they first met.

Fireworks had been blazing over the South Shore and the music and lights from the bars had danced through the streets, onto the beach where girls sat on the hoods of cars, drinking warm beer; Chandal had been one of them. Casino lovers danced with silk shirts open, smiled and made passes. At the other end of the strip was an amusement park with a merry-go-round. She'd ridden on it until her head was dazed and there was no beginning or end. And when she looked out to find her friends, she saw Justin. They had walked on the beach in a quiet mood, heard the music and laughter from the bars, and saw the fireworks light up the sky. Chandal had paused, allowing the image of Justin to intensify.

He stood, a shower of sparkling light forming a halo around his strong face. A lock of his thick black hair had fallen across his forehead, accentuating the scar. A powerful face, yet gentle, kind. The scar adding mystery, excitement. They made love that night, warm, passionate love, and were married and settled on Eighty-fifth Street within three weeks.

God, you're handsome! she told him now silently.

He strode past her and surveyed the pile of magazines lying on the tiled floor. "Where the hell could it be?" Chandal swung her right leg onto the edge of the tub and began to massage in skin cream. "Yep," Justin mumbled, "I'll be glad to get out of here."

"I'm stiff. I've got to get back to dance class," she said, digging her fingers into her thigh. Justin brushed past her. "You're getting us into a mess; you know that," she said calmly.

He doubled back at the door. "What kind of mess, Del?"

"It's crazy." She lowered her right leg and raised the left. "Wanting to move into that ugly old brown stone with two ugly old ladies."

"They're not ugly. They're interesting-looking old bags. We'll probably bore them."

"You don't bore me," she said. "How're you going to bore two old bags?" She handed him the lotion and turned her back. "I believe the shoulders are next."

"You're wrong. I believe the kiss was next." He kissed her and she smiled. "Justin, about California—"

He slapped her on the backside. "I think I was looking for something." He went back into the living room, slumped down, and checked under the couch. Then he eyed the table—pushed newspapers aside. The headline of *Variety* caught his eye: "Thr. Boom Biz, N.Y.C." Pidgin English, folksy show-business talk, meaning—theater was doing financially well in New York City. Justin was not. After directing *The Awakening,* a Nazi war trial play, his twenty-seventh in ten years, he was still nowhere. He was just another name, another director at the bottom of everyone's list.

Justin Knight, age thirty-five, an also-ran.

"Shit!" he muttered.

He had reached that magical middle ground, not young, not old, where men usually begin to analyze themselves, find the need to regain contact with their lives to remind themselves where they had come from and decipher where it was they were now.

Justin wasn't any different.

Something tangible—yet mysterious—had begun to stir in him, some terrible strain that accompanies the

6

realization that there is such a thing as the bogeyman called failure. It did something to his stomach, turned it over, made it queasy. It also made him feel raw and defenseless, and in some way resentful that he had not been prepared to understand failure when he was a child. To understand it, to fight it, and to survive.

But in Madison, Wisconsin, in the late 1940s, failure was a way of life and the only meaning of success was escape. To buy a one-way ticket out of Madison, that tired old town where the day was twenty-four hours long but seemed longer.

In 1951, he had been six years old. Colors spread out before him like assorted crayons in his brown tattered pencil holder which he carried back and forth to school each day, but never did get to use, except during lunch hour, when the other kids ignored him. Color green trees everywhere, yellow flowers aplenty, pink, blue, and red. White picket fences, brown and orange earth.

He would sit under the large elm tree at the far end of the schoolyard and color, and color, and color until his eyes could see things only in those terms. He was never sad—he was dark blue. He was not lonely—he was gray.

Momma said that color didn't mean much, but he knew that she was lying, for each time she told him that, tears flooded her eyes.

"Momma, how old was I when Poppa died?" he asked.

"Oh, you were just a bit of a thing," she'd say and go on about her work.

Drunkenly. Stupidly. In a car crash. At the age of thirty-six. That's when his father had decided to buy his own one-way ticket out of Madison. Justin always felt that way—that it was his father's decision, not God's, to pass on to another life. "You start out with nothing, and that's the way you end up." Justin's father had said that, and then he was gone. And then the colors started mixing together faster than Justin was able to sort them out.

Down the street lived Sam Jennings, who used to

beat his children with a strap. He always looked to Justin like he was crying. His children never did. He cried for all of them. There was Franky, Michael, Jonathan and Marsha. Of the four children, Justin liked Marsha the best.

Once, when Marsha and he were coloring colors together, Mr. Jennings came up behind her, picked her up by the hair and slapped her hard across the face.

"I don't want you playing with this white trash!" he said, and dragged her back to the house. Justin remembered feeling afraid every time he passed his house after that for fear he would come out with the strap and beat him. He never did.

Life went on as usual.

Mrs. Jennings, who was not at all like her husband, would come over to Justin's house evenings and talk to his mother. He would lie in bed and listen to them cry together. He colored their tears silver, and slept in rain showers many a night. Nights seemed long, like growing up, colors became more important. Blue police uniforms, black cars, bigger black dreams, and huge white folks.

Suddenly, without warning, Justin lost the sight of his right eye. The doctors came from far and wide; they had all heard of this special little boy who had contracted a rare disease. He was famous—and blind in one eye.

Colors lost their shine. He lost his patience with people. He just didn't want all those doctors looking at him. He had one eye; that was enough for him. After all, he was fourteen at the time. At fourteen, you can see plenty with one eye. "Mom, please, I can see fine. Please, I don't want the doctors here anymore," he said and kept on saying it.

"You'll do as I tell you!" she screamed at him, and kept screaming until she broke down, took him in her arms and squeezed him until he could barely see from the other eye.

"I love you—I love you, and want you to see," she told him. She was a wonderful woman and Justin would never forget her. She died shortly thereafter of

8

anemia. The year was 1959. Justin looked at her still face framed in white satin, smelled the scent of roses, red roses, that lay across her coffin, and for the first time, through his tears, he realized that he could see with both eyes. He had wished instead that he had gone totally blind. No, Momma, I'll never forget you.

"Thr. Boom Biz, N.Y.C." Justin shook his head, and somewhere deep, a voice whispered—*Momma.*

Chandal carefully worked her pantyhose up her thighs until they snapped into perfect tautness against the honied skin of her legs. Then she let her full skirt fall back into place. She wore her hair pulled back, tied with a ribbon. She had a preference for wearing it that way, though Justin had told her he didn't like it; it was too casual for a woman her age. Really! Twenty-six years old hardly qualified her for "a woman her age."

She drew back, caught sight of herself in the full-length mirror, letting her hands run down her hips as if to smooth her dress. Her red-tipped fingers were spread full, giving the motion a sexual significance. Her body was thin-boned. She wasn't actually a ravishing beauty, but she liked what she saw. Full-busted, thin-hipped, men were always attracted to her. She focused sharply on her breasts, the roundness of them, and could feel the nipples rise slightly. She blushed, staring at herself in the mirror. But then, disbelieving, she allowed her gaze to move away, move throughout the room. She was certain someone was standing there, motionless, watching her. Some hidden observer. The room was empty.

"What time is it?" Justin called from the living room.

Chandal blinked at the clock. "Ten-thirty."

"Damn! I promised the old ladies that we'd be over there by now."

"Do you want me to call?"

"Forget it."

Chandal pirouetted into the living room, making the hem of her skirt flare. Facing Justin, she stopped the

9

spin so suddenly that the skirt snapped above her knees, causing him to start.

"Jesus!" He shook his head.

"How do I look?" she asked.

She wore brown leather spike heels, sheer stockings, and a long-sleeved pale green dress, which clung from her breasts to her hips as though magnetized. Then it shot open into a full skirt that fell below her knees like an inverted tulip. A gold pendant hung from her neck and wire-thin golden bracelets wrapped around her wrists.

"Great," he said, remembering to breathe.

"Do you think they'll like me?"

"Is that what you've been worried about?" He smiled and put his arms around her. "Honey, I've never met anyone who didn't like you. Come on, let's go."

"What about the notebook?" she asked, half-heartedly. "Did you find it?"

He moved to the side table, opened the drawer. One last look. "Find it? Are you kidding? It's impossible to find anything around this dump!" he said, shuffling papers.

Chandal placed her hand on Justin's shoulder. "Justin, how will we know what California is like, unless we go there?"

More shuffling of paper. "Del, we've been all over this. California would be a bust, and you know it. No security, odd jobs, another small apartment. Again! Who needs it?" He straightened up and closed the drawer. Yes, he knew the thing to do, the only practical thing to do, was to take the brownstone. The spacious New York brownstone! "Well, that's how it's going to be," he muttered to himself, meaning that he had absolutely made up his mind.

"Let's go," he said.

"What about the notebook?"

"I think I remember the figures. If not, I'll fake it."

Chandal picked up her long red coat. Good-bye, California dream. Childhood memories. Singing her song for Aunt Mildred. Aunt Mildred, with the henna-colored hair, the slightly damp white handkerchiefs, and the dead eyes. "She's going to be in the movies someday," her mother had said, winking to her sister after Chandal had finished her song. Chandal saw the wink, but took her deep, graceful bow, anyway. "Some actress! What do you think, Milly?" Chandal's aunt stuck up her nose and said, "Women are meant to be beautiful. And quiet." Still, Chandal's dream persisted. College. "You're stage-struck, Chandal; that's not good." Her mother's watchful eyes, worried now. Graduation. Go straight to summer stock, earn thirty dollars a week as an apprentice. September. Hooray for New York! Then Chandal who? Forget acting, settle down, live a nice normal life. And now, one last chance for the old dream. I want to go to California, Justin. I want to act, she had pleaded. He had smiled; that's why we should stay right here in New York. But I'm not an actress in New York, she had reminded him—I'm a secretary! Chandal had tried for three years to get work as an actress. But her hair was too short, too long, her pictures weren't right, she was too thin, too tall—just not right.

Justin saw the strange look on Chandal's face as she did the last button closed on her coat. "Hey, honey." He put his arms around her and crushed her close to his chest. "Don't look so sad. You'll see, everything is going to be okay. Listen, as soon as we settle in, get a little money ahead, we'll take a look at California. Fly out there for a couple of weeks. If we like what we see, we'll move."

Chandal forced a smile. "Promise?"

Justin kissed her. "Promise."

They left their apartment, headed up Eighty-fifth Street toward the park. The street was clean, tree-lined, and quiet. A concerned block association, headed by Nickles Mayo, a man of many talents, kept it that way. Often Nick could be found repairing holes in trees, nailing up signs, reminding neighbors of their civic responsibility. Today, although it was windy and cold, he was crouched on his heels taking a picture of a young tree that had survived its first storm.

"Hey, Knight—wait a minute." Nick (the kids

11

called him St. Nick) let his camera swing loose around his neck. Looking like an old walrus with his chins spilling over his coat collar, he had bow legs and eyes that jerked each time a sin was committed on the block. He smiled past Chandal's ear, his interest focused on Justin, who stood with his hands in his pockets and inspected the street. "I need your help," he said, laying his hand on Justin's arm.

"How's that?"

"The trees—look at them."

Justin glanced around and said, "I don't see anything."

"That goddamn Jew with his car—he keeps backing into them!"

"I don't have the time right now, Nick." Justin said hurriedly.

"But they're dying!" he said and turned to Chandal. "Dying!"

Chandal nudged Justin. "The trees will be all right, Nick. Justin, couldn't we—" She stopped talking and squinted down the street. There were the two trees Nick was talking about, not the frail little tree he had been kneeling in front of. The two trees in front of the brownstone. They were dying, or dead already. "Weren't those trees just put in, Nick?"

"Three years in a row, we paid for new trees!" said Nick, fairly jumping up and down in his agitation. "Something's got to be done."

Justin was edging away, taking her arm, in a hurry to leave. "Look, Nick—what can I do? I don't even know the guy. Call the police. Maybe they'll help you. Okay? We have to go."

Justin pulled Chandal along up the sidewalk as Nick shouted after them, "Why won't somebody do something?"

It was Sunday, the seventh of January.

Chandal's first glimpse of the brownstone had a sobering effect and left her with a sense of pervading gloom. The building, made of dark-streaked brick, sat quietly back, recessed between two newly renovated structures, making it appear all the more rundown.

12

The column that held up the railing was cracked, ready to fall at the slightest touch. Excessive neglect and deterioration were the building's principal features.

Chandal paused at the foot of the steps. Was it the building's obvious shabbiness that had unnerved her? She could imagine the bleak, echoing hallways, in a kind of dark wood, and the high ceilings in another color, maybe a faded olive-green.

She was compelled to scan more closely the face of this ancient structure. Windows, long and narrow, were surrounded by remnants of decomposed vines; vacant eye-like windows, black with soot, that almost entirely sealed off the outside world. She followed a crack, which extended from the roof of the building and made its scar-like way down the wall in a zigzag direction, until it vanished just above the second-story windows.

The only color visible to her eyes was a faint glimmer of stained glass, whose distorted Gothic images seemed to dance in place directly above the front door. The two separate glass panels were scarlet—a deep blood red. Staring harder at these strange images, she felt an atmosphere peculiar to the immediate vicinity—an atmosphere which had no affinity with the neighborhood, but which reeked of the dull, sluggish reality of the two sisters who lived within.

A world condensed to a small plot of real estate, with narrow windows, at which a stray face sometimes appeared, a bodiless face, detached, mysterious, above the thin line of blackened brick that formed the window ledges. Chandal was reminded of those eerie paintings of Little Orphan Annie—big eyes and horrid yellow light which threw everything into silhouette.

"Christ!" breathed Chandal, and she dared to conjure a memory, two years back. Rain. Her umbrella torn inside out. She'd turned her head and seen without warning the old and wrinkled face of a woman of seventy peering out from the rain-stained window on the second floor. Motionless, the woman stared at her. A vacant stare. Sockets void of light and life. Uneasily,

Chandal had moved away down the street into the safety of her own building. Now, two years later, she was about to meet the person belonging to those eyes.

"Justin, wait a minute," she said, following him reluctantly up the gray slab steps. "Shouldn't we think this over?"

He pressed the bell. "What's to think over? In five years, it'll be ours."

"Ours?" She shrank back.

"Well, they didn't come right out and say it, but the implication was there all right. Comes the time, we can buy it."

They had only walked a short way, but already the frozen wind had cut through them. Chandal hunched her shoulders together for warmth and tried to bury her chin into her coat. Above the dull brass knocker on the heavy door a shutter flicked open and a face peered from the hole and then withdrew. A safety chain rattled and the door opened.

Chandal was relieved to find that a younger woman stood at the door. Introducing herself as Elizabeth, she cheerfully ordered them inside out of the cold. In her early sixties, the woman moved like a young girl. She was very thin and her clothes had lost their shape, but she kept smiling all the time. Despite her appearance, she seemed happy. "And is this Chandal?" She beamed. "Am I right?"

"Yes." Chandal forced a smile.

"Yes, Chandal," repeated the woman. Her deep voice was warm and cajoling. She turned to match her guess with a look, smiling to herself at her excellent memory. She asked the young couple to wait in the parlor while she went for her sister, who was asleep upstairs.

It was an old ladies' parlor, dingy, faded, depressing. Across the room, Justin warmed his hands against the radiator. Chandal wrapped her arms around herself and sat some distance away in a threadbare chair.

An Oriental carpet covered the floor. It was worn in spots, and now more gray than red. The wood floor,

14

visible at the edges of the carpet, seemed in good condition, although it was hard to tell from the thick layer of dust that covered it. The couch and chairs were covered with thin flowered cloth, the low tables had numerous handmade doilies, and the atmosphere was dark, dank, and smelled of the faint vapor of imminent death.

"Hey, come on, don't look so down." Justin felt perfectly at home. "Did I tell you? They're really two nice old ladies."

Chandal shook visibly. The sudden heat of the room made her face burn. She wiped her lips with the back of her hand—they were chapped and slightly cracked. Dammit! She was starting to cry. She clung to the narrow arms of the chair—the tears drew back and allowed her to smile slightly. "She was nice—wasn't she?"

"Sure."

Chandal stared idly at the narrow mahogany pedestal, on top of which sat a gnarled Gothic figure with its face half in shadows. It sat with its legs folded, partially hiding its cloven hooves, and gazed back at her. Lodged neatly at the base were symbols, harsh twisted lines, abstractions.

"Chandal . . ." The voice whispered to her softly and she found herself staring down the darkened hallway just beyond the living room door. The hallway seemed to go on forever. She strained her eyes, trying to see into the darkness. Her eyes blurred.

"Chandal . . ." The voice more distant now, far off.

Who was calling her? She turned. Justin had picked up a magazine, was casually flipping the pages. The windows were closed and locked. She shifted positions in her chair. Then, faintly at first, as if looking through a yellowish filter, she saw the door at the far end of the hallway move slightly.

The voice beckoned, wishfully—almost inviting. And then the door at the far end of the hallway slammed shut. The sudden sharp thud of the door startled her. "Chandal . . ."

Chandal stood up. "Justin, I'm leaving!" She was

15

stunned to find the old woman blocking her way. She could hardly keep from staring into the woman's eyes. It was the color, or rather the lack of color. So pale as to be almost transparent. Chandal stifled a sharp gasp. God! She forced a smile. The woman returned her smile with a slight gracious curve of the lips, touching her on the shoulder so lightly, it seemed the contact of a spiritual being.

Wrapped in an old woolen sweater, she wore no makeup and allowed her gray hair to go wild upon her head. She took her spectacles, thin and gold-framed, from her nose and squinted at them blindly.

"I'm sorry to have kept you waiting," Magdalen said, letting up the shade at the window, though this added very little light. It served primarily as a social gesture rather than accomplishing any practical purpose. It was still necessary for her to switch on china lamps, hand-painted, on tables at either end of the couch. Feet shuffling, she explained that she was ill and that she had to take medication which sometimes put her into a deep sleep that was difficult to wake up from. "So you've decided, then?" she said softly, abruptly changing the subject and listening closely for the answer. Her breathing was not rhythmic, but self-conscious, as if she had to remember to breathe.

Justin was the first to speak. "Oh, yes. We're very excited about it."

He looked toward Chandal, which encouraged her to add, "Yes. We've always wanted to live in a larger space. Our apartment isn't very big."

"Please, sit down. Elizabeth should be along shortly." Her voice was warmer than Chandal had imagined it would be.

"Here, honey—let me take your coat." Justin laid both their coats over the back of the chair and sat in one of the two high winged-back chairs at opposite ends of the couch. Chandal sat in the other.

"Is it very cold out?" Magdalen asked, seating herself on the couch, letting her black woolen skirt fall in a genteel fashion about her slim body. Each breath was shallow, centered in her chest.

16

Chandal watched, wondering where she had seen— now she had it. The clear picture of her father lying in bed, so thin, and getting thinner. He was almost gone by then; Chandal felt her mother knew that. Chandal believed that her father knew it, too. The next day it happened. In the evening, at dusk, he had some sort of seizure. The blanket that covered him rose and fell with his harsh spasmodic breathing. His arms and legs jerked in short, sudden motions. He recovered momentarily, rested comfortably a short while, and Chandal knew if there were things to tell him, this would be her only chance. "He seems to be okay now," Chandal's mother said in a low whisper, hoping it was true.

Chandal tried to approach his bedside, but the presence of death kept her at bay. It was something she could almost see moving toward him, taking hold, lulling him into submissiveness. He was so alive, he was still so alive. Yet even though he smiled, even though he made his eyes sparkle one last time, Chandal knew the time had come. She drew back and felt ashamed that she hadn't had the strength to hold up under it all. Her last words to him were: "See you in the morning."

He died an hour later of lung cancer.

"And so you can understand, then, why we dislike winter." Magdalen paused. "Does it affect you in the same way?"

Chandal turned to face her. How long had the woman been talking? "Oh, I had pneumonia when I was ten." She wondered why she'd said that.

"Is that all?" mused Magdalen, smiling slightly. The room fell into silence, which was blithely broken by Elizabeth clattering down the stairs from the second floor, tea tray clutched in both hands.

"Tea!" she said cheerfully, coming into the room, ready to capsize with each step. The cups were delicate, and she poured proudly from an antique teapot. Chandal felt once that Magdalen had made an almost indiscernible motion to take the teapot when Elizabeth had first set down the tray, but apparently the

17

gesture had gone unnoticed. Elizabeth had begun chatting brightly, offering tasteless dry biscuits on a thin porcelain plate. Still, there had been a faint flush in Magdalen's cheeks as she looked at her sister reigning over the tea tray. As if today, it should have been her right to do the honors of pouring the tea, serving the guests. A moment later, a deep, loving look passed between the two women, so that Chandal could see the alliance of their souls. Yes, surely she had imagined Magdalen's annoyance. She refocused on the conversation. Elizabeth was speaking. Scatterbrained, Chandal thought. Magdalen was probably the more intellectual of the two. Yet Elizabeth's voice was strangely compelling in its own way.

"Oh, yes—we've had other people interested in moving in with us," Elizabeth said, seated properly on the couch next to her sister.

"Oh, I hadn't realized that," Justin said, sipping his tea.

"Oh, my, yes. There were three others. The first was a young man. A student of music. What was it he played, Magdalen?"

"The violin."

"Yes, that was it exactly. But, no, thank you! Mind you, we like music, but we want to be able to turn it off from time to time. And then there was an unmarried woman. Oldish, wouldn't you say she was, Magdalen?"

"Yes."

"She was a foreigner. Russian, I think. We just wouldn't have felt right. Couldn't understand her, really. Accent and all. We think it would be nice to have someone to have a little chat and a cup of tea with from time to time. What use would her company have been to us? Don't you agree?"

Justin said, "Oh, sure. You wouldn't want just anyone living here."

"Exactly." Elizabeth laughed, and Justin along with her.

Chandal smiled, smoothing a wrinkle from the skirt

18

of her dress. "You said there were three. I was just wondering—"

"What?" Elizabeth asked awkwardly.

"That there were three people interested. You mentioned only two."

"Three? Did I? Oh, no—I'm wrong. Two others, not three. You know, you are a lovely girl. Isn't she, Magdalen? Pretty. Very pretty."

"Thank you." Chandal blushed.

"How old are you? Nineteen?" asked Elizabeth.

Chandal nodded. "No. Twenty-six."

"How old do you think I am?"

"I . . . really don't know."

"Well, there's really no need to tell you. When you get to be . . . well, I'm rundown, as they say. Can't sleep. I've also put on weight. Horrible, isn't it? I eat because—"

"Elizabeth." Magdalen silenced her with a sudden jerk of her hand.

"I'm sorry, Magdalen. But I do look rundown. Tell the truth."

Magdalen smiled patiently. "A little pale, perhaps."

Then the social amenities were over, and Elizabeth began with the restrictions. She hoped they wouldn't be keeping terribly late hours. So jarring to awaken in the middle of the night and hear your own front door opening and closing. Of course, they would understand if occasionally— Then there was Magdalen's health. She really shouldn't be kept up too late with loud parties and the like. Chandal asked about renovation, redecoration. Elizabeth gave Magdalen an almost imperceptible glance. Magdalen pursed her lips in annoyance and nodded her head. Of course, it would be quite all right, Elizabeth said hastily. They were to do just as they pleased. You don't mean that, thought Chandal, gazing at her pink-flushed face. You really don't want us here at all, do you? In the next moment, Elizabeth changed again to happiness and smiles, urging them to feel at home, to make themselves perfectly comfortable and happy in the brown-

19

stone. Of course, they could use the basement. Magdalen and she had no use for it whatsoever. Finally, hesitantly, Elizabeth mentioned the rent as $600 a month. Chandal squeezed Justin's hand—he said nothing. Or perhaps, if they wished it unfurnished, then—$500? Unfurnished, said Chandal hastily, imagining away the gloom and the musty furnishings. Elizabeth nodded. Yes, it would be all right. Now, there was one more thing; she was afraid she must stress its importance—under no circumstances would the young couple be allowed to venture upstairs to the second floor.

There was in all of this a touch of something not quite right. Chandal couldn't put her finger on it, but it was there. Once she thought she had heard the sound of soft padded footsteps moving above her. Or was it because Elizabeth had just mentioned the second floor? No, there they were again. Chandal could hear them clearly now, a shuffling sound, slow and steady. She glanced at Justin, disconcerted. He was preoccupied, listening to Elizabeth explain that the second floor was their home. That no one had ever been allowed up there.

Chandal looked down at her hands. They were trembling. A dull ache had formed behind her eyes, a heavy quality, as if she had been drugged. She felt dizzy.

The shuffling above her grew louder.

She turned and saw Magdalen staring at her. Behind the woman's pale eyes flickered some kind of understanding. A reaching out to Chandal.

"Do other people live here?" asked Chandal suddenly.

"No. We live alone." Magdalen smiled.

"But I can—"

"Father purchased this building in . . ." Elizabeth looked to Magdalen. "When was it?"

"Nineteen twenty-three."

"Yes, a city tax sale. For eighteen hundred dollars. Imagine. He had planned to rehabilitate it, then sell it for profit. Well . . ." Her head leaned sadly to one

20

side. "Business turned from bad to worse, as they say, and here we are."

"Imagine, honey—eighteen hundred dollars." Justin tried to join in the conversation.

"They both died within nine months," Elizabeth said, sipping tea.

"What?" asked Chandal.

"Father and Mother. Both gone within a year. Magdalen and I have lived here ever since."

Chandal couldn't imagine why no one heard the footsteps. They were there. They were still there. She spun her head around toward the hallway. Watching. Listening. But there was no one in the hallway. She fiddled with the doily on the arm of the chair. Elizabeth was speaking to Justin now. She watched him shake his head and laugh.

The footsteps above had stopped.

Chandal listened. Yes, they were gone. It was then that she noticed the way in which Magdalen stared at Justin. For a long time, Magdalen seemed unable to take her eyes from him—so much so, that at last Elizabeth leaned over and was obviously going to whisper something but changed her mind. At that point, Magdalen pulled back and politely refocused her attention on Chandal. "May we pour you more tea?"

"Oh, no—thank you." Chandal indicated that she still hadn't finished the first cup. She took another sip. An avid coffee drinker, she had an aversion to tea, even good tea, as this was, she noted conscientiously. Exotic. From India.

"Oh, Magdalen—may I show them your collection?" asked Elizabeth, the tiny charm bracelet tinkling around her wrist, as she tugged on her sister's sleeve.

"Collection?" asked Justin.

"Oh, my, yes. Magdalen has an absolutely stunning collection of butterflies. Especially from the family *Papilionidae*. The tiger swallowtail—magnificent. And the colors—radiant. Oh, please."

Magdalen made a gesture of assent.

"We'd love to see them," said Justin. "Isn't that right, Del?"

21

Chandal was caught by Justin's sudden question, having been intrigued by the way in which Magdalen moved her hands. Long and thin, her hands created graceful patterns in space, stopping abruptly and floating to rest in her lap. "What?" she asked, reddening at her belated response.

"Magdalen's collection of butterflies. Would you like to see them?" He nodded conspicuously.

"Oh, yes—please."

Elizabeth padded briskly from the room and up the stairs to the second floor. Chandal rubbed the side of her arm, waiting for someone to say something. Magdalen had begun to stare at Justin again. Justin smiled politely at her. She returned the smile.

"The statue, the one on the pedestal—it's very interesting." Justin made a half-gesture toward the wall directly behind Magdalen.

"Elizabeth and I had it made—a young artist friend years ago. It's been in our living room ever since."

Chandal shifted uncomfortably in her chair, refusing to look at the statue.

For a moment there was silence.

Then all eyes moved in the direction of the staircase as Elizabeth had now reached the lower landing and exclaimed, "Here they are!" Beneath a glass enclosed carrying case of oak, she proudly displayed Magdalen's collection. "Aren't they lovely?" She laid the tray carefully into Chandal's lap.

"Yes, they are," Chandal said, gazing into the glass tray. How fragile, she thought. How sad and how fragile. Wings transparent, stuck with pins. Wings that once flew. A butterfly coffin. How grotesque. Chandal turned to Magdalen. "They're very pretty."

"Thank you." Magdalen looked pleased.

"Would you care to see them?" Elizabeth asked Justin, reaching for the tray.

"No, don't bother. I'll come over there."

Justin stood and moved behind Chandal's chair. "They're fantastic. And the colors." He took Chandal's hand in his. "How do you—"

"If you'll excuse me now, I feel a bit tired," said

Magdalen, standing slowly, each part of her body seeming to rise at separate intervals. "Elizabeth will show you out."

"Oh, yes—of course." Justin wondered if he hadn't said something to upset the woman.

"Magdalen is ill, you understand. She—"

"Elizabeth?" Magdalen beckoned.

Elizabeth moved from Justin's side, and having displayed an embarrassed smile, helped Magdalen to the landing. She whispered into Magdalen's ear. Magdalen muttered, "No," placed her hand gently on Elizabeth's cheek, and started up the stairs.

"Well, time to go, honey." Justin nudged Chandal.

"Yes." Chandal placed the butterfly tray on the table next to her chair and stood up.

Elizabeth waited until Magdalen was nearly to the top of the stairs before returning to the living room. "I'm sorry that you have to leave so soon," she said in a low whisper. "I had wanted to show you some of her other specimens. But, well—some other time."

"Thank you again." Justin took Chandal's arm.

"We'll have our furnishings cleared out by tomorrow evening."

"You really don't—"

"No, this is your home now. You just start thinking of it that way. Come, I'll show you to the door."

Later that evening, she stood motionless at the window. The sun had left the city an hour ago; dusk faded. Carefully, she drew the shutters closed, next the curtains, blocking reflections of streetlights. Muted sounds, traffic, children playing, and a dog barking all leaked through the stained-glass windows. The room fell into deep shadows.

She moved into the middle of the room, standing beside a table draped with a plain black cloth. She lit the small black and red candles which stood in cups of green glass, transparent green glass. The swaying of flames illuminated the nymph-like images, encrusted, icon images from another age, twisted, dis-

23

torted images seeking self-gratification, punishment, adorning the walls. She lit the third candle.

In the corner of the room, another pair of hands held *The Book of Ahriman* When last the demon had appeared, he had brought with him the book. "Read it," he suggested. "It will calm you."

A haze floated over the candles.

A match was put to still more candles. She then moved to the inlaid rosewood sideboard, lifted a wooden tray, carried unlit candles, small glass vials, and flowers back to the table. She took great care in their arrangement.

This done, the two women approached the table. Clad in black robes, they wore collars, necklaces, depicting the image of Ahriman. Ruby-red beads hung around their necks; bracelets and rings adorned their fingers. They sat. Placing the book flat, the one with the book began to read:

The emerald room stank of death, although death had been denied its rightful claim on Ahriman for almost 122 years.

Born in the year 1410, his father, an ordinary Italian monk, set out to seek enlightenment. Not finding solace among his fellow monks, Ahriman's father called for a demon and asked for help. He had heard of this demon from his grandfather, and watched it materialize with a stirring curiosity and fear. As the demon presented itself, it smiled and the stench was almost overbearing. It spoke: "You have summoned me to a most unholy place. Why?"

"I wish to live forever."

"All right," the demon said in a gentle voice. "But only for my purposes. Do you understand?"

"I do," said the monk.

The demon rang a tiny bell, and three women entered; in their arms, upon their breasts, and between their thighs, the monk became corrupted by magic, because he had not known how to understand what corrupt magic was. Before the

24

night was over, the monk and two of the women were dead, ravished by the only survivor—Nina, Ahriman's mother, who died nine months later giving birth to her bastard son. That had happened a long time ago, but Nina had set free something evil in the world, the secular world, the devil world, the world at large.

Ahriman, half-demon but mortal still, upon his deathbed, vowed eternal love to the devil, and for this the devil allowed Ahriman to live forever in spirit.

And Ahriman was pleased.

With a sudden shudder of ecstasy, she took hold of the flower, crushing it gently in her sweating hand. She spoke, but her voice could not be heard. *"And Ahriman was pleased."* Her hand convulsed around the tiny head of the flower, gripped tighter, until the red petals released themselves, falling to the dusty floor like droplets of pale blood. She smiled. . . .

Ahriman was pleased.

Patient maintains a rigid posture. Tendency to cover left side of face apparently believing that scars exist from the fire. There is, in fact, no scar tissue, as patient received only slight superficial burns. Facial expressions are sad, with mouth turned down, eyes dull and lackluster. Eyes are puffy and heavily shadowed, due perhaps to patient's continued fear of sleep and resistance to sleep-inducing drugs.

It is my belief that patient has undergone some sort of severe shock that has induced temporary paranoid tendencies. There is constant fear that perhaps I am one of the enemy and there is a very real possibility that I may not be able to convince otherwise. Uncertain prognosis. Recommend that patient be watched closely for suicidal tendencies.

                                        I. Luther

❧ 2 ❧

THE NEXT MORNING, THE COLD WAVE BROKE AND temperatures climbed into the upper thirties. Justin spent most of the morning sorting through papers in his converted closet-office. Chandal dismantled the Christmas tree, which had started to droop from too many decorations, too little water. For the first time since she could remember, Justin skipped breakfast.

Chandal's hand was unsteady as she removed the first ornament, a tiny, bright yellow bird. Carefully, she put it into the plastic bag. She could see Justin's back through the door. He sat leaning forward in his chair, letting his long legs sprawl under the desk. He appeared to be looking at something that disturbed him. Chandal shrugged. Bills. Justin never enjoyed paying bills.

She turned away and smiled. She had an irresistible urge to laugh and was ashamed of it; what in God's name was funny? Only her own hysterical sense of nervousness and confusion concerning the future. She was suddenly disturbed by her own restlessness.

She continued stripping the tree, meticulously, laying the icicles in one box, the heart-shaped crystals into another. Ornaments from the past. Antiques, really. A gift from her mother and father. She became aware of the sound gradually, first imperceptibly, subconsciously—then consciously. She turned and saw Justin's chest rise and fall in a shuddering, irregular rhythm. A rhythm not of his own making. It was as if someone else was breathing for him. "Justin, are you all right?"

He turned. "What?" His voice was detached. Hazy. The telephone rang.

27

"I'll get it," she said. It was her mother.

"How's the weather over there, Chandal?" Her mother always started their conversations by reminding Chandal that the East Side of New York was the only civilized place to live. Helen Briar lived by the dictates of what she imagined to be socially correct. However, she wasn't a snob. More than anything, she was socially shy, feeling always on the outskirts of activity, almost pathetically grateful to be included in a gathering, no matter how bored she might later find herself.

"The weather here's the same as on the East Side, Mom."

"But the air is clean over here. Clean air. No smog."

"Mom, about California—"

"I can't bear it. I couldn't sleep a wink last night. Not a wink. It's terrible for my asthma—no sleep. I had an argument with my housekeeper and she's leaving. Can you believe it? The third one this year. I begged her to come back and she won't—"

"Mom. Calm down and listen." She tried to catch Justin's eye. Her mother's frantic phone calls were one of their jokes. He was frowning, looking down at his desk, lost in thought.

"I'm in bed. I took four aspirins."

"Mom, hush. Now, why did you fight with Pat?"

"It was all mixed up. It started with the fish soup. She knows how delicate my stomach is. I'm on a special diet. She knows that. I begged her to come back—"

"Mom, don't go begging Pat. She's a very unpleasant woman. Let her go. We'll find another housekeeper."

"You won't be here. You'll be in California."

"I will be here. Wait'll you hear the news. We're moving to a brownstone. Right here in New York."

From that point on, Chandal had no choice but to surrender herself to polite listening. She threw in an occasional "Ah-ha" in order to keep up her end of the conversation. When Chandal finally hung up, she felt her head ache with weariness, and she hadn't the foggiest notion of what her mother had just said. All that she knew was that she had just made her mother ridiculously happy.

"How's your mother?" Justin asked.

"Delirious."

"I figured she would be." For a few seconds he barely moved.

"Justin, is something wrong?"

"No." He got to his feet shakily and walked about the living room, touching familiar objects while she watched. He ran his hand across the dining table. It appeared to comfort him, his feet solid against the wooden floor, his hand solid against the oak table. He straightened up—listened, seemed to hear all the old familiar sounds of the building, noisy radios, conversations, the kid with his trumpet on the fourth floor. He stood perfectly still, cautious, listening. He looked like a young animal about to be caught in the hunter's trap, standing alert, and stiff. He was ready to bolt at the first sound of danger. Suddenly, Chandal found him slipping on his jacket. "Look, honey—I have to go out for a while. I'll be right back." He zipped up his jacket.

"Where are you going?"

"I'll be right back, okay?" He kissed her on the forehead and left the apartment without saying another word.

Completely exhausted and concerned over Justin's odd behavior, Chandal pressed the tips of her fingers into the bridge of her nose, trying to press away the slight ache that had gathered at the center of her forehead. Her concern drained quickly, because it had nothing tangible to adhere to. However, the exhaustion refused to depart that quickly.

She allowed herself to relax, leaning against the cushioned back of the windowseat. She tried desperately to remember everything she had to do today, to pin it all down. It was no use. What swarmed into her mind were other scenes— It was nice being someone special. Someone whose opinion was important. "Yes, I have decided to back the President on this issue." She smiled. Pictured herself stepping from a limousine, on Justin's right arm—it was the opening-night gala of her latest picture. A celebration of Chandal Knight.

She would carry herself tall. Dress in a black velvet evening gown. A black evening gown! For her, the words implied a great deal. Sophisticated people. Yacht parties—glamour. Chandal let her thoughts wander; she stood upon a moonlit terrace in Cannes. Music, soft and seductive, played in the background. There were glasses of bubbling champagne everywhere; toasts in her honor. Drifting deeper and deeper into fantasy, Chandal was unaware of her own reflection just inches away in the silver-and-gold Christmas tree ornament, of the absolute sadness which had actually crept into her face. Neither was she aware that her dreams were unrealistic, unformed, and that she lacked the discipline to obtain them.

Chandal suddenly glanced at her watch, the part that gave the date. The dream was over. They were eight days behind schedule. They had to be out by the first—the landlord had already threatened official procedures. Plane tickets had to be canceled, hotel reservations, movers. The original plan—turn the key, let the movers do it. Now—they were going to do it, all of it, alone.

She unbuttoned her blouse, unzipped her skirt. She noticed that her body was a bit swollen, but not bad. Worries building, she slipped into old clothes—dungarees, Justin's plaid shirt. Where to start? What to pack? Her depression deepened. She went into the kitchen, poured tomato juice, squeezed a lemon into it. The taste was sharp and clean. Besides, she told herself, how much was her acting worth to anyone but herself? Except for Justin, who else took her seriously? She had always seen the skepticism in people's faces, the slight smiles brimming in their eyes. Still, her face burned recalling some of the lovely things she had done as an actress.

She was a little ashamed of herself now for her inability to be happy with what she had. It seemed to her a flaw, a defect in character. Everyone else around her seemed reasonably content. Nothing was as she had planned, but Chandal plunged in, anyway, trying to ignore her disappointment.

Within an hour, Chandal had stripped the tree bare. Kneeling on the floor, pressed between the black leather chair and the couch, she had difficulty fitting the last of the lights into the flimsy box. The wires tangled; two bulbs broke. Impatiently, she gathered the cord into an untidy clump and forced it haphazardly into its proper place. Legs aching, she stood up, and then clearly heard it—the distinct slow ringing of a Christmas bell, almost symbolic of a new beginning.

"Mintz?" she called. But the cat, she was sure, was asleep on top of the kitchen cabinet. The bell sounded again.

Something was odd. The silence that followed made her heart leap. With the street sounds muted, with the windows closed, the wind shut out, the silence took on its own malevolent nature.

"Mintz!"

Then she heard another sound. Breathing. Shallow, harsh breathing. Her mind swiftly changed gears. Her heart beat rapidly and her palms were sweating. The bell sounded again.

Quickly, she glanced at the tree. Hanging from the bottom branch, an ornate silver bell she had never seen before. Glistening, shimmering light suddenly blistered her eyes. A powerful pulse began to beat in her mind, straining her vision.

She cast her mind back, trying to recall the ornament, trying to remember placing it there on the tree. Somewhere in her childhood, hadn't there been such a bell ringing . . . no, not her childhood. A layer of cool air moved over her and she felt prickles rise up on her skin, making her shiver. Was she imagining it, or was that bell actually moving by itself? Violent tugs, as if trying to rip itself right off the tree. And all the time, ringing. Ringing, until—she took an unsteady step

31

backward and her knees buckled. No, she couldn't fall. She had to walk to that door, to get out of this room.

Louder ringing until she had to cover her ears, and now the air was even colder. Could that be her own breath she was seeing?

From all sides, it grabbed her. A pressure, pushing in until it was like four walls closing around her, leaving her no room to breathe. Suddenly in her mind, she saw it. A long ebony box. A casket. If the lid opened on that box, she would see her own face, stare into her own eyes.

Subtly, insistently, the pressure squeezed in, until she heard someone screaming and it was herself and she couldn't stop. A stream of liquid was pouring down her face now, down her back, rolling down between her breasts, dripping off her body, making circles on the wood floor, until she was too weak to fight anymore, and so when the cramping began—the hot, throbbing aching of her vital organs—she doubled up like a helpless child and fell sobbing and screaming onto the hard floor. "Momma!" she cried. "Momma, help me! Please help me!" Her mother's face, lips parted, smiling, eyes glowing, passed before her eyes, and somehow, Chandal's brain became more lucid in the instant, despite the pain, despite the clarion ringing of the bell. A louder thunderous peal, and the mother's face changed—features melting like molten wax. Wax being modeled into a grotesque, evil mask, wearing a look of such malignant intensity that Chandal's scream caught inside her own chest, caught and turned against her own body, swelling inside her until she thought that surely she was going to explode. The face laughed at the young silly girl and melted away again, slowly, still stretched into grotesque lines of gaiety. Another image formed. Justin. It was Justin's face. Justin's soft, tender eyes, looking into hers.

Fighting to stay conscious, to see her husband's face more clearly, Chandal stretched her hands out on the floor and began to crawl, ignoring the splinter that drove itself inside the flesh of her finger. She crawled like an animal bent on survival.

At the edge of the braided rug, just inside the front door, she felt for the closet doorknob, tried to pull herself to her feet. The final attack came swiftly, masterfully. She was knocked to the floor by a violent blow and her legs were lifted by an unseen hand. Her back smashed hard against the wood with a sharp thud. The weight on her chest was unbearable; she tried to rise, but she was solidly pinned to the floor.

Her breasts burned. It felt as if someone was ripping them away from her body. With a last final lunge, something lifted her into the air. There was a harsh sudden sound and she knew that something inside of her had ruptured, burst open as if it had exploded with grief or pain. Her body dropped flat to the floor.

And then it was over.

The bell stopped ringing. Daylight faded.

In her dream, the shudderings, the cramps began again. She felt within her less strength for the struggle and no longer resisted.

"There, there, there," someone said.

"You see, it's not so painful," said another voice, farther off in the distance.

Chandal answered, "Yes, it's easy. Very easy."

When she awoke, she found herself in bed. With a glass straw, Elizabeth forced black coffee between her lips. Justin opened the window slightly.

At four o'clock, Magdalen brought the doctor into the room. After a brief examination, he announced that Chandal was pregnant and had been for at least two months. Reassured that his wife was going to be all right, Justin thanked the doctor and the sisters for their help. By the time he walked them to the door and said good-bye, Chandal was peacefully asleep.

She was smiling now, holding to the hand of a child. A girl child, a tiny replica of herself. The child would grow, tall and tanned and lean, and she would teach it to dream the possible dreams. To educate herself, to make herself fit for a profession. Something worthwhile. And perhaps in time, there would be a man. Someone the child would love as much as her mother loved her father. A contented sigh escaped Chandal's lips and she rolled over slightly, her hair falling free of her face across the pillow. Justin sat beside her and waited.

❦ 3 ❦

BILLY DEATS LOUNGED SLEEPILY ON HIS BEDSPREAD, whose color had been ace-of-spades black. The present color was faded brown. His shoes, feet still in them, comfortably lay across a nearby table. "No shit," he said to the phone, picking up a half-burned cigarette from the overflowing ashtray and looking for a match. "You're going to be a daddy? That's cute. When did you—"

"Couple of hours ago," Justin said and watched Chandal strut around the apartment wearing only the expectant air of motherhood. He motioned her to put something on and went back to the phone. "You're invited to the celebration." Chandal bit Justin on the back of the neck. "Cut that out!" he said.

Billy said, "What?"

And Justin said, "Not you."

"When?"

"Tonight at eight. Our place."

"You got it," said Billy and hung up.

Wrapping herself in a yellow satin robe, Chandal drank cold milk. Having a child was something she'd always wanted. A fire engine roared by. Justin banged the window shut. "That makes four in the last hour. What do they do—use this street for a shortcut?"

34

She hugged him. "They're wonderful!" she said. "Everything's wonderful!"

"Honey, are you sure about tonight?"

"And why not?" she asked, reaching for the gold loving cups. Their first anniversary. She remembered Justin presenting them with great care. Candles lit, music turned down low, Justin had suddenly disappeared into the bedroom. Chandal had let her legs stretch the full length of the couch, and waited. And then Justin had reappeared behind her and placed his hands across her eyes. "Don't look."

Chandal had never thought about hands before, but when his sensitive fingers had covered her eyes, when the heat of his warm hands had caressed her cheeks, she had known how warm a pair of hands could be.

Chandal proudly placed the cups on the coffee table and smiled. When she had opened her eyes that night, they had been sitting there, exactly where they were sitting now. "I think I'm going to cry," she had said, and laughed instead and Justin had poured the champagne. They would drink from the gold loving cups again tonight.

"Del, listen." He took hold of her arm. "For one thing, you need your rest."

"And for another?"

"Well, I—"

She was determined—Justin was glad to give in. For the first time in days she was relaxed. They made a mad rush for phone books.

Justin spoke with Chandal's mother first. "A grandchild," she said in a cathedral voice. "You're a wonderful boy, Justin. Wonderful."

"You'll come, then?" Justin asked.

"Yes, of course!" she exclaimed. "Can I bring something? French onion dip? Perhaps a chocolate cake . . . No? Well, then just the French onion dip and some chips." Justin pictured the salt-and-pepper hair being hurried into curlers, the rose-colored lipstick, the still hopeful eyes. Those eyes reminded him of Chandal's eyes. He said good-bye, putting a smile into his voice. Actually, he liked his mother-in-law. There was something so fragile about her.

More calls. Anyone and everyone. In a spurt of zaniness, Justin even called his dentist. The puzzled voice on the other end of the wire regretted he'd have to decline the invitation. Chandal covered her mouth with her hands to stifle her laughing, while Justin produced a series of comedic faces, until he himself was laughing so hard he could hardly hang up the phone. When they were rich and famous someday, Dr. Bowers would be sorry he hadn't come.

In the midst of their laughter, they pressed against each other, feeling warm and close and united against the world, and then they quit laughing and put their lips together and kissed long and deep, with Justin's tongue in Chandal's mouth, and then they interrupted their own kiss with more laughter, laughing until tears rolled out of their eyes.

For a short time after this, Chandal couldn't speak. Justin observed her with a smile, which seemed right. She sat on the couch, aware of Justin watching her. They were both a little puzzled now. The laughter had gone, replaced by the sudden warm realization that they had, during soft nights of lovemaking, conceived a child.

"I think," she finally said, reaching for his hand and pulling him down on the couch close to her, "that I'm falling in love with you all over again."

"You're fantastic," he said and kissed her.

She casually waved away his claim with her hand. "No, I'm serious, Del. You're one of the most fantastic people I know."

"You love me, don't you?"

He smiled. "Yes."

The next silence lasted for perhaps five minutes. This time Chandal felt no desire to break it and had preferred instead to let Justin light up a joint. They passed the joint back and forth in silence, two or three times, nodding and winking occasionally at each other. When Justin got stoned, he preferred not to talk. Chandal glanced out the window now, murmured, "A girl—I'd like a girl," in a cheerful way. She had the relaxation that comes only from deliberate awareness—awareness that Justin and she were facing a bright future. When she refused the fourth drag, Justin seemed relieved; it was as if he approved of Chandal's now taking good care of herself. "Jesus Christ!" Justin hollered. "The party!" and he ran out to do the shopping. Chandal dusted and vacuumed. They were two young happy people in love, getting ready to have a party. In less than two hours, they shopped, dressed, cleaned the apartment, and then managed to look fairly calm by the time the first guest arrived.

"How do I look?" Chandal demanded.

"Gorgeous."

"Thank God. I wouldn't not be beautiful tonight for anything."

She opened the door—Justin's enthusiasm crumbled. It was Sissy standing there, a girl friend of Chandal's whom he'd always despised. He'd thought that she would have better sense than to show up after their last fight. Justin didn't like any of Chandal's friends, especially Sissy. He felt that they were all neurotics feeding off of each other's weaknesses.

"Can you believe it—I'm pregnant!"

"Chandal—it's wonderful. Just wonderful." Sissy's neck was wound in a yard-long silk scarf and her eyes were hidden behind dark sunglasses—affectations acquired during her recent visits to Italy. A high-pressure ad exec, she was Chandal's best friend.

The two girls moved into the room, Sissy deliberately avoiding any contact with Justin, and Chandal felt Justin's quizzical eyes following her. She turned swiftly and gave him a wink and he relaxed a little. They had to remember to stay loose with each other. Anyway, she didn't feel bad about inviting Sissy. Good Lord, Justin had invited his dentist! She smiled to herself, remembering how they'd laughed.

In a few moments, their tiny apartment was jammed with people. Billy Deats appeared, wearing faded Levi's and an unbuttoned denim shirt: something energetic and forceful in his friendly eyes, perfectly capped actor's teeth, and trim body. Justin found himself mixing drinks in the kitchen and talking to Billy.

"Five hundred a month—can you afford it?" Billy ate a cashew.

"Not really, but with the settlement from this apartment, we've got two years of rent at the same price."

Justin and Chandal were one of three remaining families left in what was once the elegant townhouse of the late Enrico Caruso. They were holding a rent-control lease and the landlord was forced to make a settlement if he intended to renovate. He did and he had. Justin had accepted $6,000. Had he known that he wasn't going to California and now that Chandal was pregnant, he would have asked for more. The other tenants weren't willing to settle that cheaply, and already Justin felt he'd made a mistake. With moving costs and a baby soon to arrive, he knew $6,000 wouldn't go far.

"Which brownstone is it?" asked Billy.

"The old one, three down from the corner. Here's your drink."

"Thanks. Isn't that funny—I've never noticed it."

"You still going with Fay?" Justin sipped his bourbon and water.

"No, man. She had no rhythm at all, if you know what I mean. She lost control of who she was. I bowed out."

"She was a nice girl."

"They're all nice. You know, I sure miss us hanging out together. Damn, those were great times!"

Justin grinned.

Drinks in hand, they moved into the living room and sat on the floor. They were joined by a dark-haired girl, slightly exotic, with heavy-lidded eyes. "How are you? Merry Christmas. I'm afraid I'm a little late," she said and let the silence hang between.

Billy wasted no time in mentally stripping her.

"My God—all these people!" she said with Southern flatness, a hint of backwoods that Justin had heard echoed in Billy.

Billy smiled and squeezed her arm. She looked at

38

him with her gray eyes and smiled back; it was going to be an easy score. "My dear angel," Billy said, meeting her eyes, "how are you feeling this evening?"

She shrugged. "Undecided."

"I was afraid of that!" Billy's enthusiasm sank, realizing that he was going to be hopelessly swimming against the tide.

Justin watched Billy squirm, remembering how long they had been friends and how much they were alike. They both came from a working-class family, took acting lessons together, demonstrated against nuclear power in Sheridan Square, argued constantly, and loved jazz. Most of the time they discovered that their mutual attraction was based on complete disapproval of each other. They argued about that, as well, which made them practically inseparable.

The young girl with the gray eyes had now snuggled up against Justin. "Christmas is always so depressing, don't you think?"

"What?" Justin blinked.

Billy shrugged. "Christmas is over, sweetheart—two weeks now!"

"I think I need another drink." Justin rose and awkwardly disappeared into the kitchen.

Chandal's mother hugged her once more and cried. A grandchild, at last. It was a blessing. Something to live for, that's what it was. Chandal reflected suddenly what a wonderful person her mother was. She had a lot of faults, yes, but what an incredible amount of love she had inside of her. Already that love was reaching out to an unborn child. Chandal shivered, remembering her hallucination, that ridiculous business with the bell. Then she'd been terrified and it was her mother's face that had calmed her. Then had come the other face to shake that calm, reduce her again to emotional wreckage. Even now, she could see that face. Twisted, evil . . .

"Chandal? What is it, honey?" Her mother's fingers dug into her arm.

Chandal gave a quick shrug, tossing away the image. "Nothing, Mom. Just thinking."

39

"Don't worry, honey. Believe me, you'll make a wonderful mother. My baby, a mother!" She dissolved happily into tears again, letting them flood down her face, washing through powder as they ran, and still she let them run, evidence of her joy.

"How about a drink, Mom? Hey, listen, go tell Justin to fix you a *piña colada* in the blender."

As the pink plump woman bustled toward the kitchen, Chandal turned her eyes deliberately to the barren Christmas tree and the silver bell that hung silently from its lower branch. Just force yourself to look at it and you'll never be afraid again. Somebody had told her something like that a long time ago. Something about death. Yes, when Chandal was a little girl, her mother had made her look at a corpse and told her if she did, she'd never again fear death. But that really wasn't so, was it? Because she did fear death. Her father's death. All death. She couldn't take her eyes off that bell. Rather nice effect. Just the barren tree still sprinkled with a few pieces of tinsel and the one beautiful ornament. Crazy to be afraid of something so beautiful. Well, new mothers had a right to be a little nutty. She tried to smile. Wasn't it all part of expecting a baby? The fear—the joy. But why did she have this terrible knot inside her chest? Like a feeling that something was . . .

"Congratulations," said an unknown black man, shaking her hand as she felt the faintness closing in. A buzzing inside her head. No, not actually a buzzing, something else. "Are you all right?" said a voice, and she turned her eyes to the lips that were speaking. The whirling inside her head cleared, like static tuned out, and from a center of clarity, she heard a recognizable sound. The clear teasing peal of a bell! She spun away from the man, feeling all the while something holding her, pulling at her. But the only thing she could think about, the only thing she could see, was the bell. The silver bell. It floated and twisted before her eyes, ringing, filling her with a sudden nausea. "Hey, hold on, there," said the voice again and she tore her eyes

40

from the silver ornament, back to the face, the kind black face.

"The bell . . . can you hear . . . the bell ringing . . . ?" she stammered, pleadingly and his eyes looked troubled, confused.

"There's no bell ringing," he murmured soothingly.

"You—you can't hear it?" she gasped, and slowly, regretfully, he shook his head.

Then in back of him, the door to the apartment opened and standing there were two old women. Magdalen stared evenly in her direction. Elizabeth hovered by her side.

"Well, look who's here, honey." Justin moved to the doorway and took Magdalen's arm. The bell quieted, stopped ringing.

"Is something wrong?" asked the black man.

"Oh, no—thank you. I was just . . . please excuse me." She swallowed hard and moved away from his concerned eyes.

Chandal's mother chuckled when she saw the look on her daughter's face. "What's the matter, sweetheart?"

"Nothing." The whole room seemed to shake with laughter. The gall pushed its way into her mouth—she rushed from the room into the kitchen.

"What's wrong?" asked her mother. She stood in the doorway, stirring the crushed ice in her drink.

"I said nothing. Leave me alone, Mom." She bent over the sink and ran the water.

Her mother smiled. "Having a baby is nothing to be afraid of. I had you, didn't I? And I'm still around to see you have yours. Honey, everything will be all right."

Chandal swallowed an Alka Seltzer and listened. Jesus! Morning sickness—at night! She was still trembling. Embarrassed—that was it. Embarrassed to be showing her mother her weakness, her fear. "I'm sorry, Mom."

"For what?"

"For acting so damn silly."

"You're allowed."

41

Chandal shook her head. "I'm confused . . . you know, really screwing things up all the time. I guess I'm just disappointed with myself."

"Why?"

"Because, Christ! Mom, I . . ."

"Go on."

"It's the same thing—the theater. I've been thinking about it all day."

She shrugged. "You don't need that, Chandal. You have a husband. A life. That's important."

"It just isn't fair. The way things turn out."

"Only God and the Pope know what's fair." She smiled and put her arm around her daughter. "So we'll leave it to them, okay?"

Chandal smiled. "Okay." For the first time Chandal felt as if she had been able to listen to her mother as a friend.

Her mother leaned over and whispered, "There's a tall, dark stranger out there. Maybe you can fix me up." She winked.

"Come on! But I think he's gay." She dragged her mother back into the next room.

"They've just ruined that word. Ruined it. When I was young—we were all gay."

Chandal laughed. It's your party, so have fun, she ordered herself. Function! It's not polite to stand around at your own party. Suddenly, she was ravenous. Recklessly, she dipped chunks of raw cauliflower into French onion dip, eating one after another. "Delicious, Mom!"

"But you're sick to your stomach. You just took an Alka Seltzer. . . ."

"The best way to treat an upset stomach . . ." announced Chandal, filling a plate with a hot Mexican casserole, " . . . is to ignore it." She giggled. "Momma, will you look at that man kneeling in front of Sissy? Just look at them. Sissy's finally found a man to give her the respect she demands."

Her mother sniffed. "Chandal, any fool can see the man's simply looking up her dress."

Chandal laughed so hard she choked and set down

42

her plate. "Momma!" she gasped when she could talk. "Did anybody ever tell you what a funny lady you are? And did I ever tell you how much I love you?"

Her mother's eyes blinked and then filled with unexpected tears.

"No crying," whispered Chandal, kissing her swiftly on the cheek. "Now watch me dance, Momma. You'll see you didn't waste all your money on those lessons."

She danced to every kind of music. Hair flying, skirt whirling, her body alive with the music. Like a dancer. A real dancer.

"You oughta be on Broadway, Chandal," puffed Billy Deats, jumping around in her wake, trying to keep up with her. "Hey, I don't know how to do this dance. Slow down! Show me what you're doing." He looked funny, Chandal giggled to herself. Funny, nice Billy Deats.

Everything was going very well. The dancers were dancing and the talkers were talking and the drinkers were drinking. Sissy was dancing, looking very pleased with the bald-headed man, the man who'd been kneeling in front of her.

Chandal danced the tango with the lights turned down and a carnation in her teeth because they hadn't bought roses. Her partner was an effeminate man, tall and thin, a man who knew how to move. He sold water beds in Greenwich Village. Everybody had stopped talking to watch while they danced their way across the floor, moving together as one person. Tonight she was dancing the tango like a panther, twisting, feeling her body, the music inside her blood. When the last note sounded, they gathered their energy together and struck a powerful pose and the applause and the whistles rang out. Looking over the sea of cheering faces, her elation dived into sharp disappointment. Justin had missed it. Why, he hadn't even looked up. He was sitting on the sofa, his face turned away, staring at Magdalen. What could she be saying to him that could be so interesting? The smile fell from Chandal's

43

lips and she took a quick step in their direction and then stopped, feeling another pair of eyes staring at her. It was Elizabeth, sitting in a solitary corner of the room over by the window, talking to no one, just staring at Chandal in the most curious way. Almost angrily, Chandal joined the small group around the candle. Someone was telling fortunes. Chandal's was something about great success and money. And something new coming into her life. As if everybody didn't know that something new was coming into her life!

Billy Deats, captivated by the fortune teller's large bosom, used the opportunity for wrestling her. "Something new!" he chortled, putting an arm around her shoulders and pretending to crush her. "How'd you get that psychic information, woman?" They fell to the floor laughing and Chandal let her eyes wander back to the sofa. They were still there—poor Justin must be having a terrible evening—being polite to that old woman. Elizabeth still sat, half-asleep, in her chair.

One at a time, people drifted out, some alone, some in twos and threes. Billy Deats left with the long-haired fortune teller. Her mother, pleasantly tipsy, left with the water-bed salesman and his roommate. They promised to put her into a cab. The nice black man took her hand at the door and looked searchingly into her eyes. She smiled back, chin up, telling him by her happiness that everything was really quite all right. Sissy, who made a funny drunk, left on the arm of her new man. Sunglasses at 2:30 in the morning! She left and then came back. She'd forgotten she had a little present for Chandal—a volume of Arnold's poems. Chandal had to read the one called "The Buried Life." The man pulled her back out the door by the belt of her coat.

"I'll call you!" Chandal said to the happy face in the sunglasses. "Just as soon as we get settled, okay?"

Finally, she closed the door and found herself standing alone in the apartment, except for Elizabeth, who had fallen asleep against the steamy window. The woman wore an expression of pain, but the rest of her body seemed totally at peace.

44

From the kitchen, Chandal heard a faint voice. Magdalen, she thought, and moved closer to the swinging door. The voice continued. "That's possible. I understand. But we must be better acquainted. We'll meet tomorrow evening at the same hour."

Through the opening in the door, Chandal saw Justin seize the woman's hand. He was about to kiss it, but Magdalen held his hand firmly, pressed it, and said, "Good night."

Justin turned sharply to see Chandal standing behind him. "Oh, honey—has everyone gone?"

"Yes."

Magdalen laid her hand upon Chandal's face. "You are very pretty," she said. Her touch was soft and old and memories of childhood rose in Chandal's mind. The mean woman next door who raised the sweet grapes and getting caught robbing her vines! The woman's hand against her face. "What a pretty child." The hand drew back and slapped hard.

"Good night," said Magdalen, and the two sisters left the apartment.

"Thanks for coming." Justin closed the front door. Flipped the lock.

"Did you have to invite Lizzie Borden and her sister?" Chandal was surprised at her angry tone.

"What?"

"Who invited them, anyway? I was right here when you telephoned."

Justin shrugged, dropped into the leather chair. "I met Elizabeth at the store. I figured—why not?"

"And so you're pleased with yourself?"

"They had a good time." He kicked off his shoes.

"Christ!"

"What's wrong with you?"

"Nothing."

"Jealous?"

"Don't be ridiculous," she said promptly.

"Then what's wrong?"

"I keep thinking about those damn butterflies!"

"Butterflies?"

"Horrible."

45

"You said they were pretty."

"Yes. Pretty horrible."

"Why are you so angry?"

"All I could think of was an insect holocaust!"

"Come over here." He held out his arms.

"No."

"Del."

"Up yours!"

"I love you."

"Do you?"

"Yes. Come on, let's go to bed."

He laid grinning in the darkness. "Del?"

"Yeah?"

"Do you think her axe is very sharp?"

"Shut up and go to sleep."

They kissed each other lightly, too tired for a full kiss. Seconds later they were both asleep.

Deep in the night, Chandal dreamed of the silver bell around which the wind roared—not a leaf stirring on the branch from which it hung. The bell moved slowly, pitching in the wind, changing shape. Yes, there was something forming, a dark shape, like a body. The image was distorted at first, but, yes—she believed that it was a body, a human body, a corpse of a young child, its eyes opened wide like silver dollars, shining, sparkling, yet so still, helpless, floating out somewhere in the distance. Chandal shuddered when she realized that its arms were not the arms of a child at all, but rather huge muscular arms which had been grafted into place. She could feel the infant's body pressing in on her, moving closer, pressing its full weight upon her eyelids as she tried to open them in panic. She could see her own body now; her breasts had grown enormous, her stomach and abdomen were swollen, protruding like gigantic mountains, her legs as round as barrels. She could feel the baby clawing at her breasts now, chewing on them—violently sucking them, the tiny blue veins running to her nipples about to explode. She could see the baby's huge hands fondling them, caressing them, squeezing them hard, harder—

46

felt the pain shoot between her eyes, in her chest, between her legs, heard it cry "Momma!" as her body
jerked in rapid succession, in spasms, as she listened
to the long, agonizing moan that dissolved into softness, into pleasure, into ecstasy. Then, slowly at first,
tiny fragments of sunlight broke through, soft slivers of
light, reducing the images to shadows, thin shadows,
transparent, gone.

🐚 4 🐚

"MOVE IT, WILL YOU? GODDAMN IT—IT'S YOUR
job. I'm doing both your job and mine!"

"Bullshit!"

Chandal stirred. Construction workers were yelling
again under her window. Two days in a row. People
sure get mean on the job, she thought. Her arm reached
out for the silver-belled alarm clock, but didn't quite
make it. She groaned and sat up. Nine A.M. Wearily,
she collapsed back on her pillow and watched the thin
slivers of daylight flicker through the shutters. She lay
still wondering if she was the same person. Yes—the
same person plus one new person. She smiled and
patted herself companionably on the stomach.

Beside her, Justin slept on.

Chandal felt spacy now, and it felt good, like being
slightly intoxicated. Smiling, she studied the flower-
shaped shadow on the ceiling. Raised her hand into the
air as if to reach out and touch it. Slowly, her hand
seemed to separate from the rest of her body. It appeared to have a life all its own. In a flood of warmth,
she found that her hand was touching her breasts and
nipples and it felt pleasant. For the first time in days,
she wanted Justin to make love to her.

In this frame of mind, she stepped out of the bed
into the chilled air of an apartment without heat.

"Damn!" She felt the radiator. It was ice cold. She turned away to look at herself in the mirror. The person who stared back at her seemed lost, far away.

Serious blue eyes, so blue they looked almost navy-blue; fine brown hair, so straight that even a perm wouldn't curl it for long; fair skin, lightly dotted over with freckles. An attractive, slender girl. But so solemn! I'll fix you, she thought. She stuck out her tongue. The person glared back at her. Then she scowled. But the face she saw scared her. Maybe it was the sudden distortion of it; she wasn't sure. She turned away from the mirror—and moved out of the room, away from the stranger she had created.

Wearing jeans and a reindeer sweater, she sat loose-limbed on the arm of the couch, holding her coffee cup for warmth. She gazed from the window and watched the people on the street below. It seemed as though they were following after each other in slow motion. She yawned and was debating whether to let Justin sleep a while longer when the doorbell rang. It was Lois Yates, a likable fat woman of forty—polite, but frank. She lived across the hall with her burly husband and two children, a young boy and girl of nine and ten, so well brought up that they passed unnoticed, like two party dolls.

"Well, we're down to three. You, us, and the dog lady downstairs. Those damn dogs!" She wandered past Chandal into the clutter of the living room—paper plates, flat champagne, and overflowing ashtrays. Pointedly, she looked at the cake box from Schrafft's that had been made into a miniature airplane and set, belly up, on the coffee table. "Those damn dogs!" she repeated.

"I know," said Chandal, uncomfortable at not having invited her to the party.

"When are you leaving?"

"Five days—the fourteenth."

"You've definitely settled, then?" She tapped a Salem from her half-filled pack.

"Yes. We took six thousand dollars."

48

"I'll die first—'that man' has got to come across with a lot more than that to get me out." For ten years, Lois had referred to Howard Bender, the landlord, only as "that man."

"Have you heard from Mr. Bender?" Chandal emptied an ashtray into the wastepaper basket and held the ashtray out to Lois.

"No. The last thing we did yesterday was file harassment papers against him. I mean, just look at what's left of our building."

Chandal had already begun to miss their apartment. It was small, only two rooms, but Justin and she had created a home. On either side of the fireplace sat two stuffed chairs, handsome and comfortable. The modern couch, designed by Krieger, sat back in the alcove in direct contrast to the stained-glass windows. These windows held gleaming glass figures of a different age and came to life each day with the morning light. Completely filled with plants, the alcove resembled an antique greenhouse. The effect lasted for only about an hour, but it was long enough. Chandal wondered, looking at the alcove now, if perhaps the landlord would sell them the stained glass for their new apartment.

"We'll miss you." Speculatively, Lois watched her, chewing on the edge of her lower lip. She was already edgy at the prospect of being left alone in the building. Abruptly she turned. "Well, back to servitude. I just thought I'd check. Thought maybe—well, if there's anything I can do, just holler."

"Right."

Lois shuffled from the apartment, turned back. "And if you hear anything from 'that man'—let us know," she said.

And Chandal said, "I'll do that."

Chandal turned to face the fireplace, massive and ornately crafted in bronze. The diamond-cut mirror which covered most of the wall overshadowed the mantlepiece and made the apartment appear twice as large. This was the apartment they had been married in and she loved it. A small ceremony—a few friends, but it was a memory she would always cherish.

49

Chandal had started stacking paper plates and cups, working her way from the couch to the mantel, when she felt that someone was watching her. She turned— the room was empty. Shrugging, she went into the kitchen for a second cup of coffee.

It was exceedingly still. She could hear the labored breathing of Mintz, who lay on top of the refrigerator, fast asleep. Then, everything seemed absolutely silent. Chandal paused, the coffeepot heavy and hot in her hand. There was someone standing behind her. She could feel breathing on the back of her neck. "Justin?" She turned. No one.

Mintz's calico head shot straight up, her eyes darting around the kitchen, wondering who had just shattered her blissful sleep. Then lazily, she yawned, then dropped her head down between her legs and started to clean herself.

"Damn it!" Chandal placed the coffeepot on the stove. Slowly, she scrutinized the room. What was wrong with her? She took a deep breath, smiled wanly, and headed for the bedroom.

"Hey, come on—cut that out!" Justin burrowed into the hot covers. Tickling the undersides of his feet always brought him to his fullest attention.

"Honey, it's late," she said, laughing.

"What time is it?"

"Nine-thirty. Now come on, get up. Get up or I'll—"

He squinted from under the covers, feeling confused. "Put some coffee on." He scrambled to his feet, his face ashen under a stubble of beard. Bent over as if in pain, he moved into the bathroom and showered. After that, he shaved with meticulous care, making sure that no hair remained on his face.

His beard grew so thick, he had to shave twice a day to stay civilized looking. His green eyes, burrowed in shadows from the party the night before, stared back at him from the mirror. He tried to reassure himself that he certainly did not look his full thirty-five years. Thirty-two, maybe, or even thirty-one. He grinned weakly. What the hell. Even thirty-five was a damn good age for a man. Chandal was always saying how all men were ugly until at least the age of thirty.

"I'll start breakfast," Chandal said, handing him his coffee.

"I don't want any."

"But you didn't eat a thing yesterday."

"I'm not hungry." The coffee was hot and strong. What I needed, Justin thought and nodded thanks.

Cup in hand, Justin wandered in his usual morning stupor from the bathroom to the living room, en route to the front window, and saw at once that the day was gray and overcast. Pausing, he sipped his coffee.

Black clouds massed above the opposite rooftops. Justin's hand gripped the cup and he had a premonition, a fear, of things to come.

Before he had time to think about it, Chandal came and sat beside him on the windowseat. "What a party!" She smiled.

"Your mother looked smashed."

"She always does at two-thirty in the morning." She laughed shortly.

"She's a marvelous lady. A little naïve, but nice."

Chandal gave him an observer's smile. "Is that where I get it from?"

"Hmm." A dangerous question, which he left unanswered.

"What does that mean? 'Hmm'?" She watched as he stared out the window. "Justin?"

"What?" He turned to face her.

"Where did you go just now?"

He shrugged. "You know me. A dreamer since puberty."

There was a long silence.

"Billy looked depressed last night," she said, to break the mood.

"That's because he couldn't remember yesterday."

"What?"

"Yeah. He kept telling me that he couldn't remember yesterday. I told him that's why I liked him—because he couldn't remember yesterday. He was all right after that."

51

"You didn't really mean it?"

Justin paused. "To tell you the truth, I feel like the oldest child in the world. I'm worse than Billy."

"What does that mean?"

Justin shook his head and smiled. "Do you know that you have an incredible knack?"

"Oh?"

"Yeah. You make me ramble. That's what it is, all right—the knack—to make me ramble."

Now in the bedroom, she watched Justin dress. He looked tired, or maybe hung over. He casually slipped his green alpaca sweater (a gift from Chandal) over his head. It looked perfect with his black slacks.

"I think I'll call my mother," Chandal said, somehow knowing that Justin wasn't quite ready to engage in conversation—not the common, everyday "this is great coffee," kind, at any rate. There was something oddly docile and indifferent in his manner. Also, the instant he moved away from her, she noticed that the room had grown darker. At the doorway now, Justin was a mere silhouette. Time stretched away, as well as space. The door seemed an incredible distance away. She wanted to call out to Justin—to stop him from leaving the room. But it was too late—he wouldn't hear her. The door closed with a dull thud.

Justin went to the kitchen for more coffee. He always needed two cups to get into full gear. Next, he moved into the living room and examined his collection of photographs that hung left of the fireplace. Most of these were theatrical photographs—but none were in color. Most days would find Justin staring at them—images from the past. Billy Deats dressed in drag, pink feather boa and sequinned gown, doing his comedy act at the Hi-Ho Club in the Village. Stars whom he had directed in summer stock—ten years ago. He remembered how everyone had said he was sure to be a famous director before he was thirty. He hadn't been, but somehow now, he didn't care.

It was a mistake trying to be somebody in the theater. It was a world of illusion, of constant disenchantment and heartaches. The ludicrous thing was always being between jobs. Even when he was working, it was always the same question: Where would the next directing job be when the present job was over?

The only sensible thing was to know when to cut your losses. Know when to get out. What kind of a sucker comes to dine every night at a beggar's banquet? A few cold franks and beans, and none too plenty of that. While at the next table, they're pouring the wine and carving the beef. "You got to suffer if you want to be an artist," Billy had said.

"You suffer, Billy. I'm getting out," Justin had replied.

"Justin?"

Chandal's voice startled him; he hadn't heard her come back into the room. He turned to find her standing directly behind him.

"You closed the door on me," she said, stone-faced.

He laughed. "What?"

"Just now. You closed the door right in my face!"

"No, I didn't." He looked honestly puzzled and hardly knew what she was talking about. "It must have closed by itself."

Chandal suddenly felt foolish.

"Well, I guess we should get started," he said and then put his arm around her. "You take the plates. I'll get the glasses."

The rest of the day passed quickly. They filled the apartment with exuberance and healthy surging vitality. Chandal half-expected Justin to produce a tambourine and break into wild Romany rhythms of his Hungarian ancestry.

At twelve-thirty, Billy Deats came over to help pack. "It smells like a high-priced whorehouse in here," he said, throwing his jacket across the back of the chair. Justin had been burning incense.

"How would you know?" Chandal challenged.

Billy smirked. "I just passed one on the way over!" He gave her a hug.

"Keep passing, Billy—keep passing," she warned, never liking to be physically handled by men, unless it was Justin.

Whistling tunelessly, he shook hands with Justin. "I'm losing my charm, man—I'm losing my charm."

Justin grinned. "Aren't we all?"

Billy spent the next hour making a list of throwaways that he could afix for his apartment. At one-thirty, there was a brief discussion about an apartment sale, but the idea was rapidly dismissed. Who would buy any of the junk they had to sell? Billy drew a deep sigh of relief. For the next half-hour, Justin made a great show of activity, but he really accomplished nothing.

In the mid-afternoon, Justin left the apartment without saying a word to anyone. Strange, Chandal thought, and decided he had probably gone for more boxes. She finished wrapping a crystal goblet in tissue and put it carefully into a box.

Justin was gone for an hour. When he returned, he wore a new safari hat. Self-consciously, he passed Chandal still wearing the hat and went into the bedroom, closing the door after him.

"Excuse me!" she said. Then she added to Billy, "I've never seen him act like that before."

Billy looked up from the floor where he was sprawled on his stomach reading *Playboy*. "Don't fool with a man in a new hat. That dude's feeling sharp!" He smiled, took a long drag of his cigarette, and looked at Chandal. "You know, you are really something else."

"What do you mean?" Chandal asked tightly.

"You really love that guy, don't you?"

"Shouldn't I?"

"Sure." Billy gave a self-satisfied shrug. "So understand that all Hungarians are fruitcakes. I know; I spent enough time with him."

"So have I," she said frostily.

"Hey, come on—don't get mad. I just meant that he's got a lot on his mind, that's all. New baby, moving, and all. He's feeling squeezed in all of a sudden. So he goes out and gets a new hat. Makes him feel good. Like he's free to do what he wants when he wants to." Billy smiled sympathetically. "He'll calm down." He went on talking; she couldn't concentrate.

Dead center in her mind was a dark spot. Although she couldn't identify it, she felt that something was slipping out of her control.

What is happening? she thought.

She kept her eyes averted from Billy and fiddled with the bookends. As Billy spoke, the past few days kept intruding into her mind until she forgot what Billy was talking about. She was moving now in absent-minded clumsiness. Billy seemed to have stopped talking; she couldn't remember when.

"Hey, what are you doing over there?" she asked. "Are you packing or reading?"

"This one article caught my attention. I was just—"

"You better throw that naked girl away before you start running a fever."

"Okay, okay." Billy tossed the magazine in the old steamer trunk. "Listen, I'm free labor. Working only for food," he hinted broadly. "I'm getting mighty weak."

"I'll fix something in a minute," murmured Chandal as she slipped into the bedroom.

Justin stood before the mirror, hat in hand, immobile. Christ! thought Chandal, a male model. His long black curly hair had been clipped close to the scalp, leaving barely enough length to be parted to the right. He drew a long breath and came to life. "What do you think?" he asked uncertainly.

"I like it," lied Chandal. "But why . . ."

"I don't know—something different, I guess. The long hair was bothering me. I just had to cut it." He ran his hand through his hair as if to make it grow back.

"Well—" She didn't know what to say. "I guess I better fix some lunch."

Billy was the first to grab a sandwich. Chandal refused to eat bread, rolled the sandwich meat up, dipped it into the mustard, and ate it crêpe style.

Justin ate nothing. Billy mentioned the new, recently discovered Artaud play he was doing at La Mama. A freebie, completely experimental. "I'm playing a blind rhinoceros," Billy said, and the conversation shifted to theater and its present deplorable state. Justin defended the director, Billy the actor, and Chandal wished silently that she had a Kleenex commercial running on TV. Billy left at five, and he took the withered Christmas tree with him. Justin threw the bell into one of the half-packed boxes. Chandal had done most of the packing.

At nine o'clock, Chandal offered to make dinner. Again Justin refused to eat. Instead, he roamed around the apartment and kept asking her what time it was. Sometimes only ten minutes had passed until he would ask again. She was beginning to worry about her husband. By ten o'clock, she was as edgy as he was. They argued. Chandal was about to leave the room when Justin stepped in her way and she stopped short.

"Here, Chandal. Here is a piece of paper and a pencil. Sit down and write."

"Justin—"

"Sit down and write," he demanded gruffly.

She tore the paper and pencil from his hand and sat. He straddled the chair opposite her.

"Five hundred dollars a month rent. Write down five hundred dollars a month rent."

Biting off a sharp retort, Chandal pressed down hard on her pencil, almost breaking the point: $500 a month, she wrote.

"Gas and Electric—fifty dollars. Telephone—thirty dollars. Food—two hundred fifty dollars. Miscellaneous—one hundred dollars."

After several more items, he asked for the total. They were going to need at least $1,200 a month to exist. He talked too loud, punctuating his words with little jerks of his body, pointing out that up until now he had been lucky to scrape together $200 a week. She tried to quiet him—loud voices bothered her. He thought she was arguing with him and said even louder that her income as a part-time temporary secretary was almost enough to buy cigarettes and a Big Mac once a week. Besides, now that the baby was coming, who knew if she'd want to work?

Dollars and cents—practicality! The discussion lasted

an hour. Outside, snow started to cover the pavement. Justin grew more angry until finally he ran to the window, stuck his head out, and yelled at the top of his lungs: "That's right, go on—snow! Snow, you son-of-a-bitch—*snow!*"

Chandal tried to calm him down, but he paid no attention and mockingly addressed himself. "I'm an idiot! Come on, Chandal—call me an idiot!" He moved closer to her. "Tell me something. Wouldn't you just like to run away from here right now?" He dropped into the chair.

"What do you mean?" She fidgeted with the pencil.

"You know—like a little girl. Run back to your mother!"

"Not really."

"Listen—I'm going over to the brownstone right now and tell those two old ladies that we can't afford it." He hauled himself up from his chair and started for the door.

"Hey, come over here." Chandal reached out and hooked her arm around Justin's neck and pulled him close.

"What is it?" He refused to look at her.

"I want your attention—your complete, undivided attention."

He turned to face her. "You've got it."

"Tell me, who's your favorite person in the whole—"

"Come on, Del—this is no time—"

"Who?"

"You are!"

"And your friend and your lover and your wife. Oh, Justin. God, everything is going to be all right. The move, the baby, the money—everything." She smiled. "What are you afraid of?" She stroked the back of his neck.

"Well, for one thing—" He removed her hand. "It was too easy. Out of the blue, Magdalen stops me on the street, never asked for a reference, about money—nothing. I could be a pimp, for all she knows. You could be a goddamn hooker! I mean, she doesn't know anything about us."

"And for another?"

"What?"

"You said for one thing . . ."

"Okay, Del, let's be honest, okay? To tell you the truth, I never figured they were going to ask five hundred dollars. I thought—two nice old ladies. What do they know about the rental market? I thought maybe three hundred—tops, four hundred."

"I know," Chandal muttered.

"You see, you're not sure, either."

"But you'd love it. A whole floor in a brownstone."

"So what! The truth is—we can't afford it!" He gave her the benefit of a direct look from his green eyes, turned, and left the apartment. Chandal went to the window and watched Justin walk toward the brownstone. He never looked back.

It wasn't until Chandal sat down that she remembered what Magdalen had told him the night before—that they would meet tomorrow evening at the same hour. She glanced at the clock. It was eleven-fifteen, the exact time the two sisters had entered the apartment. Had Justin remembered that? The picture came to her of Justin holding Magdalen's hand. There had been a feeling between them, intimate. Forget it, you're imagining things, she told herself.

Chandal picked herself up from the black leather chair, bored and irritable. Mintz, she thought, and realized she hadn't seen the cat all day. She looked in Mintz's favorite spot—the top of the refrigerator—but Mintz wasn't there. The cat hadn't touched a mouthful of food, either. She searched the apartment but couldn't find her.

Finally, Chandal discovered her hiding place, the hall closet. The cat lay perfectly still inside the heavy tweed coat that had fallen to the floor. Chandal spoke softly to her. "Are you all right, Mintz?" The cat paid no attention to her. Getting down on her knees, Chandal rubbed her head against Mintz's fuzzy one. Mintz yawned, showing her tiny pink tongue and snuggled down deeper. "Okay, Mintzy, you sleep." She

58

stood up and went into the bedroom to sit on the radiator next to the window.

For a long time, she watched the flakes of snow zigzag down the glass panes. They gathered in the corner of the window, forming tiny clusters, until the wind sent them scattering in all directions. Vague ideas passed through her head. She saw Elizabeth bustling down the staircase with the butterfly tray held securely in her hands. She saw the face of the doctor as he told her she was pregnant. Other images came and went, fragmented, half-pictures, portions left out. Erased. The filmy past kept rolling behind her eyes. Her mind wandered.

The breathing came first. It drifted in from the living room, a low, harsh wheeze. A constricted sound, it floated through the doorway of the bedroom until it reached her. It encompassed her. Paralyzed her limbs with fear.

"Justin? Justin, is that you?" But there was no answer. She took a step forward, then collapsed on the bed, feeling that she was imagining things. She draped the blanket over her shoulders for warmth.

And then she heard it. Footsteps coming toward the bedroom.

"Justin!" Her voice was nearly inaudible. She gasped. Tried to remember. Had Justin locked the front door when he left? She always listened for the click of his key; tonight she couldn't remember. Justin was in a hurry. She had turned and gone to the window—no. She was now convinced that the door was unlocked. Her heart dropped, beat in heavy, sickening thuds. She pressed a hard fist against her chest. Oh, my God—my baby. Slowly, her fingers opened and traveled down to her belly. Her face was flushed, her skin cold and clammy. Trembling, she tried to get up. She couldn't. A loose floorboard creaked. The footsteps were closer. Think, for Christ's sake! Don't just sit there. Think! She would go very quickly, very softly to the connecting door. Wait. Feel for the right instant, and when she felt the exact impulse, run for the front door, past the intruder. Run screaming down the stairs, out of the building. Someone would hear her. Maybe Jerry, Lois' husband. She took a long breath, steadied herself and picked up a heavy brass ashtray. It slipped; she grabbed for it. Her hands were wet.

Balancing easily on her good dancer's legs, she took a determined step toward the living room, another, and then another. Breathe. She had to remember to keep breathing. Light footsteps retreated—did the front door open? No, she was sure it hadn't. With a desperate twist of her body, she wrenched the door open and plunged full force into the living room.

It was empty and quiet except for the loud ticking of the antique clock. She glanced at it—nearly one in the morning. Had there been someone in her living room? She couldn't wait any longer. She had to see what was keeping Justin.

She pulled at the door—it stuck. She clicked the lock, pulled again; it still didn't open. Clicked it again and again until she no longer remembered if it had been locked or unlocked. Finally, she wrenched the door free and left the apartment.

A slight breeze moved the loose snow casually to and fro as Chandal began to walk to the corner of the block. The street was deserted and the snow had stopped.

She felt the cold night air pass over her face. She shivered. It was a cold, still, self-contained world and she was intruding her presence into it. She could feel that she was entering someone else's territory. She came to a stop in front of the brownstone. The feeling intensified to a high pitch.

She was afraid to go forward, afraid to go back. She was caught. She stood and stared. In the half-lit night, the brownstone looked gray and old. The building had many windows, none of which showed any signs of life. And yet, she could feel herself being watched. She stood helpless, shaking. And that was observed, too.

Suddenly, she felt intensely angry. It steadied her. She clung to it. Let it build. *Goddamn it!* The anger burst forth, growing, billowing, pushing—she moved forward.

She reached the top of the steps, where, on either side, a mounted figure of stone stood sentinel. Pressing the bell, she waited. There was no reply. Looking into the octagonal glass window on the door, she could barely make out a light burning at the far end of the hallway. She pressed the bell again. No answer. Perhaps Justin had changed his mind. Perhaps he hadn't come here at all. He was probably over at Billy's place spilling his guts. Angry and cold, she returned to her apartment.

The bath felt very nice. It was warm and Chandal relaxed. She pushed the water around the tub and watched it circle over her knees and then back again over her belly. Then she soaped herself all over. She dipped deep into the tub and her entire body was hidden by the cloudy water. She stopped suddenly. Someone was walking around in the living room. Her body shot straight up. Slowly the bathroom door swung open.

"*Justin!*"

"Yeah?" He appeared at the bathroom door.

"Damn! You nearly scared me to death."

"Sorry, I thought you were asleep."

She watched him disappear into the bedroom. From the expression on his face, it was hard to tell what decision had been reached. By the time she dried off, it was too late to find out. Justin was asleep.

❧ 5 ❧

DEEP IN THE NIGHT, MAGDALEN SIGHED, AND HEARing herself sigh, she turned in sudden apprehension toward the darkened doorway and came face to face with her sister, Elizabeth. The features of Elizabeth's face, half-hidden by shadows, seemed swollen, yet her childlike personality still remained embedded within its folds. With large luminous eyes and thick henna-colored hair, she was dressed entirely in white. The faded white silk sash around her waist matched the two bows she wore in her hair. The red corkscrew curls that were pasted to her forehead seemed shocking by comparison. Her legs and feet were compressed into white stockings and soft white sandals, which gave her the appearance of walking on a cloud.

"Would you like tea?" Elizabeth asked, moving softly into the room.

"I've asked you never to sneak up on me like that. Why do you do it?"

"Sneaking? I wasn't sneaking!"

"You were." Magdalen lifted her hand to the neck of her cotton blouse, pulling the opening more tightly closed. Seated, she had covered her legs and lap with an old wrapper of quilted blue satin. Her steel-gray hair was in the same state of wild disarray as it had been when she had first awakened. She wore no makeup, barely considered her condition of dress, and took pride only in the fact that she wore slick black patent-leather slippers on her feet.

"We're going up to the attic again—aren't we?" asked Elizabeth with a marked edge of wary defiance.

"No. Not tonight." Her eyes upon her sister, she waited for her reaction.

"Good. You're not well. You haven't the strength. Perhaps in a day or two—" Elizabeth broke off and moved into the room.

Magdalen believed she heard genuine concern in her sister's voice. Still she couldn't help wondering what thoughts stirred behind her sleepy eyes. "It's almost one-thirty," Magdalen said softly, feeling now that her sister's old jealousy was still within her, smoldering, through the years, as always; it would never really die. Elizabeth kept moving, past her sister, heading toward the window where she would close the shutters. Magdalen sat perfectly still, then leaned forward slightly, and stared after her.

A wash of silence broke over the brownstone.

It was the silence that each of the sisters so absolutely distrusted. After all these years, everything that had to be said had been spoken, and now there wasn't anything else. Or was there?

Magdalen recalled the first day Elizabeth had brought her home from the hospital seven years ago. Elizabeth had broken down and cried, explaining she hadn't meant to knock her forward, hadn't meant to send her falling down the two flights of stairs. Magdalen let her speak, never accepting or rejecting her statement, her mind concentrating on other matters, filled with the shock that she would probably never recover now. She would be confined most of the time to her room, eating unbearable food twice a day. At first Elizabeth had made coffee for her. Now she drank tea, along with one egg, and toast, cold and dry and buttered with margarine. That was her breakfast. Never any meat, which she was sure Elizabeth had cooked for herself while she was asleep. The second meal consisted of watery vegetables, canned desserts—everything boiled and cold.

Magdalen steadied herself and looked into Elizabeth's face, so shiny, so refreshed in a strange way. Perhaps Magdalen should have felt grateful. Her sister had never left her side. The thought made her feel remote from herself. She had heard people say that they couldn't live alone and others say that they couldn't eat alone, or simply be alone or die alone. She had also heard people mention that they couldn't do anything alone, but she had never heard Elizabeth say these things. In fact, despite Elizabeth's constant insistence that they were absolutely necessary to each other, Magdalen felt that her sister would prefer to see her dead. But this had remained a vague idea, a thought that was never spoken. Never discussed. Perhaps if she had spoken to Elizabeth that day, tried to understand her more, the silences they now shared would not be quite as long.

Elizabeth adjusted her shawl as she moved away from the window to the far corner of the room, away from

Magdalen. She thought of the white lace dress. Whiteness was pure; whiteness meant that she was not guilty. The dress was proof of it. But the dress did not belong to her. In the beginning, everything seemed pretty and light. The girl in the white lace dress was her playmate. She had always wanted a playmate. Someone special for her very own. Her mother had given her a plush panda bear, instead. She was instantly afraid of the creature. "No! Take it away! Please, take it away!" she had screamed, but it was too late; her mother had left the brownstone.

The bear's arm was raised up as if to strike her. And then fists were beating Elizabeth's face. Her own fists. But she was sure that it was the bear that was attacking her. "He's killing me!" she screamed, pounding her fists into her face.

When her mother had entered the room, she had been shocked to see Elizabeth's face streaming with blood.

A mocking voice sneered at her. "Ah, ah, stupid girl. Eat. Eat!" Magdalen stood in the doorway laughing as her mother tried to calm Elizabeth.

"He . . . he wanted to . . ."

"There, it's all right. You'll be all right now. Mother is here. See? You're all right now."

"Yes." Elizabeth whimpered and hugged her mother tightly.

Magdalen slammed the bedroom door shut, leaving Elizabeth cradled in her mother's arms.

Now the two women sat at opposite ends of the room, like bookends, listening tensely for the next sign to continue with their conversation. Remaining perfectly motionless, they waited.

Shadows shifted, the night passed, and up the broad, creaking staircase, around the mahogany newel posts and fretted balustrades, against the blackened marble fireplace, the box-paned glass, congery of antiques, cracked, chipped, charred, the silence clung like a veil of Spanish moss in a grove of dead oak. It was a silence as big as the universe.

Patient is receiving cold-water-bath therapy. At this point, I do not recommend electric shock treatments.

Note: What is reason for the obsession over hair? Demands to have hair removed, as short as regulations allow. I have permitted a slight cut, but it appears to alleviate no symptoms.

In session, there is no direct communication. Continues to talk in third person; wishes to know what the conspiracy is. Patient also reverts to childish humor to escape reality. Rejects identity.

As patient refuses to eat, force-feeding has to be induced. Due to its traumatic nature, I wish to discontinue. However, there is currently no alternative.

I. Luther

6

THE NEXT MORNING, JUSTIN AWOKE CHANDAL WITH
a kiss. First on the lips, then one on each eyelid. Before
she had a chance to wipe the sleep from her eyes, he
reassured her—a kiss after every third word—that everything was going to be all right. That the Krispin sisters
—he glowered like a vampire—had agreed to let them
live rent-free for six months in exchange for his services.
He was to help put the house in order and to act as
super. They were planning a trip to Europe soon and
would need him to maintain the building. If this arrangement was acceptable, Justin and Chandal would
be allowed to stay on there at $200 a month, just a
little more than they were paying now.

"Justin, that's wonderful!"

"Didn't I tell you exactly what would happen?" Justin
stopped short, bowed, and sat down on the chair next to
the foot of the bed. "My dear Chandal," he continued.

"Is this going to be a speech?" she asked, pleased to
find him in such good spirits.

He struck a pose. "My dear Chandal—I love you."

They made love after that, the sensational kind of
love that sent electrical charges through their bodies and
turned each gesture into a sexual promise. Justin had
always been a good and passionate lover, but there had
been an excitement that Chandal had never experienced with him before. A roughness that entranced her.

Relaxed, partially dressed now, they sat on the edge
of the bed and studied the brownstone's floor plan.
Justin had sketched it the night before, carefully mark-
ing each room and its dimensions. Where to place the
new arrival? They decided on the small room next to
the parlor.

Chandal was pleased.

Justin sat back and smiled. His gaze was locked on the soft creamy flesh of her breasts. They were full, rounded; her nipples in silhouette. Moving forward, he reached out with both hands and covered them. For a moment, she leaned back, letting him caress her gently. The feeling of warmth increased.

Chandal caught her breath and pulled him down on top of her.

"Again?" he whispered humorously.

"Yes," she breathed.

He took her in his arms and pulled her slender body close to his own. Moving faster now, locked in her embrace, he entered her. The excitement spun through their bodies, undulating, gasping, until finally they had reached a mutual climax.

"I love you," he whispered.

"Oh, Justin." She clung to him. He was himself again. Attentive. Loving. Someone she understood. And someone she loved very much.

That afternoon, Justin made arrangements to have the entire apartment painted before they moved in, soft green and brown with white ceilings. They had to hurry. Four calendar days away from moving day; D-Day, as Chandal thought of it. Justin called Billy— Billy called three unemployed actors who in turn made other calls. By three o'clock, a work force had been assembled.

"Honey, I'm about to starve to death," Justin said, poking his head into the kitchen.

"So am I." Chandal smiled, relieved that Justin was going to break his two-day fast. She brought back a loaf of black bread from Zabar's, his favorite Brunello cheese, and a bottle of Cabernet Sauvignon (she would have preferred a Rioja *reserva*). All during the meal, they played about, kissed, knocking their teeth together, touched each other. Only briefly did Chandal wonder why no one had answered at the brownstone last night.

The next three days went smoothly. Justin was hired

67

to direct a new Off-Broadway play. Rehearsals were to begin in three weeks. Back in the theater again, Justin thought wryly, one last fling. A sort of thanks-for-the-memory bow. He'd make it the best damn play he'd ever directed, and get out. What he would do after that, he hadn't decided. He ran the possibilities over in his mind. He had toyed with the idea of opening a small restaurant with Billy. Billy was too undependable. Justin would wind up doing it by himself. He liked sketching, had taken a few art courses at Cooper Union—but found it had begun to hurt his eyes. Headaches. He could still remember the violent headaches, the visits to the eye doctor. The long, endless "migraine nights" without sleep. The pacing, the waiting, the fear that perhaps he was on the verge of . . . He shook the thought loose from his brain. Anyway, he would do something.

Chandal applied for a job at the Museum of Natural History, leaving out her own recent history—*i.e.,* pregnancy. She was immediately hired. Suddenly, their money problems were solved.

Getting the first floor of the brownstone ready was more difficult. The two women complained that the painters were making too much noise. The couch was too large to take down the stairs—it had to be dismantled. Dishes were broken and Mintz escaped through the open front door and couldn't be found for hours.

Justin had also made the costly mistake of hiring a contractor to redo the floor and cabinets and modernize both bathrooms. Chandal had suggested that they restore the natural wood of the apartment wherever possible—incredible to believe that the sisters had actually painted over most of the woodwork and doors. Stripping paint was a difficult job and who had the time?

It was now Friday afternoon and Justin was doing odd jobs around the brownstone, only to keep an eye on the man who consumed brandy after brandy and, in spite of a vast consumption, remained sober.

"The paneling doesn't look right," said Justin, annoyed at the time that had been wasted.

"Nothing wrong with the paneling," the contractor said and down went another brandy. "The cabinets in the kitchen could use another coat of varnish. Better not do it now, though. Maybe tomorrow."

"You were supposed to finish today."

"Can't."

"Tomorrow's Saturday!"

"Monday, then." He drew out a crumpled cigarette and fumbled for a match. He'd done this throughout the day—groped for a match, then asked Justin for another book of matches, only to lose them again.

"Listen, I'll finish the job myself," Justin said. It was a relief to pay the man and get him away from the brownstone.

Justin didn't start getting nervous until the man actually left the building. What the hell was making him sweat all of a sudden? He laughed and told himself he wouldn't let the pressure build. He thought about going back to work, finishing odd jobs, but enough was enough. He'd been working since ten o'clock; better to let the rest go.

What time was it now? Smart, clever, he told himself. He had placed his watch down and couldn't find it. He glanced out the window. Dusk. He felt his body draining now. Empty. He couldn't allow that. There was so much to do. What, though? What was there? He laughed. Someone laughed. He felt the air leave his lungs, throat, stomach; someone laughed. Someone was laughing for him.

Sunday, the fourteenth of January, Chandal and Justin left their apartment at dawn, bundled into parkas, boots, and gloves. Everything was frozen, wet, virginal. A fresh snowfall had just covered the streets of Manhattan. Nick's trees were glistening with ice; snow lay in small piles around them. Chill breezes whipped their way up the wide street. Today, the derelicts of Manhattan would be cold and they would remember that their yearly fight for survival on the streets was beginning now, and that before it was over some of their number would have lost their pathetic struggle against nature. Cruel and glorious nature. Hand in hand, the couple walked. Chandal stopped and turned.

She looks beautiful, Justin thought as he watched her glance back at the building that they had loved each other in for the past two years.

Inside the brownstone, they found themselves alone. The house was absolutely quiet. Only a few doors away from their old home, Chandal thought, but it seems like another world. The smell of the place was strong and clean. It felt exciting and new. Justin seemed that way to her, too. She had gotten used to his short hair. In fact, he now appeared more handsome than ever. But the unfamiliarity of the brownstone made her feel uneasy, as well, like breathing something other than air—odd and somewhat frightening.

"Come on, honey—I want to show you something." Justin took her hand in his and led her to the narrow room next to the parlor. "Something special. A surprise." He opened the door, making sure to let her enter the room first.

Chandal looked and then reached out for him. A nursery—a real nursery. With loud colors, cartoon characters dancing on the walls, and a blackboard with bright chalk. An open chest filled with toys. A giant stuffed giraffe. In the center of the room was a tiny carousel bed.

All at once, Chandal felt like a little girl and thought of her father. It was one of the few times she had allowed herself to think of him since his death six years before. Without warning, a sudden, sharp anxiousness moved over her. Even as she squeezed Justin's hand, she could feel strong internal movement. A clamoring without sound. She stood rooted as her heart suddenly flipped over with a noisy click.

It was then that she realized there were other people in the room with her. Surely— No, they were there. Chandal saw, sitting on the bed, a young man—a thin, smiling, pleasant sort of man with a large mustache. Lying beside him with her head resting in his lap was a pretty young girl in a white lace dress. The man looked at Chandal and said, "Ssh! Let her sleep, let her sleep."

"What?" asked Chandal.

"I didn't say anything." Justin saw Chandal focusing intensely on the carousel bed. "Honey, are you all right? You're shaking."

"Oh—yes. I . . . the room, it's beautiful," she said. "I'm just surprised." Then, pulling herself together, she smiled and added, "It really is beautiful."

He smiled. "I wanted to show you how I felt."

Chandal relaxed. The people were gone.

"Come on," said Justin softly. "Let's take a look at the rest of our new home." Relieved, she let Justin lead her from the room.

They wandered aimlessly through the apartment and talked. Larger rooms and more of them. No rent for six months! A basement for storage, a backyard. And heat—plenty of heat. There was only one disadvantage. Mintz would have a thousand more places to hide.

"Oh, my God!" Justin ran to the front hallway. Chandal followed. In the excitement of the moment, they had forgotten to let Mintz out of her carrying case. Justin had barely lifted the lid when the cat was off and running. Delighted with her new circumstances, Mintz darted from one room to another—she would have no trouble adjusting to her new home.

"Hey, Mintz—wait for us!" Justin followed her into the kitchen.

"Where are you running to? Of all things!" Chandal stifled frantic laughter.

Mintz happily played the game of "Around the World" throughout the day. Chandal and Justin weren't that fortunate. The telephone that was supposed to have arrived on Friday hadn't. With many phone calls to make, Justin was forced to walk to the pay phone on the corner. He grew more irritable with each call.

In the afternoon Chandal went shopping at the supermarket on the corner of Eighty-fourth Street. The horror was not to be believed. The store manager glowered at her as she entered the store, determined to banish any thoughts she might have of returning any faulty merchandise. There was no milk. The meat was gristly and exorbitant in price. Everything cost twenty percent too much, except the coffee, which cost fifty percent too much. Finally, she was at the end of a long line, weary and frustrated. Three clerks lounged at the manager's stand and did nothing, while the two who were working spent most of their time gossiping to each other.

"Oh, by the way," Chandal whispered to the checkout girl, having paid her bill, "there's a man having a cardiac arrest in aisle three." The girl gagged on her chewing gum. Chandal smiled.

She left the store with $35.27 worth of groceries in one bag. It wasn't until she placed the bag on the kitchen table that she discovered the refrigerator didn't work. Obstinately, she proceeded to prepare the meal. Plugging in the blender, she blew out all of the lights to the rear of the apartment. Justin called a number of electricians, but none was available. Half-frozen, he returned to the brownstone.

"I'll have to fix it myself!" He headed for the basement, only to find the cellar door bolted, apparently from the inside. He rattled the door in frustration.

"What's the matter?"

"How do I know? I can't even see what I'm doing. There's no light."

It was the first time either of them had realized how dark the apartment really was. Facing north and shaded by higher buildings, the brownstone attracted little sunlight. The back of the building was surrounded by a high brick wall enclosing its tiny yard, further obstructing the sun.

Flashlight in hand, Justin stood in the kitchen and tried the cellar door again. It was no use; he would have to ask the old ladies for assistance. He stopped at the lower landing and looked up the frail staircase. The huge oak door to the second floor, hand carved and rich in detail, was shut.

"I don't think I should." He hesitated.

"Why not?"

"Because I'm the super, remember? They'll think I'm crazy asking them for help."

At five o'clock, Justin walked to the corner once again and checked for messages on his service. He was informed that a production meeting of the new play had been called for six o'clock to discuss casting. He returned to the house in a black mood. "Who the hell do they think they are? I'm the director—I call the meetings! It's Sunday, for Christ's sake!"

"Justin, don't say anything to them. Remember what happened the last time—"

"It's all small time, Chandal. I'm sick of small-time big shots. Oh, don't get nervous. I'm going," he said angrily, slamming his way out of the house.

Chandal stood at the front door and watched him leave. She still had work to do, and tomorrow was her first day of work at the museum. She wished now that she hadn't agreed to start work so soon.

It was nearly eleven by the time Justin returned home. He entered the house in a dreadful mood. The meeting hadn't gone well. The producers, two law students from Harvard, had insisted that Justin accept the actress of their choice for the leading role in the play. They explained that their hands were tied—her husband was putting up most of the money.

Chandal prepared a small salad with a vinaigrette dressing. They ate in the living room, one of the only two rooms in the house that had light.

"When I went in there I was calm." Justin dropped his napkin into his lap. "But when he started talking about her . . . I felt useless. Do you know? Flat."

"What are the producers like?"

"Young!" He paused. "Let's drop the subject, okay?"

"I'll make you some coffee."

"Don't bother."

"You said you were cold."

"I meant depressed." Justin suddenly placed the palms of his hands on the coffee table and sat very still.

73

Chandal inched closer to him. "It hasn't anything to do with us, does it?"

He shook his head. "No." But his hands remained motionless on the table. He forced a smile and she could see what he was going through. "I'm sorry, Del. I . . ." He stirred, pressing his fingers suddenly to his eyes. "Damn headache. I think—I need some sleep."

"I think we both need sleep."

Before Justin went to bed, he stood in front of the dresser mirror wearing only his shorts. He examined himself. He had thought he was taller. He stood on his toes and sucked his stomach in; it didn't help. He got into bed, pulled the covers up to his chin. Chandal climbed into the bed and lay next to him. In a matter of minutes, they were both asleep.

Chandal dreamed of shadows. They played tricks on her. They appeared, disappeared. They had faces. She couldn't make out the expression on each face, but she knew that they were all watching her.

Her eyes opened suddenly. Something had awakened her, something that had nothing to do with a dream. Some kind of a noise. A real noise. She was wide awake now, straining to hear. In the silence, her own heart thudded out the beat of her rising fear, while the hum of the new electric clock reminded her in its mechanical fearless way that time was passing at its accustomed pace. Now she heard it. Someone was moving quietly through the kitchen. Justin? No, he was lying next to her, fast asleep. She reached out for him—he sighed and rolled over onto his stomach. She heard the noise again, there could be no mistaking it, and in human paradoxical fashion, because she heard it, she no longer believed it was a danger. Not something to wake a sleeping husband over.

But, damn it, it sounded like footsteps. Like soft, padded footsteps.

Chandal looked around in the darkness for Mintz. The cat was asleep at the foot of the bed. It was impossible to lie there any longer—she simply had to see what it was. Reaching for her robe, she rose from the

bed as quietly as possible. She felt her way across the
dark room, fumbled for the matches on the bureau,
remembering that the rear of the apartment was without electricity. She paused to listen. If they were footsteps, they were fainter. Her courage ebbed and she
glanced toward the bed. Just for a moment, she thought
of crawling back under the covers, next to Justin's
warm body. No. She had to know what that sound was.
Walking one slow step at a time, she made her way out
of the room and then down the long dark hallway, using up the entire box of matches along the way. Outside the kitchen door, she waited, the last unstruck
match in her hand. There was only silence. She stepped
forward and scraped the match against the side of the
box. The match exploded into flame. The kitchen was
empty.

God. She let the long pent-up sigh out from between
her teeth and collapsed against the cabinet. The cellar
door groaned, swaying slightly on its hinges. That was
odd. That door being open . . . The flame worked its
way down the match stem. It burned hot against her
flesh and she blew it out. Justin had tried for an hour to
open that door, without luck. But now the door to the
cellar was wide open. How was that possible? Cold air
rushed around her bare feet and she shivered. From below came a low sound. Steady, pulsating, like a heartbeat.

"What the hell is that?"

She listened for a moment, trying to identify the
sound. She couldn't concentrate. She spread her hand
out uneasily in the dark until she found the drawer.
The sound intensified. She fumbled for the flashlight.
Strangest damn thing she'd ever heard.

Between the dish cloths, she found it. She turned it
on, the white circle of light hitting the ceiling first, then
lowering to the basement door. Holding the flashlight
with both hands, she moved forward, pushing the door
open with her foot. The circle of light bounced down
the steep wooden steps until it focused on the cement
floor below. On either side of the steps there were old
wash buckets, paint cans, and plastic detergent bottles.

She started down the cellar stairs. At the lower landing, she paused and shined the light around the room, along the dusty blackened brick walls which were cracked and pitted. The sound stopped.

Something was moving in the far corner. She flashed the light in that direction. A small door was swaying slightly, back and forth on its rusty hinges.

"Who's there?" Chandal called. There was no reply. Again she heard footsteps.

Chandal moved quickly to the small door and opened it wider. Narrow stairs which ran alongside the west wall and up to the attic greeted her. She shined the light toward the top of the stairs. A door slammed shut. She stared for a long time, until the cold around her feet reminded her that she was freezing. Slowly, she backed away from the stairwell.

Someone from behind took hold of her. She turned and came face to face with a woman. The woman's hand was reaching out to touch her once again. She tried to scream, but only gasped for air. The woman was still—lifeless. Chandal was staring at a mannequin. And behind her, a child, a man, two women. All mannequins. The far left corner of the basement was jammed with a dozen or more mannequins, some dressed, others nude.

Wedged against each other, arms and legs touching, they appeared as a commune—a family, each with its own respective role. Because of the lack of space, the air not quite fit to breathe, it felt like being in a crowded department store—suffocating. It almost made Chandal sick to her stomach. She looked again at the woman's cold plastic face—felt her eyes glittering and looking back at her. The red lips were frozen into a smile, showing teeth made out of—they're not real teeth, she said to herself. No. They couldn't be.

A hand appeared and seized Chandal by the arm.

Chandal shrieked and spun around—Justin stood beside her. "What are you doing down here?" he asked.

"God—" She caught her breath.

"What's the matter?"

"Look!" She pointed to the mannequins.

"So?" He yawned.

"What the hell are they doing here?"

Another yawn, wider. "They seem to be just standing around." He tried rubbing the sleep from his eyes.

"Justin, I'm serious. I—heard something. That's why I came down here. It sounded like . . ."

"Oh, God—it's late, babe. Middle of the night. Come on, let's go to bed."

He dropped his arm around Chandal's shoulders and led her up the stairs. She kept glancing behind her. But there was only the still figures—no sound of anyone living.

Justin scooted Mintz off his pillow and crawled into bed. "You know, I like that basement. I think I'll set up a darkroom down there. Get back to taking pictures."

"Pictures?"

"Yeah. When I was in the army, I studied photography. Won a few awards. Nothing much, but still I knew I was good." He yawned. "Yeah, I think I'll start taking pictures again."

For a moment, she eyed him rather curiously.

"Just like that?" she asked.

"Just like that." He rolled over on his side. In less than five minutes, Justin was fast asleep. For Chandal, finding sleep took a while longer. The voice inside her head kept saying: *Just like that.*

❧ 7 ❧

THE NEXT MORNING TOWARD SEVEN O'CLOCK, WHILE Chandal was dressing for work, a joke came to her. Justin was asleep. Mintz was still cuddled at the foot of the bed, but unlike Justin, she eyed Chandal's every move and craved affection. Chandal gently slid Mintz across the bed until she was face to face with Justin and waited. Puzzled, Mintz watched her. "Purr!" whispered Chandal, scratching under Mintz's ear, and the cat rewarded her with a low, contented rumble. "Good girl." Chandal smiled and scratched her again. Mintz had by now fallen in love with the world. Her purring increased as she nuzzled her nose against Justin's cheek. This loving gesture drew Justin up from the lower depths of a dream.

"Chandal," he sighed, "leave me something for breakfast." Then he patted the cat on top of the head, rolled over on his side, and disappeared under the warmth of the covers.

Chandal marveled at this episode. She laughed to herself as she walked down the street. At the corner, she noticed that she had forgotten her wristwatch. She started back to the house, but thought better of it.

Reaching the museum, she realized that she should have remembered to ask if there wasn't another entrance to get to Personnel. Now she had to walk past the guard and explain that she wasn't making a contribution because she wasn't visiting the museum; she was working there. But maybe I should pay something, she thought uncomfortably. But that was ridiculous. Justin was right; she cared too much for appearances.

"I'm going to Personnel," she said to the smiling guard. His teeth flashed snow white against his ebony skin.

"I remember you. Come right on in." He motioned her through the turnstile and the knot in her chest relaxed. Why do you get so bothered about things? she chided herself.

She walked past the huge warrior ship crowded with native fighters. In their midst stood the medicine man wearing a ferocious mask with twisted horns, red splotches under the eyes amidst the pasty white overlay on the darkly designed jaw bone and cheeks.

She stepped into the elevator and punched three, watching the door close on a happy-looking group of children. Happy to be visiting a museum, or just happy to be playing hookie from school? The elevator door opened, she stepped out on three, and made direct eye-to-eye contact with a gorilla.

She didn't like looking at dead animals. But, something pulled her toward the creature. Perhaps it was the look in his sad, dead eyes, or perhaps it was the sense that he was so old and yet had been preserved, looking like a young and virile gorilla. "See you later," she told him, and a young girl laughed over her shoulder. Chandal wheeled around, red to her ears. "Oh, my God, you heard that? You heard me talking to a stuffed animal!"

"I do it all the time myself," laughed the girl. "That's Barnabus. My name for him. Do you remember me? I'm—"

"The receptionist. Of course." Chandal shook hands. She liked shaking hands with women. "I'm Chandal—"

"I'm Sheila. Come on. By the way, if you like talking to animals, later on, I'll introduce you to Astro. Biggest python you ever saw. Reptiles—to your rear." She pointed over her shoulder.

She led Chandal to the office corridor without missing a beat. Chandal lagged behind, suddenly unsure as to why she was here, working as a full-time secretary. It was only just for a while, she reminded herself, trying to concentrate on what Sheila was saying. Pithons and warrior ships and gorillas. They were walking through a metal swinging door to the offices. There were more rooms than she'd remembered. A face emerged from one. A shaggy fat man with a lock of lank brown hair hanging down across his forehead. He pushed a pudgy finger against the middle of his eyeglasses, staring. Was he staring at her? Pop eyes, Chandal thought, trying to smile, hurrying after Sheila. A brightly lit reception room greeted them. There were four huge desks. Only one was being manned, and that by a gray-haired woman eating a Danish. Sheila introduced them. A second later, Chandal couldn't remember the name. She dragged her mind back to clarity. Through a half-opened door, Chandal heard voices, but couldn't make out what they were saying.

79

Then hostility took hold. Chandal found herself in a world she didn't like. Therefore, it must be wrong. Suddenly that world appeared frightening. For the first time she was seeing her true colors; the common work-a-day person rattled her. She was used to theater people, sleep-until-midday people. Sounds of an overworked mimeograph machine drifted across the room.

A telephone rang. "Mrs. Polen?" someone called out.

Chandal closed her eyes, hoping that everything would freeze, vanish, become lost. To have opened them would have been like looking at

"Don't worry," said Sheila. "Pretty soon you'll get to know this joint—as well as anybody can. It's great! How about lunch? You brought something? Good, then I'll show you the solar exhibit. It's terrific. You shouldn't miss it."

Sheila did not belong to the generation of big, intimidating girls who took themselves too seriously. But she had that something of the inaccessible which made her interesting. Throughout the day, she bolstered Chandal's sense of security by letting her in on bits of museum gossip.

In what seemed like no time at all, Chandal was standing in front of the brownstone. It was a little past six when she climbed the stairs.

The sun was gone as she entered the house. She removed her coat but not her sweater. The only visible light came from the crack underneath the living room door. Hand on the doorknob, Chandal heard Magdalen's voice:

"When our world-deafened ear,
Is by the tones of a loved voice caressed—
A bolt is shot back somewhere in our breast,
And a lost pulse of feelings stirs again—"

Magdalen's voice broke off. In the silence, Chandal wondered what the woman was doing in her apartment. In the kitchen doorway, someone moved. She turned.

"The touch that kills. The touch that kills," whispered the young man. Then he disappeared. He was the same young man who was in the nursery yesterday. But hadn't she imagined him? And the young girl in white lace?

Chandal threw open the living room door. Magdalen was seated on the couch. Justin sat before her on the floor, his head resting in her lap. Gently, she stroked his hair.

In the dim light, they looked like a painting. The lamp behind the rose-colored shade cast its light on Magdalen's hair, warming the gray until it looked almost blonde. Strawberry-blonde. Her face, white as a bloom of magnolia, glowed as if lit from within. Her white hand on Justin's black hair moved gracefully.

"Justin?" Chandal's body tightened.

"Oh, honey—you're home." He quickly rose to his feet. "Magdalen was just—"

"It seems that your young man was hungry. I prepared dinner." She looked exceedingly pale, but her eyes were deeper and brighter than ever and she sat erectly upon the couch like a woman of twenty.

"Oh, Magdalen—there you are! I've been looking all over the house for you!" Elizabeth emerged from the darkness like an airy shadow. She scolded Magdalen for being out of bed—she had been sick and needed her rest.

Elizabeth spoke gently after that and referred to Magdalen as "her angel." Several times, she repeated that her angel was a good and loving person and that she brought joy into everyone's life. Arm in arm, the two women left the room and began to ascend the stairs. Justin and Chandal stood in the hallway out of courtesy. Something new had been added in the hallway. The goat-like figure which once had reigned over the sisters' living room had replaced Chandal's basket vine and now sat on the teakwood sidetable next to the door.

"What's this doing here?" asked Chandal, loudly enough to cause the sisters to stop on the stairs.

"Oh, isn't it great?" said Justin.

Magdalen smiled. "Justin liked it so much, we de-

81

cided to share it with you. The hallway seemed to be agreeable."

"Oh, yes," added Elizabeth. "It appears to belong there, doesn't it?"

Chandal had a difficult time understanding her own thoughts as she sat alone in the kitchen eating her dinner. The candle on the table flickered and went out. "Damn!"

"Sorry, honey." Justin replaced the candle with a new one.

"Did you call the electrician today?"

Justin hesitated. "Yes. He'll be here first thing in the morning."

"Thank God." She glanced at him briefly, communicating neither that she was angry at him, nor that she loved him.

He began to make shadow figures on the wall in the light of the candle. "How's the job—you going to like it?"

"It's all right." She watched him hold up his thumb and forefinger and made a dog. Quickly, it changed to a rabbit. "Make Mintz," she said automatically, and he created a cat.

"She's lovely, isn't she? A wonderful spirit," he said.

Chandal hadn't been paying attention. "Who?"

"Magdalen."

She stared at Justin—it wasn't possible, it wasn't part of the world of reason, and yet there he sat, waiting for her to reply. "I guess," she muttered and turned away.

Justin picked up melted wax and began to mold it. "A wonderful spirit," he repeated.

Around nine P.M., Justin went into the bedroom, shut the door, and stood in front of the mirror for a long time, looking at himself. A glimmer of light refracted from the mirror and Justin imagined himself looking through the crystal lens of a box camera. Time passed. He had moved now. He lay face down across the bed and slept, while inside his head the strobe light fractured time, space, flooding his subconscious with a million unexplainable images. Flash. Click. The images stuck.

Chandal sat alone in the living room until nearly one o'clock in the morning. There was no satisfactory explanation for Justin's actions. Nothing would convince her that his behavior with Magdalen was normal. The honking of a cab at the curbside entrance of the adjoining building gave her a start. She moved to the window and watched two gay men laugh, kiss, and giggle their way into the back seat of the car. She closed the shutters, turned out the light, and went to bed.

In the attic, there was candlelight. Incense burned. A live pigeon lay on the altar, struggling to free its leg from the steel jaws of the trap. An arm raised, waited for the sacrificial prayer, and then plunged downward with the gleaming knife. The pigeon's head, sliced neatly from its body, rolled to one side. A spasm seized the decapitated body. The young girl knelt before the altar, holding tapers of incense. Around her were other forms, inflexible forms. The human and the inhuman mingled together. It had been ordered by Ahriman.

Slowly the young girl began to lose consciousness. A transformation was taking place. Sound, light, and shape now wafted back through her senses, making her a newly formed observer of the world.

For a brief instant, there was some echo of resistance in her. Some shrill voice protesting in dim tones. Then it ceased and she knew that she had returned to her former self.

8

PHOTOGRAPHY HAD BECOME AN OBSESSION WITH Justin. Working day and night, he had spent most of the last seventy-two hours turning the basement into a darkroom. The floor had been waterproofed, new partitions built, safety lights hung, ventilation installed. All openings were light-trapped to exclude light. A second enameled iron sink was attached to the old one, and beside that were three smaller stainless-steel tanks, eighteen by eight. "A fucking photographic paradise," muttered Justin in satisfaction, forgetting the cost, which was over $3,000.

It was now Thursday, the eighteenth of January.

Justin drove the final screw into the wall, securing the red safety light above the kitchen door. Chandal squirted dish-washing liquid into the sink.

"There, that should do it." He slid the Phillips-head screwdriver into his back pocket and crawled down from the ladder. He glanced at Chandal, who was barely speaking to him.

For the last two nights, Chandal had come home from work exhausted only to find evidence that Magdalen had been in their apartment. When she questioned Justin, he merely said that she had stopped down to borrow something.

He slipped his arms around her waist. "That sexy little red bulb, my sweet wife, is a safety light. Whenever you see it on—please do not open the door. All right?" He kissed the nape of her neck.

Chandal reached for the soapy sponge.

"What's the matter with you?" he asked.

"She came down to borrow a cup of milk?" she asked sarcastically.

84

"Oh, Jesus—that's right!"

"And yesterday, let's see. Oh, yes, sugar, and the day before that, flour!" She threw the sponge across the top of the counter."

He shrugged. "Maybe she's lonely."

"Lonely? She has a sister, doesn't she?"

Justin turned to leave the room.

"Where are you going?"

"I'd like to work on a few pictures before it gets too late." He opened the door to the basement.

"Justin, wait a minute, Just tell me why? Why all of a sudden did you get this brilliant idea? I mean, it came over you like a road accident, to go out and spend almost every cent we have!"

"Because I'm not getting anywhere in the goddamn theater, that's why! I've got to get started in another direction. Something where I can count on a steady income."

"Photography? It's just as hard to break into as the theater."

"Del, please"—Justin stiffened—"don't go putting up stop signs before I even get started."

"But three thousand dollars. What if it doesn't work? What then?"

"Honey, trust me for a while. Don't go digging for trouble, okay?"

"That's just it—I'm not!"

"You are. You're so damn negative about this without giving it a chance."

"Because I'm scared, Justin. Because I don't know what the hell is happening here!"

"We're fighting—that's what's happening here!"

"Why? Because all of a sudden I can't reach you. All of a sudden you're more interested in Magdalen, upstairs, than you are in me! Go on, tell me it isn't true," she challenged.

He never bothered to answer the question.

The phone rang. Chandal dashed into the living room. She let it ring, feeling foolish. But at least she had been spared explaining what she had meant, which would have embarrassed her even more. She was beginning to feel acutely lonely, cut off from her usual channels of communication with Justin. What was really bothering her? The sisters rearranging the hallway? Justin's odd behavior? She tried to pin it down. Useless. She couldn't get to the heart of the matter. All she knew was that she was terribly unhappy and that Justin was changing.

"Look, nothing is wrong with change," her mother said. Chandal stood shaking with the phone in her hand.

"He's a decent and thoughtful person—that's what counts," her mother added. And Chandal thought even that was no longer true. He was moody now. It was never that way before. There were silences now. Gaps in conversation that went on forever. And when he did speak, he spoke in short sentences that hurt.

"Chandal, are you there?"

"Yeah, Ma—I'm here." He used to be honest, open. He lies now. About how he feels, what he's thinking . . .

"You and Justin aren't fighting, are you?"

There was a pause.

"Chandal?"

"No, Ma—we're just fine."

"Good. Good."

Do I have to tell you that I have tears in my eyes, Momma? Can't you hear it in my voice—hear it in my breathing?

"So listen, as soon as I get rid of the flu, I'll be over. I'm dying to see what you've done with the place."

"Okay, Ma—thanks for calling."

Chandal dipped her hands into the filmy, lukewarm dish water. Brushing the suds aside, she wiped the first of her stoneware plates that her mother had given them as a wedding present. The red light over the door flashed on suddenly and cast a dismal shadow on the ceiling and across the rear window. A tear ran down Chandal's cheek and onto her lip. She tasted it and wiped her face on her arm, forgetting why the tear was there to begin with.

She was washing everything all wrong. The glasses

were supposed to be first. She concentrated on doing a better job, and when she was finished she scrubbed the sink, turned out the light, and went into the living room. There was nothing good on TV, and she wasn't in the mood to read.

Chandal reached into the sideboard cabinet and took out a deck of playing cards. She began to play solitaire. Black five on the red six, red queen on the black king. She moved mechanically now. She wasn't thinking about the cards. Magdalen and Justin floated through her mind. She stopped, shook her head, kept on playing. Her eyes never left the cards, but she made mistakes now, buried the black nine; it should have been played on the red ten. She stopped. And then suddenly it came pouring out of her, the anger. "Goddamn it!" she screamed.

The cards flew from one end of the living room to the other. She opened the closet door and slammed it shut. Next the bathroom door and the nursery door. She yelled, "Damn you! Damnyoudamnyou!" She bit down on her fist and told herself to shut up. She was in the bathroom with a cold washcloth over her face when the phone rang in the living room.

"Hello?" she said, the washcloth still dripping in her hand.

"Is Justin there?"

"Just a minute. Who should I say is calling?"

It was Harvey Fein, the producer of Justin's new play. Justin hadn't showed up for any of the production meetings, he said coldly. They were scheduled to go into casting in the morning. He had to speak with him.

"Hold on."

She laid the phone on the table and crossed to the kitchen door. The red light was still on. She opened the door, anyway.

"Justin?"

The smell of chemical fluid was strong. A soft developing light cast a glow onto the stairs. She hesitated, unable to see past the bottom step. "Justin? There's a phone call. It's important." There was no response.

She returned to the telephone and told the producer that Justin had gone to the store, that he would be back shortly. Annoyed, the producer hung up.

For over an hour, Chandal waited for Justin to come up from the basement. Impatiently, she washed out a pair of pantyhose, ironed her dress, and stared at the basement door. *One, two, three, four, five, six, seven, eight . . .*

Slapping her hand down hard on the table, she stood. "Damn him!" She reached for the flashlight and headed for the basement.

"Close that door!" Justin hollered from below.

"But—"

"Close the door!"

She kicked the door shut so hard that it shook the dishes on the shelf. Justin flung it back open.

"Didn't I tell you not—"

"Okay, Justin. Forget it!"

Chandal stormed into the bedroom, got undressed, and climbed into bed. She rolled over on her side. The clock hummed loudly. She turned on her other side. She lay awake for a long time. Finally, in a state of complete exhaustion, she fell asleep.

Below, Justin eyed the photograph with satisfaction. Too often the photographer creates a false feeling by spreading a great deal of light in a place that is normally only moderately lighted. Justin had not made this mistake. His portrait of Magdalen was perfect. The extraordinary softness of her skin, the detail of dress. Her head had been posed to form a simple diagonal—carried out by the positioning of her hand. The picture was well posed, well taken. His admiration of the portrait lasted into the early hours of the morning.

Chandal awoke. Someone was standing in the hallway in front of her door.

"No! You must leave with me now!" said the man.

Next Chandal heard a woman's voice, high-pitched, trembling. "Leave me alone, do you hear? Leave me alone!" The door to the nursery slammed shut. It was quiet now. Chandal hadn't recognized the woman's voice, but the man's voice she knew. It was the voice of the young man she had seen. She was aware that someone was in the room with her now. By the window, moving slowly. Nearer to the foot of the bed, brushing against the blanket. Chandal reached out and put on the light.

The room was empty.

She stood up, her eyes darting from one corner of the room to the other and back toward the door. She reached for the knob, opened the door, turned, and peered into the hallway. Fastening the belt on her robe, she went to the nursery, opened the door, and flicked on the light. Satisfied that it was empty, she moved down the hallway to the kitchen. Again, she sensed a presence behind her. She turned—there was no one there. She turned back to look at the clock on the kitchen wall. Three-thirty A.M.

At precisely three-thirty A.M., Justin discovered that he no longer liked his portrait of Magdalen. Over and over again, he developed a fresh print. The first was too dark; he had made the next one too light. He enlarged the next one, bringing her face fuller into the frame. He wasn't satisfied with any of them. Tearing the prints up, he left the darkroom. When he reached the kitchen, Chandal was seated at the table waiting for him.

"I couldn't sleep," she said nervously. "You want some coffee?"

"Why not? Two insomniacs are better than one."

Face flushed, he moved with small spasmodic gestures as he snatched a cup from the dish rack. Yet, he looked fresh, filled with vitality, while Chandal could hardly keep her heavy eyelids open.

"Justin—were you walking around up here before?"

"When?"

"A little while ago."

"No. Why?"

She paused. "I heard someone walking around."

"Other people live here, remember? Sounds carry—this is an old building. Floorboards creak . . ."

"Yeah, and pigs fly!" She slammed her cup down.

"Jesus, Del. Go back to bed!" He moved into the hallway, put on his jacket.

"I heard them!"

The front door closed.

It was impossible trying to reach him. She was really alone in this. She glanced at the ceiling, not really alone at all. Wearily, she dragged herself into the bedroom and fell asleep almost at once.

Throughout the night, Justin roamed the city. At Forty-second Street, he found the sidewalks crowded. He could hardly find room to walk. Passing a sidewalk preacher ranting about Jesus, he was thrown into the arms of a whore who giggled and smiled: "You looking for some love, baby?"

Justin moved past her to the corner, ducked into a glass-enclosed phone booth, and called Billy Deats. Then he walked three blocks to Billy's apartment. They spent the rest of the evening talking about casting. In the middle of pizza and beer, Billy hinted that he would like a shot at Justin's new play. Justin said he'd see what he could do.

Billy leaned back against a poster of Elton John and began to nod. The room, shaped like a coffin and no bigger, cluttered with theatrical posters of recent Broadway hits, was reminiscent of a Cocteau movie. The 1940s jukebox bought with the last of Billy's money threw crazy orange and red lights across the dirty floors and ceiling. The drapes, left from the previous tenant, had begun to fray badly. Acting books overflowed the bookshelves, lay stacked on the floor, on the chest in the corner. All of them were dog-eared: *The Actor Prepares, Acting Is Believing,* and *The Actor's Technique.*

"Let's take off," Justin said casually.

"What?"

"We could go nowhere and stay a while."

"When—now?"

"No, I mean really take off. Get the hell out of the city."

"How about Chandal? She go with us?"

90

Justin didn't answer.

"Listen, pal—you better sleep on it." Billy lit a cigarette.

"She's okay."

"Then what's the problem?" He blew smoke rings slowly.

"I don't know."

"Nervous about the kid?"

"Yeah."

"It's a big responsibility."

"No shit." The last two weeks, tonight, it had been hard. He had to wonder how much harder it would get.

"You fucking around on the side?" Billy leaned forward.

"What?"

"You scoring somewhere else?"

"No."

"You act like it."

Justin tensed. "How do you mean?"

"I mean, I've been watching you. You look preoccupied—in-love-preoccupied. Like you're thinking about some special pussy."

Justin had understood, in a vague way, that he was changing, but this was the exact moment he realized that his world had changed and that it wasn't going back. "No." He paused. "I love Del." He moved to the phone. "Can I use it?"

"Sure. Put the quarter on the table."

Justin smiled. He knew the number by heart now. The phone rang and rang. He hung up. "She's probably asleep. She's a heavy sleeper sometimes."

"I wonder why?" Billy smirked. It was six-thirty in the morning.

"Christ, I've got to get some sleep." Justin pressed his fingers to his forehead.

"You staying here?"

"Yeah."

"You sure?"

"Cooling-off period. It'll do us both good."

"You take the bed." Billy got to his feet.

91

"The couch is all right." Justin punched the pillow into shape.

Billy yawned. "Well—" He yawned again. "You two will be okay." He groped for the bedroom door.

"Hey, Billy?"

"Yeah?"

"Thanks."

Billy shrugged and disappeared into the bedroom.

Justin had been asleep for what seemed to him later to be only five or ten minutes when he was awakened by a voice. It came as a whisper first, a thin mist of air that slipped quietly into his ear. A part of him paid attention, another part fought to make the voice go away, leave him alone to sleep. The voice was insistent, and probed deeper into the shadowy labyrinth of his unconscious, demanding now to be heard. Justin resisted, his mind on the dark side of the moon.

Help me, the voice pleaded. *Help me.*

"What?" he whispered from some region of his brain. Not on a conscious plane, but in another dimension.

You must help me. Please. The voice sounded frightened. Lost.

Justin could faintly see her now, her long red hair flowing over her shoulders, her light eyes glowing in the dark. Her virginal face was pale, thin, extremely lovely. She looked almost holy. Everything in the room suddenly stopped.

Then a deep sigh escaped from her narrow lips.

She spoke slowly, softly. *"Help me,"* she whispered. *"Help me be."*

She began to move, to advance toward him, enveloping him in a sudden cloud of ether. Sweet-smelling lilac. He wanted to reach out and touch her. The tips of his fingers grew numb, and yet they burned. Was she real? Slowly, at first, he lifted his hand. She moved closer. They touched. A warm sensation flooded his body. She whispered, *"Help me be."*

Justin turned his head slightly, the sudden closeness of her blinding his vision. "I . . . I can't see you." His

92

hands groped in the dark; he couldn't see at all now. He panicked. He couldn't see—he couldn't see! He felt behind him, touching nothing. A great pressure smacked him between the eyes. He bolted from the couch. "I can't see!" He turned. "Where are you?" he shouted.

Billy turned on the light and glanced around the room.

The sudden glare blinded Justin. He placed his hands in front of his eyes trying to shut out the harsh light.

"What the hell is going on in here? Who are you talking to?" asked Billy, laughing.

"What?" asked Justin, trying to adjust his eyes to the light.

"I heard you talking to somebody!"

Justin shrugged. "I must have been dreaming." He put his hand to his mouth, yawning. "What time is it?"

Billy stuck his head back into the other room and turned back to Justin. "Ten o'clock."

"Ten o'clock! Jesus Christ!" Justin raced back to the couch and reached for his shirt, trying to put his shoes on at the same time.

Billy went to the window and threw open the drapes. "I guess I forgot to set the alarm."

"Thanks a lot!" Justin had his coat on and was out the door.

Halfway down the stairs, he heard Billy holler, "Don't forget to think about me for the play!"

"Fat chance!" Justin screamed back, flinging open the outside door. He hurried down the street, into the subway. He arrived at the casting studio in a foul mood, an hour late.

🐾 9 🐾

IN THE PEARL-GRAY DAWN, GRADUALLY, CHANDAL
had become aware of it. It seeped into her thoughts, it
was stifling, suffocating. She sprang up, went to the living room, and threw open one of the windows. It was a
January morning, crisp and cold and filled with the
crystal-clear reality that Justin hadn't come home last
night.

She stood for a long time at the window, filling her
nostrils with the sharp air. Once again, the two dead
trees that stood twisted in front of the brownstone reminded her that she was not happy here.

Shivering miserably, she wrapped her arms around
herself for warmth, and waited. Waited for what? He
hadn't come home. The memory of last night washed
back over her with a dull ache. The voices, the arguing,
the tears. She slammed the window shut.

After two cups of coffee, she faced the dismal truth.
There were few or no illusions she had about herself.
She'd been acting bitchy. Okay. She hadn't been sup-
portive. Okay. She just wished he would come home.
She'd say, "I blew it, I'm really sorry, Justin. I really
love you a lot." Everything might not be all right right
away, but it would be a start. She frowned suddenly.
Something about the telephone ringing. She must have
been dreaming. She could hardly remember sleeping
at all. But she'd dreamt that the phone rang and she'd
let it ring, hadn't picked it up. She was suddenly anxious that it wasn't a dream, that Justin had tried to call
her.

I look like a wreck, she thought drearily, afraid to
face herself in the mirror, afraid not to. When she finally forced herself into the bathroom, looked herself

94

in the eyes, it was about as bad as she'd feared it would be.

She patted makeup under her eyes, but the circles showed, anyway. Maybe it's the light, she lied to herself and concentrated on accentuating her cheekbones with blush-on. It was eight-twenty-five A.M. She'd have to hurry. She brushed her hair, which was shiny, but flat, refusing to take a curl from her hair iron. She flipped the light switch down hard and left the bathroom. She went in and put on her beige pants suit with the dark brown knit shirt. The pants were too tight. She gave herself a lecture for missing a month's worth of dance classes. She remembered the baby. God, she had forgotten it. Forgotten she was pregnant. She patted her stomach softly.

In the kitchen, she got out rye bread for toast. Two slices were browning in the toaster when the doorbell rang.

It was Lois Yates. "Lois, I—"

"Please, may I come in for a minute?" Lois clutched her pocketbook, her hands wrung tightly around the gold-plated handle.

"Why, yes, of course." Chandal glanced back in the direction of the kitchen.

"I'll only be a minute." She moved into the foyer, past Chandal, who had by now sensed that something was wrong. "You should salt the steps—they're slippery," Lois said tonelessly.

"Justin hasn't had the time." Chandal closed the door. "Come into the kitchen. We'll have coffee." Leading the way, she listened to Lois' pattering footsteps behind her. They made her nervous.

Lois eyed the apartment as they moved along. "I noticed the living room. It's big."

"Do you like it?" Chandal asked, removing the cold toast from the toaster.

"Yes—pretty. How many rooms?"

Chandal placed a second cup on the countertop and poured the coffee. "Five. Two bathrooms. Also the basement." She reached for the milk. "How do you take your coffee?"

95

"Oh, black. Just black."

"Here you are." She handed her the coffee cup.

"So, everything is all right, then?" Lois asked.

"Oh, sure. Great." Chandal wasn't sure if Lois had detected the empty tone of her voice. "You wanted to see me. Any particular reason?" She glanced at the cellar door.

Putting her coffee on the countertop, Lois opened her purse a crack and drew out a cigarette. "To tell you the truth, I'm scared." Her shaking hand jerkily lit the cigarette. She held her hand straight out in front of her. "I guess you can tell." She quickly put her left hand into her coat pocket and drew in a deep breath of smoke.

"Why, what's wrong?" Chandal sipped coffee.

"The dog lady, she's moved out. Just like that, a few days after you left. We're alone in the building now."

Chandal wasn't paying attention. She thought of last night—voices. Maybe from the street. Lois moved through the kitchen, her cigarette crushed between her two fingers; the other hand, inside the pocket, moved her alpaca coat up and down against her side. "I'm sorry, I—"

"No, it's all right. I have to get to work, but I still have a few minutes." Chandal looked at the clock. "You were saying that you and Jerry are alone in the building."

"Yes, alone. 'That man,' he won't leave us rest now. Every night, three, four o'clock in the morning—someone knocks on our door. But when we open it, there's no one there. Then they start with the phone calls. Yesterday, all day—using filthy language. I don't know how much more we can take." She snuffed her cigarette into the ashtray and reached for another.

"Well, how can I help?" Chandal set her empty cup inside the sink.

"Justin, he always got along with 'that man.' Ask your husband to call him, please."

"Are you sure that Mr. Bender is responsible?"

"Who else would it be? I mean, the caller didn't introduce himself, but I'm sure 'that man' put him up to

96

it. Please, we only want what's ours, that's all. Six thousand dollars isn't enough. We have children. Please, have Justin call him, speak with him. He'll listen to Justin."

Chandal moved closer to her and placed her hand on Lois' arm. "All right, I'll have Justin call him."

"You won't forget?" she asked hastily.

"No." Chandal's smile was reassuring.

Lois clung to Chandal's hand. "You're a good friend."

"It's all right." Chandal glanced at the clock again.

"All right, I'm going now. I know that Justin can talk some sense into 'that man.' I know it.' She backed into the hallway. "Thanks." Her hand gave a sudden little jerk indicating good-bye. Chandal watched her leave the house.

"Boy, is he angry! Jesus Christ, look at him—he's mad!" The young actor watched Justin walk up and down in the next room.

The Equity representative, who was a genteel homosexual, quit working his crossword puzzle and closed the door. He glanced at his watch. It was going to be a long day. After six years, he knew it was going to be a very long day. Insight, having monitored countless interviews, he had it. For example, he had a fairly well-founded idea that he was never going to make it as an actor. Not now, at fifty-three, with his effeminate nature well advanced, too visible to be aesthetic for most shows, he wasn't. He couldn't even get dinner theater work and in a way, he was relieved. It was terrible to spend a whole career traveling from one dinner theater to another. In a tired way, he'd rather make thirty dollars a day as an Equity Rep.

An actress, chunky in the thighs, with a pasty face, came to the desk. "You're number one hundred forty-four," the Rep. said, and handed her a card.

"What number are they up to?" she asked, holding her wad of gum between her thumb and her forefinger.

"They aren't," he said. "They haven't even started

97

yet. I'm giving them a few more minutes and then something's got to be done."

"Jesus!" A stubby little actor collapsed in a metal chair. "I got here two hours ago, just so I'd get out early."

Save your time, thought the Rep. You haven't got a chance. He had a good eye for who had a chance and who hadn't. This fellow had no more of a chance than he himself had. He could feel the sadness of the room, the shabbiness of people who hadn't the money to put up a good front. Actresses with too much makeup, old men trying to pass for young men, trying to pretend vitality. It's sad, the Equity Rep. thought, when hope goes. He felt terribly angry with the people who were keeping these actors waiting. They'd already been waiting far too long.

Inside, the two producers tried to calm Justin down.

Not that I'm upset, Justin thought, but I really feel like knocking you on your fucking ass.

It wasn't easy to calm down. When you consider that he'd been busting his ass in the business for ten years and still hadn't gotten a break. Why had he thought it was going to be any different?

Harvey Fein posed himself in the chair near the mirror. The chair was a cheap wooden chair that creaked with the slightest movement. The chair was creaking now. Fein winced. He wore an English tweed worsted suit of blue, immaculately tailored, with out-of-date bell cuffs on his trousers that covered a portion of his expensive Gucci shoes. His shirt was a pale blue, matching his blue pinstriped tie. He eased back in the chair, flinching slightly as it creaked, and then placed his diamond-covered hands on top of his knee and crossed his leg. No more than twenty-six, maybe twenty-seven, he stank of money. "I think we should all calm down," he said.

"All right. I'm calm." Justin squeezed his fingers together, pressing them tightly into his palms. "But let's not waste our time kidding ourselves; I've directed over twenty-five plays. This is your first time out. You don't hold an open call without a stage manager!"

"But that costs money," Fein's overweight partner chimed in.

"No shit?" Why am I doing this? Justin asked himself, dropping his jacket into the chair. Why am I crucifying myself?

Bernard Stark, Bernie for short, hadn't meant to upset anyone. A few years younger than Fein, he took his bookkeeping seriously. All he ever really wanted was to please people. That's why he decided to do this play. To please people.

Pimples! Justin thought. A pubescent accountant. God!

"I don't know," muttered Stark. He turned, gestured to Fein. "Maybe we can help him."

Fein played with his diamond ring.

Justin began to wonder why in God's name he was putting up with it all. "Listen, you!" He pointed his finger at the fat kid in the dark blue pinstriped suit. "A director shouldn't have to conduct an open call. An actor every three minutes. What can they tell me in three minutes that I don't already know? I'm broke, I'm starving, I'd love to do your play! Damn!"

Fein lifted his lean body from the chair, and in a soft, low voice said, "I'm sorry, but we don't have to take this abuse. If you don't like the way we do things, you should step down as director."

"Gladly!"

And that was the end of that. Justin hit the door, brushed through a sea of people, and hollered—"Next!"

Justin had a hard time keeping his eyes open as the number 10 bus lazily made its way up Central Park West. Producers! that was a laugh. Produce my ass, Justin thought, sliding farther down in his seat. They weren't bull-shitting him. There was only one real producer—the older kid. Who, no doubt, got his money from his father. The invisible man. The play was just one more nice expensive present for the Harvard brat. Jesus, he despised that kid. You work and you work and along comes an imbecile with a wad of bills in his hand and a fat-assed, pimple-faced yes-man at his side and he takes it all. Goddamn this business. Goddamn that black-haired, eye-glassed, suited, vested, sanctimonious adolescent. Some kind of a genius, probably, without a granule of common sense. Ambitious, ruthless, smooth, Harvey Fein.

Passing the museum, his thoughts shifted to Chandal. On top of everything else, now he had to feel guilty. He could hear the conversation in his head. The baby, the money, ad infinitum, but at the bottom of it all—he was sorry. Ashamed and sorry. He made his way down the aisle, feeling his eyelids weighting down. He needed sleep.

Stepping from the bus, he felt the cold air hit him in the face like a parental slap. Hastily, he pulled up his collar and headed for the brownstone. He had acted like an ass. A real ass. Childish was a more accurate description. He had just created an ugly scene. Anyone observing would have regarded him as a son-of-a-bitch, a really spoiled brat. This made him mad, because he wasn't that at all. He knew that. Deep down inside his guts, there was a nicer person. Still, he hadn't given those two guys half a chance. Why? What the hell was wrong with him lately?

He took the concrete steps in front of the brownstone one at a time, slowly, stopping on the third step, trying to figure it all out. He dreaded telling Chandal that he had just lost his job. That would be the worst of it. Justin suffered a sudden shiver of apprehension. Moving into this building—had it really been the right thing to do? Normally, he had jumped into things without giving them a second thought. Even after they hadn't worked out, he still never looked back with regret. Yet, here he stood, shivering with fear.

Objectively, he could see that Chandal had been right. Suddenly he couldn't justify his own reasons for taking the brownstone, and wished now that he hadn't. He despised himself for this thought, not for any other reason except that what he was feeling was something terribly akin to self-pity. His father had always moped around the house feeling sorry for himself, and look where it had gotten him.

He slipped the key into the lock, wishing Chandal was home. He needed her and wished that she was here to take away the self-doubt.

The brownstone was unusually still.

Justin sat down in his leather armchair, closed his eyes, and repeated to himself again and again: I do love you, Chandal. I do. His eyes rolled back under his lids and his head fell forward. As he slept, he watched himself rise, cross to the foot of the stairs, and start upward to the second floor. After walking down a long corridor, he entered Magdalen's bedroom. There she lay in flowing white, with her hands resting comfortably across her chest. Her face was pale and calm; her eyes blazed with youth. She smiled.

"I will not be with you much longer," she said softly. "But, if I must leave you, I wish it that you should not forget me; therefore, I want you to have this." He felt the sensation of touching her and of his caress being returned.

She wore two rings on her left hand, both identical. She drew one of the rings from her finger and gave it to Justin. "I want you to wear it and think of me when I am no longer with you."

A sharp pain shot through Justin's chest and tears welled in his eyes. He would awaken later that evening and not remember any of this.

❧ 10 ❧

WILD CRIES ECHOED DOWN THE CORRIDOR OF THE museum as Chandal covered her typewriter. Thank God it was Friday. She watched the guard escort four unruly youths from the building. Arm in arm, they lurched away from his grasp and dashed around the corner to cause more trouble.

Chandal's appointment with the doctor was at six.

"You look done in. What's the matter—you sick?" asked Sheila, helping Chandal with her coat.

"Oh, no. No—I'm just not sleeping well lately."

Sheila opened her mouth to ask why, but the look on Chandal's pale face as she turned away forbade questions. Opening the door for Chandal, she said, "Have a nice weekend."

Chandal nodded her head. Sheila had become a good friend in a very short time. She'd covered for Chandal during the week, typing when Chandal's fingers couldn't find the keys, sorting out the important correspondence from the mundane, suggesting the best way to handle cataloging, tagging, doing the inventory. What to eat, where to go. Yes, Sheila had been a good friend.

Something different, Chandal thought, from Sissy. Sissy had changed when she started to climb the executive ladder. She was not quite ruthless. Only a little more aggressive, less sensitive to their friendship, less time for lunch, less time for phone calls.

Sheila, on the other hand, had come to peace in her life. That was it. She had accepted who she was and was willing to share herself with others. There was a calm that seemed to follow her about. An openness. Chandal had responded immediately to this calmness, allowing it to stabilize her own anxiety. With Sissy, there was always a hectic flush to the atmosphere, as if something was about to happen. That's what had first attracted Chandal to her. The excitement. At first, it was a relaxed kind of excitement, an excitement that was nice to be near. But lately, Sissy brought a falseness into the room with her, a pretentious air of importance, displayed in the way she dressed, the way she talked, the sunglasses, always the sunglasses, and more. Sissy's thoughts were on success. Not just in order to succeed, but success for power's sake. It was as if she were trying to prove something now. To her ex-husband? To her constant stream of boyfriends?

"Hey, you going to be all right?" Sheila asked, still hanging comfortably in the doorway.

Chandal turned, nodded tensely, and left the office.

The room was large, with lots of windows and light. Wearing a white gown, Chandal sat on the doctor's examining table. Dr. Axelrod had just completed her checkup. It had been a slow and very thorough examination, painful for Chandal, who had never learned not to tense against gynecologic probings. The nurse had also jotted down a medical history and had taken urine and blood specimens. The doctor was now standing with his back to Chandal, talking to the nurse and making a few notes on her chart. Absently, Chandal ran her hand through her hair, straightening it.

"Well, any questions?" The doctor's face was kind, his lips curved into cheerful lines.

"What? Oh, I'm sorry. I was—"

"In another world," finished the doctor, chuckling. He studied her for a moment and then made a notation on her chart. "I've given you a prescription that should give you a little more energy. Nancy will give you a diet and make another appointment." He indicated his pretty nurse with the tip of his pen and Chandal wondered instantly if they were having an affair. "All right?"

"Oh? Oh, yes—thank you." She stared at the doctor but didn't move.

"You are in deep thought today, aren't you?" He laughed.

"Doctor, do any of your patients, I mean—during their pregnancies, start to imagine things?"

"Like what?"

"Nothing specific." She looked away.

"I think I understand." He sat beside her on the swivel stool. "This is going to be your first baby, right?"

She nodded.

"Keep in mind that it is not only a physical experience, but an emotional one, as well. Fear is sometimes involved. Extreme anxiety often triggers the imagination." He saw the uncertainty on Chandal's face. "Is it a personal problem?"

She said nothing.

"Be patient with yourself—and with your husband. I was a nervous wreck during my wife's first pregnancy. Take my advice—relax. Everything is going to be just fine."

Chandal felt oddly relieved. "Maybe you're right. I'll try," she said. "Thanks, Dr. Axelrod."

"You're welcome. And next time, we'll talk again —if you're still imagining things."

Only a few blocks from the brownstone, Chandal was forced to take a cab. It was snowing hard and the sidewalks were iced over, making it impossible to walk. She snuggled down into the back seat. She was in a better mood and anxious to be with Justin.

When she arrived home, Mintz was waiting for her.

"And how are you? I'll bet anything you're hungry!" Moving down the hallway, Mintz in her arms, she saw Justin asleep in the easy chair. Poor Justin, she thought. He's tired. I don't think I've ever seen him sleep sitting up before. Not that I forgive you for staying out all night, she said silently, but not harshly. Tiptoeing past his sleeping body, she went into the kitchen, fed Mintz, and plugged in the percolator. After freshening up, she woke Justin.

"Oh, hi, babe—you just get in?" Justin looked around the room, to get his bearings.

"Yes, and you should see it out there. It's a blizzard! I made some fresh coffee." She kissed him on the forehead. "I'll be right back."

Of course, thought Justin. He was in the living room. He got up and stretched just as the telephone rang. "I'll get it," he said. "Hello?"

It was Harvey Fein, the producer. Anxiously, he asked if Justin would reconsider. He was sorry and hoped Justin wouldn't hold it against him. "Tell you what," said Harvey, "we'll hold the last open call ourselves Saturday. How's that? You don't have to be there. Take the weekend off—relax." They agreed to start fresh first thing Monday morning. Actors through agents only—readings. Differences settled, they hung up.

"Who was that?" asked Chandal, bringing the tray.

"Oh, the producers. They just wanted me to know how pleased they were with the way things are going."

Settling down on the couch, Justin and Chandal continued to talk over coffee. After comparing notes, they decided the rest of the world was crazy and they were happy to be alone together. "Very happy," whispered Justin—"and very hungry." She laughed, picked up the coffee tray, and moved toward the kitchen. The phone rang again. This time, it was her mother. "Here you go, honey." Justin handed her the phone and lowered the TV.

"Hi, Mom. How are you? When are you coming over?"

Her mother told her in gloomy pleasure that she couldn't. "I can hardly move—the worst pain. I'm so sick. I can't tell you how I'm suffering."

Chandal told her to stay in bed, call the doctor, and take fluids. She'd get better quickly.

"I won't," whined her mother.

"You will." Chandal smiled. Barring sickness from her thoughts, she hung up.

"Ma got a bug?" Justin laughed.

"Right on schedule. She's been healthy for almost two whole days now."

Justin helped her with the dinner, and afterward they watched the George Burns special on television. Justin couldn't stop laughing, except to kiss Chandal. They drank Brandy Alexanders and ate lemon chiffon pie. It was the first pleasant evening they had spent together since they moved into the brownstone.

"I like this, Del. Just sitting here alone, you and I."

"I do, too," she said and reached for his hand.

"I'm sorry about last night," he said sheepishly.

"So am I."

"Are you mad at me?"

"Not entirely. But maybe I should be."

"Maybe you're right. It's hard to argue the point."

"Where'd you go?"

"Billy's."

"Figures."

"I missed you."

"Did you?" Chandal sank deeper into the couch and looked at him as he rested his arm around her shoulder in a gesture of tenderness and such complete reconciliation that she took his hand, kissed his fingers. "I love you," she said, and noticed that his eyes had lost their usual forcefulness. He was softer, reaching out, trying to explain himself. With both his arms around her now, he explained that Chandal in Latin meant "the place of the altar—a sanctuary." Chandal smiled, still holding his hand, enjoying the softness of his touch.

Without realizing it, her eyes had been focused on the unusual ring that Justin wore on his little finger. She couldn't take her eyes from it. "Justin, where did you get that?"

"What?"

"The ring—I've never seen you wear it before." She lifted his hand.

For a split-second, Justin thought that she was playing a joke, that she had placed the ring on his finger while he was asleep. But, as a director, it was his job to be able to tell when people were acting and when they were not. She was not. He sat up and smiled. "Do you like it?" he asked.

"Yes—it's beautiful."

"Well, it's yours."

"What?"

He looked at the ring again and then screwed it off his finger. "Just what I said. It's yours." He could already see the tears. "Hey, come on, don't cry."

"But—"

"No buts about it. I wanted to surprise you. I'm not sure it's the right size. If not—we'll have it cut down. Okay?"

She nodded.

Justin placed the ring on her second finger and reached over to kiss her. Suddenly the living room

106

door flew open and smashed against the wall, sending Chandal's picture crashing to the floor. A shrill moan cut through the brownstone.

Mintz leaped up on the back of the chair and started to hiss violently. Her claws dug holes in the chair's black leather.

Chandal stood, knocking the coffee tray to the floor. The shutters on the front window smashed open and slapped against the wall. The left front window cracked, a sharp zigzag crack that ran quickly down the window like a sudden flash of lightning. Chandal shrieked, crushing a saucer under her foot, trying to reach Mintz.

Everything was exploding around her; the sound of metal and glass hit the room, and wouldn't stop.

"Christ—what's happening?" Justin spoke. Something started to ache in his head. He skipped a breath, panicked because he couldn't breathe, stopped—swayed to his feet.

Chandal clung to him. "Justin? Justin!"

"I'm all right!" he said, trying to get his bearings. Chandal reached for Mintz.

Mintz's head shot forward, her sharp teeth bared, her body twisted, contorted in agony. Her eyes dilated, she hissed, a stream of yellowish liquid spewing from the corners of her mouth.

"No, don't touch her—" Justin grabbed Chandal's arm. He could feel how rigid her body was. He started to speak, stopped. His head was now turned slightly to one side, listening.

The animal-like cry continued without pause and in full breath for almost a minute, until finally it died away like an echo into nothingness, replaced by the loud buzzing of TV static. The vertical had slipped within the picture tube, leaving a sudden jerky movement and strange shadows flickering across the four walls and the ceiling of the room.

"That's the damnedest thing—" Justin flicked it off. "I'll check the front door. It must have blown open."

Chandal carefully picked up Mintz, patted her

107

gently, and tried to reassure her that everything was all right. The cat remained motionless in her arms.

Justin appeared in the doorway. The front door had been securely locked and remained so. They both had heard the horrible sound, but were unable to explain what had caused it.

"I better see if they're all right upstairs." Justin moved unsteadily to the staircase.

"No!" Chandal let Mintz drop to the couch.

"Why? The same thing may have happened up there. They may need help."

"But what if it didn't?"

"What do you mean?"

"Maybe it just happened down here. A sudden wind—"

"From where, Del? Everything is locked tight."

"Justin, don't go up there." Chandal was visibly shaking.

"You going to be all right?"

"Yes. But don't go up there, okay? If they needed help—they'd have called down."

Justin ran his fingers quickly through his hair. "I suppose you're right."

After cleaning up the broken glass from the living room floor, Justin put out the light and went into the bedroom. Chandal sat before the mirror, removing her makeup. Mintz rested comfortably at the foot of the bed. He switched on the radio and found a jazz station, sank into a chair, and listened.

Soft music filled every corner of the room. It was relaxing, full of unexpected flights and long, graceful sustainments. Without known melody, it swung in alternate directions, each direction a confirmation of life, and filled them with a reassuring calm. Time passed.

Chandal glanced into her mirror and saw Justin standing behind her now. "You look nice," he said.

She smiled. "So do you."

"Take my hand, Del."

She looked up into his eyes and took his hand. "Are you tired?" she asked. She received no answer except his hand holding hers firmly for a moment. Then he pulled her up and kissed the ring on her finger. She could feel the heat on the back of her hand where his lips had pressed. Getting undressed, they slipped between the dark blue sheets. The glow from the reading light on the side table filtered down over Justin's body. His chest was huge and strong and covered with matted hair. Chandal saw that he was looking at her and she was glad to be lying beside him.

Taking her in his arms, Justin's chest met her softness. He began to kiss her eyes and mouth. He smiled, slipping down to kiss her breasts. Her hips moved closer to him in anticipation. Justin moved slowly, enjoying her completely, until he finally entered her.

"I love you, honey," he whispered. Their bodies moved together, damp with sweat.

"Oh, Justin." She pulled him to her hard.

Eyes closed, Chandal clung to the back of Justin's neck. "Yes," she whispered, "yes."

He was holding her buttocks firmly now, raising them. In this position, Justin felt bigger, penetrated deeper; her pleasure increased, feeling as though he were puncturing her deepest, innermost walls, and she moved with him with almost total abandonment to pleasure. She shuddered as she imagined his penis growing larger, thought how incredibly good Justin had become as a lover. Her whole body heaved with pleasure. Suddenly she became self-conscious. A pain rippled through her vagina, then another. Justin was pushing too hard now. Something was wrong. Frightened, she opened her eyes.

The bell hung in midair over Justin's shoulder.

"Yes, yes," Justin moaned.

"Justin!"

"Take it easy," he said.

Her nails ripped into his back. All she could feel was pain.

"Take it easy!"

The bell shook violently—challenging her, the tremors of sound running through her body.

"Honey," Justin sighed.

"Justin!"

"Yes!" Justin's body stiffened in a long release, and fell limp.

Chandal gasped for air, trying to breathe, trying to move his huge body.

The bell was still there.

Chandal couldn't breathe; she was suffocating. She opened her mouth. "No—*No!*"

Justin looked up. "What's the matter, Del?"

"There! Behind you!"

Justin turned, pulling the covers quickly over the lower part of his naked body. "What?" he asked.

The bell was gone.

Chandal let her body go limp. Sweat ran from her forehead, down into her eyes, across her lips. "Oh, God—God."

Justin reached for her. "Honey, are you all right?"

Justin's face, sweating and handsome, his short-cropped hair tossed casually back. Thank God he was there. She threw her arms around him. "Justin— hold me!"

He took her thin frame in his arms, crushing her close to his chest. "Baby, baby—it's all right. Everything will be all right."

Slowly, she relaxed.

"I love you, Del." He could feel her heart pounding. He ran his hands through her hair. His fingers played with her ears, her throat, her cheeks.

"Thank God for you," she whispered, gripping him with all her strength, her mouth closed on his. She closed her eyes, felt Justin run his hands along her bare arms, felt his hand slip along her back. Nothing mattered now and they became lost in each other's arms, until Chandal had reached a fulfillment that consumed her like a deep and wild ocean. Then quiet. Loving quiet. Then sleep.

11

THEY SAT ON THE PARK BENCH AND FED THE PIGEONS.
Dowdy, proud, scrawny, fat-breasted—the pigeons
pleased Chandal very much, taking the popcorn from
her hand the way they did.

The snow had stopped sometime during the eevning,
leaving mounds of smooth, unmarked white powder
over most of Central Park. The sun had replaced the
dark clouds and everything sparkled.

"Lord, what a day. *What a day!*" Justin suddenly
scooped up a handful of snow, frightening the poor
pigeons half to death. En masse, they rose off the
ground, wings fluttering like sheets hung to dry in the
wind, and put considerable distance between themselves and the crazy man.

"Justin, now look what you've done!"

"So what? They were eating all of my popcorn!" He
grabbed her wildly and kissed her. She pulled away.

"Justin, people are looking at us!"

"So what? Can't a guy kiss his wife if he wants to?"
He turned to the nearest person, a whiskery old man
sitting at the opposite end of the bench, and repeated
the question. "Shouldn't I have the right to kiss my
own wife? Shouldn't I?" Like the pigeons, the old man
quickly put distance between himself and Justin. Chandal couldn't help but laugh.

"Let's do something, honey," said Justin.

And she said, "Like what?"

"It's Saturday. Come on, think. What do people do
on Saturdays?"

She thought. "Their laundry?"

He smiled, dropped to one knee, and snapped her
picture.

111

"Justin, don't—I haven't any makeup on!"

He took another picture.

"Cut that out!" She kicked snow in his direction.

The camera kept clicking.

"All right, Justin, you asked for it!" She jumped on top of him, driving him back into the snow.

"Honey, the camera."

"Too bad—shithead!" She sat across his chest scooping handfuls of snow into his face.

"Help—rape!" he shouted.

Chandal stopped and stared down at him. "Ohmy-God!"

"Honey, what is it?" He sat up. Chandal looked dazed.

"Lois Yates," she muttered.

"Where?"

"I just remembered. She stopped by yesterday. I forgot all about it. She wanted you to call Mr. Bender. She said he's got people crawling through the building and making obscene phone calls at all hours of the day and night, harassing her. She said tell him she's willing to be fair. She'll settle. Justin, will you call him?"

"Sure, as soon as you get off my chest."

They both brushed the snow from their coats. "Is the camera all right?" she asked.

He pointed it at her. "Let's see . . ." She smiled for him. "It seems to be okay."

They walked a little way through the open base-ball diamonds. If it had been summer, there would have been six baseball games going at one time. They stopped to watch a New York crazy dressed in jog-ging attire trying to get his kite in the air. They moved past the pond, which was frozen over, and around to the other side, where they climbed the snow-covered steps to the weather station.

"Do you realize that Mom hasn't stopped by to see our new place?" Chandal plucked a twig from a tree and stuck it into her mouth like a toothpick. "She hasn't even suggested it." She sat on the wall. "That's kind of odd, don't you think?"

"I've always thought that your mother was odd." He closed the camera into its brown leather carrying case, smiling.

"Up yours!" she said lightly.

"She told you she was sick, remember?" He slung the case over his shoulder.

"But you don't believe she is, though, do you? I mean really?"

"No, honey. I don't think so. I think your mother is just fine."

Chandal frowned. Her mother's apparent hypochondria was starting to cause her concern. When had it really begun: the headaches, the pains in the back, the long, drawn-out nights without sleep? Just after Justin and she were married. Was that it? Were her constant ailments simply a way of getting attention? Chandal really hadn't been spending much time with her. Not much time at all.

She had always held a picture in her mind of her mother as a younger, healthier woman. Remembered home life orderly and secure because her mother had kept it that way. If voices were raised, her mother always saw to it that it was behind closed doors. Most evenings as a little girl, Chandal knelt with her mother in front of the television, while her father read the evening paper. Sometimes she'd fall asleep with her head in her mother's lap.

Then there were the street fairs and the movies her mother had taken her to. Some Saturdays, during the time her father worked on Wall Street, they all came into the city together and went to the zoo, or for a ride on the Staten Island Ferry. In the summer months, there were all-day outings at Far Rockaway.

Chandal never forgot those outings with her mother, and the boundless energy that she had displayed. But now, she led a lonely life.

"Hey!" Justin exclaimed, snapping her out of it. "She's fine. She's fine." He grabbed her hand. "Come on."

But if she was fine, that brought Chandal full cycle,

113

back to her original question. Why hadn't her mother come to visit them at the brownstone?

They spent the rest of the afternoon at the skating rink, where the rumbling of the skates on the ice filled the air. Men in tight ski sweaters did tricks, each believing himself surrounded by empty space. Near the mechanical organ, a woman huddled to keep warm. It was her job to change the music rolls. Banners and brightly colored streamers were used for decoration.

Chandal drank hot coffee, happy to be standing on the sidelines. One hand held the cup, the other clung to the metal railing.

"Come on—try it!" shouted Justin, swooping by, his sharp blades cutting the ice.

Chandal hurriedly finished her coffee, sure that she would be able to skate. It was something that she'd always known, that her feet would glide smoothly, sure of their control. She stepped hesitantly onto the ice and immediately her ankles collapsed and her feet lay flat against the ice as she hobbled to the middle of the rink. She glared down at them. It was the damn rented skates! Halfway around the rink, Justin skated gracefully backward and motioned her to join him.

"I can't!" she screamed.

He grinned back at her and held his hands up to his ears, shrugging.

"I can't!" she bellowed again, and people close to her turned and looked, which sent the blood rushing to her cheeks. Walking on her ankles, she began to make her way back to the railing and fell directly into the path of an oncoming skater who leaped into the air, clearing her by inches.

"Watch out, lady!" yelled the man over his rapidly disappearing shoulder. She crawled the rest of the way to the rail on all fours and hauled herself up.

"Never do that," said the attendant. "If you crawl on your hands like that, a skate could take a finger off just like that!" He snapped his mittened fingers and left her to shudder, hanging limply over the rail.

114

Justin passed her with a disapproving frown on his face. "You're not quitting?"

"My ankles are killing me," she snapped.

But he never heard her. Already he was cutting a fancy figure, heading for the center of the rink to join the better skaters.

Suddenly she heard it. The sound of the bell.

All other sounds faded from her ears. She was alone in deadly silence. The sky dimmed while she watched. Her legs gave way, pitching her forward.

Instinct saved her. Her arms reached for the railing. Her fingers wound themselves around hard metal and she hung there gasping, faceless skaters weaving around her. She saw them darkly, waiting, listening for the summons. The summons, she thought, in another part of her mind. What kind of summons? The rink came alive with sounds of laughter. It came at her from all directions. People laughing at her.

"Justin?" she murmured, a pocket of chilled air caught midway in her lungs. Her eyes started to clear. The faceless people began to have wide, smiling mouths. She took deep, cold breaths and waited for the round, staring eyes to form above the mouths. Light began to come back to the sky.

She steadied herself, the cold sweat rolling down from her neck, focusing, looking for Justin. The skaters were only skaters again. Not laughing at her at all. Justin, she thought, still staring, where was he?

And then she saw them—the silver-belled tassels on a little girl's white skates.

Chandal's breath released sharply. The little girl cut circles before her, floating easily, her tiny body gracefully maneuvering in space, the bells on her skates gently ringing.

Chandal began to laugh, the sound choking in her throat.

She turned; the little girl was gone.

The next morning, the sun rose like a huge orange coin and cast its light on the Hudson River. Houdini had done it. Justin flapped the window shade open.

115

Sunday. Fragments from the past. He dared to resurrect the little attic he slept in on Spring Street when he was a kid. The tiny window above his bed. He would lie there on Sundays for hours just listening to faint voices filter up from the rooms below. They were muffled; he couldn't tell who they belonged to. It was peaceful and eventually he would fall asleep. Outside the window there was a church with stained-glass windows that caught the sun just right. He went over there one day; he was maybe six or seven. "Hey, is anyone home?" The church had been empty except for an old derelict asleep in a pew.

Justin dressed and left the bedroom.

Chandal shivered and drew the covers over her shoulders. She nestled into the pillow to sleep again, but couldn't. Raising her head, she glanced at the alarm clock, moaned, and returned to the pillow.

The traffic outside sounded far away as she fell half-asleep. As time passed, she could lie comfortably only on her side, the weight of her breasts against her thin frame causing a pressure that had become more annoying in recent days. Face pushed deep beneath the pillow, her breathing became shallow, slow, almost nonexistent. Her breath, which by now should have frightened her, had a hypnotic effect upon her; a delicate glaze formed over her lips, her face, masking her like a spider's web.

Thinly veiled, she floated through the silence of the room on two separate planes, each plane having its own special sound, a special silence, not total and complete, but composed of elements beyond her control. The first plane was more conscious, more familiar, where the sound of the electric clock hummed, street noises filtered in from the window, the TV going in the living room. These sounds were the familiar, and needed no special attention.

The second plane was more imposing: it was the deliberate silence caused by someone else in the room with her. Watching her. There. She could feel the subtle shifting of body weight. Not Justin. Lighter, quicker. Slithering.

116

Chandal had let her body relax past the point of readiness. She would be unable to respond with split-second awareness. Time passed slowly. Her body lay comfortably suspended, yet she dozed uneasily. Her eyes kept trying to open, the sound slipped nearer, slid under her bed. Her eyes shot open. She awoke completely.

She crawled from the bed naked. Uneasily, she slipped on her bra and panties and dressed in blue jeans and a jersey. She moved into the bathroom, brushed her teeth, combed her hair so that one curl fell carelessly over her forehead. Moving swiftly through the bedroom, she smoothed and straightened, collecting water glasses from beside the bed. At the doorway, she gave the room one last glance, like a night clerk checking a motel room.

In the kitchen, Chandal fixed waffles for breakfast and orange juice in cold frosty mugs, but Justin would not smile. There was a bleak look in his eyes, and she felt that he had shifted moods again. He changed so rapidly, so completely, from one moment to the next. Chandal watched him move around the table, preoccupied in setting up a model for a still-life photography shot. He had placed an open Bible on the table. Beside it lay a half-melted candle and a glass of red wine.

"That's pretty," she said, pouring the orange juice.

"Pretty?" Justin gave a sharp bark of laughter. "Everyone to his own taste." His face was set in a tense expression and gave no indication that he was aware she was there in the room. He backed away from the table, squinted, then leaned forward and slowly moved the glass of wine to the right of the Bible.

"You know what would look good—right in the middle of that open Bible?" said Chandal, inspired. "A withered rose."

"That's what's wrong with your acting," said Justin. "You overstate things." But he saw that she was hurt and told himself to calm down. He took an interest in Mintz and started to follow her about the apartment,

117

snapping pictures. The cat couldn't find a single space to call her own. Peeved, she hid under the couch, where she finally fell asleep.

Justin wasted no time in developing the pictures. The red light above the kitchen door flashed on and the apartment fell silent. Chandal was growing to hate the red light. She was even jealous. It represented time spent alone.

She drifted around the apartment looking for something to do. She watered the plants and sprayed them. They weren't doing well. Not enough light, she thought. She ran the vacuum and dusted. Finally, she decided to call her mother. Her mother picked up the telephone on the first ring—not a good sign. After exchanging hellos, Chandal's mother explained in a husky voice that her flu had gotten worse.

"I've never had anything like it, Chandal." Her voice went on like a flood released, and Chandal sighed and sat down to listen.

" . . . a ringing in my ears. Like bells. I told Alicia . . . did you meet Alicia, Chandal? I can't remember whether—"

"What kind of ringing in your ears?" asked Chandal, gripping the phone. "Did you say bells?"

"Like bells," said her mother firmly. "It made me just sick. I was shaking like a leaf. Alicia said she heard the same thing once when she had an inner-ear infection. But I don't think it—"

"Was it more than one bell?" asked Chandal tensely.

Her mother paused. "I think it was only the one bell." Her voice sounded pleased. Chandal was taking such an interest. "Yes, it was one bell and not such a large one. I could almost see it in my mind. A fairly small bell. It was—"

"Silver," said Chandal softly.

"Why, yes. How did you—"

"I just—guessed, Mom. You get some sleep, okay? I have to go now. . . ."

"That was just wonderful the way you guessed that, Chandal. Just wonderful. I can't wait to tell Alicia. . . ."

"Good-bye, Mom. I'll talk to you tomorrow." Chandal hung up the receiver. *I'm rundown,* she thought. *I'm putting meaning to things that don't have meanings. People's ears ring. So what else is new?* Her head was hot and her hands clammy. She took three aspirins and lay down on the couch. Every few minutes, she got up, looked into the kitchen—the red light was still on. She decided to start dinner, but discovered that there wasn't anything in the house to eat.

Shopping list in hand, she looked at herself in the hall mirror. Suddenly, there were two people in the mirror—herself and a young girl who stood high above on the second-floor landing, watching her.

Chandal turned. The girl was still there.

"Angel, where are you?" Elizabeth's voice filtered down from above. The girl turned, passed through the open doorway, and closed the door behind her.

The girl from the nursery—Chandal had thought she'd imagined her. Yet, there had been a girl standing on the landing just now. She'd seen her.

Taking a step forward, she was hit with a sudden dizziness. Ahead of her, the stairs stretched out like a spool of unraveling ribbon. Bracing herself against the wall, she tried to catch her bearings. It was no use. She was going to be sick.

Chandal was still in the bathroom when she heard Justin yell.

He took the steps leading from the basement three at a time. "Honey, wait until you see it!" He ran from one room to another trying to find her. "Honey, where are you?"

When Chandal stepped from the bathroom, he could see that she was sick and insisted that she lie down. He would call the doctor.

"Justin, please—I feel fine," she said with a sour grin.

"Honey, are you sure?"

"Of course I'm sure. Now, what was all the yelling about?"

Proudly, he produced a photograph of Mintz. It was priceless. Justin had caught Mintz at exactly the right

119

time. No photographer of animals could have asked for more. He had brought out the texture of her fur, casting highlights, and had caught each drop of water that hung from either whisker.

But Chandal did not look pleased.

"What's the matter? Don't you like it?" asked Justin.

It wasn't the cat that she was looking at. There in the background, she could see the face of the young man. She looked at the picture more closely. There wasn't any doubt—it was him.

"Justin, there, in the background—what do you see?"

"What?" Justin took the photo from her. "What are you talking about?"

"Directly to the right of Mintz's head, in the background. What do you see?"

Justin examined the photograph. "I don't see anything but an out-of-focus cellar door!" He grew tense. "You can hardly see it, though, the way the picture is composed."

"I don't mean the door—I mean in the doorway!"

Justin looked again. "Are you crazy? There's nothing there. It's pitch-black."

"There—right there!" she screamed, pointing to the open doorway in the picture.

"Those are shadows!"

"Justin, that is not a shadow."

"No? Then what is it?"

For almost an hour, she tried to convince Justin that it was the face of a young man. At first Justin laughed and told her that she was seeing things. But she persisted. Finally, in a fit of anger, Justin tore up the photograph. "There! I've destroyed the goddamn picture. Now, I don't want to hear another word about it."

"Justin, I tell you that there are other people living in this house—that man and a young girl. I've seen them. Both of them."

"Oh, really—then why haven't you mentioned it before?"

"Because I thought I was imagining it. But—"

"I hate to tell you this, but you are!"

Chandal made up her mind. She would never mention it to Justin again. Her manner would become guarded and deferential, quite unlike her. It was a few minutes past eleven when Chandal crawled into bed. She lay there for a long time and thought about the picture.

In what followed, she seemed to discover the absolute belief that she was right, that the couple was very much part of this house. A tiny understanding began to form within her as she tapped the memory of the first day they had spent in the brownstone. Justin had taken her to the nursery—the couple was there; she'd seen them. Together, they were there, as if this was their home. Chandal was sure that the nursery had been their bedroom at one time.

After much tossing and turning, she fell asleep, curled up in the corner, the blanket pulled up over her head.

In the basement, Justin had once again begun work on the portrait of Magdalen. He scarcely understood the earnest desire which he now felt, but he knew that he had to perfect her picture. Her soft eyes gazed back at him. Beautiful eyes and yet . . . something different from what he saw when he was with her. He looked back into the developing tray. *See me as I am,* said a soft voice. He frowned, looked at the picture. Sometimes it seemed to him that he had captured two images on the film. A woman within the woman. If he were to look long enough, he was sure that the images would blend, become one woman. *Your mind is the camera,* whispered the voice. *My mind is the camera,* thought Justin, as though he were learning a lesson.

❧ 12 ❧

LOIS YATES STOOD IN THE DOORWAY OF HER OWN apartment and smiled. "It's wonderful. I don't know what Justin told him, but Bender has decided not to renovate. He's moving people back into the building. Look—isn't it great?"

Chandal muttered, "It's nice."

"Oh, this is the young lady who's taken your apartment."

Chandal turned to find a tall, thin girl with cameo-pink skin and large green eyes set off by dark lashes under light red hair standing next to Lois. Her figure accented through the bright sheerness of her pale green blouse; her breasts were high and pointed and sharply divided; her waist, tiny, cinched with a wide leather belt which clung to the short green skirt under which, it appeared, she wore very little.

"How pretty you are," Chandal murmured, vaguely aware that it was a strange thing to say. An older woman would tell a young girl: "How pretty you are." A girl would never say it to another girl on first meeting. Nor had Chandal ever before been so conscious of another woman's body.

"Oh, thank you," said the girl, not seeing anything strange in the remark.

Lois lifted her two hands, coaxing the girls to become instant friends. "Chandal Knight—Bonnie Barrett."

"How are you?" Bonnie smiled.

"How do you do?" Chandal shook her hand.

"I won a beauty contest, you know. In Canton, Ohio. Winning that contest meant a lot to me. It was one of the loveliest things in my life; it really was. That was

122

four years ago." She paused for a moment to embrace the passing of time.

"How about coffee, girls?" Lois asked.

"No, I have to get to work," said Chandal. "I only stopped by because I saw the moving truck outside." Had Justin called Bender? Chandal wondered.

"I hope they haven't broken everything." Bonnie paused. "Oh, I've got to run—" She dashed down the stairs.

"She's a sweet girl." Lois leaned over the wooden railing and watched her exit the building on the lower level.

"Yes, she is." Chandal paused. "Did Bender tell you why he changed his mind?"

"No, I haven't even talked to him. Just yesterday, out of the blue, I hear someone turn the key in your apartment; I thought it was you. I open the door and there stands Bonnie. She tells me she's moving in —today. Right behind her, there's an older couple —they're taking the apartment directly above me, you know, the one where the two—well, you know— boys lived. Michael and . . . ?"

"Anthony."

"Yes, Anthony, such a nice boy. Such a shame."

Chandal glanced at her watch. Eight-fifty A.M. "Well, I'm glad everything worked out all right for you."

"Oh, yes—Jerry and the kids are so happy. Please, tell Justin thank you. All right?"

"I'll do that."

The morning turned out to be a total disaster. Everything went wrong. Chandal spilled coffee on an important set of papers, broke two of her nails, and without thinking ran into a glass door that was clearly marked. She walked slower now, down the institutional-gray corridor to the ladies' room. She couldn't shake last night from her mind.

The young girl on the landing—no, she had not imagined her! A daughter of Magdalen, perhaps? The girl was too young. It was possible, though. The young man—her husband? Why conceal the fact they are

123

living there? Third—fourth floor, maybe? Boarders— the sisters are embarrassed because they had to rent most of the brownstone. But how could they hope to conceal it?

She washed her hands and patted her cheeks with cold water.

The picture was proof! The young man was there. Damn Justin! Destroying the picture like that. Does Justin know the girl is living there? Maybe his photography is just an excuse. The small door at the far corner of the basement—they could meet, who would know?

Eventually, though, she had to get back to her desk. Go on working, go on thinking, with the nausea always with her. Morning sickness—if it kept up, she'd have to get something from the doctor.

Sheila invited Chandal to her apartment for lunch. Chandal was pleased by the change. They took a taxi to save time.

Sheila had a bright studio with dark wood cabinets, a handsome sofa that turned into a bed at night, plenty of plants, and a dining alcove. Books on the occult filled her bookshelves.

"I'm a believer," laughed Sheila from the kitchen, seeing Chandal's eye on a volume of mysticism. For lunch, she fixed a fruit salad, corned beef sandwiches with kosher dill pickles, and rum-raisin Häagen-Dazs ice cream.

After they ate, Sheila showed Chandal her collection of pictures: Sheila at graduation; Sheila with her brother; Sheila at a wedding party.

"Me as a virgin," Sheila said, handing Chandal a chromium frame. It enclosed a picture of a naked baby. Laughing, Chandal returned the picture to the bookshelf.

"Do you believe in those things?" Chandal loosely indicated Sheila's collection of occult books.

"I don't know—sometimes." She reached for the dish cloth.

"Like when?"

"Well, it sounds strange—but, one night I woke up

124

and saw my mother standing in my room—she was in Florida at the time—and she called my name. Then she leaned down and kissed me and said, 'Don't feel sad, I'm well and happy!' Then she moved toward the window and vanished. The next morning, I received a telegram that my mother had died during the night." She shrugged. "It makes you think, if you know what I mean?"

"Yes." Chandal watched as Sheila wiped the dishes and put them away. Sheila's story made Chandal nervous. The unexplainable, completely beyond understanding—it was beginning to become nerve-wracking. Strange, Chandal thought, that she had come to Sheila's to get away from her worries, and now the most trivial conversation had ended by upsetting her. She sighed, the strangeness surrounding her. She could feel it, taste it, everywhere she went now. It was there.

Sheila stacked the dishes on the top shelf. Was there such a thing as too much intensity? Look at Sheila. She had had the experience, had just talked about it in a personal way, yet she was going about her work, wiping the counter clean, folding the cloth, putting it on the rack to dry. Of course, Chandal was feeling all the tension because she had no explanation for why she saw the young couple that morning, the young man in the picture, the voices at night—no explanation whatsoever. Now she had noticed it, could not stop seeing and hearing and feeling these people; it was as if their presence were a constant throbbing in her brain, hammering out their message.

"Sheila?" Chandal's voice was too loud for the room.

"Yes?"

"I . . . do you . . . " Something stopped her. "It was a nice lunch. Thank you." She had wanted to tell Sheila about her worries, what she had imagined was going on within the brownstone. Instead, she blushed and discarded the thought.

In the silence Chandal fought off her embarrassment; how difficult it was to speak of the feelings

125

growing inside of her! But God, she had to tell someone.

"Well, all done." Sheila smiled. "I'll be right back. Then we'll go." She strode into the bathroom and closed the door. She was humming a tune.

The silence in the room was complete, not only in the room, but inside Chandal's head, as well. She was no longer thinking of anything.

The breathing came first. It caught her off guard, a blistering, harsh, in-the-pit-of-her-stomach breath. Hot steam that pushed up into her mouth, gagging her. The odor, the taste followed—vile-smelling acid that scorched the roof of her mouth.

She gasped. She tried to scream. But something was moving inside her throat, traveling from her stomach, winding its way upward, trying to escape from her mouth.

In a panic, she tried to open her jaw and couldn't. She felt something slithering up and down her windpipe. She turned her head slowly, twisting it to one side of her neck, gagging, and forced her mouth open wide. Her tongue shot back, out of control. It slapped against the roof of her mouth, shot outward, licked her lips until her jaw loosened, her head dropped slightly, and her breathing came back to her in short spurts. "Sheila!" she whispered hoarsely, her body falling limp against the arm of the chair. That was the way Sheila found her.

"Did you call . . . ? Oh, my God!" Sheila looked with shock at the redness around Chandal's mouth and neck, at the panic in her gaping eyes. "Chandal, are you all right?"

"What?" she asked, in a short gasp for air.

"What is it? What happened?"

Chandal's eyes darted around the room. "I don't know." She moved her hand to her chest. "Whatever . . . it was—it's gone."

"What is?"

"I don't know." Chandal's heart raced. "It felt like someone was forcing a tube down my throat. I . . . I couldn't catch my breath—trying to get it out."

126

Sheila moved to her side. Placed her arm around her shoulder. "You'll be all right." She squeezed Chandal's hand, and Chandal managed a nervous smile in return. "Maybe we should get you to a doctor."

"No!" Chandal whirled around, her eyes wide and filled with fear. It was still in the room. Whatever it was, it was still there. "Sheila, I have to talk to you. But not here. We still have a few minutes. We'll walk back, okay?"

Sheila glanced at her watch. "Sure. Whatever you want to do."

Sheila strode along the walk, her hands stuck neatly into the pockets of her woolen coat. She looked perplexed. "And you actually saw them in the nursery?"

"Both of them. She was asleep. Her head rested in his lap."

"Then they vanished?"

"Yes." Chandal frowned.

"What did you do then?"

"Nothing. What was I supposed to do?"

"And you were awake?"

Chandal stopped. "Sheila, you're not listening to me. Justin and I had just entered the front door of the brownstone. I was nowhere near the bed."

Sheila squinted, turning slightly away from the sun. "Jesus, that sun's bright."

"Sheila!"

"What?"

"You think I'm crazy, don't you?"

She shrugged. "You said you and Justin were into smoking grass. Did you have any——"

"Oh, don't give me that drug bullshit!" she said angrily. "All right, just forget it. Okay?"

Chandal took several steps—stopped. "Hey, I'm sorry."

"It's okay."

"Sheila, I thought you said you were a believer. Then why don't you believe I saw them?"

Sheila cleared her throat slightly. "I didn't say you didn't see them, but——"

"But what?"

"They don't seem to have any connection with you. At least with my mother—" Her voice lowered, she spoke objectively. Detached. "It was personal. There was a reason."

"I've thought about that." The crisp, cold air stuck in her throat. "Maybe there is a connection." She exhaled, her breath vaporous in the frosted air.

"In what way?" At the crosswalk children played, wrestling each other into the pile of snow next to the fence. "Hey, watch it!" Sheila scowled at them

"I don't know." Chandal continued across the street.

"What?" Sheila walked next to her.

"I don't know in what way they're connected. But I feel they are."

Sheila suddenly grabbed Chandal's arm. "I don't want to pry, but are you and Justin getting along all right?"

"Yes," Chandal lied. "Why?"

"Because that could be the cause of the problem."

Sadly, Chandal shook her head. "Believe me, Sheila, you're a good friend, but you're a rotten psychiatrist."

"Why?"

"This had nothing to do with our getting along."

"How can you be sure?"

"I . . . can't." The image of Justin's face, moody, tense, passed before her eyes.

"So, maybe I'm a better psychiatrist than you think. When people aren't getting along, they imagine—" She stopped herself.

"I know. They imagine all sorts of things." Chandal locked her fingers together, tightening her gloves. "So you think it's all in my head?"

"I think it's good you got it out in the open."

"Got what out in the open?"

"That Justin may be the cause. I mean, it's possible, right?"

"Maybe."

"So now you can deal with it."

"But if the couple is real—what then?"

"Then . . . they're real, and you'll find a logical explanation for them being there."

In the museum, the attendant smiled, the gorilla scowled, the medicine doctor looked paler than ever, and they were both back in the office fifteen minutes late.

"We'll talk later, okay?" Sheila hung up her coat.

"Yeah—later."

Chandal continued to have a difficult time at the office. She completely forgot to inform the vice president of an important message, costing the museum a valuable acquisition. She misplaced a priceless document, which was later discovered in the wastepaper basket, and she broke a third nail. Things dragged on in this way for the rest of the day.

Then a new element was added to her confusion.

During the last hour, she received a call from her mother. Her flu had gotten worse. She would have to go into the hospital for a complete checkup. Nothing serious, but the doctor wanted to make sure. Chandal promised that she would visit her tomorrow after work.

Just prior to leaving the office, Chandal was confronted by a V.I.P. and asked a flood of questions. She felt relieved to have most of the answers.

"And your name is?" he asked with a smile.

"Magdalen." She gasped and covered her mouth with her hand. At the same moment, he'd glanced over at the nameplate on her desk. "Did you say—'"

"My—my name is Chandal Knight," she said quickly.

When Chandal left the building soon after, she was still tense and could feel the nausea begin again. Why had she said that? "Oh, my God," she whispered, her fingers gripping her pocketbook. "What's happening to me?"

Moments later, Chandal sat in the kitchen and stared at the basement door. She felt as though she were "it" in the game of Blindman's Buff. Waiting for her stomach to settle, she kept thinking of the young man's face hidden away in the shadows of the picture Justin had taken of Mintz. The face kept appearing and reappearing in her mind. Wavering between belief and disbelief, she tried to busy herself. She fed the cat, watched TV, reread the note Justin had left her that morning. A scrap of paper not even an entire page, stating coldly: "Back at nine P.M. tonight. Justin." Her body seemed to be burning now. Something began to materialize. She had a clear impression that there was an altar, behind a small door, but she could see it, nevertheless. The image came closer, grew clearer—there, on the altar, the head of a goat. Baring his teeth, the goat smiled and then the image vanished. She glanced at the clock—eight-fifteen P.M. She couldn't stand it any longer. She had to have another look at the picture Justin had taken.

She hit the light switch at the bottom of the basement steps and the safety light flickered on. At first, she had a difficult time finding her way around, but she finally managed to locate where Justin kept his negatives. It wasn't until she turned the developing light on that she saw Magdalen staring at her!

Justin had blown her picture up and put it on the far wall. In the dark shadows, it appeared life-like. She glanced at her watch. Eight-twenty P.M. Justin would be home soon. If he caught her down here he would be furious. She'd have to take that chance.

Magdalen stared down at her from the wall, her eyes gently reproving. Such a pale print. It gave her an ethereal appearance, yet the picture was powerful, mesmerizing. As if her eyes owned the room. As if she could see what Chandal was doing. As if she thought Chandal was wrong to be down here where she didn't belong, snooping into things that didn't concern her. Chandal moved; the eyes followed her.

She quickly placed the negative in the enlarger. Mintz sprang up before her eyes. Adjusting the enlarger, she blew up only the portion of the picture that she was interested in. Finally, only the doorway leading to the basement remained, and there it was—the face of the young man. She shot the picture.

Suddenly she heard a thumping sound. It was coming from the wall closest to the mannequins. She had to hurry. She placed the blank white piece of photo paper into the developing tank and waited. The sound continued to get louder as the image became clearer on the paper. What was causing that sound? she wondered.

She placed the picture into the fixing solution. It would have to remain there at least five minutes. The sound grew louder.

She stumbled past the mannequins and reached the spot where the sound was coming from. She placed her hand on the wall—it was red-hot. But the rest of the wall was cold. She looked at her watch—eight-thirty-five P.M. The tips of her fingers were burned and blistered. She couldn't wait any longer.

Removing the picture from the solution, she could clearly see the face of the young man. She turned out the light—hurried up the stairs and into the bedroom. Placing the picture in the lower drawer of her dresser, she heard a key in the front door.

When Justin entered the brownstone, Chandal was sitting in the living room, reading a magazine. She stirred, looked at Justin, and smiled. Justin sensed immediately that something was wrong. He knew that Chandal's smile was counterfeit and he wondered what she was up to.

"Hi, honey," he said gently.

"Hi."

He went to the closet and hung up his coat. "Did you have a nice day?"

"Dreadful."

It wasn't until Justin removed his hat that Chandal noticed that he'd had his hair cut even shorter. "Do you like it?" He'd noticed her stare.

"You look like you're enlisting in the army." She gave a weak laugh.

"So you don't like it."

"Oh, you'd look handsome if you shaved your head. Hey, wait a minute." She tried to be light. "I'm joking. The way you're going, you'll take me at my word. Seriously, you look fine."

131

Justin smiled.

"How was your day?" she asked.

"Oh, great. They finally got a stage manager. Thank—" He broke off and hung his hat on the peg. "Everything is great, though. We saw some interesting actors. Not really much talent, but interesting. They've lined up another thirty for me to look at tomorrow. All Broadway talent—at least that's what Fein told me."

"You see, he's not so bad."

"He sure has a lot of money."

"Oh?"

"He's dying to produce a hit. All that money, and still he wants to prove something. Strange."

Over dinner later, she asked, "Do people change, Justin? I mean really change."

"Yes, I believe they can."

"I don't know."

She thought about that through the dinner dishes, and when she drew a hot bath, scenting the water with bath oil, and then lying in bed sinking into darkness. Do people change? Finally, the thought crystallized. We're changing. The exhaustion, the dead weight of her eyelids closing over her eyes shut out any furtherance of the thought. Over and over again—We're changing—a floating image over her head of two people who were Justin and herself and yet not them at all. We're changing, she thought wearily, a tear rolling down her cheek, and then she fell heavily asleep.

Upstairs, Elizabeth moved to another seat next to the elegantly dressed, pretty young girl and began fussing with her hair. She pretended that the girl was a doll and in that way recaptured lost moments of her childhood, escaping the harsh reality of the gathering years.

Suddenly, it had become summer. It was vacation time. Lush green pines and spruce trees shaded their country home in Larchmont, New York, lily pads adorned the pond. She gazed at her reflection in the clear blue water.

"Don't stay in the sun too long, honey! We can't have our little girl coming down with sun poisoning!" Her mother stood in the garden amongst the roses, her face placid as always when speaking to her daughter.

That was her favorite daydream, the country home, the vacations spent in Larchmont. Sometimes, she could sit beside the young girl for an hour or so, imagining the slight breeze moving through the trees and the sound of her mother's voice. Lately, though, she found herself less and less able to conjure up those blissful memories and found herself drawn to another part of her past. Magdalen's fits of anger at the attenton her mother would shower on her favorite child. Yes, she was the favorite.

The young girl suddenly jerked Elizabeth's hand from her hair. "Get rid of the past!" she told Elizabeth with a scowl. "Wipe it from your mind, old woman." With the arrogance of youth, the girl rose, swept across the floor to the large, ornate mirror, and, in a sudden shudder of ecstasy, admired what she saw within the antique frame. She was not a doll! She was real—Elizabeth would have to get used to it!

Elizabeth's mind skipped a beat, dropped quickly into an abyss. A deep, dark pit, the walls close, suffocating. She was curled into a fetus position. Her mother was out, her father away on business. "Please, let me out!" she screamed. Her sister laughed. "You wore my dress again, didn't you? Didn't you!"

"No, please—I won't wear it anymore, not anymore, ever. Please let me out!"

"No!"

"Dear God, dear God, please let me out!" Elizabeth whimpered, fumbling for the doorknob, fumbling to embrace the small shaft of light that filtered under the closet door.

Then the light in the next room was shut off. Elizabeth heard her sister laugh. The sound was vulgar in its delight. "Good night, sweet sister."

133

"No, please—don't leave me in here. Please. *Please!*"

The loud ticking of the mantel clock began to count off the minutes, the hours. She listened to it, her body twisted, squirming in pain. "Please let me out!" she muttered, the air in the tiny closet getting thinner.

"I can't breathe, please—I can't breathe." Tick-tock, "I can't breathe," tick-tock—"please." She sat trembling in the corner, chewing her fingernails, ripping the nails away, biting the tips of her finger until she drew blood. The taste of blood was thick on her tongue; she tried to wipe it away with the back of her hand, but the taste of blood had remained.

The young girl turned away from the mirror now, stared at Elizabeth. Watched the tears fall from her eyes. "Silly old woman. You'll never stop being a child, will you? Silly damn old woman."

Patient cried today during session. There is on my wall a modern painting symbolizing the evolution of man. Patient's eyes were fixed on the picture during the first half of the session. Hands were folded tightly in lap, as in prayer, and legs were close together in old-fashioned modesty. Religiosity with accompanying superstition makes patient afraid to communicate for fear of punishment.

During word association, I said "darkness." Patient said "death." I said "death." Patient said "old." I said "old." Patient pointed to self and began to cry. Shortly afterward, patient was returned to room.

The seclusiveness and fear continue. Patient is not willing to spend time with others. Despite obvious progress, patient continues to be hyperactive, continues to relate through childlike stories in the third person.

Psychological testing will be utilized during next visit; however, attention span is poor; therefore, only short intervals will be devoted to eliciting new material.

I. Luther

❧ 13 ❧

By early morning, clouds had gathered over the city, promising snow. Inside the brownstone, everyone slept.

"How delightful! Eh?"

"Nothing better."

"Come along; let's start; but be careful."

Chandal sat up in bed. Someone was talking in the hallway. She strained to hear the rest of the conversation.

"People must be stupid to kill themselves like that."

"It's life."

"No—it's death."

She glanced at Justin, who was still asleep. Carefully, she reached across his body and shut off the alarm. It was just about to ring. Justin had set it for five-thirty A.M.

"Justin?" she whispered. "Wake up." She poked gently at his back, but he covered himself with the blanket and rolled over.

The door to the nursery clicked open and then closed. Chandal waited for further sounds—there were none.

Hurriedly, she got out of bed, put on her robe, and walked quietly into the hallway. She could barely see, but didn't want to put on the lights. Feeling her way along the wall, she moved closer to the nursery. She paused to listen. Inside the room, someone laughed.

Chandal flung the door open and quickly put on the light. The room was empty. Unconvinced, she walked into the room and saw the imprint of a stretched-out figure on the bed. The pillow was deeply indented, as if a head had lain there, and the blanket at the foot of the bed was wrinkled.

Suddenly she could feel the presence of someone standing by the window. She turned and saw a vague grayness near the curtain. It was like a quick flick of mist, hardly enough to speak of, and yet it was definite, and in a part of the room where there could be no reflection of any sort.

"What are you doing?"

She wheeled around and came face to face with Justin.

"I said, what are you doing?" He was annoyed that Chandal had woken him up.

"Oh, nothing. I—"

He never waited for her reply. Instead, he stumbled into the kitchen, drank a glass of water, and returned to bed. Chandal wondered why he'd set the alarm for five-thirty if he hadn't intended to get up. Not being able to sleep, she sat alone in the kitchen and drank coffee. Justin never got up until he had to, not even then. What did he intend to do at five-thirty in the morning? She sat without stirring and let the image of her last birthday flow over her. June 3. Five-thirty A.M. Justin had rustled her out of bed, demanding that she dress quickly. He had planned a special surprise. Groggily, she had dressed, had left the apartment half-asleep, heading for the subway.

They had gone to the racetrack—what a wonderful feeling to watch the young geldings exercise, exercise boys sitting high in the saddles, the horses' nostrils breathing fine fire as they cut through space. "God, Justin—they're magnificent!"

Justin had smiled. "Damn, I always wanted to own one. Honey, promise me, if we're rich and famous someday, we'll own one."

They had kissed. "I promise," she had said. They had lain in the thick green grass. Her eyes were closed against the sparkling blue overhead. She had said to herself that she had to be rich and famous someday just to get Justin that horse.

Chandal gripped the cup more tightly, about to move back into the reality she hated. God! Eight-thirty! She slammed the cup into the sink, dashed into the bathroom, showered, dressed, and glanced at the clock. Justin had reset it for nine. That made sense.

When she left the brownstone, he was still asleep.

Chandal could feel that they were watching her. She sat at her desk in fear, afraid that she was about to be fired. Carefully, she put a sheet of paper into her typewriter. Her reception this morning hadn't been a friendly one. Sheila dropped in from time to time to lend moral support, but it hadn't helped. Oh, God—she'd typed the same sentence twice. Self-consciously, she tried to make the correction and botched it. She'd have to type the page over. She tried to whisk it unobtrusively away. Chandal knew that she had made a mess of things yesterday. She'd have to do better today.

Lunch hour, she decided to drop off the ring that Justin had given her. It was several sizes too large and would have to be cut down. She put the ring back into her purse and set out toward the Broadway area, following the streets and looking for a jeweler's shop.

She finally found one at Eighty-seventh Street and entered, rather shaken and tired from her lack of food and sleep.

"Is it possible," she began, "to have this ring made smaller?"

The man took the ring, examined it, turned it around several times, took a magnifying glass, called a clerk, made some observations to him in a low voice, placed it on a blue velvet pad, and looked at it from a distance to admire it. He then commented on the unusualness of the ring and said that he could have it ready by five.

"That'll be fine, thank you," said Chandal.

"Name?" He prepared to write up the ticket.

"Chandal Knight."

"Address?"

"Three West Eighty-fifth Street."

"Three?" asked the man dumbfoundedly. "Are you sure?"

"Well, of course, I'm sure—why?" Chandal stiffened.

"But isn't that where the sisters live? What was her name? Magdalen, yes! And her sister, Elizabeth."

Chandal explained that her husband and she had moved into the brownstone and now occupied the first floor. The man interrupted her and started off on recollections, moving quietly among old things and ancient happenings.

"Heavens! But she was such a pretty thing at nineteen, and charming and well informed—ah!" The old man's faded blue eyes lit up like a Christmas tree ornament. "I have never seen anyone quite like her—never!"

"Why didn't she marry?" asked Chandal.

"Why?" The man paused. "Why? She didn't want to. Yet she had plenty of opportunities. But for some reason—she never did. Her sister, Elizabeth, was company enough for her, I guess." His candid, tranquil expression turned to gloom and he fell into an awkward silence.

Chandal thanked him again and left the shop.

At the corner of Eighty-second Street, she heard a familiar sound. She stopped. There it was again. Looking up, she was relieved to see that it was a wind chime hanging from a second-story window. Her thoughts moved swiftly to the picture that she had hidden in her dresser drawer.

She decided not to return to work. She made two phone calls, one to the office manager informing him that she was ill, the other to Sissy.

Sissy's voice was filled with the usual energy, determination, and humor. She was busy, she was always busy. "But I always have time for you, ducks. What are you sounding so tragic over?"

Chandal felt her self-control vanishing. She covered the receiver and leaned against the door.

"Chandal?"

139

"Sissy, I need your help. I'm . . ." Her voice cracked.

"Where are you?" asked Sissy sharply.

Chandal drew a long shuddering breath. "I'm going home. Can you meet me?"

"I'll be there in a half-hour. Are you okay?"

"I'll be fine. Just come."

"Depend on it, love. I'll be there."

Chandal hung up feeling stronger already. She let herself out of the booth, started to walk, consciously willing herself to relax.

It had been a lonely time at Duke before she met Sissy, well into her second year. Sissy had been wild and exciting. Never satisfied, she always wanted more. More parties, more dates—it had all been fun. She was attractive and popular, and Chandal enjoyed standing next to her just to see how many and which men would stop and talk to her. It was like standing in her shadow, but it made Chandal feel a little prettier.

Sissy had spent a lot of time smartening her up. She picked out her wardrobe, rearranged her hair, selected her boyfriends. Sissy had always said, "It doesn't make any difference if you're right or wrong —just as long as you're positive."

Positive. How long since she'd lost the power to be really positive? Lost the power to be herself? Sissy would help her, she thought. Sissy would help her just like she used to. Chandal started walking, suddenly in a hurry to get home.

Justin had left the brownstone earlier that morning with the rotten taste of being poor in his mouth. After scraping off the front steps and emptying the garbage, he walked downtown "dialoging it" all the way. The hammer blows of the workmen patching up Broadway rattled the windows and shook the streets. He left word on the service for Chandal to meet him at the Sacred Cow at seven P.M. for dinner. The Sacred Cow was their favorite restaurant, class at affordable prices. A theatrical crowd, singing waiters, people they knew at the bar. Billy had introduced Justin to the Sacred Cow. They had a lot of memories there. The guy at the bar who was writing a novel on bar napkins. He'd been writing the same novel for twenty years, he said. They'd tried to figure out how many napkins that would be. Billy had sprung for dinner the night before Justin and Chandal were married. Justin and Chandal and Billy and what's-her-name. An agreeable blonde with a commendable figure. Another name on Billy's long list. Memories. A lot of memories.

Thirty minutes late for casting, Justin stumbled into the dark and jammed rehearsal studio at Seventy-second.

"You're late," said the stage manager, making a note on his clipboard beside Justin's name.

Justin turned and focused on the thin, fanatical face. Jesus, after all these years in the business, fooled again. Yesterday the guy had looked like a gem. Good credentials, intelligent, good-natured, and now —damn. Like a thousand other bums, he was one more with the gift for pretending to be other than he was.

The stage manager's weak eyes glittered behind his glasses. "They're waiting for you," he said and glanced at Fein, who sat silently with tight lips, legs crossed, arms folded, beside the small table. A row back sat Bernie Stark, a tense smile hovering on his lips. His hand fluttered in greeting.

Good ole Bernie, thought Justin. Trying to make the best of a piss poor situation.

"Get me a cup of coffee, will you?" he said to the stage manager, who lifted his brow disdainfully. Justin didn't give him a chance to challenge him, as he took his seat at the table.

Fein pushed over the list of actors, his diamonds catching the light. "It doesn't look good, keeping these people waiting," he said stonily.

Justin glanced at the sheet of paper as he lit a cigarette. "Sorry, I got hung up. If they get the job, they won't care." Justin forced a grin. "How you doing?"

"Okay." Fein relaxed. "Glad you got here."

Bernie looked happier. He took a package of Life Savers from his jacket and put two into his mouth. "Want a mint?" he asked.

"No, thanks." Good God, thought Justin, listening to Bernie suck the mints, his heavy breathing filling the room. Was he going to have to listen to that all day? Fein and Stark. The Shuberts, they weren't. "Come on, let's go," he said. "Who's first?"

The stage manager called an actress who hustled up to the table trying to look sexier than she was and handed Justin a five-by-seven index card. Justin eyed her coldly.

"Miss Richards. Sit down, please."

"Thank you," she said, dropping herself into the chair like a bundle of loose rags. "Gee, I really like the script. It's great, you know."

"Tell me, Miss Richards—"

"You can call me Billie."

"Sure. How tall are you?" asked Justin, his mind elsewhere.

"Five-ten."

Justin never heard the answer. By some untraceable miscalculation, he had not seen Magdalen since Thursday, or was it Friday? He could not remember. "Here, read this." He handed Billie a script. Magdalen's image kept flashing before his eyes. With an effort, he concentrated on the actress as she read for the role of Carole, a repressed lesbian. Looking away, he watched Stark lean forward, Life Savers in hand—he was clearly impressed. Justin's lips tightened and he made a cryptic note on her card. This actress uses tricks. With her—what you see is what you get. He looked up—the actress put a hand on her hip and gave a practiced toss of her head, sending her mop of long tangled hair swirling around her face. Justin shook his head. Harvey gave a significant nod to Justin—Justin felt like laughing in his face. Goddamn empty people, he thought. "Okay, that's enough." The actress sat down. "Do you have previous theater experience?" he asked.

"Mainly modeling, but I'm willing to learn." She

gave Justin a coy smile and adjusted the straps of her bra.

Justin angrily glanced at the two producers. After ten years in the theater, he was still dealing with amateurs! He looked back at the girl and smiled. "Would you remove your clothes, please?" Justin's smile grew wider as Fein and Stark squirmed in their chairs.

"Hey, wait a minute—whaddya mean take my clothes off?" she asked.

"I'm curious to see how you look in the nude."

She considered. "Do I have to take my pants off, too?" she asked.

"I want you to disrobe completely," Justin said offhandedly, tossing his felt pen on the table. *She's a real bitch,* said the voice within him. *Make her suffer.*

The girl unbuttoned the top button of her blouse. "Is it artistic nudity?" She moved down to the second button.

"Oh, sure," said Justin. Behind him, Stark sucked in air noisily, absorbed in the girl's hand as it finished undoing the blouse.

Billie Richards giggled, shrugged a shoulder free. "Am I doing okay?"

Harvey put his hand on Justin's shoulder. "Miss . . . uh . . . Richards, would you mind waiting outside, please. . . ?"

The girl looked hurt, moved out of the room, still half-dressed.

Justin shrugged Fein's hand from his shoulder. "The next time you put a hand on me—"

"Ssh! Calm down," said Fein, his face darkening. "Listen, Justin, we have our reputations on the line here. . . ."

"Can it." Justin picked up his pen, his cigarettes.

"Let's talk about it." Fein continued to plead his cause, showing calculated humility, learned no doubt from his rich father. Stark brooded silently in a corner. Justin allowed himself to be appeased. Casting continued. By lunchtime, Justin had seen thirty actresses, none of whom he liked.

*

It was getting more difficult for Chandal to relate to her surroundings. Standing in the hallway of the brownstone, she had the feeling that she'd never been there before.

Mechanically, she stared down the long tunnel-like hallway. She pictured Justin wandering from the kitchen to the spare room directly opposite. Did the spare room door just close? She wasn't sure. Did she wish to believe that it had? No, that would mean she was hallucinating. Living room to her left, door open —it all looked familiar now. Bedroom to the right. Reality, no matter how grim, was better than illusion, she thought. None of this connected. Without knowing why, she felt a kind of panic. The nursery! Crushed between the spare room and the living room, it remained womb-like, hidden. A room of secrets, she thought. Without removing her coat, she approached the nursery door, paused, and then entered.

Again, as before, Chandal felt another presence within the room. Her conflict welled up inside her and she felt at the end of her resistance. She knew she wasn't imagining it—the covers on the bed had again shown the impression of a frail body. She was positive that she had straightened the bed before leaving the room this morning.

The next moments were lost in a mumbling confusion. She was half-convinced that Justin was all part of this, but she didn't understand exactly how.

She closed the nursery door, opened the bedroom door.

The picture was exactly where she'd left it. In the lower drawer of her dresser. She stared at the face in the picture for a long time. Then, without realizing it, she began to hum a song to herself that she'd never heard before. She was still humming ten minutes later and rocking unsteadily, back and forth on her feet, when the doorbell rang.

When Sissy entered the front door of the brownstone, she couldn't believe what she saw. Chandal had large, black circles under her eyes and her hair was wind-blown and disheveled. With coat half-on, half-off, she stood trembling and barefoot, twisting one foot on top of the other.

"Oh, my God! Chandal, what's wrong?"

Chandal could not move from the doorway. Yet, she wanted to run. Her face was flushed and tears streamed down her cheeks, but her legs remained rooted.

"Oh, baby—here, let me help you," Sissy soothed. She removed Chandal's coat and sat her down in the living room. After helping her force down two aspirins, Sissy went into the kitchen and put on a kettle of water for tea. Then she called her office and told them that she would be unable to return to work. All this took twenty minutes.

Placing a hot cup of tea in front of Chandal, Sissy brushed a few hairs away from her face. "Come on, drink this."

Chandal stared at her.

"What's wrong, for heaven's sake? Come on, you can tell me."

"Sissy, I think I'm going out of my mind," she finally said.

"Why—what's happened?"

"Come with me. I want to show you something." Chandal took Sissy by the hand and led her to the bedroom where the picture lay on the bed. She picked it up and stared at it for a moment and then handed it to Sissy. "This picture—what do you see?" she asked.

Sissy looked at the picture blankly. "I don't see much of anything."

"A face—you don't see a face in that picture?"

After carefully considering the possibility, Sissy's answer was still no.

Chandal snatched the picture back, threw it into the dresser, and slammed the drawer shut. It took Sissy the next ten minutes to calm Chandal down.

"You don't understand—it's not just the picture," said Chandal. "There have been things, other things. Incident after incident. First the bell; next the voices; then Justin acting funny—none of it makes sense!"

145

"But I don't understand what you're talking about." Sissy felt helpless—Chandal wasn't making any sense.

Suddenly Chandal insisted that they leave the house, that she was sure people were listening to their conversation. She put on her shoes. They moved outside and walked toward the park. Chandal looked back over her shoulder every third step.

They went to the playground and Chandal walked around for a while, breathing in the crisp air. It was a sharp, frosty day and she started to feel a lot better. She watched two boys on the parallel bars and thought they looked like little bears, all bundled up from head to toe in their woolen outfits.

Sissy sat on the bench and talked to a stranger while Chandal explored the entire playground alone. From time to time, Sissy would glance around to see if Chandal was all right. She was surprised to see Chandal playing ball with the children. There were three of them, and the very dark boy yelled out for Sissy to join them.

"I don't know how!" she shouted.

"Don't worry, I'll show you!"

After throwing the ball around, Sissy missing it on every occasion, Chandal decided that they should all go to the zoo. The boys declined. "How about you?" asked Chandal.

Sissy smiled. "Why not?"

The afternoon sun touched the plateglass windows and turned them a pinkish-gold, the kind of gold found in the early days of color films. The girls kept shifting from one side of the street to the other trying to keep warm.

They entered the zoo at Sixty-fourth Street and Fifth Avenue and were immediately hit in the face with a balloon. The Yum Yum hotdog man was doing a great business, having positioned himself alongside a green and moldy sign that read: "TO THE ZOO AND CAFETERIA." The next sign told them that they had to be out by seven P.M. Chandal hadn't said much, but it was obvious that she grew more relaxed as she removed herself from the vicinity of the brownstone.

The closest building to the entrance was the Monkey House. "Let's go inside," said Sissy. "I think I have some relatives in here." What she came up with was her grandfather. The sign said that this unique creature was a Wanderoo, but Sissy declared that she knew otherwise. His face was covered with a huge mop of gray hair that resembled a beard, and his two bloodshot eyes rolled around in his head in search of all the answers.

"Yep, that's Gramps, all right. I'm sure of it!" Sissy laughed and they moved on to the next cage, where the mandril was wolfing down a handful of lettuce. The sign explained that his colorful markings helped to make him sexually more attractive to the dully colored female.

"With a face like that, he needs a little color!" Sissy exclaimed.

Chandal suddenly felt a hard gaze on the back of her neck. She turned and discovered a huge chimpanzee staring at her from the next cage. He looked middle-aged and appeared to be going bald. He expressed surprise at seeing Chandal, then fear and anger. Something akin to the emotions Chandal had experienced in the last two weeks. He had hands for feet and made her feel very uneasy.

"Sissy?"

"What?" She turned to face Chandal.

"Do you believe in the supernatural?"

"The supernatural?" She shrugged. "Like what?"

"You know, things we know nothing about. Things that you can't see, but that you know are there."

"I don't think so—why?"

Chandal smiled weakly. "Nothing. It's not important."

They stood outside for a moment and watched a young man who wore clown-face makeup passing out free balloons with a big sign across his chest which read: PLEASE TIP. People would pass him a quarter and he'd go into his routine, that of making clever remarks while shaping a balloon into a small animal—a mouse, a dog, or a lion. He accomplished this in a matter of seconds.

Chandal had a sick feeling in the pit of her stomach. Sissy insisted that she eat something. Five minutes later, they sat inside the cafeteria. Sissy had French fries—the salt was nowhere to be found—a flat beer, and a cheeseburger, too well done.

Chandal ate very little. "I don't think Justin loves me anymore." She had a hard time looking at Sissy.

At first Sissy laughed, sure that Chandal must be joking. Then she discovered how serious she really was. "Don't be silly—you're imagining things."

"I am not imagining things!" Chandal slammed her cup on the table, then glanced around. Her voice was starting to carry and people were paying attention.

As Chandal bent low to speak with her, Sissy asked the usual list of pious, disrespectful questions. "Is he seeing another woman?"

"I think so—yes."

Sissy paused. "My ex . . . " she said in a trembling voice. She removed a Kleenex hastily from her bag and dabbed around her eyes. Just the mention of Sissy's ex-husband was enough to evoke tears, and Chandal stared at her, wondering. Two years since their divorce was final, and still Sissy—sensible, intelligent Sissy—could go blurry-eyed at the mention of Kevin Steele's name. "When it comes to other women," Sissy went on, sounding like she had a cold, "don't trust a husband. Not any husband. Men are such dreamers. Marriage, even the best marriage, isn't . . . " Her voice went on and on about married men and Kevin Steele, most specifically, who had been caught after an office party making love to a temporary secretary.

Chandal's mind started to wander as Sissy talked on. Men and women . . . She found her gaze fixed on a little brown-haired girl who played with the tail of a bronzed lion. Another child rode the lion's back, pretending that the ears were reins. A third little boy came over and slapped the lion in the face in open defiance of all who looked on.

"But in your case," Sissy continued, "you're about to have his baby."

And Chandal said, "It wouldn't mean anything if he didn't love me." She changed the subject. "By the way, how did it all work out? With the man, I mean. The one you met at our party."

"Oh, that. He was tacky," brooded Sissy.

"Oh, I don't know. I thought he was rather nice."

"He had a cheap little image of me in his mind that I didn't like." She paused. "My book—did you like it?"

"What?"

"The book of poetry I gave you at the party."

"Oh, yes. It was all right." She hadn't read it.

"What do you mean, all right?"

"You know me. I'm not usually much interested in anything that doesn't have a plot."

"Pity." Sissy shook her head in honest bewilderment as a young Puerto Rican boy came through the cafeteria, the disco music on his radio ripping through the air like a buzz saw.

"Look, let's get out of here, okay?" Chandal said. They left the cafeteria.

"You're not thinking of divorce, are you?" asked Sissy.

"No!" Chandal ducked into the Elephant House. Sissy followed after her. They stopped in front of an Indian elephant named Tina, who was sucking up hay faster than it could be laid down.

"Then what are you going to do?" persisted Sissy.

"I don't know. What would you do?"

"Leave him, naturally."

"Naturally."

"Who is she—do you know her?"

Chandal didn't have the answer.

They moved outside, past the First-Aid/Lost Children station and ended up looking at Ginny, who was eating up every dry leaf she could scrounge. She was, it was noted, a female eland who was presented to the zoo by Gordon's Dry Gin Company, March 23, 1976.

"Sissy, I want you to do me a favor."

149

"Sure, anything."

"I want you to stay at my place for a couple of nights, okay? It's important to me."

Sissy agreed and they started to walk again, past the golden pheasant, the wood duck, the Barbary sheep, and the antelope. A little boy said good-bye to the antelope; the antelope seemed to regret the child's departure. Sissy said good-bye to Chandal and left. She would return to the brownstone at eight.

Chandal watched Sissy wind her way through the American flags, the plastic Micky Mouse dolls, the stuffed shark toys, and Donald Duck.

In an atmosphere of chattering voices, birdsongs, and chill, Chandal left the zoo, via the back exit, and walked home through Central Park.

At three P.M., Justin abruptly left the producers in charge of the casting call. He offered no explanation. Silently, Fein took a brown handkerchief from his shirt pocket and blew his nose. Stark sat still, impotent in impatience.

Standing on the second-floor landing of the brownstone, Justin paused and then knocked lightly. Elizabeth opened the door and stared at him with an obvious air of displeasure. "Yes?"

"Is Magdalen at home?" He fidgeted with the zipper on the front of his leather jacket.

Elizabeth nodded.

"May I see her?"

Without saying a word, she indicated that he should wait there. Justin could hear every step down the long hallway, and every moment he waited his position became more unendurable. Guiltily, he thought of Chandal and the baby. He was growing uneasy when suddenly light footsteps interrupted his thoughts. Elizabeth appeared at the door and asked him to step into the apartment. He looked at her closely to see if she suspected his real emotions, but her face was calm and, without the slightest expression, she said that Magdalen was much better today and would see him. She turned and led the way.

150

Justin followed and all at once he noticed that the apartment was strangely familiar. The portraits that hung on the walls—he knew them by heart. The antique chair, the mirror, the white drapes—all were familiar. Magdalen's room was at the far end of the hall, to the right—precisely where Elizabeth led him. He knew that, too.

And somehow he knew that he'd been expected. That he was keeping an appointment he'd been expected to keep. He breathed in deeply. The sweet smell was soothing to his senses. Part of him dropped peacefully away and with it went the brooding, the sadness. He fell under an unseen protection. Yes, all was well and exactly as it should be. They stopped in front of Magdalen's door. He could hardly wait to go inside, into the warmth of Magdalen's presence. Expressionlessly, Elizabeth swung open the door and he passed over the threshold, feeling the air fanning back against his neck as immediately she closed him inside the room, shutting the heavy door from the outside.

Self-consciously, he straightened his jacket, noticing the room. He knew it as well as his own bedroom. There was the fire burning in the fireplace, the small table with his books, the rack of pipes that Magdalen had asked him to smoke. For an instant, he almost turned to leave. But instead, he turned to the white figure lying so quietly upon the bed.

"Come in—don't just stand there!" Magdalen cried out in a clear voice.

Justin moved closer. "I thought I'd lost you," he said in a low voice.

Below, Chandal took off her coat and hung it in the hall closet. She glanced at the stairs leading to the second floor. Perhaps it would help if she talked with the two old women, she thought. She had started up the stairs toward the second floor when she caught sight of Mintz. The cat always knew when Chandal entered the house and was there to greet her.

"And how are you?" She picked the cat up in her arms and moved into the kitchen. Her dish was empty. She fed Mintz and made herself a cup of coffee. She wished that she hadn't asked Sissy to stay with her tonight. What would be accomplished? The entire situation had become ludicrous. The best thing to do was to talk it out with Justin. She wrote him a note telling him that she would be home right after her visit to the hospital. She was careful to add "I love you," and after her name, she drew a heart with an arrow through it.

Folding the piece of paper, she placed it between the salt and pepper shakers on the table. Mintz had finished her food and was cleaning herself off. Exhausted, Chandal went into the bedroom to lie down.

She thought of the picture in the lower drawer. No, she'd had enough confusion for one day; rest was the best answer. The pillow felt soft and warm, and before long, she fell asleep.

Justin left the brownstone not realizing that Chandal was right there in the bedroom sleeping. Had he known, he would have been less conspicuous.

Chandal sat up in bed when she heard the front door close. She glanced at the clock—five-fourteen P.M. She went into the bathroom and showered. She soaped herself immaculately, accounting for every inch of skin surface. She repeated this several times, the entire operation taking twenty-five minutes. She combed her hair with the utmost of care, making absolutely certain that not a single strand was out of place. After brushing her teeth twice, she washed her hands and then carefully combed her hair again, making sure that the bangs were perfectly straight. When she stepped from the bathroom, she looked like an entirely different person. It was six-forty-five P.M.

Prior to leaving the brownstone, she tried to call Sissy. She wanted to tell her not to come. There was no answer. Having forgotten to call the service, she was unaware of her dinner date with Justin at seven P.M.

Justin picked his glass up off the bar, rested his elbow on the sleek black marble surface, and let his eyes move around the room slowly. There were eight, maybe nine people sitting in the Sacred Cow. Chandal was not among them.

He turned back to the bar and contemplated the glass in his hand. In the center of the small dining room a young girl sat down behind the piano and began to play.

"Look at me, I'm as helpless as a kitten up a tree . . ."

He hummed the tune to himself, in snatches, staring about him, frowning. Why was Chandal always late? He had felt the headache coming on, but now it had worsened. He rubbed the sleeve of his jacket across his forehead, trying to drive away the pain. He closed his eyes, letting the thin edge of the melody soothe his brain.

When he reopened his eyes, two men had taken seats on either side of him. Neither spoke, but Justin felt that they were together. They both ordered beer.

Justin poured the rest of his drink down his throat. It went down the way it always did, hot, curling, and lodging solid in his stomach, where it stung. Then the two men began to speak.

"Nice place," said the man to Justin's right.

"Yeah," the man to his left answered.

"Justin Knight." To his right.

"Correct?" To his left.

Justin smiled faintly, leaned back, and squinted at the two men. He knew neither of them. "I don't think—"

"Richards." The tall, thin man flashed a broad smile.

"Morgan." The other man, squat and barrel-chested, followed suit. Both men were corpse-pale and moved with jerky, haphazard gestures.

"What's your problem, Knight?" asked Morgan.

"Problem? I don't have a problem," Justin said uncomfortably.

"Well, you're going to have," said Richards, his face tight. "I mean, it isn't nice, you going around shooting your mouth off, telling people to take their clothes off like you did today. She happens to be my wife, and I don't like it. It makes me look bad."

Billie Richards, Justin thought. The girl from the reading today. A no-talent broad, a model or something. Slightly aged, simpering fool of a would-be starlet. Justin's fingers tightened into a fist. So Billie Richards was married to this goon.

Richards leaned over to Justin. "Do you know what I do for a living, Knight?"

Justin shook his head.

Richards reached into his pocket, took out a handful of dirt. Dumped it onto the bar. "Construction. That's what I do. Construction. All day, every day, six in the morning to three in the afternoon, seven days a week. I get home, I'm tired from busting my ass all day long. I need to catch some sleep. I don't like it when my wife wakes me out of a sound sleep, hysterical. Crying that she wants me to do something. What the hell is wrong with you!" He thumped the bar with his fist.

"Relax, Johnny," Morgan said, his cigarette starting to burn his finger. He snuffed it out and lit another. "That was a dumb thing to do, Knight. She's a very serious actress. But then, how would you know? You never gave her a chance."

"Chance, ha!" Richards exclaimed. "This dumb bastard probably has the play already cast. Now don't you?" he asked heavily, his broad, flat face constricted as he squinted, watching Justin, waiting for the answer.

"Not really." Justin tried to remain calm. "How did you know where to find me?"

Morgan smiled. "We called the theater. They gave us your home number. We called. Your service said you were meeting your wife here at seven. Who the hell are you, the President? You're not hard to reach."

"Look, let's stop the bullshit!" Richards poked his finger into the middle of Justin's chest. "Her name is Billie—Billie Richards. When you call tomorrow,

154

you tell her you want her to read for the play again. It'll make her happy, and I can get some sleep. Right?" He let Justin draw his own conclusions.

They both rose to their feet in unison. "You want some advice, Knight?" asked Morgan. "Take a walk, think about it—it'll be good for your health. Shmuck!"

Justin watched as they turned and walked away, up the stairs, out the front door. Morgan whistled. Justin watched them get into a checkered cab and drive away.

Without expression, he looked down. Christ!

He ordered another whiskey. The hostess, a small, well-built brunette dressed in black and gold, gave him his drink; he asked for another and then another. The minutes slipped away.

"Damn!" he muttered, watching the Scotch shimmering in the light; pale and trembling, in the glass. Once it starts to crack, there's nothing you can do about it, nothing; it keeps squeezing in on you from all sides—crumbling down on top of you and there's nothing that can stop it. Once you blow it, there's no second chance. Why did he ever tell her to take her clothes off? He didn't even seem to remember. And now these two jerks.

His hand, resting on the bar's edge, tightened: a hard, dark fleshy ball. Yet, it really didn't matter. None of it mattered. His fist unclenched itself, moved easily around the glass. Nothing mattered anymore. He could sit there and nurse his drink and let things take care of themselves.

That's right, the voice said inside his head. *Everything will be taken care of.*

And then all the headaches—racing ambitions, half-caught visions, words, glances, sudden violent apprehensions—were gone. The young business execs, the singing waiters, the hat-check girl were all around him now, and it was business as usual.

He caught a glimpse of himself in the mirror behind the bar. He hardly recognized himself. Had he changed? Uneasily, he finished the last of his drink, tipped the hostess three dollars, and left the Sacred Cow.

Chandal stopped at the front desk to ask the number of her mother's room. The woman behind the desk was busy, alternately hopping from the switchboard to the sign-out patients list. Periodically, she let out a whoop and said, "Sorry, my mistake."

Chandal took a seat and waited. A teen-age boy, his arm in a cast, sat down in the chair next to her. He glanced at the travel posters that hung on the wall.

Two interns stopped to discuss a patient. The younger of the two read aloud from a chart. "Blood study—negative. Urine analysis—normal. Chest X ray —normal. Blood pressure—110/76. Ears, nose, and throat are normal." They disappeared into the elevator.

Chandal stiffened. She thought of her baby and prayed that it would be born healthy. Oh, my God, she thought, what would she do if the baby were born abnormal—deformed?

"Miss?"

"What?" Chandal turned toward the desk.

"What's her name?" asked the nurse.

"Oh, Briar. Helen Briar."

"Third floor—D. Through the doors and down the hall."

"Thank you."

Chandal had to sign the register once she crossed over into the new wing. The nurse informed her that her mother had been placed in an oxygen tent— nothing serious, merely precautionary.

The third floor was a beehive of activity. People rushed from one room to another—a well-known news commentator was about to be operated on. What terrible loneliness he must feel, thought Chandal as she entered her mother's room.

It was difficult for her mother to speak through the plastic covering, and the noisy air pump made matters worse. This was the first time Chandal had ever seen her mother seriously ill. It frightened her.

156

"Is it still cold out?" her mother murmured.

"Yes."

"Are they giving you good heat in the new apartment?"

"Not really."

"It's going to be a gloomy winter, then."

"Yes."

Chandal's mother went on to explain that she'd had chest and stomach X rays; that they'd had her drink six pints of chalk. She stopped talking after that, but suddenly Chandal could feel her starting to panic.

"Everything's going to be all right, Mom," Chandal assured her.

"I know."

"I'll be by tomorrow. Is there anything you need?"

She shook her head. "If you can't make it tomorrow, then the next day, okay?"

"Seven o'clock tomorrow, without fail."

Reassured, her mother smiled.

Chandal sat for the next half hour and watched her mother sleep. She studied the white face, strangely young and vulnerable in sickness. What are grownups but children in old bodies? Oh, God, fragile bodies. Bodies that quit. Lungs that quit breathing, hearts that stopped beating. Let it be all right, she prayed, wishing she could reach through the plastic tent and take her mother's hand. Let everything be like it used to be.

By the time she left the room, she was exhausted by her own fear. She stopped at the desk and listened to her own voice, weak, drained of emotion, asking the nurse, how was her mother, really? The bright, energetic nurse had a message from the doctor. Chandal was to leave her phone number; he would contact her in the morning. Chandal scribbled her work number on the pad.

"That'll be just fine," said the nurse, brimming over with good spirits, and Chandal reflected that she was probably a very good woman. She would bring life into a death room, deceiving the patient into hope.

Into believing that somehow this nurse would keep the patient alive another day. And then the moment of truth would come and the patient's eyes would widen in surprise when he heard the sound of his own death rattle.

Her hands clenched in her pockets, Chandal left the hospital.

When she arrived home, Justin was in the basement—the red light over the cellar door told her so. The note she had left for Justin earlier had been torn to shreds and left on the kitchen table. It was a sign of things to come.

Unaware that Justin had already eaten, she began to prepare dinner. It was then that she realized that she'd forgotten to pick up the ring. No matter. She'd pick it up in the morning before work.

By the time Justin came up from the basement, the dinner was almost ready. Justin looked around the kitchen, laughed, and walked into the living room without speaking to Chandal. She was too tired to argue with him. She began to eat dinner alone.

While Chandal washed the dishes in the kitchen, the front doorbell rang. It was Sissy. Justin called out caustically to Chandal that her girl friend had arrived. Wearily, Chandal said that she'd be right out and told Justin to make her comfortable.

Without saying a word, Justin conducted Sissy into the living room. He glanced disapprovingly at the overnight bag she held in her hand.

"Nice space," she said, putting down her bag.

"Thanks." Justin shrugged. "Can I make you a drink?"

"Yes, please. Scotch and soda would be nice." She removed her coat as Justin mixed the drinks. He watched her sit, cross her legs, light a cigarette.

"You just come from dinner?" he asked, dropping ice cubes into the glasses.

"Yes—that's why I'm a little late. We had to sit through a one man monologue."

"When did you manage to eat?"

"During the yawns."

"Of course. Justin smiled briefly and handed Sissy her drink. "Well, here's to success."

"Thanks."

They both drank.

"God, I'm exhausted," she said, kicking off her high heels.

"Why are you here?" His voice broke off, hanging in the still air.

Sissy grimaced, curled her lower lip. "Hasn't Chandal told you?"

"No," he said coldly.

"I thought she'd tell you."

"Tell me what?"

"Perhaps you should ask her that." She sipped her drink.

"Are these cryptic comments meant to annoy? Or are you, after all these years, speechless?"

"Not at all." She twisted uncomfortably in her chair.

"Which? Speechless, or trying to annoy?" He smiled.

"My, my, multiple choice. There was a time when a statement from you went without question."

"Well?"

Sissy smiled. "Neither. I just feel there is something dreadfully dull about the telling and retelling. Chandal had something to say—let her say it to you directly."

"Why not you?"

"It's none of my business."

"Three cheers for bullshit!"

"It's nice to see you again, Justin. The fact that I can't stand you really has nothing to do with this." She held up her glass. "Mind if I have another?"

"Help yourself."

She slipped her heels back onto her feet and crossed to the cocktail cart. "By the way, I'm inviting you and Chandal up to my cabin in Pennsylvania for the weekend. Any weekend. Just for the record, you've been invited."

"I can't think of a better way to ruin a weekend."

Sissy sloshed her drink around, sending the ice cubes banging into the sides of the glass. "Why is it whenever you and I are together in the same room, there seems to be a hectic flush to the atmosphere?"

"I hadn't noticed."

"It dazzles—intrudes. It's not very comfortable, especially for Chandal."

"Is that your professional opinion?"

"I'm not going to fight with you, Justin."

"Why not? We'll square off, take five paces—turn, and pelt each other with ice cubes."

"Why act so frightened all the time?"

"Frightened. Of what?"

"Conscience, perhaps."

"Ah, yes. Well, let us not speak of conscience. It's a very unhealthy subject."

"For some, yes; others, no." Sissy was smiling wryly, staring, puffing at her cigarette absently, when Chandal entered the room.

Justin raised his glass to Chandal. "Well, here's looking at you, babe." He downed his drink in one gulp and left the room to return to the basement to work on his portrait of Magdalen.

"What was that all about?" Chandal asked.

"Beats me."

Chandal sighed. "I am glad you're here. Come on, I'll get you settled in."

"Sorry I'm late," Sissy said, following Chandal to the spare room.

"It's all right," Chandal said, trying to be cordial. "I'm sorry I haven't had time to clean the room." There were still unpacked boxes in the spare room and debris piled everywhere. She explained that Justin was a collector of junk and that already the room was jammed full of his latest findings: a New York street sign, an old chair, two lamps, a desk, and three large picture frames, minus the canvas. However, the room was warm and the bed was comfortable.

Sissy reacted immediately. Without explanation, she turned and left the room. "I'm sorry, Chandal, —I can't sleep in there."

"Sissy, I'm sorry about the mess—"

"It's not the mess! I just can't sleep there, that's all."

Chandal could see that Sissy was shaken. Had she seen something in the room? Sissy insisted that she hadn't—she merely preferred to sleep on the couch. She left no room for discussion.

They prepared the sleeping couch and then sat silently together in front of the television, pretending absorption.

"How's work going?" Chandal asked during a commercial.

Sissy's eyes were far off, distracted.

"Sissy?"

"Oh, I'm sorry." Sissy pushed her hand through her hair. "Just a little headache or something. What were you . . ."

"I was wondering how your job's going. Are you going to get another promotion, do you think?" Chandal watched her face somewhat enviously. Why hadn't she gone into business? No, she'd wanted to be one girl in a million who makes it in show business. Instead, here she was, one of the 900,000-plus who hadn't.

She had a sudden image of herself as Abigail in *The Crucible*. She'd felt so physical as Abigail, electric and vital. It hurt like hell to think about herself in that part—the rave reviews, everyone saying, "Chandal, you're going to make it," her own heart synched into the chant—*I'm going to make it, make it, make it*—and then, of course, she hadn't. She'd only worked one time after that, just after having met Justin. Was it his fault, or was it hers? Was she using him to cop out? Was she really as good as everyone said she was in *The Crucible*? Did she used to have it and did she lose it? Did she ever have it?

The old cold sweat popped out across her forehead and she couldn't block out the memory of that night, the first dress rehearsal night of *Traps*. The play that they said was going all the way. Justin out in the audience and Chandal standing backstage waiting to make her entrance. The part that could do it for her, could make her a star. Her heart was moving in heavy, painful lunges and her breath was uneven, com-

161

ing in great gasps. She stood there in her long emerald-green dress, cut low in the front, looking like a knockout, and the only thing she could think about was how scared she was. The fear was bigger than her, exploding in her stomach, her bright green bodice jerking in and out with it, the fear shooting through her bloodstream. Her mouth was dry and her tongue felt coated.

The stage manager said softly, smiling, "Stand by, please." And she turned wildly, staring, wondering at how calm they were. The light man's hand so steady on the dimmer, the tech crew playing poker in the hall. *I can't go out there*, she thought, with dead frightening certainty. *I can't take a step. I'll fall.*

"Are you ready?" whispered the stage manager, winking.

She could not respond, could not say a word as a pain ripped through her chest, sending her against the back wall.

Arms grabbed her and shook her. "That's your cue. For God's sake, Chandal!"

"I can't!" she managed to gasp, feeling that her lungs were flat, completely out of air. Sweat rolled down her face.

"They're out there ad-libbing!" the stage manager said furiously, contempt in his voice.

Her knees were water. She slid wearily down the wall and buried her face in her hands.

"The producer's out there!"

She shook her head. Never even looked up to see him calling for the curtain to be rung down. She could feel the eyes staring at her, but she kept her face covered. Only when Justin came did she cry. They stood there holding each other, her arms straining him against her, her hot tears wetting his shirt, blackening it with her mascara. He was the only thing in her world that hadn't toppled over, ceased to be.

She'd lost the job, naturally, and the dream after that was only make-believe. She never really believed in it again. Perhaps that's why no one else had, either. Too tall, they'd said. Too thin. Excuses. She knew what they were seeing—the fear. An actress who couldn't really cut it.

Lucky Sissy, she thought now. Sissy had never been afraid of anything in her life. Suddenly it was vitally important to know if Sissy was going to get that promotion. Because if she did, would they be in completely different worlds? Was she going to lose Sissy, too?

"Sissy?"

"What?" Sissy said blankly.

"I asked if you're going to be promoted again."

Sissy said yes, she was going to be promoted. And within two years, she'd be a vice-president. The executive V.P. had practically told her so. Her voice was mechanical, flat—as if she was not paying much attention to what she was saying.

At eleven P.M., both girls showered and went to bed.

Sometime later, Chandal awoke to find that Justin wasn't in bed. What time was it? Three-thirty in the morning! She slipped on her robe and checked to see if Sissy was all right. Sissy was gone. She had left a note saying that she was sorry, but that she would explain when she next saw Chandal.

Chandal crossed to the kitchen and turned on the light. Mintz looked up from her box and yawned. The cellar door was closed, but the red light wasn't on. Where was Justin?

She opened the cellar door and turned on the light switch, but the cellar remained dark. The bulb must be out, she thought. She was about to close the door when she heard a very low, very soft moaning coming from the cellar. Her first thought was that Justin had hurt himself in the dark.

"Justin? Is that you? Are you all right?" She called out anxiously.

The moaning continued. Chandal reached for the flashlight and made her way down the cellar stairs. Abruptly she stopped. Someone had completely torn apart the basement. Several of the mannequins had

163

been smashed to pieces, developing trays were over-turned, and photographs were scattered everywhere. Someone had taken the large portrait of Magdalen and slashed it with a knife. "Justin, where are you?"

The moaning was coming from the wall, the same spot where she had burned her hand. She moved closer, stepping over the developing trays. She could feel the heat from the wall as she drew nearer.

Suddenly the small door in the corner flew open!

Chandal spun around as the door slammed off the wall. The moaning stopped. There was no one there. Cautiously, she crossed the room and entered the narrow passage. No sooner was she inside than the door slammed shut, locking her in the stairwell. She tried to force it open, but it was stuck. From above she heard a whirling sound. Flashing her light to the top of the stairs, she could see a black mass ready to descend on her. She frantically pushed on the door. The black mass moved in a circular motion toward her. It made a high-pitched whistling sound that was deafening. She pushed on the door—it flew open.

Chandal was still sitting in the living room shaking when the sun came up. She had waited all night for Justin to come home. He never had.

❧ 14 ❧

THE FRAGRANCE OF LILACS HUNG HEAVY IN THE dust-filled attic air. The morning light clustered below the horizon, then fractured the rooftops with its brilliance.

Adjusting her lace shawl, the old woman moved away from the window and sat in her rocker. She stared at a heap of odds and ends and remembered eventful dates. There was so much recorded in her memory.

Eyes vacant—thoughtful, she watched herself wander arm in arm with a young man through the lush green park. Sunday, early summer—people were rowing on the lake. Stopping at a small sidewalk café, she held his hand under the table and sipped white wine from a crystal goblet, sitting beneath a canopy of pastels. Children played among the tables and their laughter was everywhere. Gentlemen passed by and tipped their hats, envying the young man—she was well known and popular. Then she heard her sister's voice say, "Ah, yes—the attic. The room for old things. Everything that has outlived its usefulness will be stored there."

On a bleak and dreary day in 1928, Marjorie Bennett Krispin, age thirty-nine, was lowered into the frozen ground next to her husband, Alexander. Magdalen and Elizabeth, young and frail, stood motionless, each embracing her private grief in silence. To Magdalen's right stood Dr. Steven Rock, handsome and aloof. With a sudden move of companionship, he took Magdalen's arm and whispered into her ear. Elizabeth's eyes flickered, the tears blurring her view of the doctor's face. Nothing seemed to make sense now. She felt panic. Later, she realized it was because she knew she'd never be able to live with it— Magdalen's marriage to the doctor, his running the brownstone like his own, his flirtatious little gestures. Yes, he had made her life unbearable, and, yes—he'd have to be punished for it.

In opposite rooms, the two old women continued to reflect, and later, much later, a pair of old hands turned to page three in *The Book of Ahriman*.

1. Everything in this world has to be worked out in pain, even pain itself.
2. Everything vanishes.
3. Everything passes into the awaiting arms of Ahriman.
4. Life comes anew to thee who worships His power and awakens to keep an ancient rendezvous.
5. To live again, to plunge thy soul into His

hands, to venture forth, without fear, toward the perfection of Ahriman, is to live forever in His glory.

6. And then Ahriman spoke: Behold in me thy own glory, and I will not deny the existence of thy spirit.

7. Behold in my glory, and I shall be pleased.

8. Behold in my glory, and I shall be back for thee.

9. Behold in my glory, and I shall set thy spirit free. Together, we shall go abroad and triumph, and will not be put back.

The old woman shuddered with ecstasy. She had secretly stolen away from the far reaches of her sister, and had begun to worship the demon privately. To love it, caress it, as a mother caresses a newborn child.

She would make love to it, convince the demon that she should be the chosen one, not her sister. Her eyes dropped back to the fragile yellowed page, where words were sweet, encouraging.

She would study the scripture, comprehend its meaning, its true meaning, and when the time was right, apply her knowledge to her best advantage. Yes, her advantage, not her sister's.

Chandal had a difficult time remembering what day it was. She looked blankly at the calendar hanging on the kitchen wall. Wednesday, the twenty-fourth of January. Wednesday? Why did she think it was the weekend? Suddenly she felt that something had been added, as though there was more to her than her usual self. Was it the baby? She reached for her stomach. No, she wasn't any bigger, yet some new dimension had been added.

It wasn't until she caught sight of the cellar door that she remembered. Trapped. The stairwell had been her jailer—deliberate, malevolent. And the horrid sound. And the havoc. Let him tell her she'd imagined *that!*

Drained and numb, Chandal moved into the

darkened bedroom to get dressed for work. She stopped. Jesus. Someone was lying in her bed. She switched on the light. Justin. "What's happening?" she muttered. She knew he hadn't come home last night. Or had he? When she was down in the cellar, maybe? But then why—? Chandal did not move, did not flicker an eyelash as she stared at Justin's back. Laugh, she thought, cry—do something, for Christ's sake! Get up, Justin—tell me what's happening— please. Frenzied, Chandal attempted to reach out and wake him and stopped. She took a breath and forced herself to calm down.

At a little past nine, Chandal was sitting moodily behind her desk pretending to be engrossed in her work. She was disturbed, puzzled—and found herself staring expressionlessly at the blotter.

The white light on her telephone flashed on—her extension. She picked up the receiver. Dr. Margolin, her mother's doctor. There was a lump in her throat when he introduced himself. Nerves. Strange. She hadn't known just how worried about her mother she really was.

"I hope it's good news," she ventured into the phone and she could hear his hesitation.

Actually, he said in his carefully concerned-but-not-involved voice, it wasn't good news or bad news. The truth was, he didn't know. Didn't know? What kind of illness could it be that he wouldn't *know?* Chandal wondered.

"Don't worry, Mrs. Knight." Uncomfortable. Something else—some kind of phobia about bodily contact. Her mother couldn't tolerate being touched.

"How do you mean?" asked Chandal.

"Well, she insists on placing the stethoscope herself during my examination. I would say that at present this phobia borders on the delusional, inasmuch as your mother feels that touching may result in death."

"But—that doesn't even sound like my mother!"

"Tell me, have you ever noticed other types of neurotic behavior prior to her illness?"

167

"No—none. Perhaps a touch of hypochondria. Why?"

"Well . . ." he hesitated. "I don't believe I have to tell you that repressed emotions can be extraordinarily strong. I thought perhaps—"

"Perhaps what?"

"It appears to me that your mother is deeply disturbed, emotionally. It doesn't appear to be a recent emotional instability. Her state is too advanced. There should have been evidence of this prior to her becoming ill."

"What kind of evidence?"

"I'll be honest with you. Has she ever appeared suicidal?"

Chandal gasped and couldn't speak for a moment.

"Mrs. Knight?"

"Yes, I'm—here."

"I know that's a tough question to answer, but I think it's important that I know."

Chandal shook her head. "No. Not that I know of."

"Are you sure?"

"Of course I'm sure. My mother has always been the stable one in our lives."

"I see here that your father died some years ago."

"Yes."

"Did that have any unusual effect on her?"

Chandal gripped the phone tightly. "Unusual. What does that mean? She cried, she took it badly, yes, but not in the way you mean." Her hands were starting to sweat. She changed the phone to her other ear.

"I see. Well, perhaps her anxiety is purely a hysterical symptom. She may be frightened at suddenly being confined. This is her first serious illness, isn't it?"

"Yes."

"Well, there you are, then," he said in a cheerful voice. He concluded the conversation by stressing the need for patience and understanding in what appeared to him to be an unusual case.

Chandal paced the office. Confused. Nervous. She finally managed to type and place two notices on the bulletin board. She had just tacked the second notice

168

into place when the telephone rang again. It was Sissy. "Are you mad?"

"If you mean crazy, maybe. If you mean angry—no."

"I couldn't help it," said Sissy. "I just felt uncomfortable there."

"Sissy, be honest with me. When you went into the spare room last night—did you see anything?" Chandal tried to choose her words carefully. "I mean, anything unusual?"

"Not that I can remember. Why?"

"Then why did you refuse to sleep there?"

"Well, if you must know," she said promptly, "the room was too small. I suffer from claustrophobia."

"So, when you said you were uncomfortable there, that's what you meant?"

"That and other things." Evasive!

"What other things?" asked Chandal bluntly.

"To tell you the truth, Justin made me feel unwelcome. And then I thought, when he comes up from the basement and sees me lying on the couch, what then? He'd make some smart-ass remark—we'd argue—who needs it? So, I decided to leave."

"I see," said Chandal disbelievingly.

"Lunch on Friday?"

"Right."

"Got to fly—bye-bye."

"Yeah."

Two of the museum's more established employees stood at the water cooler conversing. Chandal could sense that they were discussing her. Secretaries had been discouraged from accepting private phone calls during business hours. In less than forty-five minutes, she had received two.

Chandal spent the next hour poring over rare books, the latest to be added to the museum's small but impressive library. There were books of poetry, math texts, horticulture manuals, and books on ancient Greek history. Even in those days, Chandal thought, everybody was an author.

When she was about to enter the last of them into

the log, her phone rang again—it was Justin. He sounded excited and happy.

"Come home for lunch. I've made a shrimp casserole."

"Justin, I can't."

"Of course you can. I want to see you!" he chortled.

"But Justin . . ."

Across the room, Sheila cast an uneasy glance at the executive manager's open door. Chandal caught the look, hastily whispered she'd be home for lunch, and dropped the receiver back on the hook. It was only then that she remembered the chaos in the basement. He hadn't seen it yet, or he'd never have been in such good spirits. Come to think of it, what was he doing home? Wasn't he casting today? She frowned. A beep from her telephone intercom pulled her back to her surroundings. It was the executive manager. He wanted to speak with her in his private office directly after lunch. The message was loud and clear —she hadn't long to go at this particular job. The manager's door slammed shut; further emphasis.

"Does he want to see you?" Sheila indicated the executive manager's office with the tip of her pencil.

"Yes," Chandal said in a thin voice.

"When?"

"After lunch."

"And the condemned girl ate a hearty meal."

"I know."

"Chandal, I've been thinking about—you know, your problem. I was wrong. Me of all people, I should have believed you." Sheila drew a long breath, bent closer. "You should get help."

Chandal drew away.

"No, let me finish. I don't mean a psychiatrist— nothing like that. I mean from someone who deals in these things."

"What things?" asked Chandal softly.

Sheila didn't answer. Her eyes moved in little jerks, as if she were expecting someone to be listening. She shoved a folded piece of paper into Chandal's hand.

"I wrote down a woman's name, Chandal. She's very good. If there's anything going on, she'll know."

"How?"

"She'll know, that's all. I wrote down her phone number. Call her."

"I'll think about it," Chandal said, slipping the paper into her purse.

"Good. And when I get back, you should have something to tell me."

"Back? Where are you going?" asked Chandal.

"The bosses are giving me my vacation early. I told you."

"I don't remember."

"Out of the blue, they switched it. Somebody probably had a hitch in their plans. I don't care. I need to get away. I've decided to take a run up to Vermont. Do some skiing. No paperwork, no office managers, nothing but pure white snow as far as the eye can see." The smile fell from her lips. "See this woman, Chandal. You'll find out what you need to know."

"Do you really think she can help?"

"Sometimes yes, sometimes no. I think it's worth a try. You let me know as soon as I get back. If not, I know some other people who can help you."

Chandal sighed.

"Try not to worry." A faint smile came to Sheila's lips. "I'm going to have a wonderful week of skiing and you—you probably just need a marriage counselor."

Chandal looked deep into Sheila's eyes. She hesitated. "Sheila, just in case she can't help me . . . could you . . . could you give me the other phone number? Just in case."

Sheila shook her head. "Not yet. Not until you've seen the woman. These people won't talk to you unless . . ." She gripped Chandal's hand. "It'll be okay. Everything will be okay."

Chandal watched Sheila hurry off to lunch, a distracted frown playing over her face. She certainly didn't look as if she thought everything was going to be okay. She looked worried as hell. Chandal picked up her coat and made her way slowly toward the exit. Maybe Sheila was crazy with that "I'm a believer" nonsense. Maybe both of them were.

Chandal shrugged it off. She wasn't in the mood to worry about it. Like Sheila said, it was all going to be okay. It had to be.

In the meantime, she felt happy to be going home to spend time with Justin. It seemed like ages since they'd sat down together over lunch and talked.

A sudden feeling of joy made her walk differently. Her feet moved more rapidly; her steps were surer. Everything about her felt fine. More than fine.

When she got home, Justin was at the door to greet her. He immediately handed her a large bouquet of pink and white carnations and kissed her. Chandal was intrigued by his performance and hardly knew what to say. "Gee, I like this!"

"You deserve it, honey. Come on—lunch is on the table." He took her by the hand and led her into the kitchen. The room was immaculate. Everything had been scrubbed and cleaned. Dirty dishes were now washed and put away. The floor had been waxed. For the first time, Chandal noticed how cheery and pleasant her kitchen really was! "My Lord—what's going on?" she gasped.

"I finally decided to get our new home in order. Do you like it?"

"It's beautiful."

And it was. Having rearranged the table by the window, Justin had managed to make the room appear much larger and easier to live in. He had mounted a cabinet over the sink, divided the area between the stove and refrigerator, and hung several plants from the window. It looked perfect.

Justin offered her a chair, after which he sat down and they began to eat. They had shrimp casserole, sliced cheese, and white wine for lunch. Chandal attacked her meal with relish and even ate several slices of French bread before she gulped down dessert.

When they were finished, they remained seated at the table—Chandal started to talk. She mentioned her mother's condition first. Justin was disappointed that she hadn't told him before. She apologized, saying that she'd only found out today how serious it was. The conversation shifted to other things, including last night.

"Justin, have you been down in the basement to-day?" she asked cautiously.

"Yes, just for a little while."

"And you're not mad—or surprised?"

"At what?"

"At what? The way it was torn apart like that. I wonder who could have done such a thing?"

Justin smiled. "What are you talking about? There's nothing wrong with the cellar."

"Justin, last night—I saw it." Was he joking?

"Come on. Let's see what you're talking about."

Justin casually opened the cellar door and flicked on the light. It worked. Together, they entered the basement. It was more perfectly arranged than the kitchen. Nothing was damaged and the mannequins stood upright and still. The developing trays were in proper order and the floor was free of photo paper. Magdalen's portrait had been replaced by a large, snow-capped picture of Central Park.

"Justin—I saw it! This entire room was a mess."

"Well, if it was, the good fairy must have cleaned it up!"

Chandal moved to the small door. "This door—someone pushed it open. When I went to see who it was, the door closed. I was trapped inside the stair-well."

"Honey, look at it. The hinges are all rusty. That door hasn't been opened in years. Here, I'll show you." Justin forced the bolt open and pulled on the door. "You see? It doesn't open."

"Here, let me try." No matter how hard she tugged, it refused to open. Frantically, she looked around. "That wall—Justin, there is something behind that wall over there." She passed through the row of manne-quins and indicated the spot where she had burned her fingers.

173

In order to humor her, Justin examined the wall. Then he tapped at the spot she indicated with a hammer. The sound was the same the length of the wall. "Honey, this is a solid wall. There can't be anything behind it." His gaze was candid.

Chandal was startled and afraid. Finally, she said in a deeper voice than usual, "You're lying to me, Justin."

"I'm what?"

"You heard me. You're not telling me the truth." She grew pale—her breathing became faster and sharper. "Justin"—she swallowed hard—"why are you doing this to me?"

Justin did not reply. Instead, he left Chandal standing alone in the basement. Overhead, she could hear his footsteps as they made their way to the hall closet. Next she heard the front door slam shut.

"Justin!" she screamed, running up the stairs. She wanted to apologize for acting so silly. It was too late. By the time she reached the front door and opened it, Justin had already vanished.

She turned and closed the door. She could feel Magdalen's presence—she was near. The living room. But when she opened the door, the room was empty. Mintz scurried across the floor and jumped onto the back of the couch. It was then that Chandal saw it lying there, Magdalen's lace shawl. Justin had been with the woman again today.

Chandal backed away from the room and moved into the bedroom. Quickly she opened the bottom drawer of her dresser. The picture of the young man was gone. Chandal was sure that Justin had removed it. He was no longer to be trusted.

At the office, she felt indifferent to her surroundings. Her meeting with the thin-haired and black mustached executive manager was direct and to the point. Fascinated, she stared at bald spots on his head, barely hearing his voice.

"I hate to say this, Mrs. Knight. It's not pleasant —but we're not completely satisfied. In fact," he concluded apologetically, "I may say we are rather *dis*-satisfied." His lips curved in the slight smile that some people give when they have just delivered bad news.

"I'm pregnant," she said in soft revenge and color forced its way into his face. Delighted, he said. He was simply delighted. She kept smiling, disliking him more and more. He said that changed everything. He understood. She smiled.

Back at her desk, Chandal drew a doodle on her ink pad. It resembled a goat's head. She made heavy black marks with her magic marker until it was covered over. She understood nothing. God help me, she thought. No, she'd help herself.

Later that evening, the bus Chandal had taken wound its way through a narrow residential street and then made a left hand turn onto Hadly Avenue in the Bronx. Both sides of the wide avenue were lined with smallish brick buildings from another age. The street lights glowed brightly against the surrounding darkness.

Chandal turned, looked through the back window of the bus, making sure she hadn't missed her stop. The woman on the phone had said One Hundred Twelfth Street and Hadly. There were still twenty blocks to go.

Upset, almost desperate, Chandal had called the woman who dealt in psychic phenomena. At first the woman admitted to knowing no one by the name of Sheila Marsh.

"But you must—she gave me your number."

The woman still refused to acknowledge that Chandal had the right number until money was mentioned. Then, grudgingly, the woman agreed to see her.

The corner of One Hundred Twelfth and Hadly was a chaotic sea of rubble. People in all states of dress and disfigurement were milling about between the doorways and between the parked cars.

Chandal had been instructed to go into the small restaurant on the corner where she was to call the woman letting her know that she'd arrived. Then and only then would she be given the woman's address.

What Chandal found when she entered the restaurant was one of the most commodious pubs in existence. Social activities centered around the pool table and the counter. The mutters, shrieks, and music made it difficult to hear over the telephone.

"What?" asked Chandal, covering one ear with her hand.

"You'ro late!" snapped the woman. "It's eight o'clock."

"I know, I'm sorry, but—"

"What?"

"I said I'm sorry!" Chandal was almost screaming. "The bus took forever!"

The woman sullenly gave Chandal the address. She advised her not to bring anyone with her and to have the fifty dollars in cash for the visit.

"Yes—all right. Thank you." Chandal hung up and left the restaurant without looking around. She walked directly to the woman's apartment building, a tiny tenement without charm. She climbed the stairs and knocked on the door.

"I'll be right there," the woman said as Chandal glanced at the broken letter "D" that hung crookedly on the battered door. The door opened and Chandal was greeted by a large pair of almond eyes belonging to a small Italian woman with a spine as rounded as the letter "D."

"Yes?" she asked coldly.

"I'm Chandal Knight—I just called."

"Come in," she ordered, leaving Chandal standing in the doorway alone. Trying to subdue her nervousness, Chandal entered the room and closed the door.

"Sit down," the woman said, herself already seated, with dangling arms and limp outstretched legs, in a dirty armchair. Her head was covered with shocking silver hair which gave her the appearance of being some eternal mother of a great order.

Chandal sat in the center of the room, her hands resting on top of a wooden table.

The woman eyed her suspiciously. "What do you want?"

Hesitantly, Chandal described each incident, starting with the bell, and concluded with the chaos in the basement last evening. The woman listened attentively until she was finished.

"You're pregnant, are you not?" she asked suddenly.

"Why, yes. How did you know?"

"It doesn't matter. I can't help you." She rose to her feet.

"But—"

"*No!* You shouldn't have come here—not carrying a child." The woman appeared frightened. She went to the small stool near the window, sat down, and closed her eyes. There was a momentary silence. Then she began to mutter to herself, something unintelligible. Something like a prayer. When she finished, she opened her eyes and said, "Now go!"

"You can't just send me away—"

"Now go!" repeated the woman, her voice snapping like a whip.

"You can't act like this and then not tell me—" Tears gathered in Chandal's eyes.

The woman looked at her for a long time. "I tell you this," she said finally. "You must go somewhere far away."

"But why?" asked Chandal.

"That I choose not to know. But your danger is great. Trust no one. Best . . ." She chewed her lip and thought. "Yes. Best to go far away—tell no one where." She took up her torn coat from the sofa. "I'm going to take a walk now. When I return—you are not to be here." She left the apartment, ignoring the money in Chandal's outstretched hand.

All the way home, Chandal kept her hand in her coat pocket, fingers curled around the tightly rolled bills. That the seer had not taken the money had made her words more ominous, more real.

It had been snowing for over an hour by the time

177

Chandal reached the brownstone. She wished to God that she hadn't talked to the woman. She was more confused now—it was worse than ever. And she felt guilty for not having gone to visit her mother in the hospital. Goddamn it—the ring. She hadn't picked it up yet.

She sat in the living room for a while and barely stirred. She knew where she was, but her feeling of emptiness cut her off from everything around her. She had checked to see if Justin was home. He wasn't. The red light over the door wasn't on. Mintz placed her little face on her lap and began to purr. It was the only thing that kept Chandal from crying.

Upstairs in the attic, the young man's face glowed, the feeling of love spread through him. He felt warm and comfortable. It was easy to let go, to forget the other life and to exist only in this moment, where the smell of incense was sweet. Later, he must reexamine his volumes of medicine, his logs of experiments. It had been so long now. But there would be time. As for now, it was so delicious to lie before this woman, his head resting in her young lap, and to feel her hands, white as magnolia blooms, stroke through his thick black hair, loving him, loving him.

Below, Chandal fell asleep on the couch with Mintz cuddled in her arms. In her dream, faceless worshippers knelt before the altar. *Ahriman,* said a voice. Another voice, familiar to her memory in some way, explained that when first they had summoned Ahriman, god of darkness, he had appeared as a thin shadow. Now, when the Woden tin whistle sounded, he sprang before them in flesh and savagery.

A whistle lifted to old lips. Chandal opened her mouth to scream, but could not. In a flash of fire, the goat appeared, advanced toward her smiling. Her body was naked and trembling. *Ah!* said a voice. The goat's eyes burned black, passionate. She could feel his hot breath. Closer. Her heart began to beat faster. Candles were lit, wax dripped, reds and yellow

—smells scorched her nostrils. A circle of shadowy figures moved around her. Pointed thin fingers whispered—*Ahriman. Ahriman. Ahriman,* Chandal whispered and turned over on her side. Silently, Mintz jumped down from the couch and gently padded into the kitchen.

PART TWO

"Because I have communed with those who know . . ."

❧ 15 ❧

CHANDAL AWOKE TO FIND JUSTIN STANDING OVER her. For a moment, she didn't know where she was. Her whole body ached and she felt as if she was burning with a fever.

"Good morning, honey."

"Morning? What time is it?" Her body shot forward until it rested awkwardly on her elbows. Justin continued to observe her in an amused sort of way.

"It's seven-thirty."

Chandal glanced at the alarm clock on the night table. Night table? She looked up at him questioningly. "How did I get in here to the bedroom?"

"When I came up from the cellar last night, I found you sleeping on the couch. I spent the next half-hour trying to wake you up. When that didn't work, I carried you into the bedroom. You mumbled something, got undressed, and crawled into bed. Don't you remember?"

"You were home last night?"

He smiled. "Of course—where else would I be?" He went into the bathroom and turned on the light. He began to shave.

Chandal yanked herself to a seated position. "But I checked—the red light wasn't on."

"I know," he said, popping his head out of the door. "The bulb burned out. I just replaced it." He wiped the lather from the corners of his mouth. After a slight pause, he continued. "Listen, honey, I'm sorry for storming out of the house like that yesterday, but I did go to a lot of trouble. I wanted you to be pleased. Instead, all I heard was some nonsense about the basement."

182

"It wasn't nonsense, Justin! The place was a mess," she pleaded. She reached for her robe and felt the stiffness in her body.

"Maybe you only wished it that way."

"I don't understand what you mean?"

"Look, I know I've been spending too much time down there. You get lonely, so—you get jealous."

Chandal looked into his eyes. She could see that he believed what he was saying. She hesitated, then said, "Justin, the night before last, there was a picture, a large picture of Magdalen, and it was hanging over the developing trays."

"I know. So?" He disappeared into the bathroom.

"Yesterday, it was gone." She tied her robe and crossed to the bathroom door.

"Right. I didn't like it—so I tore it up."

Chandal watched as the razor glided smoothly over Justin's face. When they had been first married, she had watched him shave almost every day. It had been one of her favorite times with him. "When did you take the picture of her?" she asked, dropping down on the edge of the tub.

"A couple of days ago. Magdalen saw me taking pictures in the yard one day. She said she always wanted to have her picture taken. So I took it. I figured she'd been so nice to us that I'd do her the favor." He rubbed his hand under his chin and considered his image. "You know, I think I'll grow a mustache!"

Justin was right. The two women had been very understanding and generous with their offer. She couldn't even remember thanking them.

The phone rang in the living room, giving Chandal a start.

"Who the hell could that be at this hour?" Justin had a slight edge to his voice.

"I'll get it," she said.

Justin threw the towel on the edge of the tub and slapped his face with after-shave lotion. After a moment, Chandal returned to the bedroom.

"It's for you."

"Who is it?"

"He wouldn't say."

"Damn!" Justin brushed past Chandal and entered the living room. "Hello!"

"Is this that great and famous director—Justin Knight?" The voice carried with it a certain mocking tone.

"Who is this?"

"I'll give you one guess—shmuck! It's Richards. You know—Billie Richards' husband."

"Look, I don't want you calling me."

Chandal stood at the living room door and, in a low voice, asked him who it was. Justin covered the mouthpiece and indicated that she should be quiet.

"Why, did I wake you up? Tough! The important thing is you forgot to call my wife for that reading, shmuck! She feels real bad."

"We don't start call-backs until next week." Justin could feel the anger at the pit of his stomach. He sat down on the couch to calm himself.

"I want you to call her, anyway—now! Tell her you like her, you want to read her special. If you don't, someone might just tell that pretty little wife of yours to take her clothes off—and it won't be at no audition, either. Understand, shmuck?"

"Hey, goddamn it—"

Richards hung up.

"Son-of-a-bitch!" Justin slammed the phone down.

"Honey, what is it?" Chandal was frightened at how angry Justin was.

Without answering her, he grabbed for his jacket on the coat rack. "I'll kill that bastard!"

"Are you going to tell me what's happening?"

"Oh, nothing. Just some jerk. A real smart ass!" Justin pressed his fingertips into the sockets of his eyes, then ran them up to his forehead.

"Honey, are you all right?" She came close to him and laid her hand on his shoulder.

"Sure." He smiled. "Listen, what are your plans for the day?"

"I have to work, naturally. After that, I planned to

184

pick up my ring and then go to see my mother at the hospital."

"Tell you what, I'll be finished casting around five. I'll head over to the Sacred Cow—I'll meet you there. I really should go with you to the hospital, okay?"

Chandal agreed, after which Justin gave her a long kiss.

"Oh, by the way," she said, suddenly remembering, "did you call Bender?"

"I tried. Lucky stiff's in Florida. Be back on Friday." He kissed her again and left the house. She walked around the apartment after that trying to get her bearings. She shrugged—Bender must have changed his mind. Then she fed Mintz, had her coffee, and showered.

The hot water spurted down upon her and she relaxed into a delirium of non-motion. Enough. She scrubbed herself vigorously with Ivory soap, held up her arms to wash off the last spots of lather, and chafed herself down with a rough towel. She liked the play across her body as she drew the towel up, and for a moment she wondered if she was still in good shape.

She swung open the closet door, lined with a long mirror. She glanced at herself doubtfully. Her stomach was only beginning to protrude slightly. She had always wondered if she was pretty. Cute, maybe, but pretty was something else and better. She looked at herself sternly. "Listen, you—you're okay. Besides, pretty girls are usually a lot of silly idiots!"

She yawned slightly, heard the seer's voice stealing into her brain. *"Go far away—tell no one where."* She was probably referring to California, Chandal thought. But why tell no one?

She dressed in a light gray sweater and skirt and a red scarf, which she then exchanged for yellow—it was less conspicuous. There was something harsh and violent in the seer's voice which had frightened her last night. *"You shouldn't have come here—not carrying a child."* How did she know I was pregnant? Chandal thought.

185

She sat in the kitchen and ate two poached eggs and bacon, cut thick. She tried to be nonchalant about last night, not give it any more thought. Silly woman! Winning her own argument by this simple declaration, she smiled, put the dish in the sink, and was about to leave the house when she heard someone calling her from the top of the stairs. It was Elizabeth.

"Yes?" she asked, standing in the foyer.

"I hate to disturb you, but do you suppose that I might be able to borrow a cup of sugar?"

"Sure. I'll get it for you." Chandal crossed into the kitchen and got the sugar. When she turned around, she was surprised to see that the old woman was standing right behind her. "Oh, here you are."

"Thank you, dear." Elizabeth took the cup of sugar.

"Don't mention it." Chandal started for the door to put on her coat. Suddenly she thought: Why would Bender give us $6,000 and then—?"

The old woman stopped her. "Can I ask you a question? I mean, can we talk for a while?"

"I'm afraid I must—"

"My sister is trying to drive me crazy."

"What?" Chandal was taken aback by her frankness.

"She's like the devil reincarnated. Oh, she's always nice to me and we always have a good time together. But when I ask her for a little money, she laughs in my face. I told her that I needed money—that I wanted to go out and buy nice things. She wouldn't let me. I was so angry that I became violently ill right there in the den, so she locked me in the attic and wouldn't let me out. Things are changing so fast. Are you listening to me?"

"Yes." Chandal paused for a moment. "But why do you say she's like the devil?"

"Because she's so sure of herself. She has traveled all over the world and she knows about history. She has me figured out to a T. She sits there and tells me what I believe and what I've done. Things she couldn't possibly know. And when I got sick, her face turned a deep red and she was laughing and no one could

186

hear her except me. And the man, he's there, too—both of them. It's impossible to accept both of them, and I can't love one for the other. He and Father are so much alike, yet so different. Do you know what they do together? Magdalen and this man . . . they—"

"Please, I don't think you should be telling me all this."

"You don't understand, do you? I guess there are some things people just can't understand. I'll just have to wait, then."

Chandal watched her climb the stairs to the second floor. Before entering her own hallway, she turned to Chandal and said, "Please don't tell Magdalen that we've had a chat, all right?"

"All right."

"And then maybe we can talk again tomorrow. I won't disturb you if you have things to do, but if you have time, we could see a little more of each other. I'd like that. I . . . get lonely from time to time. I'm not very good at being alone. I get nervous."

"If I have the time. It would be nice."

"I mean you've been living here for—how long has it been now? It seems forever, doesn't it?"

"Yes."

"And we have never sat down to tea. I'd like that. I really would."

"Maybe over the weekend."

"Yes, the weekend." Pause. "If you don't mind my saying so, you should eat more, my dear. You're too thin. And exercise more. Then perhaps you would be able to act again. Why, some of the greatest actresses in the world overcame all kinds of physical problems. Sarah Bernhardt wasn't very pretty, not in the least. And look, they called her 'The Divine Sarah.' Did you know she died in her son's arms? Did you?"

"No."

"In Paris. And they put her body into a rosewood coffin that she had built for herself before she died." Elizabeth stood there for a moment as if to pay her last respects to an old friend. "Well, I'm keeping you, aren't I? The weekend, then?" She smiled.

Chandal nodded.

The old woman closed the door, leaving Chandal alone in the foyer. Simultaneously, Chandal's picture on the living room side table fell over. At first she thought it was Mintz, but the cat wasn't in the room. She placed the picture back upright, crossed into the hallway, stared at the second-floor landing for a moment, and then left the house for work.

Throughout the day, the snow rapidly disappeared due to the rain, but freezing temperatures persisted, making the streets dangerously icy. Due to hazardous weather conditions, Chandal was let go from work an hour early. She immediately seized the opportunity to collect her ring.

As soon as she entered the small shop, she felt that something was wrong. The man who had waited on her was not there. Only the goldsmith who sat in the rear of the store, jeweler's glass over one eye, examining a watch, was present. Chandal stood trembling from the cold and the rain, waiting patiently for him to acknowledge her.

"Yes?" he finally asked, removing the glass from his forehead.

"I . . . I dropped off a ring here on Tuesday—to be made smaller. I'd like to pick it up."

"Do you have the ticket?" he asked unpleasantly.

"Oh, the ticket—yes." Chandal fumbled around in her pocketbook for the ticket. "I don't seem to have it with me."

"I can't give it to you without the ticket."

Chandal dumped her entire pocketbook upside down on the counter and started frantically pushing articles aside. "Please, I need the ring today! It's important to me." Having gone over each item twice, she became tense, angry. "Look, I can describe the ring!"

The goldsmith let go of the watch he had been holding, grabbed a huge wooden case with both hands, and under his breath started to mutter to himself.

"What?" asked Chandal.

188

"Name, name—what's the name?" His eyebrows went up.

"Oh, Knight. Chandal Knight."

The man grew furious as he rummaged through the little brown envelopes. His pudgy face turned pale and he began to sweat. Then he hesitated. "Knight, Chandal?"

"Yes!"

"Address?"

"Three West Eighty-fifth Street."

He took the small brown envelope, opened it, and dropped the ring onto the soft blue velvet pad on the counter.

"Yes, yes—that's it," said Chandal, picking up the ring.

"Eight-fifty."

She paid the man, and as he put the money into the cash register, she asked, "The owner, is he here?"

"He's sick."

"Oh, I'm sorry to hear that. Is it anything serious?"

"Serious," he repeated. "Just like that, he collapsed. Next thing—he's in the hospital with tubes everywhere. Brain like a vegetable. It doesn't pay, I'll tell you that. You work and work, for what? To wind up like that?" The man sat himself back down behind the small workbench at the rear of the store, picked up the jeweler's glass, and went back to work.

"Well, thank you. You did a nice job."

"I didn't do it—he did."

"What?"

"The owner—he worked on the ring. Last piece he did before his stroke."

Chandal stared at the ring on her finger. The small detailed carvings on either side formed a strange triangular pattern and gave the ring an ancient appearance. The top part of the ring remained shiny and smooth. Odd, she thought, that Justin would pick out that particular ring.

"Did you forget something?" the goldsmith asked.

"Oh, no—thank you."

The freezing rain tore into Chandal's face, making

it impossible to go any farther. She stepped into a nearby doorway, hoping that the rain would cease, or that at least she would be able to hail a cab. Neither was the case, however, and she huddled in the doorway for a little more than an hour.

Justin peered from the window of the Sacred Cow, wondering what was keeping Chandal. He had called her office and had been informed that she had gone for the day. He ordered another drink and waited.

"You look tired," said the barmaid, pushing a double Scotch in front of him.

"I am." He took a sip.

"How's casting going?"

"Terrible."

"Why's that?" She cleaned the empty glasses off the bar.

"Because all the good actors are in California, that's why!" He shrugged. "Who can blame them? Look at it out there." He had been talking about going to California for the past three years. Twice he had accepted directing jobs in Texas and Chicago, thinking that he would go on from there. Each time, he'd found an excuse for not going. This time, it had been the brownstone.

"I see you're starting to grow a mustache." She put a fresh bowl of peanuts in front of him.

"Yeah. What do you think?"

"I can't tell yet, but I think it'll look okay."

He couldn't get Magdalen out of his mind. All day, he'd wanted to see her. Why? That's what he kept asking himself. Both parents were dead by the time he had reached his fifteenth birthday, perhaps that was it. But it was more than that. He did not think of her as being older.

He remembered their first meeting. Three years ago. It was autumn and the air was fresh and clean. The sun shone on her silver hair as she hesitated, one hand on the railing leading up the steps of the brownstone. As though she'd called, he walked up to her and smiled questioningly. "My package," she said gently.

190

"Would you be so kind—" He'd lifted the parcel to the top of the steps and she'd taken his hand in hers. "Thank you," she said. Even then, she was more than a nice old lady. He was unable to forget her.

Two months later, he'd married Chandal. Hurrying on with his life, always when he passed the brownstone, he watched. Sometimes he thought he could feel someone peering at him from a remote window, but he had not seen the woman until that eventful day. In few words, she'd asked him to bring his wife, to move to the old building. She knew her timing was perfect; he could tell. Joy had come to him, sending thoughts of California scattering. "Not see her again! I only live when I'm with her!"

"What?" asked the barmaid, looking around to see who Justin was talking to.

"Nothing." Justin paid the tab and stormed out of the Sacred Cow.

"Are you all right?" The smallish man stared at Chandal. By this time she was completely frozen and had squeezed her hand so tightly that the ring had cut into her finger. The palm of her hand was covered with blood.

"Oh, yes—I think so. I must have cut myself without realizing it."

The man insisted on helping her, but she refused his offers. Wrapping her hand in her handkerchief, she moved to the curb where she got into a taxi. When she arrived at the Sacred Cow, she told the driver to wait.

Inside, the barmaid informed her that Justin had just left. Chandal glanced at the clock—it was six-forty P.M. Why hadn't he waited? Surely he could see how bad the weather was. Goddamn him!

Chandal returned to the cab and headed for the hospital. The driver drove like a madman, skidding, grazing the safety islands in the middle of the streets. At each near miss, the driver turned around, raised his shoulders, and winked at Chandal.

Once inside the hospital, Chandal went into a

booth and telephoned home. After letting the phone ring for some time, she hung up.

When she came into her mother's room, her mother was sitting up in bed waiting for her. They had removed the oxygen tent and on the table a fresh bouquet of flowers was in evidence.

"Didn't I tell you exactly what would happen?" her mother cried. "I knew you wouldn't be here yesterday—I knew it!"

Chandal was surprised by her mother's outburst. She had never spoken to her like that before. Chandal barely had a chance to sit down before her mother went on in detail about the horrible treatment she was receiving from the nurses.

"I warned them that if they don't let me read, I'll go home. And they'll never see me again."

"Mom, don't be silly. You need care. How would you manage home alone?"

"Don't you worry, little girl!"

Seeing that her mother was determined to leave the hospital, Chandal suggested that she stay at the brownstone for a while. Her mother refused and deliberately made herself uncomfortable by kicking the covers partially from the bed. Chandal got up to straighten them.

"Don't touch me. Don't you dare touch me!"

"I wasn't going to touch you. You see me adjusting the covers, don't you?"

"Stop being cute."

"I don't know what you're talking about."

"The business of answering a question with another question."

"I didn't hear you ask a question!" Chandal was beginning to react hostilely.

Now her mother spoke in a low, childlike way. "Do you really want me to come and stay with you?" she whimpered.

"I said so, didn't I?"

"All right, I will."

It was nearly ten o'clock when Chandal stepped

from the cab in front of the brownstone. Relieved to be home, she paid the driver, carefully climbed the icy steps, and entered through the front door.

She spent the rest of the evening straightening up the spare room. From time to time, she crossed into the kitchen, where the red light over the basement door was always on now. She wanted to let Justin know that her mother was coming to live with them, but, Lord, how could she tell him? It was after twelve when she finally went to bed. Justin remained in the basement.

She lay in bed unable to sleep. She pushed the pillows around. Her breasts were starting to swell, the nipples red and aching.

Last night, no—Tuesday night; the days were becoming all mixed up in her mind. Even time. Sometimes a minute seemed like an hour, and then again sometimes hours slipped away, like tiny droplets of water running down a windowpane on a rainy night, mingling with countless other droplets, losing their significance. She gathered in a breath and imagined that there was a sickish sweet odor of lavender to the air.

She felt her heart racing. I'm isolated. Cut off from everybody. Perhaps that was really why she had insisted that her mother come live in the brownstone. Sick or otherwise, her mother always made her feel safe. Yes, her mother's presence would calm things, bring a certain sense of order into her life. Or would it? She rolled over, buried her head in the pillow.

The last thing Chandal heard before she slept was the seer's voice—*Go far away—tell no one where*. Chandal made up her mind. As soon as her mother was well, she would press Justin to move. If not California, Florida, or— She fell asleep, her thought incomplete. . . .

. . . The crying wasn't really crying at first, just a whimpering, a childlike sobbing that went unnoticed, until the thin shadow in the corner grew in intensity, in sharpness, and then Chandal saw Sheila standing in

193

the doorway of the office, Kleenex in hand, weeping. Her eyes glistened with tears.

She appeared to be covered with a white haze that rose from the snow-covered floor of the office. How strange. The office was completely covered in icicles, crystallized into a purplish-blue ice palace.

"What's the matter, Sheila?" asked Chandal.

Sheila looked away down the hallway, turned back to Chandal. "Help me."

"What?"

Sheila moved into the hallway out of sight. Through the thin walls of the office, Chandal could still hear her sobbing. Chandal stirred from her chair. She went to the hallway. She looked down the long corridor, watched as Sheila disappeared around the corner to her left. Her green woolen dress trailed off behind her, leaving a light flicker of color, a green dot before Chandal's eyes.

She followed, the hue of purple and blue light parting, as if she were walking through a thick fog, and then closing in behind her, shutting her off—allowing her no passage back to the office.

As she rounded the corner, she saw Sheila standing frozen, suspended in the "Exit" doorway, whimpering in pain. Something suddenly seemed to reach out and grab her arm, hurling her into the stairwell, dragging her up the stairway, her image splintering into fragments—gone.

"Sheila!" Chandal screamed, running toward the exit. The door slammed shut, blocking her way. She pulled on the door. It wouldn't open. But she could still hear Sheila crying. Higher up, above her.

Breathlessly, Chandal raced to the stairs to the right, started to climb. She climbed without thinking, up the labyrinth of stairs, stairwells, hallways, higher, the sound of Sheila's crying always just ahead of her.

She paused for a moment to catch her breath. Her legs shook, her hands and face numb from the cold. She pressed on.

At the end of the corridor on the fifth floor, she watched a door swing shut. It closed with a loud thud,

194

and then the hallway seemed to fall into an ominous silence.

Chandal felt increasingly drained of energy as she moved cautiously toward the door. The light had fallen away into a reddish glow, making it impossible to identify anything clearly. Chandal used her hands now, feeling her way down the long hallway to the door.

She placed her hand on its brass doorknob and shoved gently. The huge oak door swung open, slowly, until it stopped itself midway between open and shut.

Chandal saw Sheila standing at the far end of the room. She was still crying, but making no sound. Her chest heaved in short, spasmodic thrusts, her hands reaching out to Chandal for help.

"Sheila, come here." Chandal beckoned her to move forward, to move away from the huge airshaft that dropped down to the basement six floors below, directly behind her.

"Help me!" Sheila screamed.

"Sheila!"

"Help me!" And then something sucked her body straight back, smashing it against the wall, then letting it drop into the abyss below her.

"Sheila!"

Chandal moved forward. Stopped. She couldn't bring herself to look into the blackened hole that opened up before her.

Red fumes swarmed before her eyes.

Her body remained frozen, her limbs unable to budge. Her head was nearly exploding.

And then around her, she felt the eyes. Thousands of eyes all watching her. In panic, she spun—and saw she was standing in a room filled with paintings. Ancient painting from another age. Panels, flat, faded— Christ's face tender and compassionate; the Virgin Mary with the child, the image blackened, halo, hands, only the child's eyes seeming untouched by age; Christ upon the cross, body limp, blood flowing freely from his wounds; nude bodies, twisted, tormented, fighting to free themselves from the raging, flooding river; a mummified body lying in its bier, grief-stricken mourners frozen in despair and a human skeleton astride a white horse, lance in hand, smiling, and Christ, and pigs, and angels, and Christ again, and again . . .

And Chandal burst out crying in her sleep. The dream was over.

While patient did permit psychological testing, cooperation would be best described as
limited. Sarcasm, accompanied by a resentful
attitude, made little else known to us.

Nevertheless, there were enough Rorschach
and T.A.T. responses to permit some theoreti-
cal conclusions. Patient found being read aloud
to more tolerable and at times became involved,
even interested, in the material being read.

General knowledge is extensive and charac-
teristic of a scholar. However, the naïveté inherent
in a child is always present. Narcissistic preoc-
cupation and much infantile omnipotence also
present. There is also much sexual confusion,
especially regarding own sexual identity. Evidence of considerable hopelessness and under-
lying depression.

Conclusion: patient seems to be responding
to treatment at least superficially, though many
safeguards to protect ego are employed. In view
of patient's previous trauma, prognosis must still
remain guarded.

I. Luther

❧ 16 ❧

THE SKY WAS HAZY WITH SMOG AND THE SUNLIGHT was diffused in a yellowish smoke of its own. Already a chill burned her hands and face and tugged at her coat. She felt herself go lightheaded and dizzy, but she clenched her teeth and moved on.

The intense cold seemed to put the day in tune with her own feelings. She sniffed. The wind carried a sudden, strong pungency of tar to her nostrils. She lifted her eyes slightly to take in three workers huddled around a generator for warmth, its motor coughing in a sharp, even rhythm—chuk-ah, chuk-ah, chuk-ah—as the steamroller smashed tar into submission in the street outside the front doors of the museum.

It was Friday, the twenty-sixth of January.

Chandal nodded to the attendant.

"Good morning, Mrs. Knight," he said with an open smile.

Down the hall to the elevator. She glanced around the museum. Lots of people here already. The freshly painted sign on the front desk read: SUGGESTED CONTRIBUTION: $2.50. God, they keep making it more money every time you turn around.

She kept working on trivial observations, hoping to drive away the memory of last night's dream. Slow elevator, dark hallways. She reached the office, removed her coat. The trouble with this place is the closets. They're not big enough, she thought. She pushed her coat in between the others, barely managing to get the door closed. Saw Sheila falling. The door sprung back open; she pushed it shut. Saw Sheila falling. The door popped open again. The hell with it!

"Morning," she said on the way to her desk.

"Morning," accompanied by darting, flickering eyes.

"Morning." Chandal sat.

"Morning," accompanied by a mocking smile.

Up yours, sweetheart! Chandal dropped into her usual slack position, elbows leaning on the desk, hands toying with her bangs.

The office boy hurried by on his way to the Xerox room.

"Where's Sheila?"

"Called in sick." He smiled.

Chandal looked down and regarded her nails. "Sick?"

"Yeah, and the boss is p.o.'ed." He snorted once, grinning.

"Why?"

"He thinks she just said that to add a few more days to her vacation." He sat on the corner of her desk.

"She wouldn't do that."

"You think she's really sick?" He slouched down lower, fooling with her pencils in her green plastic cup.

"Listen, don't you have work to do?"

The young kid grinned. "Sure. Sure I got work to do. Loads of it."

"Don't you think you should get started?"

"That's what I like—nice friendly people!" He got up in a huff. Chandal watched him go out the door and turn right down the hallway. The same doorway she'd watched Sheila walk through last night in her dream.

She picked up the phone and dialed Sheila's number. Waited, tapping her thin fingers nervously on the blotter. No answer. She hung up.

The moving had started again, that subtle shifting of weight within her body, the buzzing and then the sudden stillness . . . impossible to figure out, and the day continued. She called Sissy, canceled lunch—"I just can't, Sissy. . . . Yes, all right, next week. I'm sorry . . . it's hard to explain. Yes, next week." And saw Sheila falling. God, I don't know what's the matter with me. I'm sorry, shall I retype the letter? That'll be fine. Called Sheila. No answer. Be sensible, Chandal . . . and then saw Sheila falling. Called Justin. No answer. Typed another four letters. Called Sheila. No answer. What time is it? You're kidding!

She stood in front of Sheila's building. She stared into the lobby at the heavy-paunched doorman; he sat hunched over, reading a magazine. She tapped on the glass with her key. The dark-looking man gazed up at her with visored eyes, blank, remote. Chandal indicated that she wanted to speak with him. It took him forever to crack open the door. "Yes?"

"Ah, Sheila Marsh—is she here?"

"Not sure, Miss. Should I buzz her?"

"Yes, please."

He let Chandal in and moved to the intercom. Pressed. Waited. Pressed again.

Come on, come on, thought Chandal, her two hands twisted into fists inside her coat pockets.

The old man flashed her a charming smile. "She's not home."

"Are you sure?"

"She doesn't answer."

"She was supposed to go away on vacation. You didn't happen to see her leave during the day, did you?"

"I just came on."

"Oh, I see. Thanks."

It had been an awful day. Chandal walked forward in a kind of stupor, watched as the man anxiously opened the door for her, fearing that she was going to perform some outrageous outburst. She stood for a moment, like a mummy, seeming not to care what happened next. And that was the frightening thing. She was starting not to care. Without definite purpose, without instruction, cut off and isolated, she stood there in the hallway fighting to care, fighting to understand. What else could she do?

"Any problem?" he asked.

"No. Not really. Thank you."

He stared at her for a moment, his mouth slightly open. "So that's it, then?"

"Yes. That's it."

Chandal left the building. The old man went back to his reading and she saw Sheila falling.

Six-fifteen P.M. Chandal stood in the lobby of the hospital and waited. Hesitation, procrastination. The point was she still hadn't told Justin her mother was coming to stay with them.

What followed was a bureaucratic nightmare.

Dr. Margolin hadn't signed a release form. "Can't I just take the responsibility?" asked Chandal. Glares from the nurse behind the desk. "If you want to pay the bill in full. The insurance won't protect you."

She tried to reach the doctor by phone. No, he wasn't home, said his bored-sounding wife over the telephone. "He's at the Harvard Club."

"Hello, Harvard Club?"

"He's having dinner."

Finally the doctor's annoyed voice came on the line. Words like inadvisable, foolish. "All right"— finally, reluctantly, he agreed, dripping suggestions of I-wouldn't-want-to-be-you. "But I wash my hands of the responsibility. Good luck."

The out-patient clerk had misplaced her mother's records. It took forty minutes to locate them and another thirty minutes to finalize the bill. It now had to be approved. The administrative assistant had gone to dinner. He was the only authority capable of signing the final release. When he returned, a discrepancy was found which had to be checked. The entire procedure took three hours and fifteen minutes.

After that, Chandal's mother insisted on walking out of the hospital of her own free will. The head nurse demanded that she be placed in a wheelchair. A nasty argument took place, the head nurse won, and Chandal's mother was put into a wheelchair and delivered to the lower lobby. Exhausted, the two women left the building, collapsed into a waiting checker cab and rode side by side in silence.

Arriving at the brownstone, Helen Briar sat tense and uneasy as the cab driver got out, removed her suitcase from the trunk, and dumped it briskly on the frozen sidewalk. She looked the other way as he held the passenger's door open, waiting for the two women to emerge.

From inside the cab, Chandal could sense the driver's annoyance. His breathing labored heavy in the darkness as his fingers tapped nervously on the outer edge of the door. "Come on, Mom." She stepped into the street, turned, and extended her hand to her mother, who refused to move. Instead, she took a faded brown envelope filled with old photographs from her pocketbook and began shuffling them.

"Look at this one, Chandal. Remember?"

"Mom, the man's waiting."

Helen shook her head. "No."

"Hey, listen, lady—I gotta make a livin'." He shot Chandal a bland and discouraging gaze.

"No. Justin won't want me here. I know it."

"Of course he will." Chandal handed the driver an extra dollar and indicated that he should carry the valise up the steps.

"Are you sure?" Helen asked.

"Positive."

"But you should have told him. You really should have." Helen refused to look at Chandal, preferring to stare at the top photograph—Chandal as a cheerleader at Columbia High School, the red and gold colors sparkling in her memory.

"Mom, he was asleep when I got home last night." Helen looked up sharply, as if questioning Chandal's last statement. Chandal wondered if her mother knew that she was lying.

"What if Justin disapproves? What then?"

Chandal smiled. "He won't. I promise you." Gently, she helped her mother from the cab and closed the door. Fingers clenched tightly around Chandal's arm, Helen paused for a moment to take in her new surroundings. Behind them, the front door to the cab slammed shut, an engine suddenly revved up, then sped away. Most of the neighboring buildings loomed dark. A dog barked somewhere, encouraging others. When they stopped, there was a moment of silence, followed by Helen's sigh. "Come on, Mom," Chandal said.

Arm in arm, they climbed the slab steps. It was six minutes to ten. Chandal glanced sideways at Helen and slipped her key into the lock. At the last possible moment, Helen broke away, ran down the steps, and into the street. Instinctively, Chandal hit the doorbell to alert Justin, then dashed after her mother. "Mom, please, what is it?"

"I don't know. I don't know . . ." she said. Her words trailed away, her two hands clutched tightly around the collar of her coat. Half-dressed, Justin appeared at the doorway.

"Justin—help me!" Chandal tried to take hold of her mother.

"No, leave me alone!" Pulling away, Helen almost stumbled and fell. Chandal screamed. "Mom!"

Justin was down the steps, taking hold of Helen's arm. "Helen, here. Let me help you."

"No, I'm afraid. I can't. When I'm ready—not now!" She struggled to free herself. Justin tried to convince her that everything was going to be all right. That he wanted her to stay. A small crowd gathered to watch.

"Are you sure? Are you sure I'll be all right in there?" she asked, trembling from the cold.

"Of course. There's nothing in there to hurt you." Justin steered her by the elbow closer to the brownstone.

"How do you feel, Mom?" asked Chandal, opening the front door.

Her mother started to cry. Justin allowed the two women to enter the brownstone first. He turned to see the people still staring at him, Nickles Mayo standing center in the crowd.

"What the hell are you looking at? Jerks!" He slammed the door in their faces.

Wearily, Chandal gave Justin the facts, having settled her mother into the spare room. Her voice appeared to be echoing in her head as she spoke, sounding shrill and harsh. Out of stillness and darkness, any sound becomes inflated, she reminded herself. Justin never said a word, allowing her to talk—to rattle on.

Finally, he asked, "Are you all right?"

"Tired, that's all."

"Oh."

"Why do you ask?"

He paused in the living room doorway, preoccupied, a fingertip pressed to the middle of his forehead. He glanced up the outer stairway to the second floor. He gave a helpless little shrug. "It's going to be hard—I mean, with your mother living here."

"I told you, I had no choice." For a moment, she eyed Justin rather curiously. What was he thinking?

A stare and a conciliating nod. "It'll be all right. We're both tired. Distracted, I guess." He held his arms out to her. "Come on, let's get some sleep."

"Okay." She relaxed. What else was left to say? Justin hadn't been exactly warm toward the idea of her mother's moving in. But to discuss it now would only make things worse. She could only hope that he would soften. She would use the weekend to get close to him, very close. He had been preoccupied; she knew that. The move had taken a lot out of him. He was always nervous when casting a play; she knew that, too. She also knew deep down inside the pit of her stomach that Justin needed her. That they both needed each other. Above all, she knew it was important for them to maintain contact with each other, genuine contact.

They turned off the lights and went to bed.

For the next two days, Chandal's mother spoke to no one. She ate her meals in silence and then went to her room to read.

"What's wrong, Mom?" asked Chandal.

And she merely replied, "There's something terrible

in this house." She didn't know what it was, but the feeling was strong.

By Sunday evening, Chandal's ring was causing a skin rash around her finger. Soon it spread to her wrist. She switched the ring to her other hand but the rash recurred even more quickly. There were red welts, as if she'd been bitten by a thousand mosquitoes. But smaller. Tiny. Just so many of them. "Justin, look at this." She held up her hand.

"What is it?"

"I don't know. It itches." She scratched. "It seems to be caused by the ring."

"Doesn't look good. I wouldn't wear it—until it clears up."

Chandal placed the ring in her glass powder box on her dresser and covered her hands and wrists with bacitracin ointment. In the next hour, she straightened the house and cooked dinner. The house was filled with the smell of corned beef and cabbage. "Honey, taste this." She slipped a piece of corned beef into Justin's mouth. "What do you think?"

"Great." He dropped into the kitchen chair.

She wondered if it didn't need a pinch more salt and added some. "By the way, did you know that Bender's decided not to renovate? He's moving people back into the building."

"When did you hear this?" He drew a pipe from his shirt pocket.

"I don't know. Monday—or Tuesday, I guess."

"Nonsense." He stuck the pipe into his tobacco pouch—filled it with Arnold's Mixture.

"No, I went over there. I met a Bonnie—what was her name? Miss Ohio, or something. She's moving into our old apartment."

"What were you doing over there?" He lit his pipe. It took six matches in all. He was new at it.

"I saw the moving truck outside, and—" She stopped, sniffed in the aroma—dry leaves burning? "Justin, what's that?"

"What?"

"That thing hanging from your mouth!"

"What does it look like? A pipe!"

"When did you—" She wasn't fond of pipes, cigars either, especially while eating. Let it pass. "It's odd, isn't it?"

"What is?"

"First he gives us six thousand dollars—then he changes his mind. It doesn't make sense." She pushed back her hair.

"Landlords always do what's best for the landlord. He knows what he's doing."

"Justin, six thousand dollars? Nobody throws away money like that. I don't care if he's a millionaire."

"He probably wanted a tax shelter."

"I don't think so. I think it's more than that."

He drew a long breath. "Suit yourself." He paused to relight his pipe, then added, "What did she look like?"

"Who?"

"Miss Iowa."

"Ohio."

"Oh, yeah."

"A silly-looking thing, really. I never could understand how they do that. Being brought out and introduced like an unusual heifer or a prize sow."

"I don't know—I think being Miss America would be a real gas."

"Oh, sure. Here she is, folks—champion human sow of America! Besides, she'd never get it; they raise them better in California."

"Bull!"

She paused. "Well, anyway, I think she's silly." The front door closed. She stepped into the hallway. Whoever it was had gone.

She glanced back at Justin. "Justin, I've been thinking, do you suppose we could build a partition in the foyer? You know, with a door. This way we would have complete privacy. Now that Mom's here—"

"I don't think it's a good idea."

"Why?"

"Because we'd insult them, that's why."

"But—"

"We can't, Del."

"Justin, they'd understand. This way they could come and go as they please. What's wrong with that? I think it's a good idea."

He looked away, then glanced back at her quickly, as if to catch her questioning him. "Well, I don't!" He lifted himself to his feet, started to leave. "Jesus! I live here, too, remember? Partitions! Mothers!"

She pressed her lips together and watched him go. The tension between them—she could feel it deepening, strengthening itself like an athlete who has done all the right exercises to make himself fit. Now Justin was pouting, angry over her mother's coming. Angry that he hadn't been told ahead of time. Damn! He was right. She should have said something. Stay calm—it'll be all right.

At dinner, Chandal's mother ate sparingly. Chandal could see she was forcing herself. At dinner's end, her mother finally spoke. "In the hospital—I awoke, there were flowers."

Chandal smiled. "Yes, I noticed. They were pretty."

"Do you know who brought them?" her mother asked.

Chandal shrugged, turned to Justin. He hadn't the answer, either. "I don't know."

"I do." Her mother rose.

"You do?" asked Chandal.

"Yes. A demon." She folded her napkin, laid it carefully beside her plate, and returned to her room.

Justin shook his head. "I needed this, right?" He pulled himself up with slow deliberation. "Well, when it comes to her, you're on your own." He dropped his napkin on the table and went into the bedroom.

She was still thinking about it as she dried the last dish and put it carefully inside the cabinet. What could have made her mother say such a thing? She ripped off the yellow rubber gloves and laid them in the soap dish. People's minds when they get older. Or pregnant, she added wryly, thinking of the state of her own mind. Like mother, like daughter, probably. She dried the area around the sink and laid the towel on the rack.

She went to the door of the spare room and knocked. "Mom?" No answer. Sleeping? She opened the door a crack. Her mother was sitting on the bed reading. "Mom, can I talk with you for a minute?" Her mother turned sharply to the next page. "At the table—you said a demon brought you those flowers."

"That's right," she said without taking her eyes from the page.

"How do you know?" Chandal sat on the bed beside her.

"Did you bring them?"

"No."

"And Justin—he didn't either. My friends, I asked them all. No, they said—they didn't bring the flowers either. The demon brought them."

"What demon?"

"Her! She heard me say I hated cut flowers—that's why she put them in my room. Oh, she denied it. But I know it was her."

"Who?"

Her mother leaned over and whispered into her ear, "The nurse."

"Oh, Mom, that's silly."

"No, no! The little girl told me. She said she saw her, watched her put them there while I was asleep. She always waited until I was asleep and then slipped into my room to do things. Change things around. Take things."

"But that's her job, Mom—to see that you're all right."

"My Bible. She took my Bible. The little girl told me so."

"Maybe the little girl lied."

"No! The woman was a demon!" She slammed her book closed.

Chandal sighed. "Okay, Mom. If you need anything, let me know." She left the room, closing the door.

Sitting at the kitchen table, she tried to understand what was wrong with her mother. Afraid of being old—dying? Lonely? She'll be all right, Chandal thought. She held out her hands. They were rough and ugly. The rash was still there, but not as irritated. She missed her ring. She wanted to wear it. It meant something.

She went to the bedroom and rummaged through her jewelry box until she found what she was looking for, a tiny silver chain. Running the chain through the ring, she hung it around her neck.

Justin lay across the bed, reading his script.

"There, how does that look?" she asked, stepping away from the mirror.

"Fine." He barely looked up.

"You're angry, aren't you?"

"About what?"

"That I didn't tell you about Mother."

"It would've been nice." He turned away from her, his face tight.

"Justin, I was afraid to."

He turned back to her. "Afraid?"

"Yes," she said in a sudden, cold tone.

"Of me?"

"I can't help it. No matter what I do or say, you jump down my throat. It scares me. We seem to be always on the verge of arguing. I have to watch everything I say now."

"That's interesting. I hadn't realized I was capable of frightening people."

"Justin, can't you see—"

"I'm going downstairs—work on a couple of pictures." He tossed the script aside and started to leave the room.

"Justin, please. Not again tonight."

"Why not? You have your mother. Let her keep you company."

"Justin, don't run off now, please."

"Why stay? I frightened you, remember?"

"At least try and understand me for once. Okay?"

"Understand what?"

"My problems."

209

"Your problems?" He drew out the words sarcastically.

"Yes!"

"And just what is your problem? That you're not acting these days? Whose fault is that?"

"That's not it at all."

"That I haven't asked you to be in the new play? Sorry, Del—I can't take that chance."

"Who the hell cares about being in your play!"

"All right, then, let's run down the list. Sissy's too busy to keep you company? I'm too busy to keep you company? Your mother is sick? We didn't go to California?"

"I'm suffocating here!"

"Wonderful. Then open a window and stop acting like a baby!"

"Justin, there is something in this house—"

"Yeah, two people fighting, two people upstairs listening, an overfed cat, and a sick mother. Sorry, Del, but I'm up to here with your problems!"

She made no effort to stop him as he left the room. Christ! Damn him, damn him, *damn him!* She flung the pillow across the room. The pain moved quickly up her back into her neck. She rolled her head around, stroking the back of her neck with her right hand. Lie down, she told herself. Relax. Sleep. No, there was some reason why she couldn't do that. Don't sleep. She couldn't remember. . . . Eyes blinking closed, she let her body slide down, bury itself deep in the soft mattress. Now, why was it she shouldn't sleep? A warmth settled down on top of her. She slept.

The face smiled warmly, even tenderly. It was Sheila. Her face was replaced by the haggard and deep-lined face of the seer from the Bronx. The seer spoke: *"You shouldn't have come here—not carrying a child!"*

Mother's face. She looked down at Chandal from above and grinned—an inane, silly kind of grin. Her mood changed suddenly and the expression on her face became serious. She pleaded, *"Help me!"* But

Chandal was unable to move. The mother screamed, *"Oh, God—help me!"*

Chandal's body shot upright. She was drenched in sweat. She felt stiff and sick to her stomach—and then she became frightened. "Mother?" she whispered. She got up and moved quickly to the rear of the apartment.

It was nearly one A.M. when she opened the door to the spare room. Her mother was asleep. Nothing in the room was out of order. In fact, the room possessed an extraordinary calm.

She closed the door softly and started into the kitchen. She heard someone moving around in the living room. "Who's there?" There was no answer. Someone was still moving through the room. She edged her way down the hallway until she stood in the open arch of the living room.

The young man sat in the corner chair, crying. Seeing Chandal, he dried his eyes with the tips of his fingers. "They are together. They are—" At that moment, he became startled and exclaimed, "Watch out—behind you!"

She spun around; no one was there. When she turned back, the young man was also gone. Suddenly she could feel someone gripping her shoulder. She shrieked. With a violent tug, the ring was torn from around her neck.

By the door, a form, white and spectral, moved. It looked like the young girl. Quickly Chandal followed her from the living room and watched her disappear into the basement. She followed.

Blindly, she felt her way down into the cellar and fumbled for the light at the foot of the steps. With her hand on the switch, she hesitated. A light image broke the darkness. Chandal's hand moved swiftly. The safety light illuminated the room. The figure was gone. The basement was vacant.

"Justin?" she called, frightened to make herself heard. His equipment looked untouched—no sign of photo paper, no dampness from dripping negatives, nothing. She felt rather than heard the long intake of

211

breath. The air was held and then released. Yes—the young girl. Chandal could see her plainly now, standing perfectly still behind one of the mannequins. Her body stiff, her eyes wide open, she resembled the other lifeless forms.

Chandal stepped closer. "Please, I know you're there. I won't hurt you. I just want to speak with you."

The girl maintained a rigid posture.

"Can you hear me? I promise—you'll be all right." She moved closer, could see that each mannequin resembled someone she knew: Justin; the old man in the jewelry store; her mother; and Sheila.

The young girl moved, her mannequin head turning slightly at first, until it finally managed to rotate completely around to face the wall. The rest of her body remained facing front. Chandal edged slowly toward her.

The girl's head suddenly spun around on her shoulders and snapped into a frontal position. Her expression was distorted and ugly—she hissed at Chandal, who jumped back and became entangled in the arms of another mannequin.

The girl darted forward, red hair swirling behind her, entered the small door, and disappeared up the back stairs. Chandal fought to free herself. Breaking away, she went to the stairwell. The girl was on the third-floor landing, heading for the attic. Chandal followed.

The girl's steps made sounds now—hurried, rushed sounds. Chandal climbed after her, conscious of her own breathing, the bursts of breath hitting the chilled air as she exhaled. It was getting colder. She climbed.

The girl looked back, then quickly away—she had reached the top, disappeared through the attic door. It was colder up there than in the basement.

Chandal stopped at the door, hesitated—shivered suddenly.

Above her now, a face, vaguely visible, teeth bared. Chandal hadn't noticed. She caught her breath—the only sound.

Then the silence was fractured. She heard a female

voice; low. "I will not be disturbed here. I will not be disturbed."

Chandal stepped into the attic—not a whole lot of light to see by.

In the darkness—shadows, loomed antique objects, old relics.

Then Chandal saw her, the young girl—crouched in a corner. "Please, don't run away. I want to talk with you!"

Slowly the girl rose and faced her. But it wasn't a young girl at all—it was Magdalen!

Magdalen charged at Chandal and, in a man's voice, screamed, "Leave us alone, you bitch!"

With one violent shove, she sent Chandal toppling down the stairs, falling backward, until her body came to rest on the third floor landing.

❧ 17 ❧

MINTZ LICKED CHANDAL'S FACE, A FACE MUMMIFIED by grief. The doctor had just informed her that she'd lost her baby. From the foyer, low voices could be heard.

"Will she be okay?" asked Justin.

"Well, there were a lot of nasty cuts—but nothing serious," said Dr. Axelrod. "She lost some blood, but she'll be okay. Keep the bandages on, and we'll remove the stitches in a few days."

At the front door, pulling on his tweed coat, the doctor asked in a soft voice, "Tell me, has your wife still been imagining things?"

Justin stared at him blankly. "I don't know what you mean."

"During her visit at the office, she seemed nervous, on edge. She asked me if it was normal to imagine things. I never did find out what those things were. I thought perhaps you might know."

"My wife used to be an actress. I'm afraid her imagination sometimes gets the better of her."

"I see." The doctor eyed Justin curiously. He had recognized the cold tone in his voice and wondered at Justin's lack of emotion. "Well, good night, then," he said dryly.

Justin closed the door and peered through the small window, making sure that the doctor had really gone. Putting the porch light out, he went into the kitchen, where Chandal's mother sat crying.

In the bedroom, Chandal listened to their voices and knew that they were talking about her. She really wasn't interested.

Her mother's voice was full of tears. "What could have caused her to go down there? What?"

"I don't know," said Justin in a monotone.

"Oh, God—she's getting so helpless—to fall down the basement stairs like that!"

Chandal knew she hadn't fallen down the basement stairs—it was the attic stairs. But who would believe her? She turned over onto her side and went to sleep. She was part of her own dream now and couldn't hear her mother's weeping. She found herself in a room with Elizabeth and Magdalen. It was a tiny room with wallpaper that represented an ancient stag hunt. The burning logs were intense, white-hot, and furious.

Elizabeth sat near the chaise longue and pretended to polish her nails. Magdalen walked back and forth near the window. She looked different than Chandal had remembered her. Her hair was drawn back over her ears; a pretty necklace, a new face, a tailored skirt and blouse of beige. On her finger—two rings. The exact type of ring that Justin had given to Chandal.

"Sit down, please," Magdalen ordered. "I'm afraid that I must be frank with you. I'm not one of those women who pretend. Justin doesn't want . . ."—she stressed this—". . . He doesn't want you for his wife any longer."

214

Elizabeth broke into a wild scream of laughter. Magdalen ordered her to be silent.

"You're still angry, aren't you, Magdalen? Because I told her about him. What you two are up to." She pointed her thin finger at her sister.

"You whore! You miserable whore!" Magdalen slapped Elizabeth savagely.

"No! Please stop! Please!" Chandal pleaded.

"Hey, honey, wake up. Del, wake up." Justin sat on the bed next to her.

But she pretended to be asleep. She didn't want to talk with Justin. Not just yet. She felt him leave her, heard him go into the living room. She lay there. She dozed off again. She was at the park with Justin. Everyone was happy. She laughed; he kissed her. It was a perfect day. She was awakened. She heard her mother go to bed. It was morning.

Chandal wept, partly because her baby was dead, and partly because she had all but forgotten she was pregnant the past few weeks and felt now as if she had been responsible for the baby's dying!

Her face became slightly distorted as she tried to stop herself from crying. Her brain became a small planet, isolated, alone and turned in on itself. For a moment, tiny images flooded her mind, a soft little face, hands, feet, holding the child to her breast, letting it suck the heart-warmed milk, loving it, caring for it—oh, God! She yearned to put her arms around her child, to comfort it as it cried, as it struggled with gawky arms and legs to discover the world around it.

Chandal's muscles tensed beneath the covers. She strained to sleep, to let the images remove themselves from her mind. Strained as if trudging uphill, a long hill, to peace.

Days and nights passed. There were the quiet, safe times when she was alone, free of thought. Then there were the terrors, the seconds of panic, when she imagined the young man standing beside her bed, beckoning to her, trying to reach out to her.

And then it happened. Deep into the fourth night.

Chandal's eyes flickered rapidly. She was asleep and yet very conscious of her physical body. Almost as if she had risen out of her body and now floated a level above it, looking down. She saw her sprawling limbs— her arm hanging over the side of the bed to the floor, her one leg outside the covers. Her hair tousled over the pillow. Her body was deeply asleep. She hovered over it protectively, waiting.

Suddenly a pale light filtered over her sleeping body.

Steam hissed gently. An unseen hand smoothed her hair, loving the silkiness of the fiber, brushing it away from her face. A long sigh released itself. Impatient arms seized her thin sleeping body and turned it face up.

Chandal dropped lower to the bed, feeling weak. Her vitality had lessened dangerously. She had been suspended in a realm where time had ceased to have measure and, while thus suspended, she had stayed outside her body too long. She had to get back, quickly.

A long triumphant hiss came from the lips of the sleeping girl.

Chandal knew what had happened. An alien presence had gained entrance. Filled with dread, she sank lower, hung weakly over the bed, and then dropped. She began to absorb herself back into physicality.

A hot, forceful gush flew at her, denying her entrance to the body, pushing her viciously into the atmosphere. Chandal was trapped. She looked down, feeling her spiritual power fading, becoming nothing. The force was covering the body with a field of energy. It was oozing over the girl like slime, cutting her away from Chandal.

Chandal tried to gather her power for one last try, before she ceased to be. She was scattering in all directions now like smoke. It was so hard to stay in focus.

"I'll help you," said an urgent, silent voice. "Follow me."

Chandal drifted vaguely toward the voice. Below

her was a vicious battlefield. Two spirits fighting over her body. A slash of red went across her cheek. Blood trickled down in a fine line.

Invisible fingers plucked at the slime. Electricity sparked off the sleeping body.

"You bitch!" screamed a voice.

Rapidly the slime unwound from the girl. Pure ugly energy reshaped itself into a funnel, poised at the nostrils of the girl.

"Now!" cried the voice.

Chandal dived rapidly, fighting through electrical currents, hardly able to maintain a center. She knew the body so much better than did the alien force. It was her only weapon.

A shriek went through the air.

She rapidly gained control of her body. Felt her body coming back to life. The force slithered in after her, slithering down her throat. She gagged, trying to throw it up.

Get out, she said. Get out.

The force was down in her.

Get out, she said, weakly, tears slipping from her eyes.

Angry, vicious fingers reached deep into her gut and wound themselves around the force and pulled.

Blackness.

At four A.M., her eyes opened slowly. The sheet was wet with sweat. Weakly, she let her body go limp and surrendered herself to deep, almost drugged sleep. She never noticed the gash on her right cheek.

The next two days passed quickly. She barely stirred from the bed. She let herself be carried along like some mysterious object caught in the current of a river. Unclaimed.

Unnoticed, the separation grew between Chandal and her mother. Chandal requested privacy, shutting her mother out from the room with no explanation. Once her mother tried to embrace her and Chandal freed herself from the entwining arms without a word. Finally, her mother, neglected and frightened, decided

217

to leave. No one stopped her. Early the next morning, in a state of exhaustion, she went to her room, packed, and left the brownstone.

Convalescence was long. Chandal had no reason to stir from her room. After a week, she still refused to leave the house for any reason. Things dragged on—soiled linens, combs, and hair curlers lying about, and everywhere piles of dirty dishes. Justin hadn't complained of the untidiness. He hadn't noticed it. He saw only through the eyes of Magdalen. Magdalen, who had consumed him. Magdalen was his world now, and his love for Chandal was barely a remembrance.

At the end of the second week, Chandal began receiving bad news from her mother. Each phone call brought with it a new horror: the latest, that her mother had to return to the hospital; the doctor felt that it was serious. Chandal felt no affection for her now and started refusing to speak with her.

Since Chandal had stopped working, she had let her nails grow out and, not knowing what to do with her hands, she began picking at her face. Her body began to look flabby and unattractive. She started wearing wigs to cover up her unkempt hair. Theatrical wigs. Wigs that had lain in boxes for years.

It was the morning of February 12 when she realized how dreadful looking she had become. Justin had just gone off to his first day of rehearsal on the new play. He had assembled an all-star cast. Billie Richards was not among the players.

Sporting a fully grown mustache and an extra-short haircut, Justin left the house in good spirits. His only comment to Chandal as he left was an offhand remark that his home was not a hospital!

Justin had a new vitality. He walked faster, the kind of stride that comes with being proud. Proud of what? wondered Chandal. He really hated the new play; she was sure of that. He hadn't much money left in the bank, the brownstone was a mess, and his wife had just lost his child. What the hell did he have to be proud of? Did he ever want the child? She sank into the black leather chair in the living room. Was that it? Was Billy right—that all Justin really wanted was his freedom?

She sat back and asked herself the question that most people are afraid of. And yet it was the only question left worth asking. Why should she go on living? Why not just end it?

She wondered if she were capable of answering the question. No. Yes—she guessed it was really quite simple. You just go on doing what was expected of you. You eat the next meal, open the next letter, go to work the next day, come home, have dinner, answer the telephone . . .

Yes, the phone was ringing.

She picked up the receiver. It was a woman from the museum.

The voice on the other end spoke hesitantly at first, then told her almost in a whisper that Sheila Marsh was dead. They had discovered her body at the bottom of a canyon. She had apparently fallen to her death while skiing. "It's such a regrettable accident, a tragedy, really. . . ." The voice continued pouring into Chandal's ear and she could see Sheila falling, her body bouncing off the snow-covered rocks, the blood sprinkling the snow with tiny drops of red.

"They tried for days to find her, but the storm caught them by surprise. They were shut in for days. . . ."

No, Chandal thought. Not rocks, not mountains. The room in the museum—that's where she died. In that room, down that airshaft—that's where Chandal had seen Sheila fall.

"We're really all still in a state of shock."

"Yes. I understand," Chandal said, the tears streaming down her face.

"Please, I'm sorry. I must hang up." She pressed her finger down on the disconnect button, paused. She ran the seer's phone number across her brain. Lifted her finger, dialed, waited. The flat, mechanical voice on the other end informed her that the number had been disconnected.

She hung up, searched in her pocketbook, found the small slip of paper Sheila had given her. She had dialed the right number. She would try again. Same voice, same information—the number had been disconnected. She hung up.

Suddenly Chandal felt a kind of shattering inside her and wondered if she wasn't going to crack, right here, right now—have a breakdown. She began to cry again in jerky, nervous spasms. "What do you want from me?" she screamed. *"What!"*

It was a relief, to finally scream out like that. It was like removing a tumor from her soul. She stood, uncertain at first. She hadn't the foggiest idea what to do. Who to turn to, where to go. She had only herself to rely on now.

She stared at herself in the bathroom mirror, tears rolling out of her eyes, stinging as they ran onto the irritated skin on her face. Awkwardly, she pulled off the short auburn wig and met her own eyes in the glass. The room in the museum. Was it really there? Had she only imagined it? She had to know.

Quickly, she soaked her skin in cream, applied a light layer of natural makeup and lipstick, putting a Kleenex to her mouth to blot the color. She brushed her hair, brought it to rest on the top of her head. She slipped into a loose green dress made of soft material, put on her fur-lined jacket, and left the brownstone.

She hurried to her bank and inquired the amount of her balance. It was a fraction over $400. After stopping long enough to cash a check for $50, she moved across the street to the drugstore—bought a pack of cigarettes. The awkward little man with the intelligent face behind the counter handed her the change.

She stepped to the far corner of the store, feverishly tore open the pack of cigarettes. Her hands were shaking.

She nervously reached for a cigarette and lit it. She hadn't had a cigarette in years. She'd tried to smoke right after her father had died. It seemed her way of being an adult for her mother. Her mother had told her that she was her little girl, after all, and preferred that she didn't. Chandal had insisted, smoked two packs a day, until her throat felt like sandpaper and had finally given it up as a lost cause four weeks later.

The green-and-white-tile floor moved under her feet now, as she paced back and forth in front of the stamp machine. She gave herself ten good reasons why the whole thing was impossible. She tried to explain away the young couple in the brownstone. Sheila's sudden death, her mother's unexplainable illness. She had trouble filling in all the details. She heard herself speaking and thought: crazy, crazy—silly—crazy!

She exhaled, dropped the cigarette to the floor—crushed it. Lit another, and became aware that she was being observed. Silently, the two faces behind the counter stared at her, tracked her movement. The little man politely apologized silently for inconveniencing her, disappeared behind the counter for a moment, and returned with an ashtray. "Forgive me, but would you mind—"

Cigarette still in her mouth, Chandal left the store and headed for the museum.

❧ 18 ❧

"YES?"

Chandal turned. Standing in the doorway to her right was a little woman of indeterminate age whose worn face, white hair, and general drained appearance proclaimed unmistakably that she had worked hard the better part of her life. Frail and thin, there was definitely an air of nonentity about her. "Can I help you?"

221

"Oh, I . . . I work here. Second floor."

"Public Relations?"

"No, no—just a secretary."

"I see." The woman stiffened.

"Hi. I'm Chandal Knight." She extended her hand.

"Miss Fry."

From the stairwell, a guard appeared. "Twenty minutes, Rose."

"Thank you." Miss Fry smiled, and the guard disappeared as suddenly as he had appeared.

"Well, if you'll excuse me . . ." She half-turned and turned back. For a moment she eyed Chandal rather curiously. "Was there something you wanted?" There was the drawl of the South in her voice.

There was a short pause while Chandal collected her thoughts. "I . . . I came up here because I thought I might be able to see the paintings in that room." She indicated the huge oak-paneled door just ahead of her.

The woman gave Chandal a peculiar flat look. "Paintings?"

"Yes. There are paintings in that room, aren't there?"

The woman seemed lost in thought for a moment, then said, "Who told you that?"

"Sheila. Sheila Marsh. She—" Chandal broke off, having a hard time completing her sentence. "She used to work here."

"You mean that poor girl who was just killed? What was it—skiing?"

"Yes," Chandal said softly.

Almost to herself, the woman muttered, "How did she know?"

"What?"

"No one was supposed to know about those paintings. Not just yet." She looked at Chandal again and there was once more that lost expression.

"I don't mean to cause anyone trouble." She shrugged. "I heard that they were beautiful. I just wanted to see them."

The woman shifted her weight uncomfortably from

one foot to the other. "No one is supposed to know they're here. That's why I thought you were from Public Relations. It's been placed entirely in their hands, just how we go about handling the news that we've purchased them. Until then, no one is supposed—"

"I won't tell a soul. I promise." Chandal mustered a perfectly innocent smile.

"I don't know."

"Just one little look." Her eyes widened. "You know how it is—curiosity."

In a few seconds the door to the room had been unlocked and both women now stood amidst a rare collection of icon art. The room was exactly as Chandal had remembered it to be: the paintings, the room, the airshaft. It was all the same. Chandal shuddered.

"Isn't this one beautiful?" The old woman pointed to a three-panel painting of Saint George and the Dragon; his spear plunged into the dragon's mouth, the tip protruding from the back of its neck.

"Yes, beautiful." Chandal hadn't been looking at the painting at all. Something had changed in the room.

"They're all regarded as sacred and all very old. Of course, it's not possible to be very sure of their actual date. Sixth century, I'd guess."

What was different? Chandal wondered.

"Can you imagine the Church forbidding the painting of such beautiful images?"

That was it! The images had changed. The paintings were different, or at least they appeared to be different. "The human skeleton—riding a white horse. Is it here?" Chandal asked.

"Human what?"

"Skeleton. On horseback. I don't see it."

The woman looked nervously around the room.

"And the people caught in the flood, and the picture of the coffin. I don't see any of them."

"You must have been misinformed. We have no

223

such paintings here." She flashed a nervous smile. "Well, we must hurry on."

"That airshaft. What's it used for?"

"Oh, years ago we stored sculptures up here. They were unloaded into the basement and then raised on pullies up here. The floor is too old now." She paused, watched Chandal eye the pitch-black hole. "Shall we go?"

"Thank you. You've been very kind."

The woman turned off the light and locked the door.

Outside the Museum, Chandal was immediately swept away by a crowd of youths dressed in dungarees, war-surplus coats, and denim jackets, with a scattering of beards, mustaches, and boots. She took them to be students let loose for the day in the city.

She slowly made her way up Central Park West. The sun made the park look alive and she thought perhaps that she would spend the morning there. It was a mild day. Chilly, but the sun shone brightly, making her world, for a brief moment, seem a little lighter. By the time she reached Eighty-fifth Street, she had changed her mind. If she'd been dreaming, how did she know that the room was there?

She turned left and walked toward the brownstone. The seer. Why had she disconnected her telephone? Chandal wished now that Sheila had given her the number of the other people. They will help you if the woman doesn't, Sheila had said. But, maybe Sheila shouldn't have given her any number at all.

Chandal could still see the expression on Sheila's face when she had left for lunch that day. Tense. Nervous. She'd had nothing to be nervous about, had she? Unless—unless she knew she was in danger.

Chandal gazed at the wrinkled face, the familiar features of the mailman who was just dropping a letter into the mail slot. She stopped at the foot of the steps and waited for him to finish.

"Morning." He tipped his cap.

"Good morning," Chandal said, and felt better. Somehow, when he had said "Morning" there was a connection with reality, some part of reality that was not hostile, that was plain and simple and needed no explanation.

Chandal turned, watched the melting snow run down the gutters into the sewer below. Listened to the trickling of water, dropping down into the bowels of the city. There was the sound of cars, people—all of it real, unhurried, undisturbed.

Chandal was sure Sheila had mentioned other people. Were there actually people who would be able to help her?

Already she was beginning to get tired again. Something was going terribly wrong, something inside of her. A loss of vitality—no, more than that. She was letting go of everything. In some way, she had to find new strength. To gather herself together. Never in her life had she let herself look so—

"Watch out!" screamed a man's voice, and instinctively she jumped back. Leaped away from the brownstone, sure in the instant of danger that whatever was threatening her would have emanated from that building. And because she was young and her instincts were good, the empty clay flowerpot missed her, missed her by inches as it hurtled downward and smashed to bits on the sidewalk. The mailman, ashen and wobbling on his legs, had made his way down the steps, his chest heaving in his agitation. They looked at each other, embarrassed suddenly at their mutual recognition of their own mortality.

"I don't know what made me look up," muttered the mailman, shaking his head.

"You—you saved me. Saved my life."

"I don't know what made me look up," he repeated helplessly. He pointed up. "Hey, listen, tell those people . . ."

"I will," she said. "I'll tell them." She turned her gaze upward. A hand was just closing the third-story window. Had that flowerpot really fallen off the ledge? It had come hurtling down so fast. Of course, it had been an accident. Almost a deadly accident. She thanked the man, moved up onto the stoop, fished for

225

the key in her purse, and let herself in. She remained motionless, staring at the second-floor landing. She had to speak with the two women—now! More angry than frightened, she climbed the stairs and knocked on their door.

"Just a minute," called a faint voice, and there was the sound of something heavy being moved across the floor and the sound of a door opening and closing. Chandal let her fingers wander over the rich design of the doorframe. She recognized the artwork as good. No, better than good. She looked closer. All kinds of naked, plump figures—Renaissance. And animals. No, she thought. Just one animal, carved again and again. What—?

The door opened slowly, only a few inches at first; then Chandal saw that it was Elizabeth. Dressed in dusting cap and apron, she appeared to be cleaning the silver. With surprising pleasantness, she invited Chandal inside. They entered an intimate but comfortable living room, where Elizabeth invited her to sit down. "My, you do look well." Chandal knew that she was lying. "How do you feel?" Elizabeth asked.

"Fine. And you?"

"I'm an old woman. Never ask an old woman how she feels; she's liable to tell you. Now, what can I do for you?"

"Just now, when I—"

Suddenly the telephone rang in another room. Excusing herself, Elizabeth put down her cleaning cloth, hurriedly took off her cap and apron, and left the room, leaving the door open.

Chandal couldn't hear the conversation, but she did hear Elizabeth talking excitedly to someone on the other end. Chandal seized the opportunity to study the room carefully, not knowing exactly what she was looking for. There was a table with sewing upon it, another small table with books. All the furniture in the room was good and solid. There was little ornamentation—nothing more.

"Oh, dear—I am sorry. Now, where were we?" Elizabeth stood in the doorway and smiled.

Reluctantly, Chandal gave up her search. "I was saying that one of your flowerpots on the third floor just fell and nearly hit me!" Chandal was surprised to see how angry she still was.

"Oh, my. I've told Magdalen many times that we should have them removed. They're so heavy, you know. Perhaps Justin—"

"Someone was up there by the window." Chandal watched as Elizabeth's face hardened and became grim, her lips held very tightly together, as though she were forcing herself not to utter a word. "Did you hear me? I said there was someone at the third-floor window just now!"

"But who could it be, I wonder?"

"Magdalen—is she home?"

"No." Elizabeth turned away abruptly and, without a word, crossed to the small table and sat.

"Does anyone else live with you?"

Elizabeth's face brightened and she spoke in a changed voice. "Oh, yes. Murray. Murray has been with us most of our lives."

"Is he here now?"

"Oh, yes." She made a little gesture with her head toward the door.

"May I—"

Elizabeth rose, walked to the door, opened it, and went out. She paid no attention to Chandal, who was left standing at the table, her sentence unfinished.

After a moment, Chandal heard whispering from the next room. Then a scraping, clawing noise. Then she heard a door shut and there was complete silence. Only when a cry came from the next room, a cry like that of a wounded animal, half-moan and half-bleat, did Chandal go to see what the woman was up to.

Staring into the next room, Chandal saw Elizabeth standing by a cage which contained a huge parrot resting comfortably on one leg. Elizabeth smiled. "This is Murray. Murray, say hello to the nice young lady." The parrot cried out on cue. "You see, he is very intelligent."

Chandal wasted no time in eyeing the new room. It

227

was some sort of reference library with medical books piled everywhere.

Elizabeth stood at a bookshelf near the corner of the room, her back to Murray, and watched Chandal closely. "You are wondering what all this is, aren't you?"

"Yes, I was." Chandal felt embarrassed that the old woman could read her thoughts so clearly.

"Magdalen's husband used to be a doctor of sorts. This was his room. Actually, it was mine, and that's when all the trouble started."

"Husband? But I thought neither of you had ever been married."

"Oh, no. Magdalen was married. To the young Dr. Steven M. Rock. Oh, a fine doctor's wife she made!"

"And he lived here?"

"We all did. For a while. Oh, yes—there's a history to be told in this house. Actually, they lived on the first floor, where you live now. I lived here on the second floor by myself. Then he needed more room for his books, so he brought them up here. We never did get along." She turned and placed the cover over her bird. "Say good-bye, Murray."

The bird cried out good-bye.

Elizabeth smiled. "Intelligent bird, don't you think?"

"Oh, yes. Yes." Chandal's mind was racing. She wanted to ask a hundred questions, but knew that the old woman would only tell her what she wanted her to know, and nothing more.

"I never did tell you how sorry we were that you lost your son like that."

Their eyes met. Son? thought Chandal and moved aside as Elizabeth walked from the room.

"Please, I—" Chandal followed her. "How did you know that I was to have a son?"

Elizabeth went back into the living room and began to polish the candlesticks. She worked without looking at Chandal. "Magdalen said it was to be a boy. She knows these things."

Chandal continued to question her about Magdalen's husband. Elizabeth had no idea how much time had passed since he'd first stepped foot into the "ice house." She referred to the brownstone as the "ice house" because as a child, she always remembered being cold. When asked about her mother and father, Elizabeth vaguely remembered that Magdalen had hated her mother and loved her father. As for herself, she couldn't recall how she felt about them.

"Why did Magdalen hate your mother?" asked Chandal.

"Because she refused to let her marry the young doctor. But then she died and they were married the day after the funeral." She held up the highly polished candlesticks. "Aren't they pretty?"

"Yes." Chandal paused for a moment, then asked, "Down in the basement, there are mannequins. What are they used for?"

Elizabeth eyed her cautiously. "When the young doctor died, Magdalen and I decided to become dressmakers. It was easy enough, and we both like pretty clothes."

"What did Magdalen's husband die of?"

"Cancer," said Elizabeth simply. "Just like that. Such a young man, only thirty-three. He died upstairs in his bed on St. Valentine's Day."

"Upstairs? I thought—"

"When he became sick, he wanted to be closer to his laboratory. His work. The stairs, you know. He couldn't climb them. So they moved their belongings upstairs to the third floor and slept in Magdalen's old bedroom—hers as a little girl. It was the winter of 1930. They were married only a year when he died. Would you like a cup of tea?"

"Yes, please." Chandal needed more time to sort out the details.

"Sit down, please. I'll be right back." Smiling, she left the room. Chandal listened to the hollow footsteps padding their way to the rear of the apartment.

Mechanically, she unbuttoned her coat. Chandal was momentarily frustrated. Her eyes regained their purpose when she noticed the large black book resting on the rosewood sideboard cabinet. There were papers

229

protruding out from between the pages; an ink pen lay beside the book, and a bottle of ink sat next to the pen. The cap was off the pen, the top off the bottle. Someone had recently been working on making notes, she thought.

She heard the tea cups rattling in the kitchen. There was still time. She moved next to the rosewood sideboard. *"The Book of Ahriman,"* she muttered aloud to herself, staring down at the gold Gothic lettering.

She quickly poked her fingers into the pages and cracked the book open. Something substantial, more powerful than her, took hold as she read silently:

Then Ahriman spoke of Joy and Sorrow.
And He said:
1. And none, save only thee who places Me within thyself, will know true Joy.
2. Only then will ye know what I am, and what great Joy may be.
3. Go forth, in My glory, with them that strive with Me; fight against them that fight against Me.
4. Let them be crushed and put under that seek to destroy My soul; let them be turned away and brought to confusion that condemn My soul.
5. Let their way be dark; and let thy will and spirit persecute them.
6. Joy is greater than Sorrow when ye embrace the waiting arms of Ahriman.
7. Let all . . .

"What are you doing?" Elizabeth's voice rang sharply behind her.

"What?" Chandal spun around and let the book fall closed.

"You mustn't pry, my dear. It isn't polite."

Under Elizabeth's calm voice, Chandal could detect a new hardness. There was a tenseness in all her smallest movements. She was, quite suddenly, not a sweet and mild old lady, but a protectress of a secret and an enemy.

Chandal watched as Elizabeth clutched her shawl

230

more tightly around her. "The tea is ready. Shall we go into the kitchen?" She turned to leave the room.

"Elizabeth, I would like to see the rest of the brownstone. The third floor—I'd like to see it."

Elizabeth turned to Chandal, her face frightened. "No! No one goes up there anymore. It's been locked for years."

"That's not true. I told you that I just saw someone up there when I first entered the building."

"That's impossible."

"How do you know unless we check?"

"But there's no light up there."

"We'll use candles."

Elizabeth saw that Chandal was determined. She felt uneasy at the idea, but decided to let the girl have her way. After all, what was there to hide? "Magdalen will be angry," she said, weakening in her position.

"You said she wasn't home."

A tiny bead of sweat ran down Elizabeth's face and as she raised her hand upward, it was trembling. She took hold of the candlesticks and gave one to Chandal. Together, they lit the candles and headed for the third floor.

Chandal watched from below as Elizabeth climbed up the stairs, disappeared around one winding corner, then appeared again out of the shadows.

"It's all right. I've unlocked it. You may come up."

The first room Chandal entered was bare. A few pegs hung on the wall—and a table with a water jug and a basin on it stood off to the right.

Elizabeth put her arm around Chandal and drew her close. Together they stood at the doorway and eyed the vacant room. Elizabeth's face was hot and wet. "Through there," Elizabeth said, pointing at the curtain at the end of a long passageway.

They reached a door at the end of the hall. Elizabeth opened it and Chandal, with her candle, scuttled forward into the darkness.

They walked to the center of the room where Elizabeth stopped beside a huge four-poster bed. She leaned down to look at the decaying mattress. Then

231

she straightened up with a little shudder. "This is where he died," she whispered.

The two women went through the door into the darkness of the adjoining room. Chandal was startled to see that around the walls were anatomical specimens mounted and labeled. There were also specimens in glass cases and a large number of packing crates, yet unopened. On the floor were bones, the skeletons of dead animals, curiosities, and brains in jars.

"This is where he conducted his work." Elizabeth placed her candlestick down on a large table, containing an array of shiny instruments: knives, long sharp steel tools, pincers, and a saw.

"Where is the room that overlooks the front of the building?" asked Chandal, repulsed by the room that she was now in.

The old woman nodded and picked up her candlestick. She led Chandal down the hallway toward the main door, which she opened, allowing Chandal to enter first.

Immediately Chandal felt damp and cold. Her candlestick flickered and almost went out. She paused for a moment, allowing the flame to restore itself. Next, she held the candlestick high in the air. She could see that she had entered into a snug room not big enough for more than four people. Its pale green walls had burst their fragile exterior paint and had erupted into sinister-looking blisters that had begun to peel badly and drop onto the floor. The tiny space was almost completely swallowed up by the badly faded Victorian couch that sat in the center of the room. Chandal's nostrils pricked with distaste, the rotten odor of decay permeating the air.

Chandal's attention moved to the red brick fireplace, ashes piled about its copper base. On its mantel sat a shiny ebony clock. The time had stopped at nine minutes past twelve. To the left of the clock sat a silver picture frame.

Chandal picked up the frame—stared. It was the young man. The young man whom she had seen on so many occasions wandering about the house.

232

The old woman moved up behind her, holding up her candlestick for more light. "That's the young doctor when they were first married."

"Dead," muttered Chandal to herself. "But I—I've seen him—"

Elizabeth's shoulders shook. She was laughing soundlessly.

Chandal grasped for control, for an image she could understand. No. There was something here beyond understanding—at least, beyond anything she wanted to understand. Another sensation gripped her. Something she should have recognized long ago. She stared closer at the picture, the image searing her consciousness. Oh, God! The young man looked like Justin. Justin was heavier and his mustache wasn't as large, but, nevertheless, they looked alike. She stiffened and felt a surge of fear shoot through her body. She could feel the old woman pressing in on top of her, her warm breath on the back of her neck.

"Do you like him?" the old woman asked.

"The window! I want to see the window!" Chandal screamed, slamming the picture down on the mantel. Violently, she moved around the room. Seeing the drapes that were drawn, she threw them open. She stopped at the cobwebbed window and looked out.

"You see, it's the way I said it would be. The window hasn't been opened for years and there is no one up here." Elizabeth remained by the mantel as Chandal tried to open the window. It would not budge.

Suddenly there was a pattering of footsteps in the darkness. Elizabeth looked around quickly, then whispered, "Someone is coming!"

The door was flung open and a sudden fire ignited in the fireplace. Elizabeth and Chandal stood together while a little light, as if from one candle, fell on their faces. From beyond the door came Magdalen's scream. "What are you doing here?"

Elizabeth quickly sat near the chaise longue and pretended to polish her nails. Magdalen moved into the room and paced back and forth near the window. She looked exactly as she had appeared in Chandal's dream: hair drawn back over her ears, a necklace, her face made up, a tailored skirt and blouse of beige, and on her finger—two rings!

"Sit down, please," Magdalen ordered. She spoke slowly, deliberately, like a woman with a passionate temper who was afraid to lose control of it. "I'm afraid that I must be frank with you. I'm not one of those women who pretend."

Chandal looked around the room. It was the same room as in her dream: the fireplace, the fire; the wallpaper that represented an ancient stag hunt; Elizabeth sitting there pretending to do her nails—it was all the same!

"Justin doesn't want you for his wife any longer," said Magdalen.

Elizabeth broke into a wild scream of laughter. Magdalen ordered her to be silent.

"You're still angry, aren't you, Magdalen? Because I told her about him. What you two are up to." She pointed her thin finger at her sister.

"You whore! You miserable whore!" Magdalen slapped Elizabeth savagely. Over and over again, she beat her around the neck and the face.

"No! Please stop! Please!" Chandal covered her face. The sound of Elizabeth whimpering cut through her brain. Magdalen spun in her direction. "You're to blame for this; I will punish you for it!"

Chandal turned; lost her temper; didn't seem to mind that she was going to pieces. "Goddamn you!" She lurched at Magdalen, who flicked her finger and hissed.

The fire went out. The candles went out. Black.

The air was cold now, but the darkness was worse and Chandal started to shake. Something snapped and struck her hand. She shuddered, pulled back. "Stop it!"

Someone was breathing to her left, circling her. Oh, my God, they're going to kill me! Snap!—the back of her neck. "Goddamn it!" She couldn't breathe, hadn't been able to take a decent breath, reached out her hands—groped and now her stomach was

234

starting to turn. Snap!—the back of her leg. She tumbled to the floor hard. Mind blank, she crawled around on all fours trying to stay alive. Kept looking; kept panting; kept reaching. Someone kicked her—she went down again. Fought hard. She thrashed her arms. Screamed—laughed. Continued to laugh, stopped only to inhale air to laugh some more.

Stopping abruptly, tears sprang to her eyes and she fell unconscious onto the floor.

❧ 19 ❧

JUSTIN HELD A HUMAN SKULL HIGH IN HIS HANDS. It was the first day of rehearsal and he wanted to create an effect. The actors waited eagerly for him to begin. Billy, who had agreed to understudy the two male leads, sat alone near the Coke machine. The stage manager, his coat off, but still immaculately dressed, was seated at a long wooden table prepared to take notes.

The hall was dimly lit.

Stepping onto the tiny rehearsal stage, Justin acknowledged the applause of his actors; he bowed, adjusted the skull slightly, and spoke. ". . . and are we to be told that Franklin here is a savage because he lived and died like a brute, and that his murderer, the honorable Professor Dorrell, is the happy creature of society because he took it upon himself to rid the world of this scum!"

At the back of the theater, the door opened slowly and two men peered in to watch as Justin continued with his eloquent description of the play.

After a brief discussion, Justin walked through the imaginary set that the actors would rehearse upon for the next four weeks. He opened the door and walked under an imaginary archway into the garden. As he moved, he heard a light voice. *"You must rid yourself of your wife,"* it whispered.

"I'm not sure of that," he argued inwardly.

"Your sorrow shall be my sorrow and we will bear it together. But you must get rid of her soon."

Justin grew more silent as he wandered through the rest of the set. He stopped suddenly, standing against the imaginary background of the very large, ornate gold-framed portrait of Professor Dorrell.

The actors watched as Justin grew pale. His body began to shake and beads of sweat rolled down his forehead.

"Hey, you all right?" asked Billy, standing on the stage beside him.

Justin looked around like a man slowly coming out of a dream, trying to grow more accustomed to the familiar things of the real world. "What?" Billy came into focus.

"Are you all right?" Billy asked.

"Oh, yeah. Thanks." Justin turned and walked back through the garden. Now his step was quicker and more purposeful. "No," he continued, "my point is that one cannot look upon him as an insignificant opponent. His medical history is, unfortunately, brilliant."

The morning rehearsal went well. Justin broke for lunch at twelve-thirty P.M. Before leaving the rehearsal hall, the stage manager informed him that the playwright was back in town and would attend the afternoon rehearsal.

"Why?" asked Justin coldly.

"Beats me. He wrote the damn thing. You'd think he'd be sick of it by now."

"What a time to meet the playwright!" Justin threw on his jacket.

"You mean you two haven't met yet?" asked Billy, sticking his script into his coat pocket.

"No. He's been in Europe. I wish to hell he'd stayed there!" It had been difficult to convince the producers

236

not to sit in on rehearsals. Now he had to convince the playwright.

Pushing their way through the Broadway crowd, Justin and Billy ducked into Charlie's for lunch. Shouts of laughter and a dribble of singing hit them as they walked through the door. The tables were packed tight with producers, actors, models, and writers.

Moving slowly into the room, Justin waved to several people he knew. All were a little tight and very talkative. Billy stopped at the bar to say hello to an actress friend. She was half-tipsy, giggling, and unpleasant.

Justin finally managed to secure a table and they sat down.

"A refined gathering, wouldn't you say?" Justin felt uncomfortable. It was the first time since he'd moved into the brownstone (two days short of a month) that he'd actually stepped into a theatrical pub, and it annoyed him.

The two men from the theater had followed Justin to Charlie's and were now standing at the bar. Each ordered Scotch and drank it slowly, watching Justin and Billy as they ate lunch. Finally, they faced the bartender and began to talk between themselves.

Justin watched Billy salt the last half of his cheeseburger and couldn't help but envy his appetite.

"What's the matter, aren't you hungry?" Billy asked.

"Not really." Justin continued to nurse his drink, ignoring the chef's salad that he'd ordered.

"I'm starving," said Billy. And Justin said, "I can see that."

Billy motioned. "Do you see Pacino sitting over there?"

Justin nodded.

Billy's appetite for food varied with his state of mind. The sight of his excellent appetite was a sure sign that he was once again an employed actor.

"What happened to you at rehearsal today? You looked awful."

"I don't know." Justin paused for a moment, then added, "Have you ever had times when you couldn't remember where you were or what you were doing?"

"Yeah, every time I'm with my girl!" He threw more salt on his burger.

"I'm serious."

"Like what?"

"I don't know. Lately, at home—I go down into the basement at night to work on a few pictures. Next thing I know, three, maybe four hours have passed, but I can't seem to remember what I've done during that time. Everything has been changed around, but I still don't remember doing anything."

"You're in love."

Justin smiled sadly. "I wish you were right."

"Why, you and Chandal aren't getting along?"

"Not really. I find it easier to talk with Magdalen."

"Magdalen who?" Billy polished off the last of his coffee, wiped his lips with his napkin, and lit a cigarette.

"Would you like more coffee?" asked the waiter.

"No, thanks."

Justin waited for him to clear away the plates before he answered Billy.

"The woman at the party. I introduced her to you."

"What party?"

"Chandal and I—to celebrate the new—" He cut himself off. Thinking of the baby had a strange effect on him. It had brought death back into his life, made him more aware of his own mortality. It shook him a little, because he couldn't see anything beyond this life. He had refused to see beyond it, just as an audience refuses to see beyond the scenery in a theater. He had thought about the baby from time to time, which brought back the headaches, which brought back the fact that he had once lost his sight in one eye. Besides, he had always secretly thought that at the moment of his own death, he would be able to get around it somehow, that he would be able to cheat death. The baby had made that seem impossible.

"You mean the old lady from the brownstone—Magdalen?"

"Yes." He was beginning to perspire.

"You find it easy to talk to her? I didn't. She kept busting my balls when I was over there painting. 'You're too loud. It's late. Couldn't you finish tomorrow?' I told her to take a walk!"

"She's a nice woman."

"To each his own." Billy glanced around, waved to the tall blonde at the bar.

Justin sat quietly and let the images of Magdalen run through his mind. He knew her every feature. He knew her birthday, her favorite music, books, food, and flowers. There wasn't a single aspect of her life that he wasn't aware of.

Again Justin could feel himself being removed from his surroundings. Then he heard a gentle voice—*I desire you—come to me.*

"Soon!" he mumbled.

"What?" Billy asked, seeing the strained lines in Justin's face.

Justin turned sharply, looked around the room, and jumped to his feet. He was afraid to sit there any longer. He gulped down his drink and left the restaurant, leaving Billy to pay the bill. When Billy went outside, Justin had disappeared.

Justin sat alone in the darkened theater trying to understand his obsession for Magdalen. The theater was completely empty; no one had returned from lunch yet. Through a small crack at the bottom of the window, he could hear the wind blowing, a soft whistling sound like a tea kettle about to boil.

And out in the hallway the shapes of two men hovered in the shadows. Footsteps started up the stairwell and the two men ducked into the bathroom to the right.

The theater door opened and Justin could barely make out the heavily built, elderly man who entered the room. He moved nearer the work light; Justin saw that his hair was long and curly and iron-gray, his face unaccustomed to smiling. "Hi, I'm Adler. J. J. Adler."

Playwrights always bothered Justin, and this one

239

was no different. He proceeded to ask Justin all the usual questions that directors hear a million times. How do you see the play being done? Have you ever directed this type of play? Do you think we need better actors? Will the audiences like my play? He removed a clay pipe from his breast pocket and lit it.

"I believe that murder—any murder—will cause an audience to think. Whether they relate to Franklin or care—that depends on the actor. We have the best." Justin wasn't sure what he'd just said, but the playwright looked impressed. Pointless going on.

The pace picked up now. Actors milled about. Billy kicked the Coke machine trying to retrieve his money. The female lead, who was still sure Justin disliked her, nodded, smiled—asshole! If her husband hadn't put up the money, there wouldn't have been a play. She didn't feel guilty for forcing herself on Justin, she decided.

Rehearsal began promptly at two P.M.

From time to time, Justin glanced at the playwright to catch his reaction. The playwright remained expressionless and just sucked on his pipe.

Chandal's mother let the phone ring many times and then she hung up. She knew Chandal was home and was deliberately not answering the phone. Why? She hadn't meant to upset anyone. Yes, she had left the brownstone, had left Chandal when she needed her. But that wasn't worth this kind of treatment. It was one-forty-five in the afternoon and already she was exhausted. She wanted to talk to someone, anyone, but there wasn't anyone.

In the room across the hall a woman was dying of cancer. Chandal's mother watched as the woman's eldest son prepared to leave.

"It won't do us any good," he said softly.

The woman said nothing. Instead, she picked up a newspaper that lay on the antiseptic white table next to her bed and began to read. The boy left without saying another word.

From where she stood, Chandal's mother saw that

the woman was crying. She understood. She rang for the nurse and waited. Chandal shouldn't treat her this way—it wasn't fair.

"Yes?" the nurse asked.

"The woman across the hall—she's in pain."

She nodded, took her hand from her blue uniformed pocket. "Thank you." She moved across the hall into the next room. Brief discussion, needle, and the woman was soon asleep.

Chandal's mother called the house again with no luck. She was furious now and took it out on the nurses. She complained about her lunch, the lack of heat in her room, and the constant noise in the hallways.

In the next hour, she suffered an extreme case of diarrhea. Each time the nurse was called, and Chandal's mother had to be helped to and from the bathroom. Annoyed, the nurse finally made some comment about her illness being psychological.

"Psychological! What's the difference? It's enough to keep me in the hospital, isn't it?"

"Well, that's true." The nurse smiled.

"Let me tell you, young lady—I'm in constant pain. Is that psychological?"

Suddenly Chandal's mother was violently thrown against the wall! Her eyes rolled back into her head and blood started running from her nose and ears. The nurse quickly rang the emergency buzzer.

Each time she reached out for the nurse's hand, she was flung back against the wall.

Then, with a sudden, violent wrench, she found herself plummeted face first against the concrete wall. Something had grabbed hold of the back of her neck and kept smashing her forehead forward.

The nurse panicked, tried to grab her, tried to pull her away from the wall. Helen turned, twisting her head violently from one side to the other.

The nurse shook her. "Stop that! Stop that!"

Helen was fighting to stay alive. She lunged at the nurse, grabbing her by the hair, clawing at her face with her fingernails.

241

The nurse fell back, stumbled, and hit the floor with a thud.

Helen's arms were ripped straight out, even with her shoulders, rendering her paralyzed. She screamed and something smashed across her mouth, sending her against the wall again, where she hung in a cruciform position, and then dropped to the floor.

By the time help had arrived, she lay on the cold slab floor in a pool of her own blood.

Chandal woke up screaming. She'd seen her mother lying on the hospital floor covered with blood. She sat staring; she didn't know what had happened. Bed, bedroom, sitting up. She was desperate for something to remember. Magdalen and Elizabeth, both of them; the first fear hit her—the attic. Then she moved her hand as the second fear hit her—her mother. The phone rang. It was the hospital. They told her that her mother was in critical condition, that she should come to the hospital as soon as possible.

Chandal slammed down the receiver and called Justin. She was hysterical. When she reached him, she tried to explain what had happened, but she wasn't making sense. Justin told her to calm down, that he would pick her up in a cab and that they would go to the hospital together. Justin left the actors with the stage manager, got into a cab, and headed north to the brownstone.

Chandal was standing outside in the freezing cold when Justin arrived. In her haste to leave the house, she'd forgotten to put on her coat. Justin helped her into the cab, removed his jacket, and wrapped it around her. She was shaking miserably and spent the rest of the time in the back seat of the cab crying.

Dr. Margolin swiftly took Chandal and Justin aside and had a difficult time explaining exactly what had happened. The head nurse was called in, along with the nurse who was in attendance when the incident occurred.

"Please," Dr. Margolin said after the two nurses

were seated, "tell Mr. and Mrs. Knight how this thing happened." His frustration at being unable to comprehend the situation himself made him edgy, causing him to fidget with the pen and pencil set on the desk. Involved in one malpractice suit already, he wasn't looking for a second.

The nurse simply told what had happened as she saw it. Chandal's mother had been irritable and depressed all morning. In order to punish herself and the others in the hospital, she'd deliberately thrown herself against the wall, causing cuts across her arms and back, several nasty bumps on her head, and internal hemorrhaging.

Chandal was furious. "I don't believe this! Just like that, my mother flung herself against the goddamn wall!"

"Honey, calm down." Justin reached for her hand. She jerked it away.

"I won't calm down! The whole thing is ridiculous!"

"Mrs. Knight," the nurse said softly, "your mother attacked me when I tried to stop her."

Only then did Chandal notice that the nurse wore a flesh-colored band-aid across her forehead, and that there were two deep gash marks across her right cheek.

"Why would she attack you?"

The head nurse moved forward in her chair. "Because your mother has always expressed a dislike for Nurse Thomas. In fact, she has stated on a number of occasions that she hates all nurses."

"But there must have been a reason. A person doesn't suddenly become violent!" Chandal fumbled for her cigarettes. The pack was empty.

"Would you like one of these?" The doctor held out a pack of Marlboros.

"Thank you." She steadied her hand, but was still unable to remove a cigarette from the pack.

"Here, honey, let me." Justin took the pack from her hand.

"If you remember, Mrs. Knight"—the doctor edged slowly into the conversation—"I told you over the

243

phone that I was worried about your mother's emotional well-being. I asked you then if your mother was suicidal."

"And I told you no! My mother has never acted like this!"

"Here you go, Del." Justin had lit the cigarette and then handed it to her.

"Thanks."

Justin slid the pack of cigarettes back onto the doctor's desk.

"Have you spent much time with her lately?" The doctor had wanted to avoid that question, if at all possible.

Chandal exhaled and came face to face with four pairs of eyes staring at her. "She just spent a week in our apartment, didn't she? She seemed all right then."

Justin moved uncomfortably in his chair. The doctor caught the movement.

"Is that true, Mr. Knight?"

Justin glanced uneasily at Chandal. "She did seem a little tense."

"Oh, for Christ's sake!" Chandal drew in hard on the cigarette.

"Del, she did."

"So did we all, but we didn't go out and attack anyone."

"Mrs. Knight, I believe your mother is suffering from schizophrenia. Some sort of ego breakdown."

"From what?" she said sharply.

"I'm not a psychiatrist. You would have—"

"So just like that, she starts inflicting pain on herself?" Chandal turned to the nurse. "Just like that, my mother flung herself against the wall?"

"That's right."

"Why!?"

"I've already told you. She had been in a deep state of depression."

"But why take it out on herself?" Chandal cried furiously. "Something isn't right here. I want to see her —now!"

244

"But she's in a semi-state of consciousness," said the head nurse and turned from the position she had taken in the chair near the door and looked at the doctor. He put his finger up to his lips and indicated that Chandal should have her way.

"Follow me," said the head nurse, rising from her chair. She led Chandal and Justin down a long corridor to the elevator, pressed the UP button. Justin held Chandal firmly with one arm. Looking into her sad eyes, he felt that he'd betrayed her. He could see the weeks of hell that she'd been going through written across her face. He brushed a few strands of hair away from her eyes and kissed her gently on the forehead.

The knot of people tangled inside the open door of the elevator made it almost impossible to step inside. There was a moment of voices shouting, cursing, and threatening.

The noise of the crowd rose. Chandal put her hands over her ears. Justin insisted that they wait for the next elevator in order to give Chandal a chance to rest. The elevator door closed and they sat down on a bench in the hallway.

"Honey, are you going to be all right?" he asked.

"I'll get the smelling salts." The nurse hurried away down the corridor.

"Oh, God! First the baby, and now this!" she said.

Justin was silent. He'd been trying to think of something to say, to make everything all right. He knew that he'd done nothing to make it easier for Chandal since she'd lost the child. Why had he treated her so badly?

He tried to recall how he'd ever managed to let things get so far out of hand. He remembered how difficult it had been on both of them to actually move, and that Chandal had really wanted to go to California. It was Chandal who singlehandedly had done most of the packing, finishing in barely enough time to move into their new apartment.

Irritated with himself, Justin turned to see what was keeping the nurse. The corridor was empty. "Honey, you wait here. I'll see what's keeping her."

"No, please—don't leave me!" She clung to his arm. and pulled him back onto the bench.

He nodded and held her hand and then saw the nurse coming toward them from the end of the corridor. She stopped to open a door and stuck her head inside. Justin could hear her speak into the room behind the door, but though her voice was loud, he still couldn't catch the words.

Chandal couldn't wait any longer; she was going to be sick. She wrenched her arm away from Justin and dashed into the bathroom, where she vomited. Her whole body was shaking uncontrollably.

The nurse snapped the smelling salts under Chandal's nose. Chandal's head shot back and she started to gag all over again. Forty minutes passed before Chandal was able to see her mother.

Motionless, her mother lay there, battered and bruised. She had a tube up her nostril and an electrical gadget recorded her heartbeat. The nurse indicated that Chandal and Justin should proceed into the room with caution.

In the center of the room stood another nurse. Behind her, standing protectively close to the bed, was a young intern. Both moved aside as Chandal advanced.

At first, her mother didn't seem to recognize her. Then tears started to gush from her eyes. The nurse moved to the bed and patted the tears away with gauze.

"Please, may I speak with her?" Chandal asked in a low voice.

"Only for a moment." The nurse moved away and stood beside the intern. Chandal moved close and sat on the edge of the bed. Justin leaned on the table at the foot of the bed and watched the thin green lines pulsate across the monitor.

"Momma, can you hear me? It's Chandal." She looked down at her and there was silence for a moment. A little girl stopped by the open doorway and peered in: almost in shadow, her hair mixed into the darkness, but her white face and pale, naked shoul-

246

ders remained visible. The intern moved behind Justin and closed the door.

"Momma, what happened?" Chandal leaned forward, hoping that she could be heard.

Her mother tried to speak, but it was only a little wind-blown whisper of a voice and Chandal could not understand a word of it. Her mother tried again; this time the whisper was louder and Chandal could begin to hear the words. But it was impossible to make any sense out of what she was saying.

"Please, I think you should let her rest," said the nurse, moving up behind Justin.

"Wait, just one more minute. She's trying to tell me something. Go ahead, Momma. I can hear you."

Then Chandal heard the fragments of a sentence.

"Punish . . . us. She has . . . punished us," her mother whispered, then fell into a state of unconsciousness. With a sudden jerk of the muscles, her mouth dropped open, as though she were continuing to speak.

Chandal looked around the room in a panic. The intern quickly checked her heartbeat as the nurse checked her pulse. The nurse reassured Chandal that her mother was all right, that she'd just fallen asleep.

Justin walked over to Chandal and beckoned her away from the bed. There was a slight knock on the door. The intern opened it, allowing Dr. Margolin to step inside. After a brief examination, the doctor also assured Chandal that her mother was resting comfortably.

Outside the hospital, the snow had begun to fall again. Chandal waited in the doorway as Justin tried to hail a cab. Next to her stood a woman with a baby in her arms. She hugged it to her, covered its small face with a blanket, and hurried over the white snow to an awaiting car. Chandal thought of her baby, but did not cry. She had no tears left.

247

❧ 20 ❧

CHANDAL SAT IN THE KITCHEN LATER THAT NIGHT and heard her mother's words, from the voice of her mind, but the wind whipped through the backyard and would not let the words finish, but blew them away.

Justin put a penny in her hand. He looked down at her and smiled. "For your thoughts."

"I don't know. I just can't help thinking about what my mother said—that she had punished us." She picked up her cigarette from the ashtray.

"She was delirious."

Chandal remembered what Magdalen had told her earlier—that she would punish her for coming into her private room. That had happened. She was there. She inhaled deeply. Her throat was dry and sore. No matter. She inhaled again, looked at Justin, and wondered if she should tell him about what had happened this morning. Would he think she was crazy? Maybe she was. She was in the bedroom when the phone rang. How did she get there? First she was with the sisters. Then— She put the cigarette out in the ashtray. "Justin, I had a long talk with Elizabeth today."

"Oh, really? What did she have to say?"

"She told me that Magdalen used to be married to a young doctor and that they lived in this house until his death." She paused, then added, "She showed me where they lived. An apartment on the third floor."

Justin turned. "You went up to the third floor?"

"Yes. Elizabeth and I."

"And Magdalen let you?"

"Well, at first she wasn't home."

"What do you mean—at first?"

Chandal could detect the tension that had crept in-

248

to Justin's voice. "She came in while we were up there. I don't know how it happened, but she and Elizabeth started to argue and she began to slap Elizabeth."

He thought, goddamn it!

But aloud he said, "Oh, Christ! Chandal, how could you? You know what she said about going up there. Now she's going to blame me!"

Chandal saw that Justin's only concern was for what Magdalen might think of him. He became furious and shouted at the top of his lungs. Throwing his coffee cup into the sink, he wheeled on her. "You're an idiot, do you know that? A damn idiot! Why did you go up there in the first place? She told you not to!"

"Because someone nearly killed me with a flower-pot—that's why!"

"What are you talking about?"

"When I came back into the house this morning, I stopped at the foot of the stairs and waited for the mailman to finish with the mail. As I stood there, a flowerpot fell from the third floor and nearly hit me. When I looked up, someone was just closing the window. When I asked Elizabeth who it was, she denied that anyone was up there."

"Of course there was no one up there!"

"Then what made the flowerpot fall like that?"

Justin crossed to the back kitchen window and flung it open. "The wind, Chandal—can you feel it? Hear it? It was the damn wind!" He shook his head, like a monstrous dog coming out of water. And then he began to laugh a high, clear yelping laugh that frightened Chandal. "You keep saying that you're not imagining things, but each day you come up with a new story!" He slammed the window shut.

She saw that Justin was in no mood to hear any-more. She wanted to tell him about the picture of the young doctor, how much it looked like him, but knew he wouldn't believe her. And the fire that had ignited by itself when Magdalen entered the room. She knew she hadn't imagined it. Any of it.

Justin stood by the window looking out. "I don't know what's happening to us, Chandal. I really don't." Then he walked up and down in the kitchen and glanced out the window every few minutes.

"What are you looking at?" Chandal asked.

"Nothing." But Justin was lying. There in the shadows, he saw a young man. He'd seen him come up from the cellar and cross to the center of the yard. The young man looked so much like himself that at first he'd thought he was seeing his own reflection in the glass. But as he watched, the young man moved about in the snow and he knew that it couldn't possibly be a reflection. He rubbed his temple. If he had a brain in his head, he wouldn't be here. He hadn't wanted to blow up like that. I'm sorry, he thought.

"I'll start dinner," Chandal said, halfheartedly rising to her feet.

"I'm not hungry!"

"But you said you skipped lunch."

"So what? I'm still not hungry." He slipped on his coat and reached for his hat.

"Where are you going?"

"The cellar door is open. I'll have to close it."

She watched through the kitchen window as Justin went into the backyard. No sooner had he stepped outside than the wind tore the hat from his head. Retrieving it, he sank into a bank of snow and almost fell. Constantly, he watched for the prowler, but he had gone.

His hat pulled down over his forehead, he finally reached the cellar door. From the steamed-over window, Chandal peered out at him. He shook his head in annoyance and disappeared down the cellar stairs, closing the door behind him.

Chandal heard him throw the large bolt into place, his footsteps descending the stairs below and the lower door closing on its rusty hinges. Silence.

Justin turned on the light in the basement and looked around. The basement floor was covered with a light coating of snow that had blown in from the backyard while the door was left open. It was the first time to his knowledge that the door had ever been opened. Who had opened it?

By the time Justin swept up the loose snow, Chandal had brought him a hot cup of coffee and was now examining the mannequins. She vividly remembered the night she'd lost the baby and was surprised to see that all the mannequins looked alike and resembled no one in particular. But there were fewer of them now. Or were there? She wasn't sure. She took a step back.

Justin had just finished cleaning up and was taking his first sip of coffee when he glanced through the small window that looked out on the wintry trees and shrubs in the yard. A young man's face stared back at him.

"Damn!" He slammed down the cup and darted for the basement door. Startled, Chandal spun around.

"What's the matter?"

"There's someone prowling around in the yard!" He flung open the first door, leaped up the stairs, threw open the second door, and practically fell into the backyard on all fours. But as soon as he reached the yard, the prowler was gone.

Justin searched around for footprints; there were none. He next looked for a way in or out of the yard. Again, he discovered that there was none.

Returning to the basement, he took off his coat and flung it over the back of the chair.

"Who was it?" Chandal asked.

"No one—just a dog!" He immediately set about nailing the basement door shut.

Chandal occupied herself with a closer examination of the room. Back against the south wall were two large kerosine drums, an empty fire bucket, and gardening tools. Next to them stood a small table with sewing gadgets and bales of wool and cotton reels. Years of dust covered everything.

Brushing the cobwebs away, she took up a piece of loose cloth in her hand. It was especially pretty material, bright red and wonderfully soft to the touch.

Suddenly she could picture the young girl sitting by the fire sewing. Hatless, but still in his cloak, the young man entered the room. The girl looked up as he came in, smiled, and put her sewing down. He crossed to her; kissed her; stood still for a moment then, looking down at her, he said, *"I love you."*

I love you, too, she replied.

"What?" Justin hollered without stopping his hammering.

"I didn't say anything," said Chandal, putting down the piece of cloth.

"Oh, I thought I heard you say something!"

For a brief moment, Chandal felt herself reduced to a tiny pinpoint of identity, as if she were the young girl whom she had just imagined, and no longer herself. Did she say, "I love you?" This was not the first time she'd felt the loss of her own identity, and with it came the feeling of solitude. Unending, alien solitude.

It was ten o'clock by the time Justin had finally nailed the basement door shut. The snow was still coming down as they entered the kitchen. Justin switched off the basement light and closed the door. "God, what a day!" He moved to the sink to wash his hands.

"I know!" She handed him a towel. "Do you think Mom will be all right?"

"Sure. She's a tough old bird." He dropped the towel on the countertop and removed his shirt. Next he sat at the edge of the chair and kicked off his shoes and pulled off his socks. Dressed in only his jeans, he leaned his head back against the kitchen wall and shut his eyes.

For the first time in days, Chandal took a close look at her husband. His mustache was fully grown now and looked dashing. His body had grown lean and muscular. The short haircut accented the sharp features of his face; his lips looked moist and sensual. She couldn't bring herself to tell Justin what she was thinking, that she wanted him to make love to her. "I think I'll take a hot shower," she said. "How about you?"

"Maybe later," he said, without moving or opening his eyes. In the silence that followed, Chandal went into the bathroom, removed her clothes, and stepped into the shower. Each movement accentuated her physical need and longing for Justin.

She turned the hot water on and let it play across her skin.

Upstairs in the attic, the old woman looked around the room with fear and revulsion. A cake of blood had dried on her cheek. Her voice was as deep as a man's and heavy and slow. She repeated over and over again, "But I tell you, he is no good, he's like an animal! Won't you send him away? If you won't—I will!"

How easy it had been. She simply had walked into his room, slowly, on tiptoes. The slightest noise would have brought attention to her being there. So she had moved quietly, cautiously, as if suspended in midair. Her hands were not trembling. The knife was not trembling.

Holding the knife so, she had walked closer and closer until she had stood over him—and with one thrust, she had plunged the knife into his chest!

Chandal had finished soaping herself and was just about to reach for the washcloth when she saw she was standing in a pool of blood! "Oh, my God!" she gasped. Stepping back, she tried to understand what was happening to her. The blood now flowed from the shower head, running down her body between her legs. She tried to rip open the shower curtain, but slipped and fell to one knee, tearing the curtain. The blood was everywhere, running into her eyes, her nose. With her arms tangled in the curtain, she couldn't free herself. The blood splattered on the walls as she flung her arms wildly, trying to escape.

Justin was brought to his feet by Chandal's horrified scream. He rushed into the bathroom and found his wife curled up against the bathroom tiles, completely naked and half out of her mind. He lifted her up and tried to calm her.

"Blood! In there—blood!" she screamed.

Justin reached in and shut off the water, which was scalding-hot, steam clouding the entire bathroom. He checked the tub to see what she meant, but couldn't see anything resembling blood. "Honey, there's nothing here."

It took nearly an hour to convince her that she had imagined the blood. The tub was checked again and again; nothing was found. Chandal looked into his eyes. She was startled and afraid.

He smiled. They sat in the living room and said very little after that. He looked at her and slowly took her hand. She was calm now, almost peaceful.

It was a little after midnight when they walked hand in hand into the bedroom and went to sleep.

The outside cellar door smashed against the ground.

Justin's head jerked slightly and then his eyes opened. A loud banging sound was coming from the cellar. *"What the hell is that?"*

Chandal never stirred as he put on his robe and went into the kitchen. He turned on the light. It was four in the morning!

Justin opened the cellar door, switched on the light, and descended the cellar stairs. He was shocked to see the basement floor entirely covered over with snow. *"Goddamn it!"*

Both the outside and inside basement doors were wide open. Angrily, Justin climbed the outside stairs, pulled the outer door shut, and bolted it. Once he had closed the inside door, he moved the large kerosine drum in front of it. Let's see the wind move that! he thought.

Too exhausted to bother with the snow, he turned out the light, crawled back into bed, and went to sleep.

When Chandal's mother opened her eyes later that night, she was floating away from her bed. The room was almost completely dark, except for a small night-light that burned near the door. The tube had been ripped from her nose, and her nose was bleeding.

Slowly, her body began to move. She tried to call out for help, but gagged on her own tongue. The more she tried to call for help, the more she choked on her own words.

254

She could sense that there was someone else in the room with her. Standing near the small nightlight was the little girl. Her pale white face was smiling now as she repeated in a singsong fashion, "I hate you, I hate you, I truly do!"

The mother's body spun around and around in a circle in rhythm to the little girl's chanting. The faster she chanted, the faster the mother's body rotated. Until finally, her body was flung through the large plate-glass window on the seventh floor. At last, she could make a sound. She screamed and kept screaming until her body broke apart on the pavement below.

The phone in the living room rang several times before Chandal heard it. She immediately woke Justin.

"What? What is it?" he asked, rising up on his elbows.

"The telephone!"

"At this hour!" He picked up the small alarm clock. "It's five o'clock in the morning!"

"We better answer it."

"The hell with it—let it ring!"

"Justin, please—answer it."

Justin looked at her and didn't say anything. Flinging the covers from the bed, he stormed into the living room and answered the phone. It was the hospital. They were sorry to have to deliver the news, but Chandal's mother had just committed suicide.

❧ 21 ❧

BUT WHEN THE SMOKE TRAILED OFF AND HER CIGA-rette was snuffed out, Chandal was still left with one thought. I wasn't there for you, Momma. I just wasn't there for you. She sat back and listened to the sound of traffic rumble outside the Medical Examiner's Building at 520 First Avenue. Morning rush hour.

She'd wanted to see the body, but they all said no. The doctor, the medical examiner, Justin—they all said no, and with each no, Chandal's imagination had created a more distorted image.

"Justin, is it that bad? Is it horrible?"

"Honey . . ." He couldn't look at her, hung an arm around her shoulders. "She's not in that body anymore. She's . . ."

"So it is that horrible," she said with dry eyes. Silence. "You know, everything went all wrong. I had a bad feeling inside me. I don't know why. I thought I didn't love her. She thought I didn't love her. But I did. I really did. I know I did, because now it hurts so much." Her voice broke.

Justin hesitated uncomfortably. "Honey . . ."

"What?" Again she was matter of fact, blowing her nose, forcing her voice to steady itself.

"God, I hate it. But rehearsals . . ."

"You go. No, really. I understand." She made a smile. She was still smiling after he was gone from her; gone in the cab, to rehearsal.

That afternoon, she sat in the front office of the Westside Holy Chapel. The funeral director, a woman of indeterminate age with deepset eyes behind large spectacles, set the form in front of her.

"Here. Fill this out," she said with insatiable and even predatory curiosity. The form was long and complicated. It covered everything from the deceased's Social Security number to the number of mourners expected at the wake. Below that were listed the number of candles, benches, chairs, and coat racks requested.

In the blank space marked "cemetery," Chandal wrote: *Fern Cliff Cemetery, Hartsdale, N.Y.* Her mother had been born and raised there and her father was buried in Hartsdale.

She paused for a moment at the next blank space. According to the funeral director, Chandal was now the plot owner. The last surviving member of the family.

"Is there something wrong?" asked the woman with a sympathetic smile.

"Oh, no. No." The last surviving member of the family. There was something she was trying to remember. Justin, she thought, taking a sharp breath. It was the link, the thing that they had in common. Justin and she were both the last surviving members of their immediate families. She felt a coldness in the pit of her stomach. She tried to think of another couple, just one couple their age, who had lost all four parents. Was it planned? she wondered. Did Magdalen know when she asked them to move in that three of their parents were dead already? Had her mother's death been arranged? Had Magdalen— She stopped. *No, I can't really be thinking this,* she thought, pushing the ridiculous paranoia away back into the recesses of darkness. *I can't believe something so insane. I can't be thinking it at all,* came another voice, a voice of caution. *It's dangerous for me to think it. They know what I'm thinking.*

She clasped her hands together, forced herself to look into the funeral director's professionally concerned eyes. *I'm fine now,* she reassured the woman silently with a forced smile. *I've just been through so much, it's made me think things that aren't possible, aren't real. But I'm fine now. See? I'm relaxed.*

But, of course, she wasn't. Today, as never before, she felt emotionally exhausted. Her mother's death had completely drained her, it seemed, of the last ounce of response. She no longer knew what she felt. Her only emotion, as always in such instances, was a lukewarm resentment against herself for not being stronger.

Perhaps she spent too much time analyzing herself, left too many questions unanswered, leaving herself scattered in a million places. She knew what she should feel, should think, but—

After a long silence, the funeral director said in a soft, kind voice, "I know it's hard. Here, let me help you."

Patiently, the woman guided Chandal to the bottom of the first page. It was finally determined that her mother would be laid out the following evening from six to nine P.M. in a closed casket. The burial would take place the following morning.

The woman, now seemingly rushed for time, turned the page and proceeded to itemize the services that would be provided: Transfer of Deceased; Securing Permits; Embalming; Merchandise—casket, clothing, flowers, etc. Total: $2,642.36.

Business concluded, Chandal was escorted to the front door, where the woman extended a limp hand. "You can be assured that we will take care of everything." Chandal left the chapel without looking back.

Around four o'clock, the funeral director called the brownstone with misgivings. The Fern Cliff Cemetery wasn't sure that they could bury her mother on Thursday. The snow had reached a record twenty-six inches in two days.

"Well, then—what can I do?" asked Chandal nervously.

"Well, the alternative is to place your mother in their receiving vault until they are able to break ground."

"Is this customary?"

"Oh, yes, indeed. It happens all the time. Last month, the grave diggers went out on strike. It was really quite a problem. But we managed."

"I see."

"We also have a problem with the church. Because Thursday is a religious holiday, they will be unable to conduct the services. I suggest we arrange for services to be held directly after the wake. Is that agreeable?"

Chandal agreed, hung up, and shook her head sadly. Walking to the kitchen window, she looked out and watched the clouds. It was an exceedingly gray day and the backyard was thick with snow. The branches on the trees were bent low from the ice that had formed on them and appeared to be ready to break at any moment.

She moved to the kitchen table, picked up a pencil, and attempted to jot down all of the things that had to be done. The paper remained blank. If they had only gone to California, surely none of it would have happened. Horrible thought—that it didn't have to happen. What was it the woman . . . the seer—what had she said? To go away. Far away. The brownstone had brought her nothing but grief. In less than a month, she'd lost her baby, her mother, and perhaps the love Justin once felt for her. Had the woman seen this? And Sheila—had she seen that, too?

Mintz came into the room and jumped up on the countertop. She eyed her empty food dish in dismay.

"What's the matter, Mintz is hungry?" Chandal smiled weakly at the way Mintz nuzzled up against her arm in answer to her question. "Okay, chow time," she said, reaching into the cabinet for Mintz's food.

Chandal, I'm sorry, the soft voice said from behind her.

Mintz raised her back and hissed. With lightning quickness, she leaped from the counter to the table and down, hitting the floor with a heavy double thud, like the impacts of two wet rags. She ran from the room, nails scratching the waxed floor in her hurry to escape.

I'm truly sorry. There it was again! She heard the voice clearly in her head; she was unable to turn around. A hand placed itself gently upon her shoulders. *Come to the cellar tonight. At ten. I must talk with you,* the voice whispered. Chandal wasn't sure what the voice was really telling her to do. She began to scream. Her mother's death had finally hit her full force and she couldn't stop screaming. There was a gaping wound opened up in her stomach and she wanted to die. Screams were followed by tears, nonstop for almost two hours.

The actress' response to Justin was a four-letter vulgarism which she had never used before, at least not at rehearsals. She retreated from the challenge

259

Justin had flung back at her by going to the frost-sheathed window of the theater.

But Justin repeated the challenge of: "Well?"

She wheeled from the window as if forcibly turned. "Okay. Have it your way, but—" She broke off and returned to the stage. For Justin, a small victory had been won, but he drew no satisfaction from it. The actors waited for his next direction—there was none. He was caught in the middle of the ebb and flow of his own emotions. He was now two personalities. And sometimes he lived in a gray shaded area between the two—as now. What was it he had been saying?

Rehearsal became a disaster. Every few minutes the playwright would stop the actors to explain that he hadn't meant for his lines to be read in that particular fashion.

Stepping onto the stage, Adler demonstrated the vocal and physical techniques needed to bring the full richness of his script to life. The actors grew warlike and started to argue. The stage manager looked to Justin, who looked the other way. By eleven A.M., the two lead actors refused to tolerate the situation any longer and stormed out of the theater.

"I don't understand actors today. It's my play; we'll do it *my* way or we'll not do it at all!" Adler slammed his script down on the table.

"You better go over there and calm him down," Billy whispered into Justin's ear.

"He's an ass."

"What's wrong with you?"

"Nothing's wrong with me. How the hell can I direct with him around?"

Billy sighed, straddled a chair, and sat down. "Hey, buddy, you gotta get your act together. We're falling apart here. You don't seem to care."

"I don't."

"What the hell is wrong with you? This can be a big play if you handle it right."

"Let him direct it if he wants to."

"Come on. What's the matter?"

Justin shrugged. "I don't know."

"Well, Christ, Justin—speculate!"

"How should I know? I can't think anymore." He pressed his fingers into the center of his forehead, the pain behind his eyes sticking like pins. "I don't have the energy anymore."

"Listen." Billy moved closer to Justin. "Just get through the day."

Justin slowly removed his hands from his eyes and stared at Billy. "What?"

Billy smiled. "You heard me. It'll be all right if you go with it. Take charge. Everything'll work out fine."

"I just have to get my head on straight."

"Sure. In the meantime, relax."

"What makes you so calm all of a sudden?" Justin stared evenly at Billy.

"Me? Calm?"

"Yeah. You're like a different person all of a sudden."

"Why rock the boat, right? Look on the bright side," Billy told him. "At least it's a job."

Justin started laughing. They both laughed.

Lunch was called as a temporary solution.

Justin swallowed a cup of lentil soup and ate a roast beef sandwich, and he awoke from his stupor. The playwright was the biggest problem, he thought, lighting a cigarette. Easily enough solved. He'd throw him out.

After lunch, back at the theater, Justin put his policy into action. The playwright was barred from the theater.

"How can I tell Adler he can't observe a rehearsal of his own play?" asked the stage manager.

"Easy. You just open your mouth and say—'Out, asshole!'"

But it wasn't that easy.

"I'll call the police!" Adler screamed from outside the locked door.

"Call God if you like!" Justin screamed back. "But you're not getting back into the theater!"

"We'll see about that!"

Justin listened as Adler slammed the outer lobby door. "Good. Now maybe we can get some work done."

"Atta way to go!" Billy began to laugh out loud. Getting to his feet, he came around the table and slapped Justin on the shoulder. "Now that's the way a director should act!"

Justin suddenly felt that he was being manipulated like a puppet. That Billy was maneuvering him. He removed Billy's hand from his shoulder. "Let's get back to work."

Billy kept on smiling, but he could see that Justin was disconcerted. He watched as Justin moved down the aisle. With a fearful leap onto the stage, like a matador entering a bull ring, Justin hollered, "We'll start at the top of Act One."

Billy's smile faded. Slipping into an aisle seat, he let his body slouch down, let his knees press against the back of the seat in front of him. He stared at Justin intently; Justin was sitting profile to him, the hard lines of his features softened in the dim light. Everything was going exactly as planned, Billy thought. Exactly as planned.

Justin spent the afternoon trying to repair the damage that the playwright had left in his wake, but his mind wandered once again. He called breaks every half-hour and spent the time thinking of Magdalen. Chandal and the death of her mother never crossed his mind.

By four-thirty, only Billy and the stage manager were left in the theater. Justin threw his script across the room and shouted, "A piece of crap! That's all it is—garbage!"

"What's the matter with you? Just yesterday you were telling me how great it was." Billy slid off the stool to face Justin.

"That was yesterday! Did you hear him this morning? The man's an idiot. If we did the play his way, we'd be laughed off the stage!"

"If that's what he wants," said the stage manager, "I think you should let him have it. After all, it's his play!"

"Listen, you! You like your job—you keep your damn mouth shut!" Justin moved toward him.

Billy stepped between them. "Hey, come on, come on! Calm down."

"Do me a favor, Billy, okay? Get lost!"

Billy and the stage manager left the theater together, leaving Justin to brood alone. After a few minutes of pacing the floor, he kicked an onstage chair, sending it crashing into the front row seats of the theater.

Unaware that there were two men watching him, he began to march up and down the stage mimicking the playwright. "The word is *beautiful!* The word should be spoken softly, eloquently, but never untruthfully. Like this ... *beautiful!*"

Applause echoed forth from the rear of the theater. Justin stopped and peered out into the darkness. "Who's there?"

"Who's there?" echoed back, but it wasn't his own voice that he heard.

"Who are you?" Justin shaded his eyes from the light.

"The shmuck wants to know who we are?" Raucous laughter filled the theater and Justin saw Richards and Morgan coming down the center aisle.

Billy Richards' husband, Justin thought, and stared at his lined and leathered face.

"Hey, Johnny," Morgan said, "look at all these comfortable seats!" He wheeled around, struck the heel of his hand against the back of the soft green velvet chair. "Nice. Real nice."

Both men were still dressed for work: construction boots, Levi's, red-and-blue-checkered woolen shirts, heavy parkas. Richards wore his steel construction hat; Morgan held his like a Frisbee in his left hand.

"Come on, Johnny—let's sit down. Watch the shmuck perform for us." Morgan dropped into the chair left of the aisle. Richards took the one to the right, placing his boots against the back of the chair in front of him.

The theater flashed before Justin's eyes. There was no back door, only side exits and the front door. The two men were positioned between him and the only way out. For a moment, Justin just stood at the edge of the stage, staring.

"You know what my wife is doing right now, Knight?" Richards let his legs slip away from the back of the seat, leaned forward. "She's seeing a shrink twice a week. You know what that costs me—having her psy-cho-analyzed?" He drew out the word for effect. "Fifty bucks a whack. That's a lot of money, but that ain't the bad part. The bad part is—I ain't getting any! Seems she thinks she's a tart. Looks like one—that's what she tells me. And do you know why? Because of freaks like you!"

"What do you want?" Justin stiffened and moved behind the table.

"Your ass, sweetheart!" Richards scowled.

Morgan rose first, slowly removing his parka and throwing it over the back of his chair. "So are you going to perform for us?"

"Yeah." Richards rose quicker, slamming his hands down on the back of the chair. "I want something for my fifty bucks!"

Justin made a sudden move to his right.

Both men jumped onto the stage, cutting Justin off from either side. Justin tried to move forward, but again he was cut off.

"How's the play going, shmuck?" Richards had his fists clenched and ready.

"Yeah, big-shot director. Did you get the actress you needed?" Morgan closed in.

"Yeah, how's the cast?" Richards stood in front of Justin now.

"Look, your wife's a good actress," muttered Justin, "but she was all wrong for the play."

"All wrong! If she took off her clothes, I'll bet she'd been all right, then—right, shmuck? Right?" Richards pushed Justin into the corner.

"The man asked you a question, asshole!" Morgan gave him another shove.

"Hey, knock it off." Justin brushed Morgan's hand aside. "I was only kidding with her that day."

"Only kidding with her. Did you hear that? Shmucko was only kidding!"

"Yeah!" Morgan shoved him one more time.

"All right, cut it out—"

"Tell me, friend"—Richards smiled—"how good was the piece of ass you finally got to do the role? Did she do you right? I mean, did the music burst open in your ears in sudden squalls when you put it in?"

Morgan laughed. "I can see the two of them now, spread-eagled she was, basking in the morning light . . ."

"And stud, here, standing above her, naked as a jay bird—all hard-on and panting . . ."

"That the truth, stud—you was panting?"

"And she was panting, just like in the movies, the two of them—panting. 'Give it to me,' she says . . ."

"And he makes her wait, right, Johnny? He knows his stuff. He makes her wait . . ."

"'Oh, please—give it to me now!' she screams . . ."

"Goddamn you!" Justin moved forward and was immediately shoved back against the wall, hard.

"And he smiles at her," Richards continued. "Oh, lord, she's really ready now. Her tits heaving, her legs spread, moaning and groaning . . ."

"She's seeing stars . . ."

"Big, pointed, red-tipped stars . . ."

"Her legs apart . . ."

"Is that what you were going to do with my wife, stud!"

Justin charged forward.

Richards smashed him across the face hard with his fist. Justin's head snapped back, and Morgan smashed a fist into the middle of his stomach, doubling him over against the wall.

Richards lifted Justin's head by the hair. "Next time you talk to a guy's wife, make sure you do it with respect!" He hit Justin again in the stomach, again, again.

Justin's arms must have been thrashing without his realizing it, because now they were grabbing Morgan around the waist.

Morgan quickly brought his knee up into Justin's face, sending him against the wall, sending the blood pouring out of his nose, running down his cheeks, across his white shirt. Half-blinded, Justin tried to wipe the blood away from his eyes, tried to breathe through his battered nose. He was starting to go under.

As he dropped to one knee, the room started to fall away. He reached out for Richards to stop himself from falling completely. Richards brushed him away and laughed.

Justin fell face down onto the stage, his gut aching, his vision blurred. He reached out, started to crawl on all fours.

"Shmuck!" Morgan kicked Justin in the ribs, sending him flat to the floor.

"So long, big-shot director!" Morgan snickered.

They left Justin lying there battered and beaten. He tried to get up and fell. He tried again and this time he staggered against the wall. The room turned upside down and he dropped unconscious onto the stage.

Intake Interview 5 (Excerpt)
I. Luther, M.D.   33236

Sessions for this time period have been canceled
due to patient's violent attack against Head Nurse
Weiss with Weiss' own scissors, at the nurses' station. When Weiss withdrew with superficial stab
wounds, patient then used scissors to cut own hair
close to the scalp in uneven chunks. When put under restraint, patient laughed.

Patient has undergone a change which makes me
think seriously of a diagnosis of pseudo-neurotic
schizophrenia.

Recommendation: patient will be allowed no
freedom outside room without an accompanying
guard.

                                              I. Luther

❦ 22 ❦

THERE WERE LESS THAN TEN PEOPLE AT THE WAKE.
Sissy, wearing black gloves and a red hat, was the
first to arrive and sat beside Chandal the entire time.
Chandal's mother had several friends who came, all of
whom spoke highly of their close friendship with her
mother. Billy arrived last, having only heard the news
in passing through the stage manager.

"Why didn't you tell me?" asked Billy, sitting down
next to Justin.

"You need my problems, right?" Justin's face was
covered with cuts and bruises. Chandal had spent most
of last night patching him up, but his lower lip and jaw
were still swollen and his left eye was black. Chandal
had wanted him to go to the hospital for X-rays, but
he had refused.

"Listen, I heard about what happened at the theater
last night. You going after them?" asked Billy.

"No."

"Why not?"

"I'll get them in another way."

"What way?"

Justin never answered the question.

Services began. The casket sat closed, a smiling
picture of Chandal's mother on its gleaming wooden lid,
a red rose in a bud vase close beside it.

Chandal's eyes kept wandering to the picture. "It's
the first time I've ever seen it—when they didn't open
the casket," she murmured to Sissy.

"I think it's better," said Sissy. "Surely you wouldn't
want to see—"

"No, not really. But at least if I could see her, I

could realize it, maybe. Believe it. This way, it all seems so unreal."

A woman started weeping. She sat in the second row of wooden, fold-out chairs. At regular intervals, she emitted a graveled cough-like sob; Chandal had the feeling that she would go on forever. Justin and the others didn't seem to notice. Chandal was surprised, as she didn't know who the woman was. Her mother had never mentioned her, nor had she brought her over to the old apartment. Chandal wanted to stop her, to reach out and shake her hard.

"She was a dear friend of your mother," whispered another woman to Chandal, leaning over the back of her chair. Chandal nodded. Now the woman's sobbing became less frequent until she fell silent. The woman next to her blew her nose. Quick eulogy and the chapel was completely cleared and dark by ten P.M. Sissy and Chandal went to the Public House, a small restaurant on Seventy-ninth Street, for a chat. A quiet evening with a friend—it would do her good.

Billy walked Justin back to the brownstone, all the while filling him in on how the rehearsal had gone that day. In Justin's absence, Fein and Stark had insisted that the actors read through the play twice for the playwright. Many things had been discussed; nothing had been decided.

Saying good night at the door, Billy headed to the East Side to meet with his girl friend. Justin lingered on the front stoop for a long time before entering the house. He had made a decision during that time that he wasn't aware of making. Perhaps, in some strange way, Billy had helped him make that decision. What was it he had said? "There's a lot of ways to pay those bastards back. Go inside, think about it. You'll come up with the right answer."

Justin quickly closed the front door and went into the kitchen. Without thought, he started gathering various items: one white candle; a cup; a glass of wine; and two dishes, one filled with salt, the other with water. Next he took a double-edged kitchen knife with a

269

wooden handle from the drawer and placed it among the other items.

Going into the bathroom, he moved a small side table center, and around the table he created a circle by pouring baking soda on the floor. Having completed the circle, he began to set the table.

Accurately, his mind continued to receive images, diagrams, messages: place the knife center on the table, blade pointing south: Image: wine, incense, and dish of salt above the knife. Diagram almost complete. Put the dish of water below the handle of the knife, place the candle carefully at the west edge of the table.

Once this was done, he took a plain piece of paper, wrote "The Tree" carefully across the top, and signed his name below. Then he put incense into the cup and lit it. Next he lit the candle.

Now ready, Justin removed his clothing and jewelry. Naked, he picked up the candle, moved clockwise around the circle, and softly spoke these words: "The Temple is about to be erected. Let all within this Temple be here of their own free will and accord."

Returning the candle to the table, Justin picked up the knife and placed its point into the dish of salt. "Salt is life. Let this Salt be pure and let it purify our lives, as we use it in these Rites." He then used the knife to lift three portions of the salt, which were dropped into the water. Stirring the salted water with his knife, he said, "Let the Sacred Salt drive out any impurities in this water that together they may be used in the service of Ahriman—spirit of darkness! Ahriman; spirit of darkness. Here do I invite you to join with me in my Rites."

Removing the knife from the salted water, he kissed the blade; then he replaced it on the table. Next he drank the wine. "Now is the Temple erected. Let none leave it, but with good reason."

Having satisfied himself that he was doing the right thing, Justin lifted both arms high above the table and shouted, "Ahriman, hear me now! Grant me that which I desire! Permit me to worship the devil and all that the devil represents!"

Once more, Justin picked up the knife and kissed the

blade, then holding it high, said, "Ahriman, here do I stand before you, naked and unadorned, to dedicate myself to your honor. Ever will I protect you and that which is yours. Let none speak ill of you, for ever will I defend you. You are my life and I am yours from this day forth. So be it!"

Sissy and Chandal sat with their backs to the front window on the wooden seat. Cheerful, forced conversation over margaritas. Sissy folding and unfolding her gloves. Chandal couldn't take her eyes off those black gloves. Black, the color of mourning. Sissy said something about the museum. Chandal stared at the gloves, sipped her drink. The sound of voices was good and reminded her that life goes on. It was the right thing to do, coming here, being with a friend. Sissy said with her busy calendar, she hadn't been inside the museum in three years. Chandal hadn't heard her. She sat with her spine against the hardback chair, her arms hanging loosely at her sides.

"You're not saying a word, honey," said Sissy in a moment, whisking the gloves away into her lap, away from Chandal's remote eyes. "Say something. Cry. Something."

"I'm not sure what to say," said Chandal, transferring her eyes to the necklace around Sissy's neck, a Zodiac sign. Libra, she thought. The necklace blurred. Tears?

"Get it out," said Sissy, and she handed Chandal a napkin.

"No, I think I'm all right." Chandal took the napkin, started tearing bits of paper from it and wadding them between her thumb and forefinger. "I always wondered how I'd react to something like this, and now I'm still wondering, I guess. It hasn't caught up to me yet."

"But, your father—"

"That was different." She laid aside the napkin and her hand was steady. She looked at the blue veins running through her hand and they reminded her of the veins in her mother's hands. She'd had big veins, too.

271

"What would you say," Chandal said, "if I told you my mother was killed intentionally?"

"Now, you can't blame the hospital . . ." started Sissy, then stopped. "No, now, wait. Maybe there is a lawsuit here. I knew a man who got a hundred and fifty thousand . . ."

"She said it was a demon," said Chandal, and Sissy fell silent, face downcast and anxious. "I believe her," Chandal added defiantly and imagined that the couple at the next table glanced at her.

"What kind of a demon?" whispered Sissy, her hand at the side of her face.

"There's something going on," said Chandal, wondering if she was talking too loud. "It has something to do with the brownstone. I'm sure of it. Before we moved in, there was this bell on the Christmas tree ringing by itself, and I kept seeing faces. Magdalen. I saw her face. It was like a demon. And she wants Justin. I've seen them together . . ."

"Magdalen and Justin?" said Sissy, her face red and shocked.

"Please, Sissy—you must believe me! I've seen them together!"

"But there's nothing wrong with that."

"Sissy, listen to me. First the baby dies, then Sheila, and now my mother."

"Sheila?"

"Yes. The girl I worked with at the museum. She said that she'd help me. She tried—gave me the name . . ." Chandal broke off, aware that Sissy wasn't paying attention to her. Instead, she had turned to the closest table, kind of nodded her apologies for Chandal's having become too loud.

"Sissy!" She reached out and gripped her arm tightly. Sissy turned to her. "Chandal, please."

"I saw Sheila die days before she actually died. I was there when it happened—I mean, when I thought it happened. But she did die—just as I envisioned it."

"I believe that you are a psychically very sensitive woman. It's incredible, Chandal. Don't you see?

You've picked up on vibrations. It's not that it's actually happening; it's . . ."

"But it is actually happening!" cried Chandal, and the host took a half-step toward their table. *It's all happening!* Her voice echoed inside her head. Now she was finally losing her control. *Shut up!* said a familiar voice in her brain. *Why should I?* she answered back to the other woman who was also occupying her body at the moment. Trying to crowd her out. Chandal fought back, attempting to push the other woman outside.

Hands touched her. Dazed, she looked at a roomful of smiling faces. Sissy's face—stretched out of proportion by a grotesque grin. The waitress' face—mystical, glowing. Also smiling. The couple at the next table laughed. Everybody laughed.

She was alone. Now, nobody on earth could see her anymore. She was absolutely invisible and alone.

She scarcely remembered leaving the restaurant.

Justin was asleep when Chandal entered the bedroom. She paused for a moment, the pungent sickening-sweet odor assailing her nostrils. At first she thought it was her senses playing tricks on her. But the odor intensified, became more oppressive. And something else. There was a faint chill in the air. Yet the rest of the apartment was warm. Suddenly Justin's face loomed up at her from beneath the covers. He straightened up, holding his breath, and stared into the darkness around him.

Something had changed.

Chandal stood motionless. She could hardly believe her eyes. His face had been completely healed. There wasn't a mark on it! All signs of violence had vanished.

In a voice that she'd never heard Justin use before, he said, "Come to bed, Chandal."

She started to speak, but Justin refused to let her. Naked, he rose up from the bed and placed his hand across her mouth and kept it there three or four minutes. Their bodies barely touched, but she felt as if Justin were making love to her.

High above, on the third floor, Magdalen stared at the specimen case. In the center of the room stood Elizabeth. They remained frozen and silent for a moment. Then Elizabeth said, "Did I tell you? He is not to be trusted."

Magdalen turned and began mounting the stairs to the attic. "We shall see."

Elizabeth followed her as she climbed and heard the voice in her mind. *I should kill him. I should kill him.*

They entered the attic and closed the door.

Outside the breeze rattled the rain gutter that ran along the upper portion of the roof. Loose-jointed, a broken fragment leaped forward, its tinny surface tapping at the edge of the building like a quick, brittle finger.

Magdalen smiled. Across the room her white lace dress hung waiting, like a ghost in the corner. Neat. Ready.

Elizabeth wrapped her shawl tighter around her shoulders. She knew what was to follow. The amount of vital energy that must flow from the essence of Magdalen if she would become . . . "Stop," she said suddenly, closing her hand on Magdalen's arm.

Magdalen's eyes jerked from the whiteness of the waiting dress to her sister's face. "What is it, Elizabeth, dear?" The endearment held a contemptuous note.

Elizabeth trembled slightly and withdrew her hand. "I don't think you should, Magdalen. Please, not tonight." She stared into Magdalen's vacant eyes. Through the thickness of her glasses, they looked far off and yet, back, recessed deep within the tiny, barely discernible irises, was a faint glimmer of ecstasy.

"My health is none of your business," Magdalen said, her voice cold and remote.

Elizabeth felt a strong desire to leave the room, but she dared not. Magdalen was her sister, the only person she had, really, in the entire world. It mattered little that she hated Magdalen, that she had hated her imprisonment all these years with a cheerless nag, performing duties within the house like a servant.

You're right, angel—it's none of my business, she thought. But deeper within the depths of her mind, she promised herself that in the end, she would have the final say. The final ecstasy would be hers.

❧ 23 ❧

THE NEXT MORNING, CHANDAL AWOKE WITH A start.

There was a loud banging coming from the basement. She reached for Justin, but he wasn't there. "Justin?"

Naked, she stepped from the bed.

It felt as if someone had torn away part of her stomach. She allowed her body to sink back onto the mattress. For a moment, she sat on the edge of the bed, dazed—not being able to quite understand what had happened to her last night.

Justin had had his hand over her mouth. They were standing still for a long time, and then slowly he removed her coat, started to undress her, his eyes hungry for her flesh.

She looked down at her breasts now. They were bruised, scratched from where Justin had sucked on them, clawed at them. She remembered now that he never removed her skirt and thrown her face down on the bed, where he ripped her panties from her body.

From behind, he violently tore her legs apart and entered her. She struggled, she remembered that, but Justin was too wanting, too strong. Each time she tried to rise, he forced her face into the mattress.

She fought harder—not being able to breathe, and then was turned suddenly on her back. Justin entered her again, harder, quicker, before she could close her legs.

Each violent thrust of Justin's body shot pain through the lower half of her body. She began to whimper. She grabbed hold of him, her fingernails tearing away the flesh from his back.

And then it was over. Finally over. Justin bolted upright, shaking, looking at her with dazed eyes. And like a little child, he dropped into her lap and began to cry. He cried like a baby for a long time, until the tears dried; there were no words, only exhaustion.

With her arms around his sleeping body, Chandal had only one thought—that she had just been raped by her husband.

Below, Justin slammed the cellar door shut. Someone had moved the huge kerosine drum aside and again the cellar door had been opened. They had also torn the outside door off its hinges. Justin moved about the basement angrily, ready to kill. It was probably those bastards, Richards and Morgan, he thought. They were probably still out to get him!

"Justin, is that you?" Chandal appeared at the head of the cellar stairs.

"Of course it's me!"

"What are you doing?"

"It's the door again. I can't keep the damn thing shut! Put some coffee on, will you?"

"All right." She wearily crossed to the stove and turned on the gas. Trembling, she filled the coffeepot with water.

Justin found himself moving about the cellar mechanically, not aware of what he was actually doing. First, he took an old jelly jar filled with nuts and bolts and removed the contents. Next he filled the jar with razor blades, pieces of broken glass, nails, and other sharp objects. He removed a small vial from his pocket, opened it, and poured the yellow fluid over the contents of the jar.

Next, he went into the backyard, cleared away the snow, and, beneath the far side of the back porch, buried the jar. "There. Now let's see those bastards try to get me!"

From the window, Chandal watched as he dug away the snow from underneath the porch and buried the jar. When he entered the kitchen, she couldn't help but ask what it was he'd just done.

"I'm protecting myself, that's all."

"By burying an old jar under the porch?"

Justin smiled at her ignorance. He wasn't going to wait for Richards and Morgan to get him. Instead, he had just sent their evil straight back to them.

Smugly, he disappeared into the bathroom to shower and shave. He took off his clothes, wrote a few lines on a pad which he left in view, and then shot hot lather into the palm of his hand.

Chandal moved into the bedroom and sat at the edge of the bed. She thought of her mother, who was by this time halfway to Hartsdale, where her body would be placed in the receiving vault. She felt vaguely a disgust and a sense of shame at the way the funeral had been arranged. "Justin?"

"Yeah?" He stepped into view. His lean, naked body hung in the doorway and distracted her. Neither of them was willing to acknowledge what had happened the night before.

"Do you think my mother will be buried properly?"

"Sure. They know what they're doing."

"I'm worried."

"About what?"

"I don't know. Maybe we should have kept her here in the city for a few more days."

"To tell you the truth, she should have been cremated!"

"What?" asked Chandal, taken aback by Justin's sharp remark.

"You heard me. Who needed a high-cost funeral? Better she was cremated, or her body given to a hospital for research purposes."

"But—"

"Look, right now she's in Drëun; she's happy. What happens to her body really doesn't matter."

"Drëun?" Chandal had a hard time pronouncing the word. "What's that?"

277

Justin stopped and stared at her. Had he said Dröun? He wasn't even sure what that meant. He put his heavy fist to the corner of his eye and rubbed. "Look, I'm late. We'll talk about it tonight." He moved back into the bathroom and shut the door. Jotting several more lines down on his pad, he stepped into the shower and turned on the water.

Chandal saw clearly that Justin had completely changed. He walked and talked in an entirely different way now and his whole attitude about life had been drastically altered. Dröun—cremation? She considered this. Magdalen, again?

The sharp whistle of the kettle brought her to her feet and into the kitchen. After a moment, the room was filled with the aroma of instant coffee and burned toast. "Damn!" she muttered, shoving the knife into the toaster.

Then out of the corner of her eye, she saw Justin leave the bedroom and enter the nursery. What could he possibly want in there? She heard him singing, moving about inside the room:

> "O'er tops of dewy grass
> So nimbly do we pass,
> The young and tender stalk
> Ne'er bends where we do walk;
> Yet in the morning may be seen
> Where we the night before have been."

Chandal threw open the door. Justin was sitting on the bed alone, smiling. He appeared to be holding something in his lap. Her eyes widened as she noticed the frail imprint of a stretched-out figure on the bed.

Instantly she remembered the first day she'd entered the nursery—she'd seen the young man sitting on the bed exactly where Justin was now sitting. And on his lap had rested the head of the young girl.

And the song that Justin had just sung—it was the same one that she had hummed to herself weeks ago while waiting for Sissy to come to the brownstone. Chandal was sure that Justin and she had never shared

278

that song together. "What are you doing here?" she asked.

"Why? What's the matter?"

"What are you doing here?"

"Honey, take it easy. I was just looking for my other pair of shoes."

"In here?"

"Look, get off my goddamn back, okay? I can't do anything without you asking a lot of stupid questions!" He stormed past her and entered the kitchen. Chandal stayed right with him. He sat and began to have his coffee.

Chandal paused for a moment, not knowing what to say. "Justin, your face—can you explain to me how it suddenly cleared up like that?"

"Cleared up? The swelling went down, that's all!"

"And the black eye—the cuts?"

"Honey, it wasn't that bad. If it makes you feel any happier, I'll let those two gorillas kick the hell out of me again!"

"It doesn't make me happy. I just don't understand it, that's all. Nothing seems to make sense anymore." She looked at him questioningly.

Justin rose and put the empty cup into the sink. Then he watched as Chandal walked nervously around the room and eyed all the dirt that had accumulated everywhere. Filth! She began to kick the kitchen wall savagely; her face was twisted with anger. "Look at this place! It's a mess! I hate it! I hate it!"

"Honey, calm down. Why are you so angry with me?" He crossed the room and took her hand in his.

"Justin, I want to leave here."

"What?"

"This house—I don't want to stay here anymore. We said we were going to California. Please, let's go before it's too late."

"Are you serious?"

"Yes. Today, right now—let's leave."

It took Justin a full minute to realize what she was proposing, which was basically to leave everything

279

they owned behind them and to jump on the first plane available for L.A.

After the first shock, Justin became more angry than she was. "Are you crazy? We've spent a fortune! Everything we own is tied up here."

"I don't care!"

"Well, I do! Listen, if you want to go to California, then go. I'm staying right here."

"Justin, we must—"

"No, I don't want to hear it. You're incapable of understanding anything when it comes to money."

"Is that the way you feel?"

"That's the way I feel!"

Chandal was in no mood to be challenged. She went into the bedroom and methodically began to pack. Everything she cared about had to fit into one bag.

Justin entered the room and watched her neatly put her entire life into one tiny suitcase. "Chandal, please—"

"Let's not discuss it, since I'm incapable of understanding it."

"I didn't mean that." He laughed slightly, trying to ease the tension.

"I don't think it's funny."

"I didn't mean to be funny. Chandal, we're quarreling now for no reason."

"Oh, really. I asked you a simple question and you treat me as though I were a baby." Flinging the last piece of clothing into the suitcase, she slammed the lid shut. "Now, if you don't mind, I would like to take a shower!"

"All right. You want to leave—leave!" He left the house without saying another word.

Chandal sat for a moment on the bed, lost and afraid. She tried to call Sissy at home, but there was no answer. Next she tried her work number. She was informed that Sissy was in an important meeting and could not be disturbed.

Banging the receiver down, she moved into the bathroom to shower. It was there that she noticed the pad that Justin had left open on top of the sink. Written across the pad were indecipherable signs.

More to hurt Justin than anything else, she dropped the pad into the wastebasket. If he needed his notes, let him find them in the garbage!

After her shower, she dressed and called the airport. A flight was leaving for Los Angeles at six-fifteen P.M. She made her reservation.

At eleven-thirty A.M., Sissy returned her call and was shocked to hear Chandal say that she was leaving New York. For no reason that Chandal could fathom, she told Sissy that it was for health reasons. What a dumb thing to say, she thought. Why don't I just tell her the truth, that Justin and I are separating?

"Listen, I'll be right over."

"No!"

It was too late. Sissy had already hung up.

The ground was covered with snow and Justin's steps made the only sound as he searched in desperation for a cab. It was colder on the corner than anywhere else on the block and he shivered suddenly. He was wearing only a thin cotton shirt under his leather jacket and his shivering grew more intense. He slapped his arms across his chest and then danced from one foot to the other trying to get the circulation going.

He was still cold.

As he was about to give up, a gypsy cab pulled to the curb. Justin knew that he would be overcharged; he didn't care. He leaped into the cab and headed to the theater.

The stage manager was waiting for him in the lobby when he arrived.

"I'm sorry I'm late," he said, still visibly shaking.

"It's all right—no one is here."

"What do you mean?" Justin removed his jacket.

"Rehearsals have been canceled." The stage manager lit a cigarette; inhaled. "Something about a change in the schedule." He went over, sat on the small couch, got up and brought over an ashtray, and placed it on the coffee table in front of him.

Justin came over and sat beside him. "What change in schedule?" Justin watched him.

The stage manager hesitated, holding the cigarette loosely in his right hand. "I'm trying to think what might be a good way to begin," he said.

"Make it simple—begin anywhere." Justin moved his fingers in and out to get them warm.

"You've been fired," he said.

For a minute Justin was surprised, but then he realized it was to be expected, but still the whole thing was ridiculous. Confused and upset, he rose and went to the center of the lobby. He rubbed his left temple as he spoke, his left eye starting to blink. "It's all right—let them fire me. But I'll fix their asses! You think getting rid of me is going to be easy?" He paced the lobby. His eye blinking was worse. "Why did they do this to me?"

"They didn't do anything to you. You brought it on yourself."

"You wanted them to, didn't you?" He rubbed his temple harder now. "I'm a talent! How can they fire a talent? Those bastards! I've had more hit shows in this town than most directors put together. Fired—I'll show them!"

The stage manager puffed on his cigarette while Justin blasted on. Then Justin grabbed him, pulled him to his feet. But the stage manager never lost his balance and then he screamed at Justin, louder than Justin had ever heard him scream before. "You're a loser! A crazy—a damn loser!"

Justin sagged.

The stage manager straightened the lapels on his suit.

"I won't let them do this to me!" Justin scowled.

"It's too late; you fucked up and now they're replacing you. The playwright's decided to direct his own play. And I'm glad. Maybe now it will stand a chance." He snuffed his cigarette and then he was out the door, leaving Justin alone in the middle of the lobby, slumped, watching the people move outside through the snowy streets.

Chandal walked to the kitchen, opened a can of cat food, and put it on Mintz's dish. Then she knocked the can opener against the sink, called her name. Mintz was inside the kitchen and eating in no time.

After Mintz finished her food, Chandal picked her up and walked to the window to stare out into the empty yard. More confused than ever, she put Mintz down, got out a few records, and had the records dusted off and the needle in place when the front doorbell rang.

Without shutting off the record player, she moved slowly to the front door. It was Sissy.

"Oh, Chandal—"

Chandal wouldn't let Sissy into the house. "Go back to work, please."

"But what's the matter?"

"I'm just trying to get my life straightened out; nothing's the matter." She took a step back, away from Sissy.

Sissy immediately moved inside the door. "I've got an hour—let's talk."

"No!"

"You'll get sick if you don't get out of this draft."

"Oh, for Christ's sake!" She let Sissy in and closed the door.

"Why are you acting so strange?"

"How am I acting?"

"What I mean is, you barely let me in the door just now."

Chandal started talking very fast. "It's not my fault. I call you up to tell you that I'm leaving New York, and before I have a chance to ask you a question, which is why I called in the first place, you hang up and come rushing over here and never stop to think that maybe I'm in no mood, no shape to deal with anyone now! I realize that's hard for you to understand, being who you are, meetings and all—important. But it's not my goddamn fault!"

"Chandal, listen—"

"No, Sissy—you listen. I tried to communicate to you last night. I really tried. You acted like all the others, like I'm crazy. I'm not crazy!"

283

"Chandal, we can discuss it."

"Can we?"

"What's that supposed to mean?" She watched Chandal now, and wasn't quite sure what she read in her face.

"Did you ever try to understand? I mean really?"

"Don't make it sound all of a sudden that your problems are my fault. We were supposed to have lunch together; you canceled that. I came right over when you needed me. What did you do? Moped around at the damn zoo all day. You got problems with Justin —it's not my fault."

Chandal felt a little shiver run up the back of her neck as she watched Sissy remove her gloves. Sissy really didn't care—not the way Chandal wanted her to.

"Sissy, the night you stayed here—you ran out on me. Why?"

"I told you. Justin—"

"No, it was more than that. Be honest with me. Please."

"Chandal . . . I am traveling in a different world from you. I'm sorry your acting didn't work out. But I just felt that night—and don't ask me why—that if I stayed around this house, I would lose everything— everything I've worked so damn hard for. I don't want that to happen."

"Lose everything? How? Why?"

"I don't know. It was a feeling, that's all. Maybe I saw you and Justin going under, like I saw myself going under when Kevin and I were splitting up. I sank to the bottom then; I was drowning and there was nobody there to help me. I had to help myself." She sighed heavily. Tears welled in her eyes. It was as if something had touched her at that moment, something tangible that had never been clear to her until this moment.

"I can't help you, Chandal." She forced herself to continue. "It brings back all the pain, all the weaknesses. I can't allow that to happen. Can you understand that?"

Sissy's face went blank.

Chandal nodded.

"Perhaps the best thing for you to do is go away. Get a different viewpoint." Sissy looked into Chandal's eyes, then quickly turned away. She had caught a faint glimmer of impatience written across her face. "You're right, I shouldn't have come over here. I'm sorry." Sissy moved to the door. Chandal walked quietly behind her. "Call me as soon as you get settled out there, okay?"

"Yeah." Chandal held the door open for her.

"You know I've often wondered," said Sissy, sliding the smooth kid gloves over her long, delicate fingers, "why we didn't move out there years ago when we felt the urge. We planned to go, remember? I don't know what we were afraid of. But then we were afraid of so many things then, weren't we?"

Chandal smiled sadly. "I'll see you."

"Write me?"

"Yes."

She reached over quickly and kissed Chandal on the cheek. "I'll see you." She turned away quickly.

Chandal watched Sissy throw back her hair, find a firm grip on the railing, and start down the stairs. She remembered the hours she'd spent trying to impress Sissy. Studying languages, learning to ride horses, talking feminist—all to gain her admiration. "Sissy?"

Sissy turned back, her scarf lifting and blowing in the wind. "Yes . . . ?"

"That night. When you left here. You saw something—felt something in the spare room, didn't you? More than what you've told me."

Protestation and confusion rose to Sissy's face.

"Didn't you?" Chandal asked.

The truth leaped to Sissy's eyes. Still she said nothing.

"You should have told me, you know," said Chandal, a mask of regret settling upon her face.

Sissy stopped where she was on the steps and watched as Chandal gave a kind of small, casual wave and then closed the front door. "I guess we've never really known each other," she muttered then hurried away up the street.

Chandal's mind immediately leaped to the picture of Magdalen's husband, Dr. Steven M. Rock. But the young doctor was dead. Elizabeth had said that he was. If so, she had been seeing the young man's spirit. Had Sissy also seen him?

Spirit? Was that even a remote possibility? Chandal couldn't stop her imagination. Was the doctor really dead? Elizabeth had lied, lied plenty. She wasn't to be trusted. None of them were to be trusted. Chandal had to remember that.

Flipping through her address book, she found the "M's"; ran her finger down the column until it stopped at McLeary, Jonas, an old boyfriend fresh out of law school who now worked for the firm of Kahn, Leafgreen, and Rhodes.

Jonas was hard to reach. The secretary's tone implied that Chandal was trying to get a call through to God, and she was put on hold.

What time was it now? Twelve-fifteen P.M. She switched off the record player, balancing the phone between her head and her shoulder.

Jonas was surprised and delighted to hear Chandal's voice. "How long has it been?"

"Three years." With a quick gesture, she swept a couple of errant curls from her forehead. If he could see me, he wouldn't be that impressed. She suddenly wished that she looked better.

"It feels like only yesterday. How are you?"

She nodded. "All right."

"Everything's okay, then?"

"Sure. Uh, you wouldn't have some time this afternoon, would you?"

He hadn't. He was leaving town and wouldn't be back for at least a week. "Is there anything that I can help you with?"

"I needed to locate the records of a doctor. Steven M. Rock. He died in the winter of . . . "—she paused for a moment, remembering what Elizabeth had said—". . . 1930."

"Your best bet is to contact the American Medical Association. If he was a member, they'd have his records."

They talked a few minutes; he promised to call her the minute he returned. She led him to believe that she'd be delighted to lunch with him at that time and then hung up. God, I wasn't thinking about him at all, she thought. Now he thinks— Her mind shifted as she dialed information. The American Medical Association wasn't listed in New York; it was located in Chicago. What Chandal wanted was the Medical Society, Manhattan, County of New York.

Second call; you want membership, I'll switch you. Membership; you want State Medical Society.

Third call; hold on, I'll give you the Medical Directory. Yes, we had a Steven M. Rock—he resigned in 1930. Call the Medical Examiner's Office.

Fourth call; hold on, I'll give you administration. No, call the Health Department.

Fifth call; yes, this is the Health Department. No, you want Birth and Death Records.

Sixth call—no! We have no record of a Steven M. Rock, M.D., dying during the year of 1930. No, not 1929, or 1931, or 1932. Sorry.

Chandal continued to call every source available; nowhere was Dr. Steven M. Rock listed as dead.

Again she glanced at her watch. Two-thirty P.M. Probably she should eat something. She went to the refrigerator; the cottage cheese had gone bad. Nothing else appealed to her. What day was it? February 15. Barely a month since she'd set foot into the brownstone. Had she packed everything?

In the bedroom, she stopped and stared at the mirror. Justin had painted the back of the mirror black! Why? And why had Elizabeth told her that the young doctor had died of cancer? If he had, there would have been a medical record of it someplace!

None of it made sense. Start at the beginning— California. They were going to California. The building was being renovated—Bender wanted everyone out. So they would take the $6,000 and—but then Bender had changed his mind. Lois was still living there. They didn't have to leave, after all. Bender had changed his mind. Why? It probably wasn't important but . . . She moved quickly into the spare room, switched on the light. Justin's old desk. First drawer, second drawer—where was it? Bottom drawer—papers, bills, lease—and there it was, the agreement they'd signed accepting $6,000. L&S, Ltd.

She went into the living room, looking at the telephone number on the letterhead. She dialed.

"L&S—good afternoon."

"Hello, uh, I was wondering if you can give me some information? This is Chandal Knight. I used to live at Forty-six West Eighty-fifth Street. We moved from there about a month ago. Do you remember?"

"Just a minute." The phone clicked on hold. Waiting, Chandal dog-eared the letterhead. Finally! "Yes, this is Mr. Bailey—can I help you?"

"Yes—hello. Chandal Knight. I lived at Forty-six West Eighty-fifth—"

"Oh, yes. How are you?"

"Fine. I-I noticed that Mr. Bender has decided not to renovate our old building."

Bailey made an agreeable mumble that she took to mean yes.

"He changed his mind, then?" she asked.

"No, the owners did. They love the building and decided not to destroy its natural beauty."

"Wait a minute. I'm confused. Doesn't Mr. Bender own the building?"

"No, he sold it about six months ago."

"But he was responsible for moving us out."

"That was part of the condition of sale—that the present owners would buy the building only if it was vacated. It was Mr. Bender's responsibility to deliver the building totally empty."

"Oh, I see. Could you tell me who owns the building now?"

"Not actually—it's part of an estate. The Krispin Estate."

288

"Krispin. The two sisters?" Chandal's hands began to tremble.

"Well—I know there are at least two sisters, but then there could be more."

"Thank you." She hung up. Chandal knew now that whatever was in store for her had been arranged for a long time.

The silence intensified. She reached behind her, felt for a chair, and sank slowly down. Were they in the Brownstone right this minute? Listening, perhaps? The danger was real; there was no longer any denying that. What exactly was going on, she didn't know, but she knew it had started sometime ago. She reached into her pocket, drew out a cigarette, and lit it. Was Justin part of it? She drew in a lungful of smoke. If he was, then he was the enemy. She blew out the smoke in rings—they were imperfect and broke apart rapidly. If he wasn't involved, he was in terrible trouble. No, she couldn't leave now. She had to stay and . . . what? She walked back to the bedroom and pulled the door shut, putting a chair under the doorknob. Idiot. Whoever they were, they couldn't be stopped so easily. Slowly she pulled the chair away, put out her cigarette.

The phone rang in the living room. Chandal remained still, letting the phone continue to ring. It was probably Sissy. She would ask Chandal to change her mind, stay in New York. Try to work things out. Her body was moving now.

She wondered how long it would take for the phone to stop ringing. She was only a few steps away from picking it up. Through one door, through the hall, past another door to the table beside the couch.

Only a few more steps, yet an all but overwhelming distance; she would have to be patient with Sissy. Humble. Show no sign of agitation.

"Hello?"

"Hello, Chandal. Is Justin there?"

"Billy?"

"Yeah." Pause. "Anything wrong?"

"No. No, I just wasn't expecting it to be you, that's all."

"Is Justin there?"

"No. Isn't he at rehearsal?"

Slight pause. "Uh, no—rehearsals were canceled for the day."

"Anything wrong?"

"No, not really. The playwright's doing some re-writes. Fein decided to start fresh in the morning. Give us all a break."

"I see." Chandal put the phone to her chest. The sweat was running down her forehead into her eyes. She wiped her eyes dry with the back of her hand.

"Chandal?"

"Yes. Billy, can you come over here?"

"When?"

"Now. Please. Justin and I are in trouble. We . . . we need help. Please Billy, it's important. Can you?"

"Sure. Sure, I can be there in an hour. How's that?"

Chandal sighed with relief. "That's fine."

"You all right?"

"Yes." She started to smile nervously. "Just a little nervous."

"Hey, come on. Relax. It's been a rough couple of months. Listen, you go into the bedroom and lie down. Rest. I'll be over there before you know it."

"Okay." Chandal could feel the tension draining from her body.

"Promise me now, okay? That you'll go inside and lie down. That you'll get some sleep until I get there."

"I promise."

"Good. Good, I'll see you in a little while. Whatever the trouble is, I'm sure we can get it worked out. See you."

Relieved, Chandal dropped the receiver into its cradle. God, why hadn't she thought of Billy before this? He had always helped them before. He'd make sense out of the whole thing.

Chandal let her body fall limp across the bed. Her frenzy began to dissipate, although it could explode again in an instant. And then, without any warning at all, she felt something snap inside her. Her eyelids flickered—heavy, moist, they closed. Now her body rocked gently in a kind of suspended animation, as though she were floating on a still, calm pond.

"*Sleep* . . ." the voice whispered.

Suddenly Chandal realized that she had made a fatal mistake. She became aware of a strange phosphorescent light that seemed to emanate from her body. She trembled. The glow became a brilliant flash—blinding, yet warm. She could see her body silhouetted against the sudden blast of light. It seemed to be suspended in midair. She began to sink, down, down, until she was lost in a deep sleep.

Justin waited. It was getting colder now. Inside Charlie's, he heard the cheers and the applause; someone had opened in a hit show on Broadway the night before.

"Excuse us." A young couple brushed Justin aside and entered the restaurant. He followed.

Inside, he dropped on the closest barstool and ordered a double Scotch on the rocks. Pipe smoke burned his eyes; the man sitting next to him resembled a chimney stack. Over a pile of used pipe cleaners and burned matches, the man shoved money at the bartender and left.

Casually, Justin picked up the pipe cleaners and started to shape little figures. A body, a head, arms, and legs. Fired me. They actually fired me! The first figure he shaped represented the playwright. He built facial features, a large protruding nose—bastard! A cocktail napkin created the suit. I'm a talent; anyone knows that! The stage manager was more difficult to create. Long hair—thinner, shorter; I never liked short people! The little figures now lay on opposite sides of the ashtray.

"Give me a knife from the dining room, okay?" he asked a nearby waiter. Justin drew a circle with the end of a burned match; the knife lay across the bar. The bartender became curious when Justin asked for salt and water. The bartender brought them and watched.

Justin waited until the bartender was called away; bent his head low and whispered, "Ahriman, hear now my plea to you." He placed the two figures into the ashtray; salt went into water; he lit a match and set the figures on fire. "Thus may they be drawn, one to the other, to be together always. As one in death. No more shall they be separated; no more let them live. But ever fast together—let them die!"

Patient's attitude since attack on Head Nurse
Weiss has deteriorated completely. Patient now
refuses to speak. Patient's last spoken words:
I asked, "Will you come to my office to talk?"
Patient's reply: "She will not be there."

All scheduled consultations will be canceled to
allow patient time for self-evaluation.

                                              I. Luther

PART THREE

"I am who I am."

᷿ 24 ᷿

CHANDAL AWOKE EXACTLY AT TEN P.M. TO THE pulsating sound that came up from the basement. She lay there, her surroundings cold and bleak. "Come to the cellar tonight. At ten. I must talk with you," the voice had said. But Chandal hadn't gone to the basement that night. She had been too busy treating Justin's battered face. And last night—the wake. Afterward, the less-than-settling drink with Sissy. This had been the first night in days that Chandal found herself alone in the brownstone. She glanced at the clock. Ten P.M.! Thoughts scattered, she leaned forward, listened to the sound. She knew it was coming from the basement wall. And behind it, yes—the young man. Of course.

She got up, went into the kitchen. The cellar door was open. She wondered if Justin had come home while she was asleep. "Justin?" she called out in a low voice; the echo came back to chill her. She knew the cellar now; that was important. She switched on the light; it remained dark below. She grabbed for the flashlight, descended the stairs, listened. A soft voice whispered, *Help me. They are taking me away.* Then the pulsating sound stopped.

Chandal watched as the thin, vaporous image started to materialize through the wall. Lying in a prone position, floating several feet from the floor, hovered the body of Dr. Steven M. Rock. Eyes bulging wide, dressed in an ancient frock coat, pleated trousers, high-buttoned shoes, he appeared before her.

The odor came next. The rancid smell of decaying meat. Meat that had been forgotten, buried away for years to rot. His body, Chandal thought. They had killed him years ago and had buried his body away inside the cellar wall. That's why there wasn't any record of his death. Yet, his body appeared preserved. Normal. Alive.

She covered her mouth to stop herself from gagging. The doctor's body started to float now, away from the wall, toward the small doorway in the corner, which opened by itself to receive him.

A bolt of anxiety shot feverishly through Chandal's veins. They're taking him upstairs! No, I must speak with him! I must!

His body floated into the stairwell, rose higher toward the attic, out of sight. "No!" She screamed and rushed toward the door. The door slammed shut, locking her out.

She grabbed for the door; it wouldn't open. I must talk with him!

She dashed upstairs to the kitchen, moved into the hallway, stared at the second-floor landing. She remembered that each floor had a doorway leading to the side stairwell.

She opened the front door to the second floor, slipped inside quickly, and passed into the first room on her right. She was starting to invent her own moves now, sure of what she was doing.

The door leading to the stairwell was locked; she moved up to the third floor, through the first empty room, through the doctor's room. She tried the door to the stairwell; it opened. She entered the stairwell, climbed the stairs to the attic. As she climbed, she remembered having been thrown down the stairs, losing her baby. Awkwardly, she placed her hand on the doorknob, cracked open the door slightly. Almost the entire attic was visible to her now, and there on the large wooden table lay the corpse of the young man.

Next to him stood Elizabeth, draped in the folds of a satiny-blue robe, working on the body. The young girl stood off in the far corner, shadowed. Candles burned and the smell of incense was strong. Magdalen—where was she? Chandal looked behind her, down the long descending staircase. It was empty. She returned her gaze to the room.

And then she saw them. The huge icon paintings that she had seen in the museum. The skeleton on horseback, a hideous smile written across his boned face. The body lying in its bier, the mourners twisted and tormented in their grief. Below that painting, the flooding river raged, turned in on the horrified people who were about to be swallowed up. There they hung, looming in the shadows, their death images flat in the gloomy light. Flat, yet alive.

So she hadn't imagined them. The paintings that she'd thought were in the museum had been in this room all along. She had seen them, maybe not with her eyes, but on another plane of her mind. It was the evil that surrounded her now that had killed Sheila. The distorted introspective religion. They're devil worshippers, she thought with quiet, resigned certainty. She wondered why she wasn't surprised, not a bit surprised, not really.

Chandal watched as Elizabeth selected bits of what looked like flesh and rubbed them over the young man's arms, legs, and face. At length, she chanted, her voice harsh and loud, resembling at once the barking of a dog and the howling of a wolf.

She stopped suddenly; the young girl stepped forward.

"Why are you here?" asked Elizabeth.

"I wish a Handparting from Steven M. Rock," the young girl replied.

"Do you desire this of your own free will?"

"I do."

"Then let us proceed, remembering that we stand ever before Ahriman."

The young girl began to call upon the furies of hell, reminding them of the dreadful, repulsive sacrifices she had made in their honor. She demanded that the corpse stand erect before her. The body did not move. From behind her back, she removed a human hand and slapped the man across his face; the stump shot blood over everything. The body rose, not by degrees, but in a single impulse and stood erect. His eyelids opened.

Chandal felt the sickness in her stomach; she was going to vomit. She took a deep breath, covered her mouth.

The young man uttered no sound. The girl commanded him to speak, to admit that he had betrayed her. If he would tell her what she wanted to hear, she would burn the body in such a way that he would never again be disturbed.

Slowly, he spoke—admitted betrayal and begged her forgiveness. With outstretched hands, he implored her to desist in the ceremony. Request denied; his body was returned to the table. The young girl's hand shot straight up and held a slimy thing high in the air. "From this fetus, let him be reborn!"

Fetus! Chandal closed her eyes. Oh, God—no! Not my baby! Please—not my child!

The young girl flung the slime onto his body. Elizabeth lit the torch, placed it to his pale frame. Soon he was writhing on fire, and in one violent gush of agony and smoke, he vanished.

Elizabeth, in a high hysterical voice, cried, "Now are you Handparted. Let all know you as such. Go your separate ways. So be it." She bowed her head.

Gagging, Chandal fled down through the building, into the bathroom below, and vomited. Her entire insides felt as though they were coming out of her. "Oh, God!" she muttered. "Please help me!" The phone rang suddenly in the living room. Chandal's head spun around to face the door. The phone continued to ring —she half-rose, fell back. She tried again to lift her body, failed. The ringing stopped.

Billy, she thought. She had forgotten all about Billy. Oh, please, Billy—call back. Please call back. She waited. Silence.

After ten minutes or so, she got up, kept her head bent low. She washed her face hard, scrubbed it; all evidence of makeup vanished. "Oh, Christ, you're beautiful," she muttered sarcastically.

She sat down on the edge of the bathtub, swallowed, and the bad taste in her mouth started to make her feel sick all over again. She opened the medicine chest, grabbed the mouthwash, rinsed out her mouth, and felt better. Again the phone rang in the living room. She opened the door, stepped into the bedroom. The ringing continued. She hurried, stumbling once or twice over the furniture, but never enough to make her come close to falling. "Hello? Hello?" The sound of her own voice frightened her. "Billy?"

It was the producer of Justin's show. Talking in short, choppy sentences, he told her that the theater was on fire, that they feared Justin was trapped inside. At least, that's what an eyewitness had reported. She should get down there right away. Hysteria came fast. Her face crumbled and she spun for the door and was halfway into the hallway before Justin had grabbed her.

"OhmyGod!" She was stunned to see him standing right there next to her.

"What's the matter? You look surprised to see me." He smiled.

"The theater—it's on fire! They told me that you were inside!"

"They're wrong. As you can see, I'm right here." There was something too calm about Justin, too constant. Chandal felt uneasy standing that close to him. His body blocked her way; she had no room to move, to breathe.

"Didn't you hear what I said? The theater is on fire!"

"I know."

"But someone is trapped inside, they said."

"So?" A look of amusement came over his face.

"Look, Justin—stop the what-about-it stuff! I'm telling you that your theater is on fire. It's your production, so can we discuss it?"

He became angry. "Wrong! It's not my theater, not my production! They fired me today! That's right— shit-canned! The playwright decided to direct his own play, so now let the bastard burn!"

Chandal started to answer, but Justin turned and walked into the kitchen. Opening the refrigerator door, he stuck his head inside, threw up his hands in exasperation. "Goddamn thing is empty!" He slammed the door shut.

Chandal appeared at the kitchen door. "You think it's the playwright, then?"

"I hope so!"

"You hate him that much?"

"Yes! How's that for a simple statement of fact?" He dropped into a chair.

"Statement of fact? I'll tell you a statement of fact! Not more than an hour ago, I . . ." She looked for the words to describe what had taken place in the attic, but something made her stop. She took an extra-long look at Justin sitting there, legs crossed, arms folded. Could he be trusted? She went one step further. Did he know what had gone on in the attic? Was he part of it?

Justin smiled. "I thought you were leaving. California, wasn't it?"

He waited. Chandal said nothing.

"Aren't you going to say anything?"

"Do you want me to?"

"It doesn't matter one way or the other. But, if you want to—go ahead."

"Okay." She paused. "I think you need help."

"Help?"

"Yes, I think there's something wrong with you. Maybe you know what it is, maybe you don't."

"Really? And what's that?"

"Magdalen."

"Magdalen?" He stiffened.

"Yes, I think Magdalen has gotten to you."

"Oh, in what way?"

"Your feelings. I think—I think you're in love with her."

"In love with her!" His body began to tremble. "How goddamn stupid can you get? She's an old woman, for Christ's sake!" He got up and left the room muttering. "You're so damn ridiculous, almost as ridiculous as that bastard playwright!"

"Yes, you love her!" Chandal followed him into the

301

living room. "Admit it! Admit that you've been with her day and night, that you can't keep away from her!"

"Shut up!"

"No, I won't. Justin, she's evil. All of them—evil!"

"I said, shut up!"

"Look at you—you're grotesque! Lusting after a seventy-year-old woman. Justin, stop a minute. Look at the facts. Not what you feel—the facts! Please!" She was speaking very fast now. "You're a young man in love with a woman old enough to be your grandmother. Can't you see how perverted that is? How sick?"

Justin lunged for her, slapped her hard on the face. "She's a goddess, do you hear me?"

"I hear you—but do you hear me?" She paused, feeling the sting from his slap. "You wanted to know what I thought. All right, I'll tell you," she said. "Let's see if you can take it. I may be completely cock-eyed about everything I'm about to say. If I am, forget it— hate me. I don't care. Something is wrong here. Maybe you're a part of it, maybe not. If not you're the only one in this building who isn't. Justin, she killed her husband. I've checked—his death isn't recorded anywhere. Why? Because they killed him and hid his body in the basement wall! I've seen it!"

"Shut up!"

"Justin, she wants you. She had our building vacated. She knew you'd come to live here. Justin—she's a witch! I've seen them—in the attic. Both of them— witches!" She stopped speaking, looked earnestly into his eyes.

He took a step forward, put out his hand, pressed her arm. He smiled. "I know."

Numbly, she stared back at him, feeling his fingers closing tighter and tighter around her arm, bruising her flesh. His eyes!

Chandal pulled her arm free. Justin grabbed her again; he couldn't keep hold and she ran to the front door. It wouldn't open. She dashed into the spare room and locked herself in. Justin pounded on the door, calling for her to come out, but she was crying far too loudly to care.

Finally, he moved away from the door.

Chandal remained in the corner of the room. Her head jerked back and forth; her mouth hung open. The brownstone fell silent and the young girl smiled. Justin laid his head in her lap, closed his eyes. The attic was now his favorite room.

❦ 25 ❦

SHE REALIZED THAT HER RUNNING SERVED NO PURpose; she couldn't escape. They were on top of her now—the mannequins, all of them, reaching out for her, pulling at her arms, face, laughing.

Chandal's eyes shot open, but only her pupils moved to take in the room. Beneath her eyelids, they slid from one side to the other looking for a sign of Justin. The room was empty.

Thin beams of yellowing sunlight forced their way into the spare room through the open spaces in the shutters. Filled with dust, they formed a strange pattern on the floor and across the piles of unopened boxes. One of her fingers moved slightly, next her whole hand; she was still alive. She had survived the night.

She listened; heard the thin, high singing of children playing in the schoolyard the next street over. The sound of their voices drifted away and she was now more alone than ever.

Slowly at first, she moved toward the door. Justin had removed the key from inside the lock. She hesitated, listened—the brownstone was completely without sound. Was Justin home? She had to risk it. Pulling on the door, she found that it was locked from the outside. She pulled even harder. The door wouldn't budge. They meant to keep her locked away now. For what reason?

Alarmed, she moved faster, back to the window, lowered her body, peered through the tiny crack in the shutters. In the window, high above in the neighboring building, she thought she saw an old man gazing from his room. She pressed her face against the cold window. Yes—there was a man! He appeared closer now, almost within reach.

Wrenching the base of the window, her knuckles whitened, the veins in her neck filled with the excess of strained blood. The man moved suddenly; he was leaving the window. "No," she muttered aloud, "please don't go!" Then, like cymbals clashing, the sharp crash of breaking glass echoed through the room. She'd shattered the window with an old wooden statue.

Cold, controlled logic stopped her from calling out. The man was no longer visible at his window—the shutters were boarded over from the outside. Through the shutters, past the thick snow, up over the fence to the sixth floor where he lived, through his closed window—how would he hear her?

The phone rang in the living room, giving her a start. Holding her breath, she waited to see if anyone would answer it.

Justin did. Was it Billy? Was he finally coming over?

The sound of his voice was calm. There was a brief flurry of words which she could not catch. Justin spoke, but never twice in the same way; he used his own voice, then the voice of the young doctor—a high voice, a low voice.

Chandal stood near the broken window shivering and waiting; her hands dug deep into her arms, wrapped around her body for warmth.

Now she heard Justin hang up, walk along the hallway, open the nursery door, but he did not go inside. He turned away from the room, closed the door and moved toward the kitchen. Chandal knew that he was coming to her.

304

"Chandal?" he said softly, standing outside the door. "Chandal, it's Steven." At the end of these words, he shoved a piece of parchment under the door. "Chandal, you must not be frightened. You will be safe with us. Just sign your name in The Tree. Then we will know that you are one of us."

She hesitated, then picked up the piece of paper. Inscribed across the top were the same symbols that were written on the pad that she'd thrown into the wastepaper basket. Under these symbols were the signatures of Elizabeth and Magdalen Krispin. Beneath them—Steven M. Rock. There was no doubt now. Justin had become one of them. His handwriting was unmistakable. Methodically, she tore the paper to shreds.

Justin spoke so abusively to her now that she took an involuntary step backward and sat on the end of the bed. Suddenly he fell silent, but did not move away from the door; his stillness was more menacing than movement.

The front doorbell rang. Billy!

Justin turned with a measured, deliberate movement from the door. "Chandal, I will let Mr. Fein in now. Do not make a sound, for his sake. If you do, I will be forced to destroy him. Do you understand?" Justin left the kitchen, crossed to the front door, and let Harvey Fein in.

Closing the door behind him, Justin locked it. Something Steven always did when he wanted to annoy a guest. They went into the living room. Justin moved to the record player and flicked it on.

The soundtrack from *Funny Girl*—loud.

Sentence fragments. They were talking about the fire. The producer was describing the bodies.

"Jesus! They were black. I almost threw up. I was there when they dragged them out, before they covered them up. I shouldn't have looked. Jesus!"

A pause.

Justin's voice, flat, emotionless. "Well, that's sad. Yes—very sad."

"I'll never forget it. The building was burning like a

goddamn matchbox. You know, it looked like something you see in a movie. No kidding. The fire shooting out of the windows. Black smoke—I mean filthy, pitch-black soot pouring out. Hot as hell. You know, I keep wondering if they were dead before . . . well, before they burned. I keep seeing them. Burning alive. Jesus, what a way to go!" His voice sounded sick, nervous. "How about a cup of coffee?" he asked.

"All right. I'll get it."

The record player was switched abruptly off, interrupting Barbra Streisand in mid-syllable, distorting her sad voice.

Chandal knelt quickly by the keyhole and peered into the kitchen. Justin came into view, looked in her direction, then back toward the living room, and crossed to the sink to fill the kettle with water.

Chandal watched the producer linger in the kitchen doorway. "Nice place you have here. Plenty of space," he said, twirling a plaid rain hat between his fingers. He was dressed in a finely tailored woolen suit. Immaculately tailored, even in disaster. "So you heard Richards and Morgan were in there last night? Hell, I know they were bastards, but even so . . ."

"I guess so," said Justin in a flat voice.

Fein paused uncomfortably. "But, how did you know they were—"

"Billy told me." Justin lit the flame under the kettle.

"Strange." Fein sat.

"How's that?"

"I just spoke with Billy a while ago. He said he still hadn't been able to reach you. That's why I stopped by."

"He called right after you hung up." Justin looked at the spare room. Chandal held her breath, moving away from the door slightly. No one had called after Justin received the first call. She knew that. There was still hope that Billy would come. That he would be able to make Justin listen to reason.

She cautiously knelt on one knee. Listened.

"Four people dead—it's hard to believe." Fein inched forward in his chair. He was practically sitting

306

on its edge. He offered Justin a cigarette, but he declined with a negative jerk of the head. Fein lit one for himself; his hand shook a bit. "Apparently, Richards and Morgen thought you were in the theater; that's why they lit the fire."

"If I was still the director, I would have been."

"I'm sorry about that."

"The way things worked out—I'm not!"

The two men faced each other in awkward silence.

"Where's your wife?" asked Fein, filling his lungs with smoke.

"California. She left yesterday."

Chandal stopped herself from calling out. She bit down hard, caught a corner of her tongue. She moved away from the keyhole briefly while she collected her wits. Oh—please! She swallowed hard.

Fein nodded, rubbed his temple. "You want to know the truth, for whatever it means to you?" He put down his cigarette. "I was against his directing his own show. It was my first play; I needed a good director—that's why I got you. I could have made it happen; I wanted a hit play. If you want something enough and you care, you can make it happen. The truth—I felt terrible about getting rid of you, but Jesus, I was alone, three against one. The stage manager—"

"Bullshit!"

"What?"

"Quit with the games. You had to trust me. I needed time to get my head on straight. I busted my ass for you guys—you dumped me! You want to know something? I'm glad the playwright burned up, the stage manager along with him. I'm glad, so what do you say to that?"

Fein delicately rubbed his cigarette out in the ashtray, smiling his still-boyish smile. "Don't try to shock me with your callousness, Justin. I was born into it. I recognize it for what it really is."

"What's that?"

"An effort to create meaning—purpose. Ambition. I recognized it in you immediately. The way you walk. The way you hold your head, your hands, always wait-

307

ing for the right opportunity. Always expecting a great fist to drop down from out of the sky and crack you on top of your head when you least expect it. So you walk around expecting it—waiting, ready."

"Take a better look; maybe I've changed."

"A little, not much. Somebody told me a funny story about you yesterday."

"Really? Who?"

"It doesn't make any difference. You were at a dinner, had too much to drink, and somebody was eyeing your girl friend. You grabbed hold of him and said, 'Just because I used to be blind in one eye, it doesn't mean I can't see now.' And you hit him. See, always ready to stop people from taking something away from you. That's called ambition." He lifted his hat from the table. "I'll be talking to you again." He stirred from his chair.

Chandal tried to speak—no words came. Her mouth felt dry. She swallowed, tried again—nothing. She stood up, stepped back, knocking a large cardboard box onto the floor.

"What was that?" asked Fein, stopping in the kitchen doorway.

"The cat," Justin said unpleasantly, ushering Fein to the front door.

"What are you going to do now?" Fein asked, smoothly slipping his hat on and straightening the brim. He looked preoccupied and kept glancing back into the kitchen.

"Ask around. Make a few phone calls. There's always work for a good director." Justin wondered if Fein believed him about the cat.

"We could try again, you know." He shrugged. "I never fail at anything. I want a hit show. You could give it to me, if—"

"If?"

"You calm down, get help. Something's bothering you that isn't right. Maybe it's your wife. So she leaves for California. Am I right?"

"That's right," Justin said.

"And now maybe everything will be okay. In a few

308

weeks, we find another show. I got friends, big friends. This time—Broadway."

Justin suddenly found it amusing that the producer had only one thing on his mind—to have a hit play. It would have been nice, Justin thought. Maybe back—when? It all seemed so damn long ago. The hope, the enthusiasm. Within the great barn-like theater, the crowd seated row after row waiting for the great event. The play. Justin's play, the one he had just directed. The play that he loved like a child, cheering for it to take flight, hoping that it would be loved. Through sleepless nights, endless rehearsals, huge scenic backdrops, half-walls, a limbo of mirror images, a world that had never lost its third dimension, Justin had only one thought. I hope they love the play.

But he soon discovered that the theater was not born out of love; it was born out of hollow clichés. When you're hot, you're hot. A star was born tonight. The play's the thing, and who you're sleeping with, who your agent's sleeping with, which critic was a friend of a friend, and if you are circumcised. Money talks, and bullshit walks. Well, not anymore.

Justin smiled. "Broadway. It sounds nice. Any script I choose?" he asked, toying with Fein.

"If I like it."

"What kind of budget?"

"Million. Million and a half."

"No shit, that's terrific!"

"I think it is."

"To tell you the truth, things have sure changed in one day. Yesterday, you dump me from an Off-Broadway show. Today, you get me on Broadway with a budget of a million and a half!" He moved his body close to the producer. "Tell me, what would you say we've been doing?"

"I don't understand?"

"Jerking each other off, pal. I mean, if we're going to do it, let's do it until we get it right!"

"You son-of-a-bitch!"

"Get out," Justin said calmly.

"Okay, all right, suit yourself. But the next time you're looking for work, don't come to me!"

Justin slammed the door in his face.

Chandal waited for Justin to make the next move toward her; he didn't. Instead, he slowly climbed the stairs to the second floor, opened the door without knocking, passed down the long hallway, and entered Magdalen's bedroom.

The spare room was quiet, dark, and cold.

Chandal switched on the light; it didn't work. She went to the dresser to find something warm to wear. Instead, she found the drawers stuffed with old magazines, back issues of *Playboy, Vogue,* and *House Beautiful.* Next she went to the closet, got down on her knees, and plowed through the cardboard box tucked away in the corner. Silently she pulled up the rags and bits of blanket from where they'd been thrown out onto the floor. She stopped suddenly, lifted out a crumpled sweater, put it on. Next she found a ragged jacket and wrapped it around herself. She stuffed the remaining bits and pieces of clothing into the window. Her hands were nearly frozen.

She didn't try to do anything after that—just waited. Better not do anything foolish, she thought. Her mind wandered. What are you thinking?

She couldn't hear her own thoughts. Her brain felt dizzy, stunned.

What are you remembering?

She removed her hands from her pockets. Blew on them to warm them.

There, there, everything will be all right now. Her mother's warm hand brushing against her cheek as she straightened the covers. First memory as a child. Near dawn, she must have had a nightmare.

She drew a trembling breath.

Where was Billy?

She closed her eyes. The spare room had grown colder.

Gathering darkness, the day was slipping by. Chandal could do nothing to stop it.

310

She was on the floor; her mother, wearing a long silk dress, was speaking into a wall telephone. Chandal had tugged at her mother's hem; a shaft of sunlight crossed her mother's shoe. Second memory as a child.

The lights were coming on all over the city now. Lights in the windows of the stores, taverns, and on street corners.

Chandal's eyes started to shut. No! She couldn't allow herself to sleep. Moonlight slanted in through the shutters, past the broken glass, and seemed to filter through her lashes straight into her eyes. Inside her head, thoughts continued to churn around and around. She was cold and frightened, but wouldn't allow herself to sleep. Yet, after a while, she must have dropped off. If she hadn't, how could something wake her up?

And it did.

"*Night . . . night,*" sighed the young girl who stood near the open doorway.

Chandal opened her eyes wide. She saw the young girl, her face half-illuminated and half-shadowed by the light coming from the kitchen.

"*Don't be frightened. I want to speak with you,*" she said in a whisper.

"*Go away,*" Chandal mumbled weakly, her arm hanging limp against her body.

With the street noise unintelligibly distant, the young girl shut the door. She was almost impossible to see now as she laughed, a high-pitched snarl, an animal noise. Chandal looked with frightened eyes at the young girl, who had now transferred herself to the far corner of the room in a single instant.

"*When you hear the sweet, thin sound of the tin whistle, the ceremony will have begun. Justin and I will be together then—for life.*" She paused for a moment to look out the window. She now wore the smile of an idiot. "*Steven and I will be together again. My sister, Elizabeth, has promised me that she will not kill him like she did the last time. She has promised to let us be happy. To live together in this house like before. She will be gone. But Steven and I will still be here.*"

311

"Justin is not your Steven!"

She smiled. *"Not the sniveling coward who went crying to you, no. But there is a new Steven now—the way I want him to be. We will be happy and you can be part of that happiness—do you understand?"*

Slowly, awkwardly, Chandal rose to her feet. "What do you want of me?"

"I want you—to become me."

Chandal's eyes were glazed. She could barely make out the young girl, who seemed lost to the shadows of the room. Chandal pushed the thought from her lips. "Who . . . who are you?"

The young girl drifted softly forward into the half-light that clustered near the center of the room. The train of her white lace dress floated ghost-like behind her, swirling about her ankles and tiny bare feet.

"Magdalen. I'm Magdalen as I used to be. I will be dead soon, but you must take my place."

Chandal looked back at her and slowly—Oh, God! —she understood. She wasn't going crazy. Magdalen stood before her—younger, but underneath it an old woman panting for life, and that was the object of it all —wasn't it?—staying alive. Take Chandal's body—use it as her own. Transfer her soul into another's body, and now Chandal's stomach was starting to cramp slightly, and that would be funny—to die before Magdalen, but Chandal would not let that happen. She tried to speak but couldn't because she was in a terrible sickening pain, around and around, but this time she knew the cause. Suddenly she vibrated in a high-pitched scream, "Never!" She gasped for air, as if hit by a fist across the throat. "Never," she murmured, barely able to speak.

Chandal's head was suddenly jerked back, held in place by the wrenching of her hair, back against her neck. Her body jerked in short movements—receiving electrical charges. Then the stillness came as the girl descended on her.

"You have no one to help you. You are alone," she hissed.

"Billy . . ." Chandal could hardly get the word out.

312

"No." The girl smiled. "Billy has been ours for some time. He belongs to us now. Sheila, foolish girl—she is gone. All of them gone." The girl drew closer, lovingly looked into Chandal's face, almost as if to reach out and kiss her. "It is you . . . and me now."

Chandal reached down into her stomach, drew deeply upon the poisonous hatred inside herself, and spat in the girl's face.

The girl laughed. A demented laugh.

Again, the girl had changed positions; she stood by the door. "You will do as I ask. In a few days, the fasting will purify you, the cold will seduce you, and I will always be present, in one shape or another." With the greatest contempt, she laughed and left the room. The door slammed shut and locked itself in one swift motion.

In the attic, Justin and the young girl stood naked before the altar. Strewn before them and about the circle were flowers—red roses and violets. Elizabeth, in her black priestess robe, stood waiting, torch in hand, and mannequins in black tunics formed the coven. The two rings were passed through the flame and placed side by side upon the altar beside the goblet of blood. Elizabeth brought the tin whistle to her lips and began to blow. The Handfasting Ceremony had begun.

From the darkness, the sudden swell of sound: the squealing and squeaking of the whistle. Chandal covered her ears to block out the sound. It was so sharp that her nose opened up and started to bleed. With one hand still covering her ear, she tried to stop the bleeding with her handkerchief. The bleeding continued. She threw herself across the bed and raised her legs into the air. Holding her head back as far as it would go, she wiped the blood from her cheeks. After a moment, the bleeding stopped.

In the attic, Elizabeth proclaimed, "There are those in our midst who seek the bond of Handfasting. Let them come forward." Justin and the young girl came forward to stand face to face.

313

"And what is your desire?" Elizabeth asked Justin.

"To be made one with Magdalen Krispin in the eyes of Ahriman."

"And what is your desire?" she asked the young girl.

"To be made one with Steven M. Rock in the eyes of Ahriman."

Elizabeth picked up the knife from the altar, raised it high. "Ahriman, here before you stand two of your followers. Witness, now, that which they have to declare."

Chandal rose from the bed, moved about the room, caged, her eyes darting sharply at every sound, the blood still covering her cheeks. Did Justin know what he was doing? Perhaps he wasn't aware, didn't actually know! She ran to the door and screamed, "Justin!"

She clawed at the door until her hands were covered with blood. Her eyes, filled with tears, strained to see. "Oh, God—please! No! Justin!"

"Repeat after me." As Elizabeth spoke, the young girl and Justin repeated her words. "I do come here of my own free will, to seek the Partnership with thee; I come with all love, wishing only to become one with thee and Ahriman. Each other's life we will defend before our own. May this knife be plunged into our hearts should we not be sincere in all that we declare. All this we swear in the name of Ahriman. May he give us the strength to keep our vows. So be it."

Chandal slid to the base of the door completely numb. Her body lay in a heap—she gasped for air. Each breath she took into her chest caused a sharp pain and it felt like she was being stabbed to death by icicles. She muttered over and over again her husband's name.

Elizabeth took up the two rings and sprinkled them with censes. She then handed the young girl's ring to Justin and Justin's ring to the young girl. "Ever love,

314

help, and honor each other and then know truly that you are one in the eyes of Ahriman. So be it."

Justin and the young girl each placed the ring on the other's finger and kissed. They then kissed Elizabeth. After this was done, they began the Ceremony of Cake and Ale, followed by games and merriment.

❦ 26 ❦

THE SNOW FELL HARD IN THE BRIGHT SATURDAY morning light. Chandal could see nothing from the crack in the shutters except the falling of the thick white flakes.

As the snow drifted and drove past her eyes, she turned and glanced through the small room; it had been crystallized; a thin veil of white frost covered everything—the floor hard and cold, a danger to walk on.

She had not eaten in three days. She was isolated, behind the shifting wall of snow. She raised her hands before her, palms upward, the dried blood covering them. They were trembling. She looked in terror, tried to move her lips, but no words came. For a moment, the room was quiet. Then from above, she heard the noise of drunken singing and voices bawling and brawling; they had continued to celebrate throughout the night and into the morning.

Lying on the bed, Chandal listened to what sounded like dancing now, heavy footsteps, and the young girl singing. The thumping lasted for almost an hour. Suddenly Chandal began to scream, but the noise above didn't stop. Screaming like a baby now, she picked up anything she could find and began flinging it at the ceiling. Justin had started to sing now, and, suddenly through it, Chandal heard the long, high, distant cry of Elizabeth which dwindled into silence.

For a moment, the brownstone was still.

Shoulders tense, Chandal stood on the bed and wondered what had happened. She waited. The stillness suggested the climax after death. Something had gone wrong upstairs—she was sure of it.

A hissing sound drew her attention to the corner of the room, and there, coiled on the chair, was a huge snake, flat head and neck raised, waiting to strike. Chandal could actually feel her heart stop, then start again; she breathed in short gasps, her breath visible in the frigid air.

The snake's black diamonds were clearly outlined by a row of creamy scales, and the creature appeared to be at least six feet long. Its loosely attached upper and lower jaws contained two rows of teeth on each side, teeth that curved backward.

The snake, now moving its head from one side to the other, lifted its elastic throat, which stretched out to receive what had been offered to it. Its eyes bulged, the skin of its neck distended, separating from time to time, breathing through a stiff tubular attachment, longing to devour its prey.

Something was slithering in Chandal's windpipe. Gagging, she tried to open her mouth. Her jaws locked. From inside her body, the thing pushed its way up toward her mouth.

The snake shot out its fangs.

Chandal was caught between two forces: one within, the other without.

Yellowish fluid began to drip from the snake's mouth, running down its scaly neck. Its eyes lit up like red glowing rubies, as its head moved in a slow circular motion.

Chandal's hands shot to her throat; she was being strangled to death. She squeezed, trying to rid herself of whatever had taken hold of her. She squeezed, harder. Suddenly something released itself from within, slithered away, sending a rush of shivers up and down her body.

Slowly the snake lowered its head, dropped from the chair, and started toward her. She stepped back against

316

the wall, looking for something to protect herself with. The snake quickly moved under the bed and disappeared. Above, the laughing and singing began again.

Chandal could not bring herself to move. She stood motionless for a long time, her physical discomfort mixed with her fear. Was the snake crawling up onto the bed? She wanted to squeeze closer to the wall, but her body refused to budge.

Shaking miserably, she finally managed to slide along the wall to the side of the bed. Just as she was about to step down, the snake's head shot straight up and lunged, fangs ready. She jumped back, leaped from the opposite side of the bed, and threw herself into the closet. Slamming the door shut, she frantically stuffed bits of rags into the space between the door and the floor.

She had made it—she was safe again, but she reminded herself that she must be on guard at all times.

Justin stood beside Magdalen's bed—she was very ill. Elizabeth, in a lazy, offhanded way, rose from the table behind Justin, crossed to the window, looked out. The snow was still falling. If she had any devotion for her sister, she hadn't displayed it at this time. Nothing reached her now except indistinct sounds, voices from the past. She gazed from the window into the yard below and thought of her sister locking her away in the closet.

"The snow won't stop. It's like the last day," Magdalen said to Justin softly.

He knew that she hadn't long to live. *I won't allow it,* he said to himself. *I won't allow it!* He bowed his head and wept.

"No! No weakness. You should be ashamed of yourself," she said, her gentle eyes reaching out to meet his.

Notwithstanding the calmness with which she spoke, Justin saw how deeply she suffered. He restrained himself from saying what was really on his mind, so that nothing he said would disturb her further. "Magdalen, we will be together again. I promise."

"She's killed herself for you already," murmured Elizabeth, "by staying in that form too long."

He reached out and took Magdalen's hand in his. Before him, at that moment, he did not see an old and withered body and face, but the beautiful apparition of the young girl with whom he had fallen in love. He imagined her long flowing red hair, her green eyes, and the softness of her pale and lovely face.

An image came to Chandal of herself inside a casket, the lid being closed. I'm alive! Alive! She shook her head to clear it of the vision. It was being locked up in this closet, this box-like chamber. No, wait. Had Magdalen put the thought there? So that she would leave the closet. The snake! Something brushed across her leg and she was quickly certain that the snake was inside the closet with her! *Get hold of yourself. Relax,* she soothed. *You've got to get out of here, that's all.* She reached for the door; her breathing came in short, labored sobs. She was not far from hysteria.

She opened the closet door, letting it swing free by itself. She saw on the dresser a single candle which flickered waveringly in the draft coming from the window. Someone had been in the room. She stepped out.

In the candle's eerie light, her shadow, forming and dissolving like an ectoplasmic manifestation, shimmered uncertainly on the different surfaces of the room. Little puddles of water were forming on the floor near the broken window.

She stopped. She sensed no other presence in the room. At first, she did not trust her instincts. Sure that the snake would appear at any moment, she stepped carefully, cautiously—she kept her fists clenched tightly, her body rigid. She wasn't sure now. She waited for it to happen; it didn't; she was no longer jumpy. The deadness of the room brought calmness; the panic was gone and she waited.

Sometime during the mid-afternoon, Chandal began rapidly stamping with both feet on the hard wooden floor. Pacing up and down, she drove each foot against the floor as hard as she could. She imagined that she

heard whispering and smothered laughter everywhere
—from the closet, behind the dresser, in the kitchen;
she poured out her life, her thoughts, everything, quite
disconnectedly. She began by saying that she was useless, that her whole life added up to zero. She'd become
laughable. At this point, she became pathetic and began sobbing, beating herself around the chest and face
for almost five minutes, getting more and more frantic
at the whispering, the laughter.

"I will not give you my body! Never. I'll kill myself
first. Can you hear me? I'll kill you all. All of you—
I'll kill you!"

Unaware of what she was doing, she flung herself,
face down on the bed, wrapped herself convulsively,
head and all, into the blanket and lay that way for the
remainder of the day.

One A.M.

The spare room stank of an amazing mixture of
smells: candle wax, flesh, camphor, perfume, incense,
and excrement. Chandal's head ached; it was like trying to breathe inside the mouth of a scavenger bird, a
vulture or hawk.

Across the room, something moved.

One of the empty wooden crates on the floor started
to rise. Midair, it hung, then in a crackling, splintering
crunch, smashed to the ground. The lid flew open and a
horrid vapor began to ooze from within. The room had
crystallized into lacy dry ice and around the box, it
started to melt, causing steam.

Chandal spun around—heard glass crash behind her
and found a vase had fallen to the floor. Then a picture
dropped and crashed to the floor. She caught a glimpse
of it in flight. Then there was a knocking and scraping
on the outside of the door and window. The sound
moved inside, under Chandal's feet. She was slapped
across her face. Again and again. The blows were distinct, like the open palm of a heavy hand. Suddenly
her hair was jerked back, wrenching her neck practically from her body.

And then it began.

They stuck pins into her body, pinched and bruised her flesh, disheveled and tangled her hair. "Oh, God—" A hand slapped across her mouth; she couldn't call out; her words choked in her throat. She struggled to remove the hand; it released her and slapped—hard!

The whistle began. Slowly, then deafening.

From the open box, a little girl grew out of the vapor and steam. First a mere mass of light, and then she grew into personal form and there she was. She curled back her lips, bared her teeth. In a voice that was shrill, yet mild and pleasant, she spoke: "Come take my hand—we will be together."

"No!"

"Whore!" Her voice deepened. She hissed.

"No!" Chandal held onto the bed.

"I will enter you!" said the little girl. Her body rose from the box, her long red hair floating around her face and shoulders. She stopped in midair, above Chandal, looking down—"I will enter you!"

Every line in the girl's face was stretched into distorted joy. Her eyes sparkled blue emerald, cold and vacant. With far-reaching hands and long fingernails, she lunged at Chandal. The tiny veins in her forehead popped with excess blood, pulsating, throbbing.

"*God!* Christ—help me!" Chandal threw herself into a praying position. Closed her eyes. Sweat-drenched and shaken, she couldn't find the words. But she heard the sound of childish laughter. A child four years old, maybe five. The laughter was at the foot of the bed. A flood of music entered the room, the kind made by stringed instruments. She looked up; the little girl was gone, but she found herself in the middle of a snowstorm. It was as if she were inside a kaleidoscope. She could plainly see the snow coming down, big fat flakes that occur when snow first starts to fall on a cold winter day. Off in the distance, the little girl reappeared, younger now, wearing a fur cap and matching coat, and beckoned Chandal to play.

"*No!*" Chandal screamed.

There was silence. It was morning.

Magdalen stood before her now, her voice hoarse

320

and thick. "I'm dying. Let me into you, you bitch! You cunt!"

The words poured from Chandal's mouth. "Hail Mary, Mother of God, blessed are the wounds of Jesus, forgive me, for I have sinned, for I dread the loss of heaven and the pains of hell."

"Let me in!"

"Hail Mary—" Chandal couldn't think. "Hail Mary! Hail Mary!" The demon now rose within Magdalen—higher—her face, goat-like—the smell putrifying—Chandal cupped her mouth and nose. "Hail Mary, mother of God, forgive me for I have sinned, because I dread—" Her arm shot back and her sweater was torn away from her body. "Hail Mary—Mother of God!"

Her body was lifted from the ground; she screamed. "God help me!" She dropped to the floor.

"Let me in you!" the goat's head shouted.

Chandal's body started to open up. She wrapped herself around the leg of the bed, pulled inward. "Jesus, save me! Jesus, save me!" The bed shook, rose in the air, and smashed down. She pulled even tighter. "Jesus, save me!" Her forehead was wet with sweat. She gasped and struggled; some force threw her back inert onto the floor. Suddenly there were loud raps like the sound of a mallet striking the walls. Each blow shook the room, sending violent electrical currents through Chandal's body. She screamed: "God, take me! Please—take me!"

The goat's head lurched forward on the girl's shoulders. Chandal was going to lose. She couldn't fight anymore. She couldn't—her head jerked up. She listened. The raps were not so loud. They were weakening. The goat's head stopped—dissolved. The girl faltered; she was barely breathing now. She raised her hand, started to slap viciously, but never completed the gesture. Her hand dropped limp to her side. Wiping her tear-soaked face with her hand, Chandal struggled to get back onto her knees; her lips began to move again. "Hail Mary . . ."

The young girl sank down—smaller, until only a child stood in the box crying. Her body lowered slowly.

The lid dropped back into place and the rapping ceased.

Sunday passed.

It was completely dark outside when Chandal heard Justin moving around the kitchen. Then she listened as he ran the water in the next room. The picture of the apartment flashed across her mind. The half-bathroom! It was almost never used—Chandal had completely forgotten it. She placed her feet squarely on the floor, rose and crossed the room.

Slowly, she opened the closet door and pushed aside the boxes. She could hear the water rushing through the pipes clearly now. Checking the walls, she saw that they were makeshift, that the half-bathroom used to be part of the spare room. There was a sudden flicker of hope. How hard would it be to get from the spare room into the bathroom? She would have to wait until Justin left the house. There was little chance she'd be able to break through the wall without being heard. The patchwork plywood on her side of the wall was barely attached. Through one of the mismatched spaces, she saw a thin sliver of light.

The water stopped; the light disappeared.

Justin stood directly in front of the crack in the wall, drying his hands. Chandal held her breath, her body rigid. Justin paused for a moment, hung the towel over the rack, then left the room, leaving the bathroom light still burning. Chandal once again stared at the small glimmer of light as her only hope.

The key to the spare room was put into its lock. Chandal recoiled, almost smashing into the closet door. She'd barely managed to get the door closed when Justin appeared in front of her. She stood motionless, waiting in the frost-covered gloom for Justin to close the door. He held a candle in his hand; he moved slightly; his shadow fell across the wall. He unwrapped a sack, flung aside a soft white dress, lowered the candle and placed it on the table.

For a moment there was silence.

"Put this on," he finally ordered.

Chandal refused to move. Not a whisper. She recognized the dress immediately as belonging to the young girl.

Suddenly he flung the dress at her. "When I return, you must be wearing the dress." He walked toward the door, stood waiting. Chandal continued to stand in silence. He walked out into the kitchen and locked the door.

Trembling, Chandal struggled to regain her composure. As soon as she did, she moved unsteadily but heavily to the foot of the bed and sat.

The house was silent for nearly two hours. Chandal knew that the time had come, that the white dress was meant as part of her transformation into Magdalen. She had to take the chance that Justin was upstairs or down in the basement and would not hear her.

She moved quickly now.

Removing the boxes from the closet, she began to pry away the boards. She became so absorbed in what she was doing that she completely forgot the need for silence. Some of the boards resisted her pull and she banged furiously on the frame until they loosened. Warm air poured into the closet. Chandal could feel her blood moving freely.

Finally, she finished. Exhausted from her efforts and panting heavily, she crawled through the small hole. She came out of the darkness of the closet like an underground animal, the sharp light from over the sink nearly blinding her.

For a moment, she was still, her head held a little to one side, looking around the tiny bathroom. Her hand suddenly unclenched itself like a jerk of the nerves after death. She tiptoed to the door, took hold of the knob, and slowly turned; she was relieved to see that the door opened. She stared out into the hallway for a long time. She was alone—everything was quiet. Soon she was able to tell her feet where to go.

Without further hesitation, she bolted from the room toward the front of the brownstone. The door to the second floor slammed shut! Chandal whirled about. She wasn't close enough to the front door to see who it was. Icy and shivering, she ran into the living room and ducked down behind the couch.

Justin appeared on the stairway. He looked like a cadaverous clown. Smiling, he stopped in front of the hall mirror. He considered his image, his long fingers rapping on his elbow. He wore a long dark coat, immaculately tailored, an ornate, embroidered vest, gold chain, high cravat, dark trousers, shining boots, and a a velvet cummerbund. On the third finger of his left hand, he wore one of the two matching rings belonging to Magdalen. Now from in back of the couch, Chandal heard Justin open the front door, enter the outside world, close the door, and lock it.

She rose quickly, crossed to the front door, peered from the small window into the street. She watched as Justin stopped in front of the brownstone to talk to a man with his two children. Justin wagged his head in the opposite direction. He winked and nudged the children, pointing out in a dumb show that their father had apparently lost his way. All laughed, then departed—the street was empty; the snow had stopped.

Chandal was just about to leave the brownstone when she felt that someone was watching her. She turned her head slowly and looked behind her. She saw nothing but her own image reflected in the hall mirror. Or was it? She barely recognized herself now. She frowned and became more on guard. She began to speak with flashing eyes, almost menacingly, bending her head forward, raising the forefinger of her left hand high above her. "Where are you? I know you're here!"

Her next instinct was to run through the streets yelling for help. Help from what? Who would believe that they were trying to take over her body? So mixed were her feelings that she picked up the goat statue from the hall table. Looking at the statue, she laughed. She knew there was no escape. Survival, hatred, confusion pushed her past her own panic. She quickly returned the statue to its proper place on the table. Only then did she realize what she must do.

❧ 27 ❧

WHEN SHE LEFT THE KITCHEN, SHE STILL HADN'T recovered from her ordeal of the last three days. "Mintz?" whispered Chandal. She looked for her cat, her eyes wild. "Mintz?" The cat must not be harmed, she thought.

She found Mintz sleeping in the bathtub. The cat jumped out eagerly; Chandal was there to hold her and hug her. "You haven't disappeared. No," she said solemnly. "You are still here." She continued to speak softly to the cat as she carried her to the front door. "Oh, you know my fears? Yes—my being afraid of them. Not important! It's important enough for them to want to keep me here, now, isn't it? Well, that's true. I see. Do you?" Chandal smiled. "Yes, I think you do —but, well—" She opened the front door and chased Mintz down the front steps. Sadly, she closed the door and bolted it from the inside.

When she came to the bedroom, she stopped to adjust the blankets, then went to her nightstand and applied her makeup. She turned out her light and left the room.

Without hesitation, Chandal opened the basement door, switched on the light, and descended the stairs. In the gloom, her eyes roved around the basement. She glanced quickly, fearfully, at the mannequins, and after a moment the glint of their stripped bone heads took shape: the seer who had refused to help her, Justin, Sissy. She spoke to them in a changed voice. "There is no need to be frightened. The celebration will be in your honor. It may well be your last. Do you know what it is to be afraid? It doesn't matter; at least, you're not alone. I've always been lonely. Oh, yes—there's lots of ways of dying. I know."

325

Magdalen screamed out in panic.

Elizabeth did not move away from the window, but allowed her sister to convulse in her own madness. "Move quickly, light the fire. We're ready," Elizabeth whispered.

With a sudden spasmodic jerk, Magdalen reached out and pulled roughly, violently, at her sister's sleeve and tried to speak. Terror looked out from her eyes. If Elizabeth knew what she was trying to tell her, she made no indication. She did not pull her arm away, but seemed hardly to know that Magdalen was there.

"My name . . . my name will be—a ghost; help me!" Magdalen fell back across the bed. Elizabeth stood over her now and smiled. Her smile was magnificent, as though she felt joyful all at once. In a singsong voice, coaxing her sister tenderly as though she were a child, she said, "Be good, be good, or I will come with my knife."

"Elizabeth, hold my hand—"

Elizabeth backed away slightly. "That isn't a hand; it's a knife. Can't you see? It's my knife. I should have killed you that night, instead of Steven. I realize that now."

Magdalen remembered that night only too well; she did not move an eyelash but looked intently at her sister.

"I loved him," Elizabeth added casually. "You never knew that, did you? Do not trust an elder sister to choose a life for you. I've told myself that over and over again. And you did—you did choose my life for me, shutting me away with the men you hated, despised. Watching them dribble and splutter on me. But Steven, you wanted him for yourself, so you closeted me, shut me away until it was safe to marry him."

"Please—" Magdalen reached out for her sister.

"I smell vinegar in the air. Have you noticed?"

"Help me." Magdalen pleaded.

"Good night, dear sister. Sleep well. I still have work to do." Her voice fell into a whisper, into silence, into the final revenge on her sister.

"Ahriman!" Magdalen screamed.

"No, dear sister. Dear, sweet sister. Ahriman is mine now."

"No! Thief! Murderer! Ahriman . . ." She reached out, tugged at Elizabeth's arm. Elizabeth seized her arm and threw her back. "Ahriman has chosen me, dear sister, not you. I will live on, not you. You, dear sister—are dead."

Chandal lurched over to the kerosine drum, opened the valve. It gushed forth and started covering the cellar floor. Then she rushed across the room, picked up the empty fire bucket, and filled it with the kerosine. Going to the small door, she stumbled and the kerosine spilled over her dress and down her legs. She entered the stairwell, leaving the door open. Walk quietly, she reminded herself. Soon, the entire stairwell was covered with kerosine.

Next Chandal hurried to a large chest, cut the ropes around the chest with a knife, and dragged away all her old clothing. Placing a shawl around her shoulders, she scattered the rest of the clothing up and down the stairs. "If anyone calls, tell them I've gone to the theater with my husband." She laughed, then spoke directly to the mannequin that she imagined was Justin. "I'm sorry I frightened you, coming in suddenly while you were asleep," she said, holding out her hand to him. Her terror vanished for a moment, although she still looked at him with dismay, evidently trying to understand something. At last, a cruel smile rose to her lips and again she began trembling and started toward the stiff, slick wooden body.

Justin slouched against the counter in a kind of self-pitying gloom, but the druggist paid no attention. When the glass door was finally opened, the druggist informed him that it would be at least another ten minutes before the drugs were ready.

Then Justin walked to the phone booth, fumbled in his pocket as he went, searching for change. Irritated, he turned to the young lady behind the counter. "Would you give me change for this, please?" He handed her a dollar bill. It took some time for her to work the register. Justin tapped his fingers nervously on the counter. Something was bothering him.

"Here you go," she said, handing him his change.

Justin crossed to the phone booth—stopped. He looked back at the young lady, and slowly, through his muddled thoughts, he recalled the fire at the theater.

"Say, if you ain't going to call, how about letting me pour you a cup of our fine coffee?"

Justin let the change slip through his fingers and dashed quickly from the store.

"Hey, what did I say?"

It took time for Chandal to maneuver all the mannequins onto the fairly narrow stairway leading to the second and third floors. But she was pleased at how nicely they looked, sitting, standing, leaning there in the darkness.

Now she lit the match.

There was a great burst of flames; she stepped back into the basement to watch and applaud.

Justin slipped his key into the front door; it wouldn't open even after he unlocked it. He looked around quickly. He would have to go into the next building, out the back, and over the wall. By the time he reached the back door of the brownstone, flames shot out from the second-story window. He saw Elizabeth fasten her shawl around her shoulders as if to embrace the flames.

Trembling, he threw open the back door and entered the kitchen. He heard Magdalen begin to scream. He raced to the front stairs leading to the second floor —they had already been engulfed in flames. He moved back into the kitchen and down the cellar stairs as the screaming continued. Choking from the smoke and ducking the flames, for the basement was on fire by the time he reached it, he screamed, "Magdalen!"

The entire basement was thick with smoke and flames shot from the small door like a volcano. He fought fiercely to enter the stairwell; it was impossible. Magdalen's distant cry dwindled away under the roar of the fire. A large beam fell from the ceiling, nearly crushing him. He jumped back, turned, and started up the stairs leading to the kitchen when he saw Chandal huddled in the far corner, a sad smile wiped across her lips. "Chandal?" He moved closer. "Chandal, is that you?"

Chandal laughed. Someone laughed. She felt the air leave her lungs, throat, stomach; someone laughed. Her? No, someone was laughing for her.

"No, I'm Elizabeth," she said softly.

Justin knew in an instant that something was wrong. Magdalen and he had been betrayed by Ahriman.

Chandal lunged forward, catching Justin off guard.

Justin screamed, frozen against Chandal's shawl because it moved now in fast, sharp stabs, stomach level, and the knife cut into his flesh easily above his velvet cummerbund, ripped his middle wide open. Justin screamed and fell to the ground, drew back on his knees, and saw, over his shoulder, the knife coming down again, over and over again, into the back of his neck, into his shoulders.

"It's Valentine Day! Happy Valentine!" screamed Chandal, sending the knife into the center of his back. Groaning, he tried to rise; the knife ripped his face, his throat; he thought he was crying as the blood poured from his eyes; he thought, he thought—

Chandal stood over his limp body and smiled. The sound of the front door of the brownstone being broken down brought her to the realization that she was saved. That someone had finally come to save her.

Out on the street, she lifted her thin white face to the heat of the flames and smiled. What a pretty fire. Oranges and reds and white-hot heat. She laughed out loud, staring up toward the second-floor window, laughed for joy to think of the two hag skeletons lying in that raging furnace. Eyes oozing from their sockets like broken eggs. Limbs and torsos melting like wax. Let them burn. Let their wrinkled flesh melt from their bones, let their blood run like a river until it boiled dry.

In a flash, the fire jumped upward, a living, blazing

weed running along the pitched roof, across the entire face of the building. Billows of black smoke curled through the air; the whole world was red and black and Chandal watched the sparks, like stars, raise toward the heavens, watched Elizabeth lurch against the third-story window with a fixed, grinning agony pressed across her lips. Through the crackling and hissing of the fire, Chandal could hear Elizabeth screaming, but remotely, a sound almost lost to her ears.

In a few moments, it would be impossible to see anything; the building would be drowned in a sudden, final outburst of flaming timber and brick. Chandal's wish would soon be granted. The Krispin sisters would be no more.

❧ 28 ❧

THE DETAILS OF THE ROOM NOW SHOWN CLEARLY in the merciless morning snow-light. No shadows, no twisted shapes in half-darkness, but only the bed with its clean white sheets, clean white pillowcase, whitewashed walls, Moorish style. And inside, lights, bright, burning day and night, so that the attendants could see any change of expression, any contradiction in attitude, but Chandal knew that she would beat them at their little game.

They had asked her questions; she had told them whatever came into her head, jokes and delightfully amusing stories. She knew that they had held it against her; that's why she was almost always alone. *Where has everyone gone?* she wondered. *What if they've forgotten me, forgotten that I exist?* She paused at the edge of the bed; the thought frightened her.

It's happened before, she muttered in her mind. *What will become of me?*

Suddenly, she thought that she saw someone at the window. She rose, crossed, brushed the palm of her hand across the barred window. *Shadows, I guess,* she whispered to herself. *Vague shadows, they frighten me. Something is happening to me, something I can't control. Half of me feels different from the other, an invisible line has drawn itself through my body; I am now divided into two people.*

Chandal moved away from the window. She could still remember the horror of that filthy little room—the footsteps at night blundering up the stairs, the whispering, and the smothered laughter screeching beyond the flowered paper on the wall. And the smell of the two old women. And one thought remained, that perhaps they were right. Perhaps she was a bit unsettled. Perhaps she should remain there, as they suggested.

Initial Intake Note: February 19, 1980

This twenty-six-year-old Caucasian female appears to be suffering from delusions. Physical examination reveals an average, thin, normally developed twenty-six-year-old.

Psychiatric Examination: patient shows evidence of hallucinating phenomena. Her memory is vague. I.Q. is extremely high. Patient enters interview situations and psychological testing in complete terror. Patient is seclusive. There is, however, some willingness to speak of less emoitonal subjects—*i.e.,* she loves to relate children's stories, jokes, speak of flowers, friends, and weather.

She continues in her need for cleanliness, neatness. A specific obsession involves loss of body control. She spends many hours reassuring herself that her body still belongs to her. There is much basic anxiety, poor identification, self-hate. In any case, we have a very fragile, sensitive young girl.

Recommendation: patient must be allowed as much freedom as possible and will be seen in psychotherapy three times a week with Dr. I. Luther.

Six-Month-Interval Note: August 20, 1980
Patient continues to spend most of her time in her room alone. Refuses to attend all sessions with Dr. Luther. All regularly scheduled sessions have been canceled.
Recommendation: continued institutionalization. It must be remembered that patient is still terror-ridden and is many months away from the time when she will face her fears.

On September 5, 1980, Chandal Knight left her room of her own free will, paused, and started the long walk down the brightly lit corridor to Dr. I Luther's office.
That's right, dear. Smile, the voice inside of Chandal whispered. *Remember, they called Sarah Bernhardt "The Divine Sarah." We must make this our best performance ever. I've always wanted to be an actress. Did you know that? In my day, it was considered risqué. But today, one can do anything. It's so nice to be young today. Smile dear, we're very happy.*

"Because I have seen what I have seen,
   Because I have been where I have been,
   Because I have communed with those who
      know . . .
   I am who I am."

Ingenious plots that will hold you spellbound to the very end. Page-turning action and plenty of suspense. Characters that live—and love—you'll never forget them.

Discerning readers everywhere are choosing these bestselling thrillers from *Pocket Books*:

_____ 80915   THE KEY TO MIDNIGHT Leigh Nichols $2.50

_____ 82678   THE GLENDOWER LEGACY Thomas Gifford $2.50

_____ 82384   A FAMILY FORTUNE Jerome Weidman $2.50

_____ 82111   SPY WHO SAT AND WAITED
               R. Wright Campbell $2.50

_____ 82479   BOTTOM LINE Fletcher Knebel $2.50

_____ 80416   TRESPASS Fletcher Knebel $1.95

_____ 81988   TRUE CONFESSIONS John Gregory Dunne $2.50

_____ 83209   KILLER OF KINGS R. Wright Campbell $2.50

_____ 82864   THE BABYSITTER Andrew Coburn $2.50

9